"Whether the situation calls for standing up to a British aristocrat or bribing a security guard with chocolate-dipped macaroons, smart, tenacious Sadie Hoffmiller won't let anything keep her from the truth behind a murder. **Intricate, twisting, and downright tasty**, *English Trifle* will whet your appetite for more of Josi Kilpack's delicious culinary mysteries."

—Stephanie Black, author of *Fool Me Twice*

Lemon Tart

"**The novel has a bit of everything. It's a mystery, a cookbook, a low-key romance and a dead-on depiction of life.** . . . That may sound like a hodgepodge. It's not. It works. Kilpack blends it all together and cooks it up until it has the taste of, well . . . of a tangy lemon tart."

—Jerry Johnston, *Deseret News*

"***Lemon Tart* is an enjoyable mystery** with a well-hidden culprit and an unlikely heroine in Sadie Hoffmiller. Kilpack endows Sadie with logical hidden talents that come in handy at just the right moment."

—Shelley Glodowski, *Midwest Book Review*, June 2009

"***Lemon Tart* was delicious!** Sadie's curiosity, determination, and good old-fashioned pluck made her one of the most delightful characters I've ever met in a book. Finding that all my guesses about whodunit were wrong made for an exciting and clever ending to a satisfying mystery."

—Julie Wright, author of *My Not-So-Fairy-Tale Life*, http://www.juliewright.com

"Josi Kilpack's new book *Lemon Tart* takes everything I love about a culinary mystery—the food, the humor, the intrigue—and blends it all at high speed with a dash of spice in the form of our main character, Sadie. **A must-read for those who enjoy well-crafted mysteries.**"

—Tristi Pinkston, http://www.tristipinkston.blogspot.com

KEY LIME PIE

OTHER BOOKS BY JOSI S· KILPACK

Her Good Name
Sheep's Clothing
Unsung Lullaby

Culinary Mysteries
Lemon Tart
English Trifle
Devil's Food Cake
Blackberry Crumble (coming Spring 2011)

Download a free PDF of all the recipes in this book at
josiskilpack.com

KEY LIME PIE

A CULINARY MYSTERY

Josi S. Kilpack

DESERET BOOK

SALT LAKE CITY, UTAH

To Lee—the best decision I ever made

Library of Congress Cataloging-in-Publication Data
Kilpack, Josi S.
  Key lime pie / Josi S. Kilpack.
    p. cm.
  Summary: Part-time detective and full-time food lover Sadie Hoffmiller has traveled to the Florida Keys to help her new friend, Eric, track down the whereabouts of his missing daughter, Megan.
  ISBN 978-1-60641-813-0 (paperbound)
  1. Hoffmiller, Sadie (Fictitious character)—Fiction. 2. Cooks—Fiction. 3. Missing persons—Investigation—Fiction. I. Title.
  PS3561.I412K49 2010
  813'.54—dc22   2010011476

Printed in the United States of America
Worzalla Publishing Co., Stevens Point, WI

10   9   8   7   6   5   4   3   2   1

CHAPTER 1

"Hey."

Sadie Hoffmiller looked up from where she was planting marigolds in the courthouse flower beds—part of the community service she'd been sentenced to after an unfortunate situation she'd been involved in a few months earlier. The sun blinded her, forcing her to lift a gloved hand to shield her eyes even though she knew the voice. Eric Burton had received the same sentence for the same reason—co-conspirators is what they'd been called.

"Hi there," Sadie responded, sitting back on her heels and attempting to smooth her hair before realizing her glove was covered in dirt and therefore made whatever state her hair was in even worse. "I thought you'd finished your community service on Monday."

The judge could have been much harder on both of them. As it was, Eric had made short work of his three hundred hours, sometimes doing up to twenty hours a week in addition to running his locksmith business. Sadie had tried to keep up with him, but she still had a few days left.

"And how would you know that?" Eric asked, giving her a playful smile. "Or have you been asking about me?"

Sadie felt her cheeks heat up for no good reason at all and went back to her flowers. "Actually I was excited to have a little peace and quiet around here. I've been counting down your hours more than I've been counting down my own."

Eric laughed out loud, making it impossible for Sadie to feign offense at their banter. He lowered himself to the grass beside her, and Sadie found herself watching him out of the corner of her eye. Spring had just come out of hiding in Colorado and the grass was still a mottled green and brown. It was warm for April, mid-sixties, and the citizens of Garrison were taking full advantage of it.

Eric lay on his back, supporting his weight with his elbows while lifting his face to the sun that was almost directly overhead. His long hair was pulled into his usual ponytail at the base of his neck, and he wore jeans and a gray, long-sleeved T-shirt with a green alien head on the front.

Sadie watched him a little too long before going back to her marigolds. Sometimes he was flirty, and now and again he was downright brazen in his attention to her, and yet he backpedaled quickly when those moments came around, leaving a bewildered Sadie in his wake.

"I told Tami I'd keep helping with Wednesday's food delivery until someone else breaks the law and takes my place," Eric said, interrupting her thoughts. "Apparently Garrison doesn't have enough of us fringe citizens."

Us? He wasn't calling Sadie a fringe citizen, was he? She glanced at him quickly and realized he probably was. He probably thought it was a compliment. "It's generous of you to keep helping her out," she said.

"It was generous of you to give her the cookies. She insisted I have one," Eric said after a few seconds. She could feel him looking

2

at her, and she imagined his blue eyes were even brighter than usual, thanks to the sun. But she didn't allow herself to look at him and instead became even more intent on the flower she was patting into place.

When she didn't answer, Eric spoke again. "What kind of cookies are they?"

She still didn't answer.

"I'm not leaving till you tell me, so you may as well fess up."

Sadie squinted at him as she once again sat back on her heels and let out a breath. "No one was supposed to know they were from me," she said quietly, embarrassed to be found out. "They were an anonymous thank-you gift. I didn't want Tami to feel indebted."

"If it makes you feel better, she hasn't figured it out yet," Eric said with a wry grin. "I'll keep your secret if you give me the recipe."

Not since Sadie's late husband, Neil, had she met a man who preferred the kitchen to the La-Z-Boy, and while Eric insisted that he loved to cook, Sadie had seen his house and had a hard time believing he could cook in such a mess. She didn't like to doubt him, but there were so many ways that Eric confused her. Cooking was only one of them.

"So?"

Sadie looked up at him. "So? What?"

"The recipe," Eric said, shaking his head slightly. "Are you going to give it to me, or do I have to tell Tami she's got to find a way to thank you for the thank-you."

"You're impossible." In some ways he was like a younger brother, teasing and goading her all the time, and yet . . . in other ways he was nothing like a brother at all. Not one little bit.

"They're my Kickin' Craisin cookies," Sadie said in surrender.

"Kickin' Craisin, huh?" Eric said, squinting thoughtfully. "Where's the kick come from?"

"Cayenne pepper," Sadie said, unable to hide a smile. She loved people's reactions when she told them the secret ingredient.

Eric's eyebrows shot up. "In a cookie?"

Sadie smiled even wider. "Just a little. You want zing not zoinks."

Eric threw his head back and laughed before sobering instantly. "Am I interrupting something?"

Sadie looked up. Pete Cunningham, her sorta-kinda-boyfriend-maybe, was blocking the sun. She smiled, but felt as though she'd been caught doing something she oughtn't. "Pete," she said, hoping that by making her voice sound lighter she could cover up her discomfort. "Is it four o'clock already?"

"Almost," Pete said. He was dressed in black slacks and a royal blue shirt that looked quite striking beneath his black overcoat. He cut a very different figure than Eric did, and he didn't look all that happy to find them talking together. He turned to Eric. "Mr. Burton," he said with a polite nod. Too polite.

"Detective," Eric said just as coolly. He pushed himself up to a sitting position while Sadie patted another flower into place.

"I've only got a few more flowers to get in the ground," Sadie said. "It's going to get cold again tomorrow, and I want to get these planted before the weather turns. I didn't realize it was so late."

Pete put his hands in his pockets. "It's all right. We've got a few minutes."

"I can finish this for you, if you'd like," Eric said, his tone suspiciously formal.

Sadie turned to look at him in surprise.

"If I hadn't been distracting you, you wouldn't be running late."

Sadie sighed and gave him a reproachful look. His gallantry was only a ploy to make the point that *he'd* been distracting her from the date she had with *Pete*. He was so not worth the thoughts she couldn't seem to get out of her head about him. However, she chose to take him at his word. To do anything else would allow him an opportunity to make even more uncomfortable comments.

"That would be great," she said, brushing off her gloves before removing them and handing them to Eric. He frowned slightly, betraying the fact that he'd hoped to draw this out a little longer. He took the proffered gloves as Sadie pushed herself up, wincing at the cramps in her knees from kneeling so long. Pete reached down to help her, and she raised her left hand toward him.

Eric put a hand on her arm. "Your shoulder?"

"Oh, right." Sadie lifted her right hand instead. As part of the unfortunate situation that had landed her with the community service in the first place, she'd torn a ligament in her shoulder. It had made remarkable progress over the last several weeks but it was still tender. Why was it Eric had remembered and Pete hadn't?

"Give me a couple minutes to clean up and I'll be ready," she said, untying the apron she'd worn to protect her clothes. She and Pete were going to Baxter's for an early dinner and then planned to catch a movie at the Capitol Theatre, which played classics on Wednesday nights. Tonight they were featuring *Out of Africa* and Sadie's best friend, Gayle, had dropped Sadie off at the courthouse for her community service so that Pete could pick her up and they wouldn't have to worry about Sadie's car.

"No need to rush," Pete said, smiling at her with those hazel eyes she liked so much. Pete was wonderful—kind, smart, supportive, and stable—everything she wanted. And yet, there was something that was either too much or too little. Because of . . . whatever it was, their relationship hadn't progressed much over the last few months. But they were in a comfortable place and for now they both seemed okay with that. "I've got a few phone calls to make," Pete continued, leaning in to kiss her on the cheek. "I'll wait for you in the car if that's okay."

Sadie nodded her agreement and looked down at a quiet Eric while Pete headed toward the parking lot. "I appreciate your help finishing up," she said to Eric, feeling bad he was digging in the dirt even though it wasn't her fault exactly. He had chosen not to wear the gloves; they were next to him on the ground while he worked bare-handed.

"I'll just bet you do," Eric said in a dull voice.

"What?" Sadie questioned, sure she'd misinterpreted his tone.

Eric sat back, put his hands on his thighs, and looked up, glancing at Pete's retreating back before making eye contact with her. "Is that really the kind of guy you want to be with?"

Sadie was instantly defensive. "Obviously," she answered, folding her arms over her chest, embarrassed. She should have reprimanded Eric for asking such an inappropriate question, but she didn't.

Eric studied her for a moment before turning back to the flower bed, stabbing the trowel into the dirt. "Huh."

She frowned. "Huh, what?" she asked.

Eric shrugged and then jammed a poor marigold into the hole he'd just dug. "I pegged you as wanting someone who was a little more real, a little more—I don't know—fun."

"Pete's real," Sadie said even though she didn't know what that meant. "And he's . . . fun."

Eric paused, then put down his trowel and stood slowly. "Is he?" he asked, hooking his thumbs in the belt loops of his jeans. His tone had changed dramatically. No longer hard, it was now whispery and . . . almost intimate. He took a step toward her so they were only a foot apart. His closeness forced Sadie to look up, and although she knew she should take a step backward for reasons of propriety, she didn't want to.

"You deserve more than a safe bet, Sadie," he said. His breath smelled like cinnamon and a hint of cayenne. "You deserve someone who will enjoy life with you rather than just live it by your side."

Behind the words was the implication that *he* was the kind of man she'd enjoy life with, and that brought to the foreground all the thoughts she tried not to think about him but had a hard time avoiding. All of a sudden it was impossible to ignore the fact that she was attracted to this man.

It made her feel utterly ridiculous.

"I'm older than you," she said before realizing she'd opened her mouth. Her face instantly burned. Did she seriously say that? Out loud?

"Are you?" he asked.

Sadie narrowed her eyes. "You know I am."

Eric made an innocent face and shrugged. "I don't know any such thing."

"I'm fifty-six," Sadie said in an attempt to convince him; the words almost stuck in her throat. It was not normal for a woman to admit her age like that, but this was an emergency. She watched his face, but he showed no reaction at all. "How old are you?"

Eric shook his head. "It doesn't matter."

He *was* younger than she was! She knew it! "It *does* matter."

"Not to me," he said. "Is that your only reason for choosing him over me?"

Sadie cast a look over her shoulder, remembering that Pete was only twenty yards away. His car must be on the other side of the parking lot, though; she couldn't see it from where she stood.

Eric took her chin in his hand and turned her head back to face him. He didn't say anything, just lifted his eyebrows expectantly as he dropped his hand. He wasn't going to let this conversation just go away.

Sadie's head was still spinning, but there didn't seem to be any option other than answering.

"I—uh . . ." She stumbled to find another reason, acutely aware of the fact that there were things she *couldn't* say. She had been an educator; he was a locksmith. She was organized; he was a slob. And she was older than he was!

"You have longer hair than I do."

Eric smiled. "I'll cut it."

This was not happening! And yet it was. She was not having this conversation! And yet she was. She didn't know what to say. And yet she spoke because it had to be said. "We're too different."

"Not really." Eric took another tiny step toward her; she could feel the toe of his boot against the toe of her sneaker. "You just have a hard time admitting that I'm the kind of guy you really want to spend the rest of your life with."

Sadie stared into his eyes and when he leaned into her, she found herself steeling herself expectantly. He was going to kiss her.

And she was totally going to let him.

Inches from making contact, however, Eric paused. "Mark my words, Sadie Hoffmiller, the first time our lips meet, it will be *you* kissing *me*."

He stepped back while Sadie tried to make sense of what he'd just said, and what he *hadn't* done. Her eyes snapped to meet his laughing ones, and the expression on his face told her in no uncertain terms that she'd proved something he'd suspected all along.

Sadie opened her mouth but could find no words. She wasn't used to being made a fool of and felt instant heat rush up her spine.

The ringing of his cell phone saved her from having to respond. It was some heavy metal song she didn't want to know the title of—AC/DC she thought. He winked at her while digging the phone from his pocket.

"This is Eric," he said, turning away from Sadie who stood with her hands balled into fists at her sides. How dare he trick her into saying things she shouldn't have said!

She narrowed her eyes, waiting for him to get off the phone so she could tell him what she *really* thought of him, but then she noticed his eyes go wide. "What?" he breathed before going silent again. He glanced at Sadie, a pleading, scared look on his face that drained her of all her anger. "Yes," he continued, "I can fax them to you in about ten minutes." He pulled the phone away from his ear and stared at it for a moment before turning it off.

"What?" Sadie asked as he turned toward her. "What's happened?"

"They found a body in Florida," he said, looking away for just a moment and taking a deep breath. "They think it might be my daughter, Megan."

Kickin' Craisin Cookies

1 cup butter
1 cup sugar
1 cup brown sugar
2 eggs
1 teaspoon vanilla
2 cups flour
2½ cups quick oats

½ teaspoon salt
1 teaspoon baking powder
1 teaspoon baking soda
½ teaspoon cloves
½ teaspoon ground ginger
1 teaspoon cinnamon
Dash of cayenne pepper
1½ cups Craisins
½ cup white chocolate chips (optional)
½ cup chopped walnuts or pecans (optional)

Preheat oven to 400 degrees. Cream butter and sugars. Add eggs and vanilla and mix until well combined. Add dry ingredients and mix well. Add Craisins, chocolate chips, and nuts, using a wooden spoon to mix (dough will be too thick for most mixers).

Drop by tablespoons or use a 1-inch scoop to make dough balls and place on an ungreased cookie sheet about two inches apart. Bake 6 to 9 minutes or until just browned—do not overbake. Allow to cool on pan 2 minutes before moving to cooling rack. Cookies should be crisp on the outside and chewy on the inside.

Makes 3 dozen.

CHAPTER 2

Sadie gasped and raised a hand to her mouth. She instinctively reached her other hand out to Eric, who grasped it and held on tight. Eric had told her briefly about his daughter—how she'd vanished during spring break in Florida three years ago. "They found . . . a *body?*"

Not a living person.

The tortured look in Eric's eyes deepened. "I've never believed she was alive all this time," he said. He looked at their joined hands for a moment before dropping hers. "I haven't *wanted* her to be alive all this time."

Sadie was shocked. "What? Of course you've wanted her to be alive. Every parent—"

"There are worse things than death," Eric interjected. "And if she's been alive all this time but unable to contact me or her mother . . ." He didn't finish the sentence. He didn't need to.

Sadie felt her stomach drop. Three years was a long time to consider what might have happened. Sadie felt a lump rise in her throat as she glimpsed just a moment of what he'd been dealing with all these years. He held her eyes one more second before looking away.

"I've got to get home; they need a copy of her dental records. They can't find them in her file."

"The Florida police?"

Eric nodded, already turning toward the parking lot. Sadie hurried to keep up with him. "Eric," she said, running a few steps. "Where did they find Meg—uh, her . . . uh . . . the body?"

"I don't know," Eric said.

He had very long legs, and Sadie was in a full-on jog by the time they reached the parking lot. He pulled the keys from his pocket and headed for his Jeep Cherokee.

"So you fax the records, and then what?" Sadie asked, still trying to keep up, physically and mentally.

"I don't know," Eric said again. He grabbed the handle of the car door and pulled it open just as Pete called out from behind them.

"Sadie?"

"Just a minute," she threw over her shoulder before turning back to Eric, who had one foot in his Jeep but was looking at her. "I—I don't know what to say," she finally admitted.

"There's nothing you should say," Eric replied, no reproach in his voice. "I'm sorry I won't be able to finish the flowers."

"Are you kidding?" she said. She paused again, struggling to find some way to . . . what? Comfort him? Support him? Say the right thing? "Are you going to be okay?"

"I just hope it's her," Eric said, his voice soft and full of regret. "I want to know where my daughter is."

Sadie nodded her understanding even though she fully realized that she didn't understand. How could she?

A hand settled on her shoulder, and she looked up into Pete's concerned face. For an instant she thought he was worried about Eric too, then realized he was likely wondering why Sadie was talking to Eric instead of getting ready like she was supposed to be doing.

She turned to Eric and accepted that there wasn't anything she could do to help him. They were only friends, but not exactly close friends—despite the almost-kiss. She hadn't even known his daughter's name.

"Good luck," she finally said, offering him a sympathetic smile. "If there's some way I can help, please don't hesitate."

"Good luck with what?" Pete asked. "What kind of help?" There was an edge to his voice that Sadie resented, a touch of envy that would have been laughable if not for the circumstances being so serious.

Eric glanced briefly at Pete, then Sadie. "Thank you," was all he said before he got into the Jeep and pulled the door shut.

"What was that all about?" Pete asked as Eric's engine roared to life.

Sadie felt an overwhelming annoyance at the fact that while Eric was facing a horrendous discovery full of complex emotions and realizations, Pete seemed to be caught up only in his own jealousy. "He just got a call saying the police may have found his daughter's body in Florida."

Pete was well aware of Eric's daughter's disappearance; Eric had told the Garrison police about it at the time of his and Sadie's arrest. Sadie felt sure that Eric had hoped the information would spark some new interest in his daughter's case, but as far as Sadie could tell, nothing had come of it.

"Oh," Pete said simply. He watched Eric's Jeep disappear around the corner. After a moment he looked at Sadie. "Are you okay?"

Sadie wasn't sure. Over the last several months she'd been involved in no fewer than three murder investigations. First, her neighbor Anne had been found dead in the field behind her house. Then, on a trip to the English country estate of Sadie's daughter's boyfriend, a servant had been murdered. And just two months ago there had been a shooting at the Garrison Library fund-raising dinner. She was like some kind of murder magnet, not a title she wanted for herself. The Library Shooting, as it had come to be known around Garrison, was what had landed Sadie with three hundred hours of community service; she hadn't exactly done what the police had wanted her to do that night. But it had all worked out for the best in the end—if "best" was the right word.

And now, here was another body. Only this body was all the way in Florida. She was glad to be on the outside of this one since there was no room in her life for more drama. But how could she not worry about Eric? As his friend, was there anything she could do to help?

"Sadie?" Pete asked.

Sadie snapped out of her thoughts and looked up into Pete's concerned eyes. "Are you okay?" he asked again.

"I'm fine," Sadie said quickly, because of course she was fine, just worried. This wasn't about her at all. "I can't imagine what this must feel like for him." Talking about Eric brought back the almost-kiss from a couple minutes earlier, and Sadie had to look away from Pete's probing gaze. She felt her face heat up all the same. Would she really have let Eric kiss her? In the more than six months Sadie and Pete had been seeing each other, they had kissed only one time— and she hardly considered it a *real* kiss due to the high-stress situation they were both in at the time.

Pete said nothing, just waited for her to look back at him. "So, no dinner and movie, huh?" he asked, sounding both sympathetic and disappointed.

Sadie opened her mouth to say, no, it wasn't a good night, and yet right on the heels of that was her own question. *Why not?* How would it help Eric for her to cancel her evening plans?

You are not a part of this, she told herself, ignoring the stab of disappointment she felt inside. Was she really so arrogant as to feel left out somehow? For being a woman in her mid-fifties, she still had a lot to learn about what made her do and say and think the things she did and said and thought.

"Of course we'll still go out," she said. She looked toward the street where Eric had disappeared before smiling up at Pete whose expression was unreadable. "There's nothing I can do," she said. "I know that."

"You're sure?" Pete asked, but she could hear the relief in his tone. He didn't seem to want her to choose worrying about Eric over spending a night out with him. Sadie hated that if he knew what had happened on the courthouse lawn a few minutes earlier, he'd be even more insecure. Should she tell him? Had he seen them?

She and Pete weren't serious—they'd never discussed being exclusive or anything—but neither of them were seeing anyone else either. Why did it have to be so complicated? The almost-kiss played in her mind again and she searched Pete's face, but couldn't determine what he might or might not have seen. He guarded his expressions well.

She wished there were a delete key in her brain for things she really didn't want to ponder on. And yet, even as she thought it, she felt her toes tingle at the memory of Eric's face so close to her own. Argh! The man had ruined her! "I just need to get those last two flowers in the ground, and then I'll clean up. I'm sorry."

"No apology necessary," Pete said, tucking a lock of her hair behind her ear. His hand was soft and warm against her skin and when he opened his palm, she leaned into it, absorbing the comfort offered by his touch. Wanting his touch, however, made her feel like a hussy—inches away from kissing Eric one minute and pining for Pete's tenderness another. "And I'll finish planting the flowers," Pete added.

She took note of his business attire. "You'll get dirty," she said, shaking her head. "I'll do it."

"I want to," Pete said, and Sadie wondered if he was feeling competitive with Eric somehow. Just like when Eric offered his help, she chose to take it at face value.

"Okay," she said. "I'll meet you at your car in a few minutes."

"Perfect," Pete said with a nod.

He turned toward the flower beds, and Sadie turned to the back door of the city offices. As she let herself inside and headed down the hall to the bathroom, however, she couldn't get Eric out of her head. No matter how much she tried to distract herself from his situation, she couldn't help but picture Eric standing over a fax machine as he sent dental records across the country in order to see if the body the police had found was that of his only child. What was it like to face such a life-altering situation? What was it like to face it alone?

CHAPTER 3

S o, what's with you and Eric?"

Sadie's head snapped up. Hadn't Pete been talking about work? "What?"

Pete was watching her closely from across the table at Baxter's. His plate was clean. Sadie had taken a few bites of her chicken Caesar salad, but mostly pushed the lettuce around the bowl while listening to Pete's voice and the other sounds of the restaurant. She wasn't hungry. "I asked about the relationship between you and Eric."

Sadie searched his tone for some kind of accusation, but it was hard to read. He probably learned that trick at the police academy: Neutral Tone 101. "I'm not sure what you mean," she said, hedging.

Pete took a breath and leaned back in his chair. "It's not a difficult question, Sadie, and I'm not looking for any specific answer. I'd just like to know exactly what Eric means to you."

"He's a friend," Sadie said, the almost-kiss racing to the front of her mind, taunting her once again. *Was* he a friend? Did *friends* try to kiss you, then tell you that you would kiss them first? She took another bite of her salad without looking at Pete but could feel his eyes on her as she did so.

The waitress took Pete's plate and asked if they were interested in dessert. "None for me," Pete said. He lifted his eyebrows at Sadie. "You?"

"No, thanks," Sadie said. She felt guilty enough for not eating the entire meal; too bad salad didn't keep well as leftovers. She gave up on the meal she didn't want to eat and pushed the salad away. The waitress took the cue and picked up the bowl before returning to the kitchen.

Once they were alone, Sadie looked up into Pete's face, realizing that it would do neither of them any favors to avoid this conversation. "How would you define *our* relationship, Pete?"

"I guess I would say we're dating," he said. "We see each other a couple times a week and seem to enjoy our time together."

"But we've been doing that for months," Sadie said. "Do you see this going anywhere?"

"I don't know," Pete said, leaning forward and lacing his fingers together before resting his hands and forearms on the table. "The answer to that question might be wrapped up in my original one."

Eric.

Sadie looked down, mostly to avoid his gaze long enough to come up with an appropriate response. She'd dropped a piece of lettuce on her pants and picked it off to reveal a splotchy oil spot on her left thigh. Perfect. She looked up to find Pete just as intent as before. "What about Eric?" Sadie asked, putting her hands on the table in an attempt to stop her fidgeting.

"You light up when he's around."

"I do?" Sadie said without thinking. "I mean, um, I don't think . . ."

Pete surprised her by reaching across the table and taking her hand. He offered her a smile. A serious, slightly sad one, but a smile all the same. "It's okay," he said. "Enjoying one another's company doesn't mean you owe me anything."

What on earth was she supposed to say to that?

Luckily, she didn't have to answer. "Look," Pete said, rubbing his thumb across the back of her hand. She felt the tenderness and warmth of his touch all the way to her toes. "I think you're a remarkable woman, but the last thing I want is for you to be with me when you want to be with somebody else."

Sadie's mouth went dry. She shook her head. "It's not like that," she said quietly, embarrassed to be having this discussion. Did Pete think she'd been leading him on? Where was a distraction when she needed one? Was it too much to ask for a busboy to drop a tray of dishes or something?

Sadie took a breath. "I really like you, Pete, and I enjoy spending time with you."

"But?" he said, when she stopped from saying it herself.

"But I don't know where it's going with us," she finally admitted. "Things are the same now as they were six months ago and, quite frankly, at my age waiting doesn't come easily."

"I agree," Pete said, withdrawing his hand from hers and sitting back in his chair. It felt symbolic to her, his pulling away. The restaurant suddenly seemed a little cooler than it had before, a little quieter, too. They both fell silent. Sadie felt horrible. She'd said too much and it didn't feel right in her stomach. And yet, she hadn't said anything that wasn't true. She'd been widowed at the age of thirty-six, and over the years, when she would allow herself to consider remarrying, she'd imagined that she'd have no doubts and no hesitation when she found the right man—much like she'd felt when she'd first met Neil nearly thirty years ago. Instead she had both doubts *and* hesitation when it came to Pete. Did that mean Pete wasn't the man she'd wanted him to be? The seconds ticked by and they both sat there, avoiding being the first person to speak.

"I can take care of that when you're ready," the waitress said, as she slid the black leather case in front of Pete. He smiled politely and opened it, seeming relieved to have a distraction.

Sadie shifted in her chair. Was it fair to have Pete pay for her meal that ended with a conversation like this?

He slid his debit card into the binder and placed it so it hung over the edge of the table a couple of inches. Then he looked up and met Sadie's eyes. He didn't look as tormented as she expected. Did that mean he wasn't disappointed? Or was he simply doing the same thing with his expression as he'd done with his tone earlier—keeping it neutral? "You and I both know that life is short," he said. "And we both know what it's like to be loved and truly comfortable in a relationship. For that reason, neither of us should settle for anything less than that. Don't you agree?"

Sadie did agree and yet she felt a lump in her throat as she nodded. "I feel like I owe you an apology or something."

Pete managed a chuckle. "You don't. I've had a really good time, and I'd rather part as friends than take it to a point where one of us will be hurt."

Sadie nodded again, at a loss for words. She felt like a junior high student and a very old woman all at the same time. "Does this mean we're not going to the movie?" she asked.

Pete smiled, but this one seemed to break his guarded expression. This time he looked sad. Sadie felt the lump in her throat thicken. "I'd go to a movie with you anytime, Sadie, but . . . are you sure you wouldn't rather check in with Eric and see how he's doing? I imagine this isn't an easy time for him. Perhaps he could use . . . a friend."

CHAPTER 4

The ride home was awkward, to say the least. There wasn't much to talk about and all Sadie could think of saying when Pete walked her to her front door was "I'm sorry."

He took her hand and gave it a squeeze. "Call me when you want to catch that movie—no strings attached."

Sadie stepped forward and he automatically reached out his arms and pulled her into a hug that felt so comfortable, so right despite the decision they'd reached. He seemed to hold her a few seconds longer than was warranted before letting her go. They shared a look and Sadie reminded herself that this really was for the best. Finally, she thanked him and waited on the porch while he returned to his car and drove around the cul-de-sac, his headlights illuminating the other houses in the circle as he made his way out. When he turned onto the street, the cul-de-sac seemed darker than it had been when they'd arrived.

Sadie pulled her jacket closed. The days might be warming up, but the nights were still laced with the chill of a Rocky Mountain winter. Pete's car was long gone before Sadie let herself into the house. She felt tears come to her eyes and scolded herself for hurting a perfectly good man. But had she hurt him? He'd been rather logical about the whole thing—perhaps even relieved. Maybe Eric was just an excuse for Pete to extract himself from a relationship he didn't want any more. And was it fair for Sadie to continue things as they were when she *did* have these feelings for Eric?

"Oh, biscuits," Sadie said as she shut the door behind her. She hated having to sort out all these thoughts. Thank goodness for the smell of cinnamon and ginger that still hung in the air from the morning's baking. Her mood couldn't help but lighten, and her eyes settled on the baking rack still full of cookies. She hadn't given *all* of them to Tami. It took three steps to cross the kitchen, another two to retrieve the milk from the fridge, and then three more to get a plate and a cup from the cupboard.

The spices zinged exactly as they should, and she savored every bite, knowing she dared not have more than three cookies. Maybe four. She'd managed to lose seven pounds over the last several weeks and didn't want to undo her progress by getting carried away.

Then again, this was a unique situation. A five-cookie situation, perhaps.

Or six.

After finishing the final cookie, her stomach rebelled at the thought of more. She obeyed, and put the rest of the cookies on a plate. Eric had liked them, and she'd promised him the recipe. As Pete had suggested, she imagined that Eric did need a friend about now. Her stomach flip-flopped, and not because of the cookies. Was visiting Eric appropriate after what had happened earlier? And yet, didn't ignoring his situation make her uncompassionate?

Besides, if these cookies stayed in the house much longer she'd eat the rest.

On the drive to Eric's house, she attempted to calm her rising anxiety using every approach she could think of. She tried to talk herself out of it, blaming her discomfort on having eaten too many cookies. And then she berated herself for being such a silly woman about it in the first place. In the end, when she pulled up in front of his house, she was assaulted by memories of the last time she had been there, two months earlier. It had been such a strange night, and yet Eric had helped her in every way he could—ending up with community service for his efforts. Didn't she owe him something now that he was the one facing a difficult situation?

After taking a deep breath, she stepped out of the car, locked it, and headed up his front steps. She glanced only briefly at the tangled bushes she was all too familiar with and then knocked on the door.

She heard the locks click. She straightened, and, when Eric opened the door, held up the plate of cookies. He looked at her first, then the cookies, and then back at her. But Sadie's attention was drawn to a suitcase a few feet behind him. She stared at it for a moment before meeting Eric's eyes.

"You're leaving?"

Eric looked over his shoulder at the suitcase and then back at Sadie before inviting her in. As she stepped inside she realized the house was cleaner than she remembered it, but that wasn't saying much. There was still a general cluttered look about the house. Piles of newspapers, jackets thrown over chairs, and a hundred and one things that didn't belong in the living room. Like the teapot sitting on the ottoman. How did he stand it? Could people with such different expectations of home and cleanliness make a relationship work?

"They won't have an answer for me until Friday," Eric said, interrupting her thoughts and pulling her attention away from the messy house. "There's a red-eye out of Denver tonight."

"What if it's not her?" Sadie asked.

"What if it is?"

"What about your work?"

"I'm not the only locksmith in town," Eric said with a one-shoulder shrug. "I already talked to The Lock Shop. They can do the rekey I have scheduled for tomorrow; we cover for each other."

Sadie was out of arguments, but didn't want him to go. Why not? It made sense that he should. If Sadie were in his place, she'd go.

"Maybe you can take these with you, then," she said. "Do they confiscate cookies at security now?"

Eric smiled. "I'll put them in my suitcase so they get checked." He looked from the plate to Sadie's face. "Thank you."

"I only wish I could do more."

Eric cocked his head to the side. "Do you really?"

"Of course," Sadie said, but even as she said it, she wondered what she could possibly do.

"Then come with me."

Sadie felt her mouth drop open. "Wh—what?"

Eric took a step closer. "I don't have anyone else to ask."

Sadie stared at him, at those deep blue eyes that wouldn't let her go. Hadn't she wondered what it was like to be Eric, facing such a difficult situation alone? And now he was reaching out, asking her to help him through it. And yet there were so many warning bells going off in her mind she couldn't hear anything else. She had broken up with Pete less than an hour ago.

Eric reached up and ran his thumb along her jaw. She held her breath and then got control of herself and took a step backward. "I can't, Eric," she said. "I've got a meeting about the spring fund-raiser for the high school tomorrow, and I volunteer with Meals on Wheels on Friday, and the Renaissance dinner with Gayle is on Saturday—"

"It's okay," Eric cut in, but the disappointment was obvious. He turned back to his suitcase and fiddled with something on the zipper. "I knew it was a long shot."

Sadie's own words rang back to her: *"I only wish I could do more."* And yet she'd said no when he asked her for help. But how could she say yes?

"I'm sorry," she said, feeling exceptionally lame.

"It's okay," Eric said, offering her a forgiving smile. He straightened and looked at his watch. "I'd better get going. Thanks for the cookies."

Oh yeah, cookies. That was all she could do to help? Really? "Do you have a Zip-loc or Tupperware or something? It will make them easier to pack."

"Sure," Eric said. "I can take care of it." He took the plate, brushing her fingers in the process.

"I'm sorry I can't go," she said again, aware of how pathetic she sounded even as she searched for absolution.

"I said it's okay," Eric said. Then he smiled. She smiled back. They stood for a few more seconds.

"Well, I, uh, better go," Sadie said. Eric just nodded. Should she ask him to call her and tell her what he found out? Was that rude in light of the fact that she was refusing to help him in the one way he'd asked her to?

"Drive safe," he said, showing her to the door.

"*You* drive safe," Sadie said. He was the one catching a flight at Denver International. She was going home. Where she'd worry about him all night long. "Are you leaving your car at the airport?" she asked. Should she offer him a ride? But it was almost three hours to Denver—six hours round-trip. That seemed . . . inappropriate somehow.

"I've got a buddy in Denver," he said, pulling the door open. "I'm going to his place first and he'll take me to the airport so I don't have to worry about my car."

Sadie turned. "That's good. Um, if you need . . . anything else . . . let me know."

Lame! Could she be any lamer?

"I will," he said.

Sadie nodded, not wanting to delay him any longer as she headed for the porch steps. She heard the door shut softly behind her and the locks fit back into place as she headed for her car.

Even though she felt sure that refusing the invitation was the right thing to do, she felt horrible about it. She knew she had a very long night ahead of her. Not as long as Eric's, though. Once again she pondered on what it would be like to be him right now.

CHAPTER 5

It took hours for Sadie to fall asleep. To distract herself after re-turning home, she cleaned, then did some laundry, and then reorganized her spice cupboard. She'd managed to collect three containers of basil since the last time she cleaned it out.

At midnight she imagined that Eric's plane was just leaving, or had just left, or was just about to leave, and the guilt hit her hard. But imagining what it would have been like if she'd accepted Eric's offer made her shake her head. What would people say if she'd left town with him? What would Pete think? Her reputation had been damaged after the library shooting; she couldn't afford to chip away at it any more than she already had.

Around two o'clock she fell asleep, certain she would have dreams about Eric since he was all she'd thought about in the hours before she went to bed. Instead she dreamed she was doing a Lysol commercial and couldn't say the word *contamination*. Go figure.

The ringing of the phone next to the bed woke her up, but she was surprised to find her bedroom filled with daylight when she opened her eyes. She reached for the handset while looking at the digital clock. The numbers read 9:09! Sadie couldn't remember the last time she'd slept past eight and therefore never bothered to set an alarm. She was supposed to be at the high school by ten.

"Hello?" she said into the phone as she swung her legs over the side of the bed, making herself a little dizzy in the process.

"Sadie?"

It only took a moment to recognize the voice. "Eric!" she said, gripping the phone tighter as a warm shiver ran down her spine. "Where are you? Are you all right?"

"I'm fine," Eric said quickly. "I'm in Florida. I need a favor."

Sadie's stomach sank. Was he going to ask her to go to Florida again? Would he understand if she tried to explain the whole reputation thing?

"Actually, two favors," he added.

"O–kay," Sadie said, hesitation in her voice.

"Remember how back in February you said you'd clean my house after you brought those stinky files into it?"

"Ye–es," Sadie said, carefully. She'd reminded him of it a few times, but he always winked and said he'd let her know when he was ready. He was going to collect on that *now*?

"Well, I'm wondering if I can trade you for something else."

Trade? What did he need more than some housekeeping?

"Clean my trailer instead," Eric said. "I just listed it in the paper, which means people will start calling on it tomorrow morning. My neighbor agreed to show it, but he doesn't know glass cleaner from furniture polish. I know you're busy, but—"

"Sure, it's not a problem," Sadie said, relieved. This was something she could do, and it would help ease her guilty conscience. "I can work on it this afternoon. Is the trailer unlocked?"

"No," Eric said. "But the key to the trailer is in the house, hanging by the back door. The house key is inside the second cabinet on your left inside the garage, and the key to the garage is around the back of the shed, underneath the third stepping-stone."

Sadie scrambled for paper and a pen in the drawer of her nightstand. "You'll need to repeat that," she said, holding the phone against her ear with her shoulder. She had to test three pens before finding one that worked. It was time to clean out her bedside table drawers.

Eric repeated the instructions, and Sadie kept her questions about the over-complication of his key hiding to herself. "Okay," she said after repeating the instructions back to him, finally finding a pause in her thoughts long enough to let a question take root. "Why are you listing the trailer now?"

Eric paused. "I need a little cash."

"Why?"

"Um, the second favor is a little easier," he said, ignoring her question. "There's a box in the corner of my bedroom closet; I need it shipped to me overnight. I can pay you back when I get home."

"What's in the box?" Sadie asked. She looked at the clock again. He'd only been in Florida a few hours. "What's going on, Eric?"

He ignored her questions. "Could you send me that box as soon as possible? I think it needs to be to FedEx by two in order to make it overnight."

Sadie tapped the pen on the notepad. "Eric," she said, slow and calculated. "What's going on?"

He was quiet. "I really need your help with this, Sadie," he said.

Sadie waited for him to continue, but he didn't. He needed money and the contents of a box and he wasn't going to tell her why. But he *had* called her for help. "What does the box look like?"

Eric let out an audible sigh of relief. "It's an old Sunkist Orange box," he said. "FedEx said they'd either rebox it or reinforce the existing one if necessary so you don't need to do anything special. I'll text you the address where I'm staying, okay? I really appreciate this, Sadie."

"I'm glad to help," Sadie said. In fact, she was fairly itching to help. How long would it take to open that box and have a look at whatever was inside?

CHAPTER 6

Unfortunately Sadie didn't have time to get to Eric's before her meeting at the high school. She took copious notes on the information discussed, but her head was across town, trying to imagine what was in that box. The meeting ended at 11:30; she made an excuse for why she couldn't grab lunch with a couple of the other committee members and made a beeline for Eric's house.

Sadie found the rock that hid the garage key and then the key to the house which let her inside. The hinge creaked when she opened the door, but she didn't even pause as she went inside, worried that if she acted hesitant a neighbor might call the police on her. She peeked around doorways until she found what had to be Eric's bedroom. She paused at the threshold, vastly uncomfortable with the idea of entering. She looked to her left and her right, as though someone might be watching, then lifted her chin, smoothed her shirt and walked into the room, feigning confidence she didn't feel. His bed was unmade—big surprise—and she tried to ignore it while reminding herself that she was a grown woman. What was there to be uncomfortable with?

There were piles of laundry on the floor and a stack of books on the bedside table. She gave them both a mere glance—intent on her destination.

It took a little digging, but within a couple minutes, Sadie found the box. It took another minute to wrestle it out of the corner of the narrow closet, and she was cursing every pack rat she'd ever met by the time she finally dragged the box into the room. She was sweating, and she rolled her shoulder, which had begun to rebel against the efforts. She'd still clean the trailer, but one day she was going to get her hands on Eric's house as well. It needed some serious attention. If the thought created a deeper concern about their personal compatibility, she ignored it for now. There were only so many things a woman could worry about at one time.

The box demanded all of her attention, and anxiety settled in her stomach as she looked at it. It didn't belong to her, and Eric had asked her simply to ship it. And yet, she'd be the one signing off that it didn't contain anything hazardous. It would be irresponsible to ship something without any idea of what that something was, right? Plus, Eric had said FedEx might have to repack the items. On the one hand, that meant he knew other people might see what was in the box. On the other hand, that meant the contents were probably not hazardous. Sadie sighed, her curiosity burning. He hadn't told her *not* to look.

That final thought was all the encouragement she needed. She squatted and, using her legs as instructed by every exercise DVD she'd ever watched, hefted the box, only to find it wasn't that heavy. It was still big, however, and she carried it to the unmade bed and put it down on an area relatively free of rumpled bedding. It would be easier to look through the box while standing.

She began to wrestle the top half of the box off, then stopped and pushed the comforter and top sheet farther away, giving her a flat surface on which she could lay out the contents. She returned to the box, slid the top off, and prepared herself for what she would find inside.

A red sweater. Two three-ring binders—one for a class on Shakespearean literature and another labeled Math 1050. The dates on the pages of notes were from three years earlier and the name typed on a returned assignment in the front pocket of one of the binders read "Megan Burton." A chill ran down Sadie's back as she realized she held Eric's missing daughter's things, but it also compounded the questions in her mind. Eric needed these items? Why?

Sadie had planned to take only a peek at the contents, but that was forgotten as she continued unloading the box, carefully placing everything on the bed in search of what Eric might need so badly. There was a box of checks—half full of new checkbooks and two used booklets that held only the duplicates of checks already written. There were two pairs of flip-flops, a Zip-loc baggie full of hair stuff: bobby pins, a hair brush, elastics, and a couple stretchy headbands. She pulled out a square tea tin about six inches tall and four inches wide containing miscellaneous receipts, some refrigerator magnets, and a couple of photos; the meager contents didn't fill it up by any means.

The Sunkist box also held a couple pairs of jeans, a black bra, two yoga DVDs, and a music box that looked as though it belonged to a six-year-old—ballerinas in pink tutus pirouetted around the sides. Sadie opened the music box and watched the ballerina inside spin around while a tinny version of "Swan Lake" filled the room. The contents of the music box seemed to be several single earrings, a silver necklace, and a few beaded bracelets.

That's it? Sadie wondered as she looked at the bare cardboard of the bottom of the box. No journals, planners, unopened mail? There wasn't even an address book or old cell phone. It was just . . . dregs, leftover items that seemed to have no value, no purpose—especially three years after the owner of the items had disappeared.

Sadie's eyes were drawn back to the tea tin and she removed the lid again, pulling out the three photos and fanning them in her hand. One was of a redheaded girl making a face: her cheeks were blown out, her lips pursed, and her eyes crossed to the extent that it was difficult to determine what she really looked like. Sadie considered that it could be Megan, but the next photo seemed a more likely possibility. In this one a dark-haired girl with bright blue eyes looked back at the camera while she leaned against the chest of a young man whose arms were draped protectively around the girl's waist. They were on a dock or a boat or something, the ocean stretching behind them and wind blowing through their hair. Both of them were strangers to Sadie, of course, but the blue eyes of the girl looked very much like Eric's.

The third picture was of a cat: a gray Persian. It looked up from a tiled floor with a red bow tied onto a lock of fur on its head. Sadie had never seen a cat with a bow in its hair before; she thought that was usually reserved for little yippy dogs.

Sadie looked at the other papers in the tin box and picked up a yellow credit card receipt from Texaco. At the bottom was a signature: *Megan Burton.* The M was fancy, almost like calligraphy, hinting at a personality behind what was otherwise just a name on a gas receipt. Sadie rubbed her thumb over the fancy lettering and wondered what had happened to this girl. She'd had a life, she was in college, and yet her ambition and goals led her nowhere. So much life now resigned to a box. Sadie wondered how many people had holes in their lives where Megan had once been.

For a few minutes, Sadie went through the contents a little

slower, looking for anything that would jump out at her and say, "Aha, this is what Eric needed!" Nothing did. If what he needed was something to sell for quick cash, it didn't exist in this box.

She began carefully repacking the items while pondering the possibilities. When she finished, placing the red sweater on top of everything else and pressing it down to ensure everything fit, she glanced at the clock radio next to Eric's bed. It was 12:13. First, Eric had been cryptic and deliberately vague. Then the box hadn't given her anything to help make sense of his behavior. Sadie hated not having the answers.

In light of those unanswered questions, her concern for Eric increased. What was going on in Florida that made the miscellaneous items in this box so important to him? Was he in trouble? If so, how much? Was there something in the box that would help identify the body? But if so, why hadn't Eric told her?

She drummed her fingers on top of the sweater, letting her thoughts flow and connect in her mind. The only conclusion she could come to was that she was not at peace with things the way they were right now, and she wasn't ready to stop looking for that peace. Not yet.

Eric had said she needed to get the box to Federal Express by 2:00. Sadie could do a lot with the time between then and now.

CHAPTER 7

Sadie pulled into the parking lot of the copy store that also served as the local Federal Express shipping office. She put the car in park and tapped her fingers on the steering wheel as she looked at the blue-and-purple sign. It was 1:36. She only had twenty-four minutes to make up her mind. She picked up her phone from the passenger seat and toggled her way to her text messages where she had stored the address Eric had sent her. After leaving Eric's house, but before driving to the store, she'd gone home and done a reverse look-up on the computer. The address belonged to a house in Homestead, Florida, which was a suburb of Miami. A little more digging led her to the owner on title: Lawrence McCallister. Sadie had no idea who he was.

She paused only a minute before calling Eric's cell phone—his last chance to explain things. He didn't answer. Shoot. Sadie was left with her quandary. However, several seconds after hanging up, while she was still staring at the store and considering her options, she received a text message.

Can't talk right now. Did u ship the box?

She texted back.

I'm at FedEx. I'm worried. What's going on?

He didn't answer right away. She waited until the clock turned to 1:40, then texted him again, aware that he probably wouldn't respond and she would be forced to make a decision with only the information she already had.

You're not going to tell me, are you?

This time he responded.

Not yet. I've got 2 go. Thanks for your help.

Sadie took a deep breath. It fairly killed her to be left out of the loop, and therefore she felt she had only one option. She turned in her seat and stared at the carry-on bag she'd quickly packed half an hour earlier. She hadn't been able to layer her clothing between tissue paper or put things in individual Zip-loc bags, but she had four days' worth of clothing. She was ready to go—but was going to Florida reasonable?

No, she answered herself. There was nothing reasonable about it. She attempted to calm herself by listing again her reasons for doing this. First, Eric needed the box. Second, Eric was involved in something he was unwilling to tell her about—major red flag. Third, he'd invited her to come with him and said there was no one else for him to ask. She'd refused him then, and still stood by the merit of that decision. But now they weren't leaving together so any impropriety seemed displaced by her genuine concern about his welfare. And the fact that she'd been invited meant she would be welcomed if she showed up. Fourth, Eric was her friend; and perhaps one day he'd be more than that. She paused. Was he *already* more than that?

She sat in silence in her car. There were so many reasons for her *not* to do this. She went through each one in her mind. But when she looked at the mental list of why she *should* go, one thing stood out to her above everything else. She truly believed, in her heart of hearts, that Eric needed her.

A moment later she threw the car into reverse and dialed the number she'd stored in her cell phone before leaving the house. She was almost out of Garrison before she reached an actual person on the line. "Yes," she said to the man who asked if he could help her. "I need to get to Miami from Denver International as soon as possible. When's your next flight?"

When she hung up a few minutes later, she had just spent $413.68 on a nonrefundable plane ticket. She was committed to the trip. Which reminded her of the next phone call she needed to make. This one was speed-dial number eight.

Gayle picked up on the second ring. "Sadie," her friend said into the phone. "How was the movie last night with that hunk-a-hunk-of-burnin' love? If you ask me, Robert Redford and Pete Cunningham are a lethal combination."

Was it only last night that Sadie was supposed to watch *Out of Africa* with Pete? So much had happened since then.

"Oh, Gayle," Sadie said, overwhelmed with how much she had to say. "I have got the story of the year for you," she said, knowing that would irrevocably trigger Gayle's curiosity to the point that she'd jump at the chance to be a part of it. Most people would think Gayle an unlikely confidant, but Sadie trusted her completely. They were best friends and had weathered many of life's storms together. Sadie knew about the unfortunate experience Gayle had encountered when she had tried her hand at Internet dating, and Gayle knew about the time Sadie had . . . well, she knew about things no one else knew. Sadie was safe with Gayle, and there was no one else she'd trust to protect her reputation. "But you have to promise me you'll keep it a secret. I'd be ruined if anyone found out."

"Oh?" Gayle said, intrigue oozing from the single syllable.

"And I need to ask a favor. Several favors, actually."

CHAPTER 8

O kay," Gayle said after Sadie had laid out every detail of what had happened last night with both Eric and Pete and had gone on to explain her plan. "So the story I'm to tell everyone is that you went back east to visit your former college roommate, Kara."

"Tara," Sadie corrected. "She lives in Jacksonville. I'll do my darnedest to get up there and even take a picture with us together so I can prove my story. It's been years since I've seen her anyway, so it's kind of like I'm killing two birds with one stone. Right?"

"Right," Gayle said. "I mean, it doesn't explain why you left so quickly or anything, but it'll work."

"It has to work," Sadie said, her stomach clenching at the thought of what would happen if certain details were filtered over backyard fences. "You know as well as anyone that I can't risk anyone knowing what I'm up to."

"You mean you spending the weekend with Eric Burton, alone in Florida, one of the top ten most romantic places in the United States?"

Sadie groaned, making Gayle laugh.

"I'm kidding," she said. "But you can't blame me for teasing just a little bit."

"I wouldn't be going at all if not for the fact that I think Eric is in some kind of trouble."

"But he doesn't know you're coming, does he?"

"Not yet," Sadie said, shifting in her seat. "I'm not sure if I should call before I head out, or after I arrive."

"Oh, you should surprise him," Gayle said. "It's way more romantic that way."

"This isn't a romance-inspired trip," Sadie said. "I'm just worried about him."

"I know," Gayle said with a flippant tone. "Some of the best romance novels I've read are because two people get thrown together in a decidedly unromantic way, only to fall head over heels in love with one another. It's my favorite kind, so you shouldn't tell him you're coming—just appear on his doorstep and *show* him how worried you are."

"I don't think things happen quite like that in real life," Sadie said. She'd already fallen for the police detective and that plot had been done a million times, yet it hadn't gotten her very far.

"Okay, fine," Gayle said. "Call him and have him tell you he doesn't want you to be there. Then you can ignore him while you get to the bottom of things—that's a much better catalyst for a future relationship."

Sadie considered her limited options. "You make a very good point," she said.

"Of course I do," Gayle said with confidence.

Sadie changed the subject back to their arrangement. "You'll get the trailer cleaned up?"

"You bet," Gayle said.

"Thank you." Sadie let out a breath. She was coming up on the I-76 and had just passed a sign that read "Denver 86 miles." Her flight left at 5:23—the timing was perfect, which must mean she was meant to do this, right? "I owe you one."

"Do I get to choose the payback?" There was a new undercurrent to Gayle's voice. A serious tone that caused Sadie to tense slightly despite herself. It was such a quick shift between moods that Sadie couldn't help but be concerned by it.

"What?" Sadie asked, worried she'd misunderstood.

"Do I get to choose how you pay me back?"

"I don't know what you mean."

Gayle paused for a moment. "Never mind," she said, laughing nervously.

"No, what do you mean?"

"Nothing. I shouldn't have said anything. So, do you want me to call you when the trailer is ready?"

"Gayle," Sadie said in a commanding, yet calm, tone. "What do you mean about choosing how I pay you back?"

Another pause. Sadie waited this one out. After a few seconds, Gayle took the bait.

"You and Pete broke up, right?" Gayle asked, hurrying on before Sadie could confirm it. "Is it the 'I hate you and now my friends hate you too' kind of breakup, or the 'We mutually respect each other and have no problem with our friends still being friends' kind of breakup?"

It took a moment for Sadie to figure out exactly what Gayle was saying. When she did, she felt the blood drain from her face a little bit. "You want my permission to date Pete?"

"Well . . . um . . . It's just that now that you'll be out of town, I have an extra ticket to the Renaissance dinner on Saturday."

Sadie was surprised by how much the idea bothered her. She was well aware of Gayle's attraction to Pete—Gayle was not subtle—but neither of them had let it get in the way of their friendship. Pete did not belong to Sadie. He never had, really. Yet picturing Gayle on Pete's arm, Gayle laughing at his jokes, Pete walking Gayle to her door at night—it all made Sadie's stomach tighten. Why? She could think of no reason not to give her blessing other than a humiliating amount of selfishness. Selfishness was wrong. Keeping Pete and Gayle from a potential relationship was even . . . wronger. Never mind that Gayle was breaking one of the cardinal rules of best friendship—never going for your best friend's guy. If Sadie had known Gayle wanted to date Pete, she may have reconsidered putting her trust in Gayle at all. But it was too late now; she'd already laid the whole plan at Gayle's feet. She was over a barrel.

"I'm sorry," Gayle said suddenly, alerting Sadie that she'd paused too long. "It was out of line for me to ask. Pretend I never said anything. Anyway, about the trailer—"

"Of course it's fine," Sadie cut in, purposely lightening her tone and hoping it would help banish all selfish thoughts from her mind. Pete had released her from any commitments they had in order to ensure she could seek out her own best future. Didn't he deserve the same consideration? "I don't have a problem with the two of you going out." She was such a liar sometimes.

"Really? Are you sure? I don't want to hurt our friendship over some super-hot detective you don't want to date anymore. You're much more important to me."

It might have sounded like Gayle was simply overstating things, but Sadie knew she meant every word. If Sadie said, "No, you can't date Pete because he was mine first," Gayle would accept that—grudgingly, perhaps—but she'd accept it all the same. But knowing that made it even more unfair for Sadie to hold either of them accountable to her prior feelings toward Pete.

"I'm sure," Sadie said. "You're both wonderful people and I want you both to be happy." If that happiness was found with each other, well, that was wonderful. Wasn't it?

"You don't think he's so devastated by the breakup that he needs more time to recover, do you?" Gayle asked, hope rising in her voice.

Sadie thought back to the very logical and unemotional way Pete had addressed the issue between them last night. "No," she said, a little sad to admit it. "I don't think he's devastated."

"Oh good," Gayle said with relief. "I wouldn't want to put myself on the altar of relationship rebounding, ya know?"

"No rebound," Sadie said, trying to convince herself she was warming up to the idea. "But you promised me you wouldn't tell anyone what I'm doing, remember? Especially Pete." Sadie felt a touch of panic. If Gayle didn't keep her secret . . . Sadie couldn't think about that. It was too late to call anything back.

"Of course not," Gayle said. To her credit, she sounded sincere in her response. Sadie had no choice but to trust her and put her faith in their years of friendship.

There was another pause; the mood had definitely changed over the last couple of minutes. Sadie finally broke the silence. "Anyway, I'd better go. Call me tomorrow."

"Great," Gayle said. "I'll call in a substitute for Meals on Wheels, and then I'll take the trailer key to Eric's neighbor when I'm done cleaning it up."

"That would be great," Sadie said, thanking Gayle and ending the call. Once she hung up the phone, she allowed her thoughts to leave Garrison, Gayle, and Pete. She needed to focus on what was ahead of her, rather than those things left behind. Gayle would protect Sadie's reputation and fulfill Sadie's agreement to prepare the trailer for sale. Sadie, on the other hand, needed to get ready for what was awaiting her in Florida.

CHAPTER 9

The drive to Denver International Airport was uneventful, except for the lingering discomfort Sadie felt each time she pictured Pete and Gayle going to the Renaissance dinner Saturday night. Would Pete accept the invitation? Part of her hoped he wouldn't—hoped he *did* have something to get over. Then she felt guilty for such thoughts. She'd given her blessing. She eventually gave herself a strong enough talking-to that she could let it go—for the most part—and fully focus on Eric and Florida instead.

Since she had to check the box as luggage—which she'd amply wrapped with duct tape and marked *fragile*—she checked her suitcase as well and had time to grab some dinner in one of the restaurants near her terminal. One would think that a chef's salad would be difficult to do poorly, but airport food was in a class of its own. The lettuce was limp, the tomatoes were tasteless, and the ranch dressing was too sweet. On her way out of the café, she saw a selection of pies in the front case. She zeroed in on the key lime pie, feeling it was only appropriate to have a slice of Florida's official state pie. Certainly it would be better than the salad.

She took a seat at a booth and smiled as the waitress set down

the pie in front of her. For whatever reason her thoughts began wax-
ing poetic and as her fork hovered over the slice of pie, she took note
of the triangular shape—the three corners. Gayle, Pete, and Sadie?
Or maybe Eric, Pete, and Sadie? She brought the edge of her fork
down and cut off the tip of the pie. Now there were four corners.
What was once a triangle was now closer to a rectangle—Gayle,
Sadie, Eric, and Pete? She sighed and put the bite in her mouth,
prepared for zippy, tangy, creamy goodness.

Instead the meringue was too sweet, and Sadie could barely
taste the lime. No zip, no tang, and the graham cracker crust was
soggy. Sadie ate half of the pie before determining it wasn't worth
the calories or the six dollars she'd paid for it. Convinced she'd have
a chance to taste good key lime pie once she arrived in Florida, she
threw away the uneaten portion and grabbed a packet of peanut butter M&M's from one of the gift shops instead. The M&M's were
really good, which spoke volumes about the pie.

The plane to Miami left on time, but since the flight was nearly
four hours long and Florida time was two hours later than Colorado,
it was after midnight when Sadie arrived. She hadn't calculated the
time quite right, so her plans of driving straight to the address Eric
had given her wasn't an option. Instead, she picked up a rental car,
relieved that she didn't need to have a reservation, and then followed
the lit-up signs to the airport Hilton.

Even at night she could feel the thickness of the air. She didn't
have much experience with humidity and she hoped it wouldn't be
too hot tomorrow. If it was, she hoped she had brought the right
kind of clothes.

It wasn't until she was alone in a strange room, in a strange city,
staring at a strange ceiling that she wondered if she should have
just mailed the box like Eric had asked and been done with it. She

hadn't necessarily meant to follow Gayle's advice of surprising Eric, but she'd managed to do it anyway and wasn't sure how to proceed in the morning. What would he do when he realized she had come in person?

And yet, despite the discomfort all these thoughts brought to mind, it was difficult to imagine having done anything different. Eric was in trouble; she could feel it. It wasn't normal to need so much money so quickly. She had a feeling that he'd listed the trailer at a price far below its value in hopes that it would sell quickly. And it would. The people of Garrison were notoriously cheap. She made a note to ask Gayle to check out his ad in the morning.

Gayle. Had she called Pete already?

With a grunt, Sadie rolled onto her side and forced her eyes closed. Morning was coming whether she was well-rested or not, but it would be an easier day if she got some sleep. Still, her stomach remained in knots as she thought about Eric not too many miles away. Should she call him and tell him she was in Florida, even though it was the middle of the night? Was showing up on his doorstep in the morning too rash? Argh, what was she doing? Her brain finally shut off and allowed her to drift into dreamless sleep.

Sadie woke at eight, then hurried to get ready. She hoped to intercept Eric before he went anywhere for the day. She ordered a good Southern breakfast from room service—biscuits and gravy—and then flung open her curtains to greet the inspiring view of office buildings and streets crowded with the downtown Miami morning commute. Lovely.

With breakfast on the way, she took a quick shower and was nearly ready by the time someone tapped on her door, announcing "Room service."

She wriggled as she sat down at the small table by the window, excited by such an appropriate start to her day's adventures even if she only had two minutes to eat, but within one bite she found herself less than impressed. She felt sure the gravy had come from a can. The next hotel room she rented would have a kitchenette, she decided. Then she'd make her own biscuits and gravy, which, if she did say so herself, were amazing.

Not wanting to make the kitchen staff feel bad—she was convinced they checked the plates and based their self-esteem on how much food was gone—she ate about half, but couldn't force herself to eat the rest. She repacked her suitcase, slipped forty dollars into her pocket for emergencies, and headed downstairs to check out.

On her way to the rental car, she grabbed a banana and a muffin from the hotel café. When she stepped outside, she was again slapped around by the humidity, which was thicker and hotter than it had been when she had arrived last night. With a little luck, she'd get used to the weather pretty fast.

Once in her car she turned it on and plugged in the handy-dandy GPS unit she'd bought at Walmart a few months earlier. She and Gayle had gone to Denver looking for this boutique they'd heard carried those darling red-bottomed shoes Oprah wore all the time. After finding themselves lost three times, Sadie had invested in a GPS system; she had no doubt it would be put to good use here in Miami.

It took her a couple minutes to program the address, and once the map was calculated, she was surprised to find that the city of Homestead was nearly fifty miles away. Living in Northern Colorado for most of her life apparently gave her a warped sense of the word *suburb*. It was nearly nine o'clock before she was on the right freeway heading in the right direction. She wondered if she'd get to Homestead so late in the day that Eric would already be gone doing whatever it was he was doing. She could only hope that wouldn't be the case. She also realized she was almost out of time to call and warn him of her arrival. This far in, though, she was worried he'd be mad and she'd feel like an idiot. She decided to take comfort in Gayle's insistence that it was romantic for her to surprise him. Hopefully the romance would overwhelm anything else he was thinking.

When she finally pulled up to the address, the butterflies in her stomach had turned to bumblebees. She took a deep breath, hoping it would calm her down, and then wondered how on earth she could have done all the things that had brought her here and not have felt this way until now? Not for the first time she wondered if there was something wrong with her, some neurological breakdown that delayed full consideration of her actions until that consideration was a moot point.

Taking another deep breath—which didn't help—she got out of the car and popped the trunk before shutting the driver's door and giving the house another look while she stretched out her back. A mini-palm tree grew next to the front door and the fenceless yard melted into the lawn of its neighbors on both sides. The grass wasn't soft like the grass in Colorado, rather it was coarser, with thicker blades. Sadie assumed that had to do with the climate. The mid-sixties temperature was something she could get used to very quickly if not for the humidity that made her feel sticky and in need of a shower despite the fact that it was just past ten o'clock in the morning.

The small square house was wrapped in peach stucco, with a single carport on one side covering a late-model Ford sedan. There was an Avis sticker on the back window verifying it was a rental car. Eric was here. Sadie's stomach flipped with the realization that their meeting was only seconds away. What would he say? What would *she* say? What if he didn't want her here after all?

Moving around to the trunk, Sadie gripped the Sunkist box with both hands and lifted it; a twinge in her bad shoulder made her wince. She attempted to shift the weight, which helped, and re-minded herself to be more careful. Though healed, her shoulder was certainly still tender and deserved her respect and understanding of all it had been through.

She had to balance the box on the bumper in order to shut the trunk, and then there was nothing else to do but go to the door and face whatever Eric's reaction would be. As she made her way up the cracked sidewalk she hoped that her assumption he would be glad to see her was correct and that this trip wasn't something she would regret.

Once on the porch, she used her elbow to ring the doorbell, then forced a polite smile as she raised her chin and straightened her back, trying to look more confident than she felt at the moment.

Footsteps approached on the other side of the door, and then the knob turned, and the wooden door was pulled open, leaving a screen to separate her and . . . the *woman* standing there. Sadie felt her eyebrows lift, and her explanation of what she was doing there fizzled out on her tongue now that she was faced with a completely unexpected set of circumstances. And then her mind made a con-nection and her discomfort multiplied by eighty-two.

Other than the eyes, which were brown, and the lines that, though not prominent, gave away middle-age, this woman looked almost exactly like the photo of Megan Sadie had found in the box yesterday.

Although she couldn't be certain, and a large part of her heart really wanted to believe it wasn't the case, Sadie suspected she'd just traveled two thousand miles to find herself face-to-face with Eric's ex-wife.

Super Sausage Gravy

1 pound ground sage sausage
½ cup flour
½ teaspoon basil (add more, if desired)
1 (12-ounce) can evaporated milk*
2 to 4 cups water
Salt and pepper to taste

Brown sausage, breaking up clumps as it cooks; do not drain. Sprinkle flour and basil over the sausage and cook 3 minutes, stirring constantly. Add evaporated milk and 1 cup of water. Bring to a boil, stirring constantly, and then lower heat, stirring until desired consistency is reached, adding more water as needed. Salt and pepper to taste.

Serve over biscuits. (Frozen biscuits work great—just thaw and bake them first.) .

Serves 6.

*Can use regular milk in place of evaporated milk and water.

CHAPTER 10

Sadie readjusted her position on the couch, hoping she didn't look as uncomfortable as she felt. She could smell something cooking in the kitchen, and her stomach, though full, was terribly distracted by it. *Chicken,* Sadie thought, *and barbeque sauce.* It was just after ten o'clock in the morning, which led Sadie to believe that whatever was cooking was in a slow cooker; the aroma was too strong to be lingering in the air from last night's dinner. The spices tingled in her nose and her mouth watered for some home cooking, but Sadie tried very, very hard to keep her focus.

Layla—that was her name, like the song by Eric Clapton—dialed a number written on a pad of paper on the end table. Sadie took it as a good sign that she hadn't assigned Eric a speed-dial number and hoped that, like most people, the two were glad to be divorced from one another. While Layla listened on the phone, Sadie took a quick inventory of the woman.

Layla was a little thick around the middle, but had dark hair that brushed her shoulders and wide, brown eyes that made her look young and innocent despite her being in her mid-forties. She was wearing a bright turquoise fitted T-shirt, white knee-length shorts, and white sandals. A multicolored beaded necklace hung against her tanned neck. She was very polished and well put-together, but seemed a little disconnected. A little too unattached to the situation at hand. Maybe the stress of all that was happening was overwhelming her emotional responses or something.

In the minute and a half since Sadie had arrived, they'd exchanged names and established that Sadie had brought the box to Eric. Sadie tried her best to ignore the vise grip in her stomach, not liking the way this encounter had come together. She didn't have verification that Layla was Eric's ex-wife because she couldn't think of a way to ask that wouldn't somehow come across as adversarial. Sadie was here, in part, because she had a romantic interest in Eric. If, in fact, Layla was Eric's former wife, then that put them in an awkward situation. It seemed best to leave things ambiguous, but the resemblance between Layla and Megan was impossible to discount. Because of all that, this moment was nothing like the fantasy Sadie had created in her mind, the one where Eric, realizing that she had come to Florida, confessed what was going on and pulled her into an embrace which may, or may not, have ended in that first kiss he'd left up to her. She hurried to blink away the scene so perfectly mapped out in her mind and hoped Layla wouldn't notice the tint in her cheeks.

Layla put the phone on the end table next to the recliner where she sat across from Sadie. If she was as curious about Sadie as Sadie was about her, she was doing an excellent job of hiding it. Layla hadn't asked about the box that sat on the floor at Sadie's feet or how Sadie knew Eric in the first place. "He's still not answering," Layla said. She picked up the remote and un-muted the TV.

"Still?" Sadie asked. "Have you been trying to reach him for awhile?"

"He left early this morning," Layla said casually, turning to watch *The Price Is Right.* Bob Barker was the host, which meant that particular episode was a rerun. "He said he'd be back by nine."

"Where did he go?" Sadie asked after several seconds without conversation.

"I don't know," Layla said, still watching the TV.

Sadie glanced at the large clock on the wall behind Layla's head while Bob Barker introduced the next item the contestants were supposed to price. It was eight minutes after ten. "So, um, Eric left from here?" she asked, trying to be subtle. "Did he, uh, stay here last night then?"

That was the only reason Sadie could think of that Layla would know he'd left early and expect that he was coming back. Plus, his rental car was in the carport. But she didn't like thinking these things, didn't like the implications she couldn't ignore in her mind. Layla, however, ignored the implications completely. In fact, she ignored everything and didn't answer, engrossed in watching the newest audience member running for the stage. Sadie's nerves had no patience for this or the questions that kept bubbling up. Eric could return at any minute and she wanted to know exactly what she was dealing with when he did.

She cleared her throat. "Did Eric stay here last night?" she asked, louder and bolder than she'd have liked to but in serious need of getting this woman's attention. Layla glanced at her and nodded, but with such casualness that Sadie questioned herself. Was Sadie jumping to conclusions again? Was she watching too much TV and developing a mind that thought the worst of people?

She decided to push *those* thoughts to the back of her mind and keep her focus on where Eric was and when he was coming back. The information would be much easier to figure out if Layla were even a little bit helpful. Eric hadn't told Layla where he was going, but surely she had ideas; she must have overheard something or noted the way he was dressed.

Layla just stared at the TV, looking bored and expressionless, but completely absorbed in the show. Maybe a doctor had given her something to help her cope with the information that the police may have found her daughter's body.

Sadie decided to wait for a commercial break. Unfortunately, when one came on, Layla seemed just as interested in the Welch's grape juice commercial. Sadie was sorely tempted to mute the TV altogether, but knew Emily Post probably had some rules somewhere on it being bad manners to turn off someone's TV in their own home.

"Do you have any idea where Eric went?" she asked, loud enough to get Layla's attention. She turned to face Sadie and although the TV was very distracting, Sadie was determined to have a conversation despite the noise. She reminded herself that the game show would be back on soon and she might very well lose Layla again.

"He didn't tell me where they were going. He said that they'd be back at nine."

Wait a minute . . .

"They?"

"Larry went with him."

Larry? Short for Lawrence McCallister, the home owner? "And Larry is . . . ?"

Layla blinked, letting the hanging sentence hang.

"Is Larry your . . . husband?" Sadie liked the idea that Layla and Larry lived together in this house. That Eric had simply slept on their couch to avoid having to pay for a hotel. She liked that explanation a whole lot.

But Layla's answer didn't give that possibility much room to breathe. "Larry used to be my husband."

Sadie was so confused. Layla *had* to be medicated—or maybe she was mentally ill. Sadie took a breath, no longer concerned with easing her way into getting answers. "So your *ex*-husbands left together and said they'd be home by nine—nine this morning or nine o'clock tonight?"

"This morning."

"They're an hour late. You're not worried about them?"

Layla's blank stare didn't waver. "They told me not to worry about anything."

"I don't mean to pry," Sadie said, inching forward on the couch. "But Eric was expecting some important information today. It's surprising he would make himself unavailable."

"He said not to worry," Layla repeated.

Sadie felt her shoulders fall. This was getting ridiculous. She was running out of ways to make the point that *she* was worried, and that if Layla knew anything at all she ought to share it.

"This box is full of Megan's things," Sadie suddenly said, going up yet one more level of boldness and pointing at the box. She watched Layla's eyes go to the box for a few moments and waited for her to make some reaction to Megan's name. Nothing. "Eric seemed to need it pretty badly."

"He said he was waiting for a box," Layla said casually, letting her eyes dart to the TV where a car commercial raced across the screen. "I'm supposed to sign for it and not open it until they get back."

When her eyes came back to Sadie's they contained no question as to why Sadie had brought the box from Colorado instead of

FedEx, but at least Sadie now knew why Layla was here—to receive the package.

A station advertisement of what was on today's lineup came on the TV and Sadie feared it would transition to *The Price Is Right* again at any moment.

"I'm worried about Eric," Sadie finally said flat out, talking quickly. "When he called me yesterday he was . . . vague about what's been going on." Sadie cringed; she sounded like his mother!

"He's always like that," Layla said, her eyes moving to the TV again. "Larry says it makes him feel heroic."

Glancing quickly at the TV, Sadie knew she might only have seconds left before she'd have to give up center stage to a new re-frigerator and Barker's Beauties. Were there any other questions she could ask this woman, unhelpful as she was?

The opportunity was officially lost when Rod Roddy's voice introduced the show. Sadie slumped against the back of the couch, reviewing what she'd learned.

"Megan is your daughter, right?"

"Yes." Layla didn't look away from the TV.

"So Eric is your ex-husband?"

"Yes."

"And he and Larry went somewhere together?"

Layla didn't answer at all this time, her eyes glued to the TV. Sadie was left to ponder on it herself. Where would two men who had been married to the same woman want to go together? Leaving early in the morning meant they probably hadn't gone to the police station. What else would be important enough to go to together—and leave Layla by herself in the process? Sadie didn't know what was wrong with the woman, but she doubted it was a good idea to leave her alone for long stretches of time.

Sadie was pondering the possibilities when she caught movement near the kitchen. She turned slightly and watched a gray cat smooth itself around the corner of the room. Sadie instantly recognized it as the cat from the picture she'd found in the Sunkist box, although it had put on some weight and no longer had the red bow. The cat looked at Sadie for a moment before jumping onto Layla's lap. Without so much as looking at the animal, Layla immediately began stroking the cat from head to tail.

Sadie watched Layla's hand glide over the cat's body in a rhythmic motion. After only five minutes with this woman, Sadie could imagine Layla sitting that way, petting the cat, for hours at a time while she blankly watched TV. The cat purred loudly enough that Sadie could hear it over the audience applauding the next contestant.

After waiting for several seconds, just in case Layla realized they hadn't finished their conversation, Sadie pulled open her purse and dug out her cell phone. She hadn't wanted to call Eric herself for fear it would appear rather vain for her to expect him to answer her call after Layla had already tried, but she had a feeling that very little affected Layla. She'd opened her contact list in search of his number when she was startled by the ringing of the cordless phone sitting on the end table next to Layla. Layla looked at the phone but made no attempt to answer; she was too busy petting the cat and watching a tiny Filipino woman guess the price on a tube of toothpaste.

"Would you like me to answer that?" Sadie asked after the second ring.

"Sure," Layla said.

Shaking her head slightly, Sadie hurried to the phone, pushed TALK and raised it to her ear, turning her back on the TV in hopes the sound wouldn't interfere with the call. "Hello?" she said.

"Hello, is Mr. Burton there?" an official voice asked.

Sadie wished he were. "I'm sorry, he's not here right now. Can I, uh, take a message?"

"What about Mrs. McCallister?"

Sadie glanced at Layla. Was her last name McCallister? She'd said Larry used to be her husband. Sadie wasn't thrilled about handing the phone over, but didn't see that she had much choice. Perhaps listening to Layla's end of the conversation would be helpful. "Just a minute," Sadie said. She held the phone against her chest and turned to Layla. "They're calling for Mrs. McCallister. Is that you?"

Layla didn't answer, but the audience burst into applause and the little woman on the TV screen raised both hands to cover her mouth. She'd won . . . something. Sadie took a couple steps forward and picked up the remote. It was very forward of her, she knew, but the phone call sounded important. She took a breath and then pressed the mute button. Layla immediately looked to where the remote had been, then up to Sadie who was holding it.

"I was watching that!" she said, and though Sadie knew she was angry, her voice showed very little inflection.

"Are you Mrs. McCallister?" Sadie asked her again.

Layla was thrown off for a moment, leading Sadie to repeat the question. "Are you Mrs. McCallister?"

"I think so," Layla said, causing Sadie even more confusion. She *thought* her name was Mrs. McCallister? She wasn't sure?

"Then, I guess this is for you."

Layla paused for a moment, but then took the phone. "Hello . . . yes . . . okay . . . I don't know . . . yes . . . okay." She hung up and stood slowly, seeming to be more worried about displacing the cat than the content of the phone call. Once she was on her feet, she met Sadie's eyes. "The police want me to come to the station." Her eyes flitted to the TV.

"It's a rerun," Sadie said, trying to preempt any ideas Layla might have of finishing the show before following the police's instructions. Layla hesitated, and Sadie pressed the POWER button. She didn't know what to make of the other woman, and wouldn't have been surprised if Layla had insisted on staying. Luckily, she didn't.

"Did they say why they wanted you to come down?" Sadie asked, glad that she had Layla's full attention now—though that wasn't saying much.

"They said it was important," Layla said.

Sadie's heart started racing. Eric had said the police would know today whether or not the body was Megan's. This could be *that* answer. And Layla was the one who would hear the news first?

"Do you need a ride?" Sadie asked on impulse, suddenly worried about the other woman's ability to hear tragic news—if in fact the news was tragic—not to mention Layla's ability to drive. Her behavior was so strange already; if the police told her the remains they had found were her daughter's, how would she react? Besides that, the rental car was the only vehicle Sadie had seen and she didn't imagine Layla was authorized to drive it.

Layla took one more glance at the blank TV then let out a regretful sigh. "Okay," she said in that same even tone. "But *Wheel of Fortune* starts at noon."

CHAPTER 11

Layla gave Sadie perfect instructions on how to find the police station, which was only a few blocks away. By the time they arrived, Sadie had drawn up the hypothesis that Homestead, Florida, wasn't all that different than Garrison, Colorado. The towns seemed to be similar in size and endowed with equal quaintness. The cobblestone streets and businesses of the downtown area were clean and well-maintained, reflecting a historical feel. Palm trees dotted the city, just as cottonwoods and birch trees grew throughout Garrison. Old-fashioned lampposts and park benches encouraged people to stop and smell the roses—or hibiscus, as the case may be.

As soon as they pulled up to the police station, a blocky building the same color as Layla's house, Layla let herself out. Sadie scrambled to shut off the car and follow the other woman inside despite the lack of invitation. Sadie didn't think Layla would object and, quite honestly, didn't know what else to do. She considered texting Eric, but what would she say? Finding the right words to explain why she'd come to Florida was much harder than she'd anticipated. Of course, it would have been much easier if he'd have answered the door like he was *supposed* to.

"Can I help you?" a Latin woman at the front counter asked, cutting off Sadie's thoughts.

Layla didn't answer the question. Instead, she looked around the room. From the attention she gave them, one would think the white walls, utilitarian desks, and terra-cotta tile made for fascinating décor. Sadie gave Layla a few seconds to speak before leaning in and answering for her.

"This is Layla McCallister," Sadie said. "I'm not sure who called her, but someone from the station asked her to come in. Perhaps something regarding her daughter, Megan Burton." Sadie cast a sideways glance at Layla to see if she reacted, but she was looking out the front door of the police station. Sadie couldn't see whether she was surprised to hear Megan's name or not.

The woman at the desk nodded and put the phone to her ear as she punched a button and lowered her chin so that Sadie couldn't hear what she said. A moment later, she hung up the phone and directed Sadie and Layla to a row of plastic chairs on the left side of the room. They hadn't reached them before a large black man stepped out of an office farther down the hall. He seemed to recognize Layla and came toward them.

"Mrs. McCallister," he said, inclining his head, which was so bald and shiny it reflected the fluorescent lighting. He put out his hand, and Layla took it, though Sadie felt sure she gave a limp-noodle handshake at best. "How are you doing?"

"Fine," Layla said in her flat tone. She seemed annoyed to be here.

The man turned to Sadie and the expression on his face was so instantly familiar that Sadie nearly startled at the unexpected reminder of Pete that flashed through her mind. This man was younger, broader, taller, and darker, but the way he held his eyes and the careful smile on his face was just like Pete. It further confirmed her suspicions that such neutral expressions were taught to police detectives throughout the country. He put out his hand, and Sadie focused on giving him a firm shake, like her father had taught her to do many years ago. Dad had told her when you gave a strong handshake, it inspired confidence and respect in the other person. Sadie hoped it was true.

"I'm Sadie Hoffmiller," she said with a nod as they dropped hands. "I'm a friend of Eric Burton's and was at Mrs. McCallister's house when you called. She asked me to drive her over." It was hard not to say more—lay out all the details—so she clamped her teeth together to prevent herself from giving in. The police in Garrison thought she was a busybody. She wanted to make a better impression on this man. She liked to think of this as a whole new start in regard to her relationship with law enforcement.

"I'm Sergeant Mathews," the man said with a nod, then extended his arm toward the room he'd just exited and looked at Layla, his expression softening a little. "My office, if you please."

Sadie tried to hide her surprise at being included. The other officers she'd been involved with had tried to keep her out of things. Of course, it hadn't worked, but they had tried. Maybe they did things differently in Florida, or maybe they could see what the Colorado police couldn't, that Sadie was an asset and not a liability to their investigation. The thought made her smile, and she walked a little taller as she followed Layla into Sergeant Mathews's office.

Sadie and Layla sat in the leather chairs across from the desk while the detective closed the door behind them. His chair creaked when he sat down, and he immediately tapped his fingers on a closed file on his desk.

"I had hoped Mr. Burton would be here by now," Sergeant Mathews began, his eyes on Layla after a quick glance at his watch.

"He said he'd be back by nine," Layla answered. She sat up straight in the chair, her hands resting on her tanned knee, crossed over her other leg. She was very still and Sadie wondered if she was nervous about what was coming.

"Do you know where he went?" Sergeant Mathews asked.

"I don't know," Layla said in that airy voice of hers. "But he told me not to worry."

The sergeant nodded thoughtfully, and Sadie couldn't help but add more information so as to help him get a full picture of what was going on. "Layla's been trying to call him, but he isn't answering," she said, giving the detective an intent look she hoped would alert him to her concern.

Sergeant Mathews held her eyes for a moment, and then nodded his understanding, encouraging Sadie to continue.

"You said he was coming here. Did *you* get a hold of him?"

"Yes, but we only spoke for a few seconds. He said he'd be in as soon as he could." He paused thoughtfully. "Do you have any reason to believe he's in some kind of trouble?"

Sadie hesitated. Did selling his trailer and wanting Megan's box count toward adequate reason for being worried about him? She wasn't sure that was what Sergeant Mathews was looking for.

"He said not to worry," Layla cut in.

"That's good," Mathews said as though to appease Layla. Sadie wondered how well he knew Eric's ex-wife, and she wished she could ask him some questions about her.

The sergeant pulled a notebook out of the front drawer of his desk and wrote something down. He paused, then looked up at both women. Sadie liked that he seemed to be giving her as much consideration as he was giving Layla.

"I would postpone this if I could, but I have a meeting at the courthouse in half an hour and I wanted to pass on the information as soon as possible." He cleared his throat. "We have the first of the medical examiner's reports," he explained. Though there was still a great deal of neutrality in his tone, Sadie could hear an undercurrent that seemed . . . relieved. And it relieved her as well. As much as she liked being a part of things, she didn't like to hear bad news. Which, she realized, was likely why Sergeant Mathews had let her come in the first place—because he wasn't going to drop a bombshell. She suspected that he also wasn't sure Layla would understand everything going on and he wanted another witness to the event. Whatever the reason, she was simply glad to be part of the in-crowd on this one and hoped she'd be able to help in some way.

Sadie still held her breath in anticipation of what he was about to say. Layla was looking at a spot on the floor just in front of her chair, her hands clasped together and back straight.

"It's not Megan," Sergeant Mathews said.

The room seemed to lose pressure instantly. They all paused for a moment and Layla lifted her head, her expression still causal. "Can I have the bracelet back now?"

What bracelet? Sadie wondered, taken aback by Layla's response. No tears of relief? No questions about who the body might be?

"I'm afraid it's still evidence," Mathews said regretfully. His eyes flickered to Sadie before returning to Layla. "There's something else."

Both women looked at him.

"We found a purse not far from the body. It's in pretty bad shape, but our forensic team has been going through it, taking X-rays and specialized photographs of the contents." He opened the folder on his desk and pulled out a single piece of paper. He slid the paper toward Layla, and Sadie leaned forward to get a peek.

The image on the paper reminded Sadie of a carbon copy, though one where the carbon had been bent and wrinkled, transferring smudges onto places it didn't belong. "Is this a driver's license?" Sadie asked. The image was enlarged, of course, and the fact that the details were all shades of the same color of inky blue made it hard to distinguish specifics.

Without saying anything, Sergeant Mathews leaned forward and tapped the photo. Sadie followed his silent instruction and squinted at the picture on the right-hand side. It was really hard to make out many features. She leaned in closer. It looked a little like . . .

"Megan?" Layla asked, also leaning forward. She jabbed her finger at the photo and looked up at Mathews, her eyes wider than usual and her expression animated for the first time. "Is that Megan?"

Once again, Mathews didn't answer. Instead he moved his finger from the photo to the date the license was issued. "We've requested an actual copy from the Department of Motor Vehicles in Texas— the state that issued this license—to verify the information, but it looks like this license was issued three weeks after your daughter disappeared."

CHAPTER 12

Sadie began scanning the image with more detail. She'd seen only one photograph of Megan so she had very little to compare this picture to. The name printed on the license was Lucile Anne Powell. "Are you sure this is her?" Sadie asked, looking back at the image once more.

"No," Mathews said, shaking his head. "The copy is too poor of quality for us to do much with it, but seeing as the bracelet was found with the body . . ." He glanced at Layla before continuing. "We think that this *could* be Megan, or someone who looks very much like her." He leaned back in his chair.

"It's not her," Layla suddenly said, causing Sadie and Sergeant Mathews to look at her. She was sitting in her chair, her back straight and her mouth thin. Sadie, sitting beside her, could see the muscles bunching up below Layla's ear, the only betrayal of her tension. Layla shook her head for emphasis and repeated herself. "It's not her." She began looking around the office as though searching for something else to focus on.

Sadie looked at Sergeant Mathews, who sat in his chair watching

Layla. He began talking again. "We'll be getting the original from Texas any time, which will better allow us to finalize the results."

Layla let out a breath and made eye contact with Mathews again. "It isn't her," she said. The emotion had drained from her words and her face, returning her to her usual flatness.

"Why don't you want to believe it could be her?" Sadie asked, instantly aware of Mathews looking at her and wishing she could bite back the words, or at least not ask them quite so sharply. *I am not a busybody. I am not a busybody. I am not a busybody.*

Layla didn't answer. Instead she stood up. "Can I go? I don't want to be here anymore."

Mathews watched her carefully and nodded. Layla headed for the door. Sadie didn't know what to do except stand up as well. She turned to the sergeant, looking for some way to close this strange meeting. She felt as though she should apologize for Layla, but she'd only known the woman for forty minutes. More than anything she worried that Layla's actions would come across as suspicious to the police, and although she didn't know this woman or understand why she was so . . . oblivious, she felt protective of her for some reason.

"I, uh, well . . . um. It was nice meeting you." She turned to see Layla heading toward the front of the police station. "And I'll be sure to relay this information to Mr. Burton as soon as I speak to him."

Mathews stood as well, but didn't speak right away. "Do you have a moment?"

"Um," Sadie looked to see Layla push her way out of the front doors. "I think maybe I should make sure she gets home okay."

"Layla's all right," Mathews said. "We all keep an eye on her; she'll probably walk home."

Sadie snapped her head around to look at the sergeant. "You keep an eye on her?"

Mathews smiled, revealing a slight gap between his front teeth that Sadie hadn't noticed before—probably because he hadn't smiled since she'd met him. He gestured for her to sit down again. "Everyone looks out for Layla. She'll be fine."

Sadie sat, holding her purse on her lap with both hands. "Looks out for her?"

Mathews also returned to his chair. "How well do you know Layla?"

"Not well at all," Sadie explained. "I know Eri—Mr. Burton. We're . . . friends and we live in the same town in Colorado."

He nodded, and Sadie felt an uncomfortable flutter in her stomach at his easy acceptance. Easy acceptance was not a trait police officers were all that good at—not the officers Sadie had met, anyway.

"But Mr. Burton told you what to expect with Layla, right?"

"Not exactly," Sadie said, relaxing her hands where they were gripping the handles of her purse too tightly. "I was worried about him and he needed some things from his house, so I brought them to him, only he wasn't there. That's when I met Layla."

"Today?" Mathews asked, his heavy eyebrows rising onto his forehead.

Sadie nodded again, shifting in her seat. "Less than an hour ago."

"And you haven't seen Mr. Burton since your arrival?"

"No."

He seemed to consider this for a few moments. "Do you mind telling me what had you so worried about him?" Mathews asked, using that careful tone police were so good at.

She opened her mouth to answer, but the words wouldn't come. Eric didn't even know she was here; he hadn't had a chance to explain what was going on yet. What would he think if she just downloaded her concerns to Sergeant Mathews? But right on the heels of that thought was the reminder of all the times she'd been the one sneaking behind the back of the police. It might have turned out okay, but it had also landed her with community service and caused her to question her own character.

Mathews was watching her and he suddenly reminded her of Pete—of the first time she'd met him and all the times they'd been together since. More than once Pete had told her that telling the truth made all the difference in a police investigation. Sadie was going to shoot straight this time around; she wasn't going to be underfoot or hiding anything.

She took a deep breath and told him about Eric's call from the day before, about the box, and about her decision to come to Florida when Eric wouldn't explain what was going on. She ended with her concerns about Eric telling Layla he would be home at nine, yet now it was nearly eleven. "He expected an answer about . . . the body today. I can't imagine that he'd make himself unavailable." She paused for a breath, finding it much easier to talk to Mathews than she had thought it would be. It was like sharing her burden, which meant she didn't have to worry alone anymore. "When Layla first told me he was gone, I assumed he'd entrusted her to deal with the information in his place, but after getting to know her a little better, I . . ." Her voice trailed off. She didn't want to slander the woman, but there was definitely something . . . off. Enough that she didn't think Eric wouldn't expect Layla to take the primary role in something this important.

Mathews nodded and wrote some notes in his notebook. "I'm surprised as well," he said, looking up at her and tapping his pen on the pad of paper. "I've spoken with Mr. Burton several times since we made the first call to him on Wednesday. I'd asked him for some personal effects of Megan's and I assume that's what's in the box. He said it would arrive today and seemed quite eager for any information I could give him. I called him this morning, after I called Layla, and he said he'd be right in, but he seemed to be a bit distracted. I have a feeling he hasn't been giving me the full story."

Sadie was sure Eric was holding back information from *her*, but why would he also be holding back from the police?

Mathews tapped his pen some more, keeping rhythm with Sadie's thoughts, and raised his other hand to rub his clean-shaved chin. "What do you know about Megan Burton?"

"I know she disappeared three years ago after going on spring break and that the police had almost nothing to go on. I know she looked like her mother."

Looked. Past tense.

"That's it?" Mathews asked, surprise flickering across his face. She could almost read his thoughts: how could she be a friend of Eric's and yet be so uninformed of the most tragic thing that had ever happened to him? It was an excellent question.

"He doesn't talk about his past much," Sadie said. *And because I was trying to hide from my feelings toward him, I didn't dare deepen our friendship by asking personal questions.* She felt bad about that now, wondering what kind of difference she could have made if she'd given Eric the opportunity to trust her with his heartache.

"You said Layla tried to call him after you arrived at her house?"

Sadie nodded, trepidation filling in the nooks and crannies of her mind as she picked up on Mathews's growing concern. "He didn't answer. And . . . did I mention he doesn't know I'm here?"

Mathews immediately furrowed his eyebrows. "You mean he doesn't know you've arrived?"

Sadie made a half-nod, half-shrug motion with her head and

shoulders, feeling as though she were about to be reprimanded. "Like I said, he was really . . . cryptic on the phone yesterday. I worried he'd tell me not to come. Then when he wasn't at the house and I met Layla instead—which was not something I expected—it kind of threw me off."

Mathews leaned forward, resting his arms on the desk as he looked at Sadie. "You're saying he didn't know you were *coming?*"

She thought she'd adequately covered that, but was feeling more and more unsettled due to the fact that Mathews was having such trouble with her explanation. Would he understand if she used the romance-novel angle Gayle had advocated?

"No," Sadie said. "I mean, he asked me to come, but I said no and then I changed my mind and decided to . . . surprise him. No one knows I'm here, well, except my friend Gayle, but she promised she wouldn't tell a soul."

Mathews held her eyes for a few seconds, and Sadie wished she dared look away. Even though she knew she'd told the truth, the whole truth, and nothing but the truth, she found herself searching her brain to make sure she hadn't misled him in any way. The fact was that sometimes the truth didn't sound so good.

The sergeant leaned back and opened the folder again, flipping through a few papers before extracting one and pushing it across the table. The title on the form was "Privacy Release Authorization Form." Sadie skimmed over the typed words until arriving at the end of the printed information. The final line was "I therefore authorize this office of the Miami-Dade police department to impart any and all information in regard to this case to the following individuals until I request that the privacy authorization be removed." Below that final sentence were two names, written in somewhat sloppy handwriting that Sadie had seen a time or two and knew belonged to Eric.

The first name was Lawrence McCallister of Homestead, Florida.

The second name was Sarah Diane (Sadie) Hoffmiller of Garrison, Colorado.

CHAPTER 13

Sadie blinked and read her name again, then scanned a little farther down the page where the printed name below the swirling signature read Eric Burton. For a few seconds she tried to come up with all the reasons he would have done this—but only one was certain.

Eric expected her to come to Florida. She wasn't sure how she felt about that, but now she realized why Sergeant Mathews had let her come in with Layla, why he'd told her all the details. And she'd thought they just did things differently here?

Mathews cleared his throat and Sadie looked up. How could Eric have known she would come to Florida when she herself hadn't known until a few hours before her flight left?

"He signed this yesterday?" Sadie asked, having noticed the date when she'd scanned the page.

"We met yesterday morning and, among other things, we discussed who would have privileged access to the case. As you can see, Mrs. McCallister is . . . *limited,* but she is still Megan's mother. Therefore it's helpful for us to have other people authorized to receive information in case, like today, for example, Mr. Burton is unavailable."

After looking at the form again, Sadie felt her embarrassment rise as the word *busybody* marched through her head. Did everyone see it but her? Did Eric somehow know she'd come?

Should she be somehow flattered that he knew her this way? She wasn't. She felt foolish, but didn't know if that was warranted either.

"Perhaps you should give him a call," Mathews suggested.

Talk to him? Sadie thought to herself. What would she say?

Mathews continued. "You must have been quite worried to come all the way down here, and after hearing these details I must admit I'm rather concerned as well. With the attention Mr. Burton has given to his daughter's disappearance, I can't understand why he wouldn't be here by now." He jabbed his finger at the top of the desk. "Perhaps learning you're in town will get his attention and help us both understand what it is he's involved in."

It was difficult to argue with his logic, so despite her own reluctance to talk to Eric until she'd sorted out her thoughts, she nodded, pulled out her cell phone, and dialed his number. Hopefully he wouldn't answer the phone so she could have more time to think of what to say.

Her hopes were dashed when, after the second ring, her call was answered.

"Sadie?" he said, a smile in his voice that annoyed rather than softened her mood.

She didn't know what to say. Finally, she settled on formal. "Hi, Eric," she said before pausing to take a breath. "I'm here."

He was quiet. "Here? In Florida?"

"Yes," Sadie said, testing the waters, trying to feel her way through the confusing thoughts in her mind. "Didn't you know I was coming?"

"Well, I hoped you were," Eric said easily.

"What do you mean, you hoped I was?"

"Well, you know, I thought maybe you'd want to come at some point."

Sadie paused and reviewed quickly the events that had brought her here: Eric's phone call, his asking her for favors but not telling her why. An uncomfortable thought came to mind. "Did you . . . set me up?"

He laughed.

Laughed! Sadie felt herself stiffening even more and thought back to the mantra she had beat into her kids' heads when they'd reached dating age, "Dating is a time to get to know another person, find out if you are compatible." She and Eric weren't dating, but one of the reasons she was here was certainly related to finding out more about him and more about how the two of them worked together. So far, things were not going well in that department.

"I wouldn't say I set you up," he said, breaking into her thoughts. "But I'm sure glad you came."

Sadie blinked, making sure she was listening carefully to what he'd said. "You told me enough to get me interested and knew I wouldn't be able to resist, didn't you? You knew I'd fall for it."

He seemed to clue into the fact that she wasn't nearly as entertained by this as he was. "I just—"

"You knew I'd look in the box," Sadie said, aware of Sergeant Mathews watching her. She ducked her head in even more embarrassment.

"I didn't *know* you would look in the box," Eric said quickly. "And I never imagined you'd come all the way out here without telling me you wanted to help. I just thought, maybe, if you *did* look, you'd want to be here. That's all."

Sergeant Mathews cleared his throat, drawing Sadie's attention. Recognizing him as the savior she needed to rescue her from this uncomfortable moment, she handed the phone across the desk. Besides, he was the one who'd wanted her to call. Mathews didn't hesitate in taking the phone and putting it to his ear.

"Mr. Burton," he said into the phone. "We've received information from the medical examiner and . . ."

Sadie tuned out his voice, closing her eyes and taking a deep breath so she could better analyze the situation. What was she angry about? The fact that Eric had set her up, or the fact that she'd fallen for it? Perhaps both.

I shouldn't have come, Sadie said to herself, folding her arms across her chest. *Busybody.*

She thought of all the things she'd done to make this trip work—the money, the time, the exhausting flight, not to mention giving Gayle permission to take Pete to the Renaissance dinner—and she felt utterly ridiculous. What had she been thinking?

"Mrs. Hoffmiller?"

Sadie looked back at the sergeant, pushing away the insecurity that crowded her mind. That was what bothered her so much—that Eric seemed . . . sneaky, purposely leaving out information to lure her in. It was her own fault it had worked, that the curiosity center in her brain was so hypersensitive, but it still felt like he'd used it against her and that made her pull back and reconsider what had brought her here. Maybe it had been a mistake to have trusted in those tingly feelings Eric inspired in her.

"Mrs. Hoffmiller?" Sergeant Mathews said again, wiggling the phone in his hand to get her attention. "Mr. Burton would like to speak with you again."

She took the phone and put it to her ear. "Yes?" she said as formally, as carefully, and as un-foolishly as she could.

"Call me as soon as you're alone," he said quietly into the phone. "I need to talk to you, but I don't want Mathews to overhear."

"Why wouldn't you want Mathews to overhear?" she asked out loud, feeling defensive and not liking Eric's assumption that she would play along with his games. Mathews raised his eyebrows. "I've told him everything I know and I have no reason to keep anything from the police."

Eric groaned slightly on the other end of the line. "Sadie," he said, his voice nearly a whisper now. "Things are complicated and—"

"Why are things complicated?"

"Sadie, please," Eric said, his voice both pleading and annoyed. "I'm sorry, okay? Can we at least talk about this before you overreact? I . . . are you still in his office?"

"Yes, I'm still in Sergeant Mathews's office," Sadie said innocently. "Is that a problem?"

Eric didn't say anything which told Sadie she'd sufficiently made her point. "Good-bye, Eric," she said quickly, then pulled the phone from her ear and clicked the END button. She could feel emotion rising in her throat and did her best to swallow it. Now was *not* the time for a self-pity cry.

When she looked up, Sergeant Mathews was watching her with enough surprise in his expression to remind her that, yes, he was human, after all, and sympathetic to her discomfort.

She smiled in what she hoped was a polite and confident way even though she didn't expect him to see her as anything more than a chump.

"You didn't tell me you looked in the box," Mathews said.

"I didn't?" Sadie said, thrown off-track as she searched her memory. She didn't remember *not* telling him, but didn't remember telling him either. "Probably because it wasn't anything important. Just some clothes, school papers, and a couple photographs."

"But you brought it to him," he reminded her. "It must have something important for him to want it and for you not to trust it to a shipping company."

"I thought he was in trouble," Sadie said quietly, feeling vulnerable. "And I can't seem to get through my thick skull when it's better to just leave well enough alone." She stood up quickly, not wanting to let her mouth run away. She was off-kilter and needed to be careful about saying too much. She thought about the other reason she'd come to Florida: because she had feelings for Eric.

Stupid girl, she admonished herself even as she admitted that it was flattering that he wanted her here. She just wasn't sure if that cancelled out everything else, and she couldn't help thinking, with a fair amount of regret, that Pete would not have used her this way—even if he'd known he could. She hoped Gayle would admire that about him.

The rising heat of tears coming to her eyes would not help anything. "I'm sorry," she said, turning toward the door. "I wish you the best of luck in this."

"Wait," Mathews said. She knew he'd stood up before she turned back to face him, but was reminded of what an imposing man he was when she had to look up to meet his eyes. He held out a notebook to her. "Will you please write down your full name, address, and phone number for the file?"

"Okay," Sadie said, taking the notebook and the pen he handed to her, eager to complete the task and be on her way.

"If I have any questions, I assume it's okay to call?" he asked as she handed the notebook back to him.

"Sure," Sadie said, but her mind was already on its way back to Miami—leaving seemed to be her only solution. Thank goodness no one but Gayle knew what she'd done. Sadie was reminded of the old fable about the dog that drops its own steak in hopes of getting the bigger one that was reflected back to him in the water. Sadie had given up all claim on Pete, a good man who may have made her happy, in order to go after the man who made her blood run a little hotter. Pete had stepped aside to let Sadie figure things out, and now Sadie felt as though she were standing alone, looking at both Eric and Pete off in the distance.

"And here's my card," Mathews said, holding the small rectangle out to her. "Call me for any reason."

She took the card and slipped it into the side pocket of her purse. She half-expected Sergeant Mathews to stop her again as she headed out of his office, but he didn't. She fished her keys out of her purse and strode deliberately to the front door, planning out the next few hours of her life. She still had the airline's number on her phone. She'd call them on her way back to the interstate and hopefully be just as lucky in getting a flight home as she'd been in getting the flight that brought her to this madness. Beyond that she could only hope that by the time she got back home, she would have worked through her feelings about all of this. She wondered if Gayle would laugh when Sadie told her what had happened. Sadie almost hoped she would. If Gayle found it funny, maybe Sadie would one day feel the same. At least Eric had the box now. She'd accomplished one of her objectives and that made her feel better.

The thick air hit her yet again when she pushed through the outer door, and she squinted into the sunlight before digging her sunglasses out of her purse, glad she'd come prepared. She pushed the glasses onto her face before heading toward her car, but then paused when she saw Layla stand up from the wrought-iron bench a few feet from Sadie's rental car. Sergeant Mathews had said Layla would walk home and Sadie hadn't given it another thought. However, the woman had a strange effect on Sadie, calling out to her motherly instincts despite the fact that Layla wasn't much younger than Sadie. It wouldn't be hard to drop her off on the way out of town. Sadie smiled as she approached the bench. Layla just watched her.

"Would you like a ride home?" Sadie asked.

"Yes," Layla said. She headed for the passenger side of the car. Sadie unlocked the door and they both slid in, pulling their doors shut at the same time. If it had been Gayle or Sadie's daughter, Breanna, they'd have laughed at how perfectly in sync they were. But motherly instincts aside, Sadie didn't know this woman. There were no inside jokes to share.

They drove in silence, which didn't seem to bother either one of them, and as they rolled to a stop in front of the house, Sadie turned to her passenger. "It was nice to meet you, Layla. I hope everything turns out okay."

"Would you like to come in? Tia made chicken for sandwiches and pasta salad for lunch."

The mention of food reminded Sadie how sorely neglectful she'd been of her stomach these last twenty-four hours. All it had had since yesterday afternoon was processed garbage. Maybe she'd find a decent restaurant on her way to the airport where she could order some *good* key lime pie—she still needed to redeem the Denver airport's interpretation. She also patted herself on the back for appropriately deciphering the smell of chicken from Layla's house earlier. But who was Tia?

No more questions, she told herself. *Go home.*

"Thank you," Sadie said with a sincere smile. "But I need to get to the airport. I'm heading home."

If she'd been on the receiving end of such a statement, she'd have wondered why the woman who had just arrived was leaving. But Layla didn't seem to notice the oddity of it. "Okay," she said, opening the door and letting herself out.

"You're welcome," Sadie said even though Layla hadn't thanked her. She watched Layla for a moment, then began pulling away when something caught her eye and caused her to press her foot on the brake instead of the gas. The screen door was in place, but the front door was open, allowing Sadie to see into the house. When they'd left, nearly an hour earlier, Layla had shut and locked the door, Sadie was sure of it. For half a second she argued with herself; it wasn't her business, it was probably the mysterious Tia who'd left it open. But Sadie hadn't even finished presenting that side of the case before her eyes were drawn upward and she saw something else.

Smoke.

CHAPTER 14

L ayla!" Sadie shouted, throwing the car into park with her right
hand while shoving the car door open with her left, running up
just as Layla reached the porch. "Don't go in there!" As soon as she'd
left the car she could smell the smoke as well as see it.

Layla turned to look at Sadie mere moments before Sadie
reached her and grabbed Layla's arm, pulling her back down the
cracked sidewalk. Her eyes weren't on Layla stumbling alongside her;
they were glued to the top of the house, where tendrils of smoke
reached for the sky—tendrils that now looked too small to be a
house fire. She looked through the screen and front door. There
wasn't any smoke coming from inside, but she noticed the wood
around the door frame had split and when she looked at the top of
the porch, she could see splinters she hadn't been able to see from
the car. Someone had broken into the house while they'd been gone.
And something was burning.

Sadie continued pulling Layla away from the house until they
reached the gravelly shoulder of the road near Sadie's car that was
still running with the driver's side door open. Layla followed without
complaint or question.

"Wait here," Sadie said. With her eyes still on the smoke, she ran toward the side of the house, noting right away that the grass didn't feel as solid as grass in Colorado did. It was a strange sensation, giving just a little bit beneath her feet.

Forcing herself to ignore the weird texture, she followed the pillar of smoke to an old oil drum that sat in the middle of the bricked patio behind the house. There were holes punched around the bottom edge of the drum, and enough soot hiding the original blue paint that Sadie recognized it as what she would call a burn can at home. She had one herself—the holes at the bottom allowed air to circulate and the can itself created a handy way to contain burning weeds and twigs.

It was a relief to know the *house* wasn't on fire, but Sadie's senses stayed on high alert as she scanned the backyard, which touched five other backyards. She saw no one as she approached the oil drum, which seemed to be smoldering rather than in the middle of an active burn. When she reached it, she found it half full of an indecipherable mess. The smoke certainly didn't help her identify any of the contents, and Sadie pulled back, her eyes stinging. She looked around, blinking quickly to get the smoke out of her eyes, and spotted a hose wound up against the side of the house. Moments later the contents of the oil can were wet and stinky, but no longer on fire. She looked into the can again and realized that whatever had been in there was beyond saving.

She lifted her head and looked through the sliding glass door of Layla's house. She could see into the kitchen and part of the living room. Nothing seemed out of place—no drawers emptied, no furniture overturned—but something had been put in this can and lit on fire, and since whoever had done it had broken into the house, it made sense to assume that whatever was in the can now had been in the house when she and Layla had left.

Her hand was mere centimeters away from the handle of the sliding glass door before she pulled back as though it too were on fire. What was she doing? Entering a crime scene? Putting herself right in the middle of the action? Again? Shaking her head, despite the fact that there was no one to see her, she stepped away from the patio.

I'm done with this kind of thing, she said to herself when she reached the grass. She turned around, leaving the fire can and the patio behind her as she made her way back around the house. *I'm going home.*

Even as she declared it in her mind, she knew it wouldn't be that simple. She had to call the police and at the very least give a statement about what she'd seen.

She groaned low in her throat at the thought of staying here longer, creating more opportunity for Eric to catch up with her. In addition to that, she worried about her own ability to keep her curiosity at bay. She was embarrassed right now, and that was enough to drown out her hunger for finding answers, but how long would it last? It felt a little like how she imagined an alcoholic felt when they went into a bar. The longer they were there, the better the chance of them having a drink. The reasonable solution, then, was to avoid the bar. But she had to make a statement. What dumb luck.

When she rounded the front of the house, Layla was standing in exactly the same place Sadie had left her. The driver's door to Sadie's car was still open, and the slight hum in the air reminded her that she hadn't turned off the engine.

Sergeant Mathews had said that people looked out for Layla, and Sadie wondered why exactly. Was Layla ill? Had something happened that kept her from reacting to things the way normal people did? Sadie wished she'd asked Mathews more questions, but the timing hadn't been right and it really wasn't any of her business. She was going home.

"We need to call the police," Sadie said when she reached Layla.

Layla looked from the house to Sadie's face, confused. "Why?"

Why? Sadie repeated in her own mind. Wasn't it obvious? But this was Layla she was talking to.

"Someone broke into your house and then put something in the fire can out back," she explained.

Layla turned her head to look at the front door. "Oh," she said simply.

Sadie paused another moment, then pulled out her phone and the card Sergeant Mathews had given her. Mourning the disruption in her plan to return home as soon as possible, Sadie dialed the number and waited.

"This is Sergeant Mathews," he said a moment later.

"This is Sadie Hoffmiller; I just left your office."

"Yes, Mrs. Hoffmiller. How can I help you?"

Sadie took a breath and began her explanation. "Well, it's like this . . ."

CHAPTER 15

The officer explained at length how Sadie was to fill out the statement form. She nodded politely, but in her mind she was recalculating her time frame. If she flew out of Miami before 2:00, she could be home in time to make some good biscuits and gravy—thus redeeming the Southern food she'd been so horribly denied—and could pretend the last twenty-four hours had been a mere blip of unreasonable thought on her part. At some point she'd have to face Eric, but the longer she could put it off the more time she'd have to come up with a plausible explanation for her behavior.

" . . . then sign here and return it to me."

Sadie smiled at the officer and put her hand out for the form he'd already attached to a clipboard. "Thank you," she said. It looked nearly identical to the forms she'd filled out in Garrison. Piece of cake.

She leaned against the hood of her car—which she'd turned off right after calling Mathews—and began filling in the blanks. Layla was a few feet away, speaking to Mathews, who had arrived after rescheduling his other meetings. If Sadie slid a little closer she'd be able to hear what they were saying. Instead, she stayed right where she was, allowing their voices to remain indecipherable.

The squeak of the screen door tricked her into looking up as an officer came out of the house and headed toward Mathews. Mathews ended his conversation with Layla and took a few steps forward to meet the officer. They were close enough that Sadie could hear what they were saying even though she didn't want to. Well, she *did* want to, but she didn't *want* to want to.

"Nothing seems out of place," the officer explained. "We've been through every room. It's clear and undisturbed."

But the door was kicked in, Sadie said to herself. Someone had a reason to get in there. And the timing was impossibly coincidental—the very time Sadie and Layla were at the police station.

She commanded herself to stop it. *No more questions!*

"What about the fire can?" Mathews asked. "Have we identified its contents?"

"Clothes," the officer said, shrugging. "And what's left of some three-ring binders; the papers inside are unsalvageable, I'm afraid."

Sadie's hand slowed.

He continued. "Officer Kerr is laying everything out, and the fire chief is on his way over to help, but so far there doesn't seem to be anything all that important."

Sadie's mind went back to her explanation to Mathews about the contents of the box. *Nothing important.* For the second time in twenty minutes she growled low in her throat and threw a mental tantrum about having to step even further into this whole situation. Mathews moved forward as though to go to the back of the house and Sadie was tempted to let him, but she was the only person here who knew what had been in the box. She couldn't withhold that kind of information.

"Sergeant Mathews," she said, tucking the pen beneath the clip of the clipboard and moving toward him. He turned and waited for her to catch up with him, watching her with careful expectation. She looked at the grass, wondering if she wanted to do this. Her experience with police officers hadn't necessarily built trusting relationships. Would Eric want her to tell? Did it matter? Was it fair to distrust every police officer she ever met simply because she'd run into a couple difficult ones?

"Mrs. Hoffmiller," he said when she reached him.

"That box I brought from Colorado," she said. "It was in the living room when Layla and I left for the police station. Is it still inside?"

"You said it was a Sunkist box, right?"

Sadie nodded. Mathews looked past her and got the attention of another officer. He told the officer what to look for and the officer went back to the house. Before speaking again, she took a breath. Hoping she was wrong about what else she had to say. "It would fit in that oil drum, I think."

Mathews had been watching the door and turned back to face her. She held his eye, but neither of them spoke. A few seconds later the hinge of the screen door squeaked again and moments later an officer approached.

"No Sunkist box, Sergeant," the officer said. "Want me to check the other rooms?"

"Sure," Mathews said, but Sadie knew that he knew as well as she did that it was a fool's errand. He nodded to Sadie. "Shall we head out back?"

Sadie fell in step beside him. As they walked, she tried to write on the statement form some more, eager to complete the paperwork even though she knew that yet one more thing was now standing in her way. Walking and writing at the same time resulted in horrible handwriting so she tucked the clipboard under her arm.

They rounded the house and Sadie crinkled her nose at the wet cinder smell of the backyard. A sheet of plastic had been laid out on the patio and several black mounds were spaced every few inches upon it. She stopped when Mathews did, just in front of the dissected mass and pointed at the item that first caught her attention. "That's the red sweater," Sadie said. "It was at the top of the box." Parts of the red yarn were still visible, probably where the sweater had been folded. She pointed to another clump of blackened fabric. "I'm assuming that's a pair of jeans—there were two of them." The three-ring binders were easy to identify since they were now metal rings attached to melted lumps of plastic, and what she assumed was the music box was still the right shape, only black. She imagined the ballerina inside was melted. It had seemed to be a memento of Megan's childhood, and Sadie was sad to see it destroyed.

"I'm going to need a list of everything you saw in that box," Mathews said, his eyes fixed on the burned items and his tone grim. "Every detail."

"Okay," Sadie said dryly. Every minute that passed made her more antsy to leave. "Do you have an inventory form handy or are they back at the station?"

Mathews looked at her strangely, and she realized that normal people didn't know the proper form for something like this. Even when she *tried* to be normal it didn't work.

"The station," Mathews said. "We'll take Layla with us. I'd like to make sure she's okay."

"All right," Sadie said, defeated. She pulled the clipboard out again. "Let me just finish this statement. The officer who gave it to me is expecting it." His name was Newman but Sadie didn't like the way Mathews was looking at her so she chose to be vague. Normal people were vague all the time.

"Sure," Mathews said, but she heard his tone and didn't like it. Until now she had been on the sidelines; now she'd somehow moved closer to the nucleus. Her trip home was getting farther and farther away, which made meeting up with Eric more probable every minute. Without saying anything else to Mathews, she began heading back to the front of the house. Mathews stayed in the backyard to talk to Officer Kerr.

Moments later, Sadie rounded the front of the house. She paused long enough to finish the last sentence on the statement form and had signed her name to the bottom when a prickling sensation began climbing up her spine. She lifted her head to look around and was immediately captured by a pair of bright blue eyes.

Eric was watching her from several feet away while he talked to one of the other officers. His hair was pulled back and there was mud on his shoes, but that was all she noticed before the prickling sensation turned into a full-on tingle and, despite her internal protestations to the contrary, she remembered what had drawn her to him in the first place.

CHAPTER 16

S adie did everything she could to avoid talking to Eric at Layla's house, which wasn't hard to do since Mathews had him cornered, firing questions at him at lightning speed. When Eric's voice started to rise, Mathews shut him down and left a couple officers on the scene while ordering the rest of them back to the station—along with Eric, Layla, and Sadie. At least Sadie got to drive in her own car, Layla automatically tagging along. Eric rode over with Mathews even though his rental car was still parked in the carport. She assumed Mathews had insisted on it.

Sadie drove slowly, giving herself a tour of Homestead on the way and hoping that Eric would already be in Mathews's office when she got to the station. Layla didn't seem to notice. By the time they arrived, Eric was nowhere to be seen and Sadie got to work on the inventory form. Layla sat next to Sadie on one of the blue plastic chairs, content to silently watch the comings and goings of the officers. The woman piqued Sadie's curiosity a great deal, but she kept pushing it away. To get the answers she wanted, she'd have to ask questions, and she was against that at the moment. She just wanted to do what she had to do and get the heck out of Florida as quickly as possible. And yet she could feel the pull of the man in the other room, urging her to stay with his silent desire that she do so.

She put all her focus into the paperwork she'd been given, but couldn't help glancing at Mathews's office each time raised voices escaped the edges of the door. She wondered what she would say when it was her turn to talk to Eric.

While part of her felt taken advantage of, another part of her wanted his arms around her as he whispered an explanation that would make everything all better. She assumed the hug-and-apology option was inspired by the part of her that didn't want to be wrong about Eric; she had to admit she liked the idea that he would trust her. She bounced back and forth between both fantasies until she was completely confused. What *did* she want?

It was vastly unsettling not to know her own mind, and she hated the idea of facing Eric when she was so unsure of her feelings. If she were open to the idea of attempting to repair whatever it was between them, it wouldn't happen here. Not under this kind of pressure, and not with how she felt toward him right now. And then she felt guilty for focusing on her internal conflict when there were bigger issues taking place around her—a dead girl with Megan's bracelet. Better to step out of this tension-filled situation than expect to get a good outcome here and now.

"I want to go home," Layla said, causing Sadie to look at the woman sitting next to her. She was so quiet it was easy to forget she was there at all. She seemed agitated and tapped her foot against the tile. "Tia made barbeque chicken for sandwiches and pasta salad for lunch." Sadie waited for her to say something about *Wheel of Fortune*, but she didn't seem to remember.

"I'm sure they'll let us go soon," Sadie assured her. After she said it, Sadie realized she'd used *us*, joining her plans to Layla's. She shook her head and went back to the inventory form. There was no *us*. Not with Layla, not with Eric. Sadie needed to remember she was not a part of this.

She bent over her clipboard, intent on finishing the list of items she'd seen in the box that she now wished she'd have left in the trunk of her rental car. No one would have known the box was even in Florida if she hadn't taken it into the house. Which brought up a whole new passel of questions. Who would have known the box was there? And who would have known its contents? Layla had barely glanced at it. What had been in the box that was important enough to be destroyed?

She reviewed her list, trying to identify anything that seemed to stand out. As before, however, nothing seemed particularly interesting and she was again reminded that the contents of the box seemed to be dregs—leftovers. She wished she'd paid more attention to the papers in the binders, and to the photos and receipts in the tea tin, but she'd merely glanced at them, not realizing she'd be the last person to ever see them in their original form. She included the details she remembered—one of the receipts was to a Texaco station, another was the yellow carbon of a credit card sale to . . . somewhere. She knew from prior experience that it was often the small details that made all the difference. Whoever burned all those details likely knew the same thing.

"Layla."

Sadie looked up and saw that while she'd been lost in her ponderings, a man had approached them. He was in his forties, Sadie guessed. What was left of his red hair was short and faded. He was wearing a lavender button-up shirt and slacks with crisp pleats down the front that screamed dry-cleaned—men who ironed their own pants never did the creases right. Sadie wondered if he was a police detective.

Layla's expression didn't change, making it impossible for Sadie to determine if Layla knew him. After a moment, Layla looked away and crossed her arms. "It's past lunchtime," she said again, and although her tone stayed the same, Sadie picked up on new tension.

"Yes, it is past lunchtime," the man said with a sympathetic nod. He looked around the room at the officers milling around. "Have they said when you can go home?"

"No," Layla said. "But I'm hungry."

The man nodded again. He was worried about her; Sadie could read it in the lines of his face, which made her think he wasn't with the police department after all—they didn't let their emotions show so easily.

He held out his hand to Sadie. "You must be Eric's friend, Sandy."

"Sadie," she replied, appreciating his firm grip while wondering who he was and what Eric had told him about her.

"Sadie, that's right. Sorry."

"No problem," Sadie assured him. "I've been called worse."

He smiled. "I'm Larry."

"Oh," Sadie said, almost as an exclamation. He looked surprised at her reaction, and she hurried to explain. "Layla mentioned you."

Larry nodded, but still looked a little bit uncomfortable. Sadie was dying to ask him questions—about Layla, about himself, about the whole used-to-be-married-but-Layla-still-lives-in-his-house thing. Never mind that despite being *limited*—that was the word Mathews had used—how was it that Layla had been married *twice*?

No questions, she told herself. *Just finish.*

"I'm going to, um, talk to someone and see when Layla can go home," Larry said, moving away from them.

Layla didn't look at him when he tried to make eye contact, but Sadie nodded and then watched him cross the room and talk to one officer before nodding and going to another one. The second officer he approached was talking on the phone, so Larry stood to the side, waiting patiently for his turn to speak. Sadie went back to her paperwork, but looked up at Larry a time or two as she made more notations.

Larry returned after a minute and directed his comments to Sadie. "I guess they have to talk to a sergeant about Layla leaving, and he's in with Eric."

Sadie nodded, suddenly remembering that Layla had said Eric and Larry had been together this morning. "Sergeant Mathews," she said, pointing toward the door. "They've been in there for nearly half an hour."

Larry looked at the door with trepidation. "I went back to the house and the officers there told me to come here." Once again, raised voices spilled out from beneath the door, and Larry shook his head. "Eric's making everything worse, isn't he?"

"He's certainly not making things better," Sadie replied, wondering what the relationship was between Eric and Larry. She couldn't stop herself. "You and Eric were together this morning, right?"

Larry nodded. "I had to go to work, though. I'm off for lunch, but have to get back in . . ." He looked at his watch. "Twenty minutes."

"Eric's rental car was at the house when I arrived this morning, but he wasn't."

"He had my car," Larry said, glancing at Layla again. Sadie tried to remember if she'd seen another car at the house after Eric arrived, but there had been several cars at the house. "A coworker took me to the house to pick it up." A crease showed on his forehead as he looked around the station again. He seemed increasingly uncomfortable.

"Where do you work?" Sadie asked.

"The Speedway," he answered.

Sadie wondered if that was a grocery store or something.

Larry glanced at the officer he'd been speaking with before. "I better go see what I need to do."

He turned but hadn't moved very far before Layla shouted, "Get me an orange soda!"

Larry stopped, clearly embarrassed by her outburst as every officer in the room turned to look. Sadie felt her own cheeks heat up.

When he didn't answer, Layla continued. "Are you going to get me an orange soda or not?"

"Sure, Layla," he said, his voice quiet, but not upset. Sadie suspected he was used to this and wondered again what was wrong with this woman.

Larry walked away and an officer directed him down a short hallway that Sadie assumed led to a vending machine. She shook her head, unimpressed that Larry was so quick to give in. Layla might be forty-something years old, but she was being a brat and her getting her way didn't help anyone. Still, she reminded herself, none of this was her problem.

After scanning the list one last time and assuring herself it was as complete as possible, she stood and took the clipboard to the nearest officer, a tall man with wide eyes and a bright smile. It was nice to see a cop smile. "I'm finished," she said, refusing to think about Eric or get too caught up in trying to figure out Larry or Layla. Instead of giving in to those temptations, she asked herself whether she would prefer an aisle seat or a window for the flight home.

Officer Sanchez, according to his name tag, took the clipboard.

"Thank you," he said with a slight Spanish accent. "Sergeant Mathews will be finished in a few minutes, I'm sure." But he shot a concerned glance at the door to Mathews's office. The voices were louder. Sadie couldn't imagine yelling at a police officer like that and wondered why Eric would be so . . . courageous. That didn't seem the right word. "Dumb" might be more appropriate.

"Sergeant Mathews has my contact information. Can you just have him call me?"

"Sorry," Sanchez said. "He specifically asked that I have you stay."

Her stomach dropped but she wasn't the type to argue with a police officer. Well, at least not today. Technically, she didn't think they could make her stay unless she was under arrest, but she was trying hard to stay in Mathews's good graces.

She returned to her seat next to Layla. Larry came back with an orange soda and unscrewed the lid before handing it to Layla, who took the bottle without saying thank you. She took a rather dainty sip and began looking around the station again.

"I should have asked if you wanted something too," Larry said to Sadie. "I'm sorry. It's been a long day."

Sadie hated adding to his stress. "You're very sweet," she said. "But I'm fine, thanks."

Larry nodded, but still looked rather disappointed in himself. "The officer said I could go back to work and come in when I finish up tonight. I wish I could stay and help with Layla and everything."

"I don't need help," Layla said in her monotone voice. "Go away."

Sadie was embarrassed all over again. Why, of all people, did Larry bring out this side of her? "I'm sorry," she said before realizing she didn't even know what she was apologizing for.

"It's okay," Larry said easily. "Will you tell Eric I came by and that I'll catch him later?"

Sadie didn't want to relay anything to Eric, but she nodded anyway. Larry could use one less thing to worry about. "Sure," she said.

"Thanks," Larry replied. "I'll see you two later, then."

"No, you won't," Sadie said a little too quick and a little too loud. "I mean, I'll be leaving as soon as I'm done here." If she said it enough times, surely it would happen.

"But you just got here this morning, didn't you?"

"Yeah," Sadie said, wondering how he knew that. Had Eric told Larry all about this woman he knew would be following him to Florida? "But I'm not staying."

Larry pulled his eyebrows together. "If you don't mind my asking, why did you come?"

"To bring something to Eric and assure myself he was okay," Sadie said, trying to sound as though that had been her only goal all along. "But I've got to get back home now that those things are taken care of." Sadie bit her tongue to keep from overexplaining herself.

"Oh," Larry said, obviously still confused. "Well, have a safe trip. It was nice to meet you."

"Nice to meet you too," Sadie replied. He stood there for another moment, then glanced at Layla and although he seemed to consider saying something, he didn't. Instead he nodded at Sadie one last time, and then headed for the door.

Sadie watched him leave and tried to talk herself out of the burning curiosity in her gut. What was Larry's story? And why was Layla, who didn't seem to have many feelings at all, so angry with him?

As the minutes stretched on, Sadie started tapping her foot and tried to keep from clenching her jaw; she hated waiting. She thought of the phone call she'd promised Gayle. She must be on pins and needles waiting to hear from Sadie—that is, assuming she and Pete weren't playing tennis together.

She shook the image from her mind. What was done was done and she needed to come to terms with that. Sadie pulled her phone from her purse. To her surprise, she'd missed a text message. To her even greater surprise it was from Eric. She furrowed her brow. How had he managed to send her a text while he was arguing with Mathews? Then she realized it had been sent over an hour ago: 11:06 to be exact. Sadie had looked at the dashboard clock during her deliberately detoured drive back to the police station at 11:32, which meant this text had been sent before Eric showed up at Layla's house.

Her heart rate increased immediately. She took a breath as she opened the message, glancing quickly at Layla to be sure she wasn't reading it over her shoulder. Layla was engrossed in her magazine and paid no attention to Sadie.

I promise 2 explain everthng as soon as I can. Plz don't tell Mathews anthng else. I swore not 2 involve cops—Meg's life might depend on it. Once I explain I think u will understand y.

Sadie blinked. *Megan's life might depend on it?*

Just then muffled voices seemed to explode into the station, causing Sadie to jump as she quickly returned her phone to her purse. Eric backed out of the room, glaring at Mathews who was only a few feet away, coming toward him. "You'll regret this, Mr. Burton," Mathews said, and Sadie noticed a sheen of sweat on his bald head. "If I have to arrest you to keep you from making a bigger mess of this—"

"If you could arrest me, you would have already." Eric turned his head as though looking for someone and immediately focused on Sadie. She saw the tiniest bit of relief soften his expression and liked that her presence could give him a little comfort. Eric turned back to Sergeant Mathews. "When I have something to tell you, I will."

He immediately headed for Sadie, who stood up quickly. "Come on," he said, grabbing her arm.

Sadie couldn't even come up with a protest before she was stumbling to fall in step with him. She glanced over her shoulder to see that Layla had stood up as well and was following behind them. She'd left the orange soda on the chair next to her, but still had the magazine in her hand. She was watching them but didn't seem upset despite the intensity of the moment.

"Mrs. Hoffmiller."

Sadie craned her head around at the sound of Sergeant Mathews's voice. Eric didn't stop, which annoyed her even further. Pulling her arm quickly so as to catch him off guard, she managed to escape from his grip. When Eric looked at her in surprise, she gave him a pointed look and turned back to Mathews, who continued speaking once he knew he had Sadie's attention.

"You said he didn't tell you what was going on and there was good reason for that. He's gotten himself in trouble, and if you go with him you'll be putting yourself right beside him. I would strongly suggest you reconsider."

"Thank you, Sergeant," Sadie said evenly. "But I'm not going anywhere *with* him. I'm going to my car, which will then take me to the Miami airport." If she were being totally honest she would admit, at least to herself, that Eric's text message had eased her of some of her confusion, reminding her just how high the stakes were. "But thank you for your concern."

She could tell Mathews didn't believe her; she sensed Eric didn't either. Did she believe herself?

Layla walked past her and when Mathews didn't say anything else, Sadie turned toward the front door, aware that every cop in the room was watching her. Eric reached for her arm again, but she stepped out of his reach and gave him a look that made her point. He hung back a step and followed Layla out of the building. Sadie didn't look back again, nor did she stop to put on her sunglasses when the Florida sunshine attempted to blind her. Instead she fumbled through her purse as she walked, nearly tripping over a crack in the pavement due to her inattentiveness and the distraction of such thick, heavy air. How did people get used to this humidity? Enough sweat had mixed with the moisture that she felt sticky all over.

Layla headed for Sadie's car and, after a moment, Sadie remembered that Eric had come to the police station in a police car and therefore had no way home either. Perfect.

"I'll give you a ride to Layla's," she said to Eric, who was a few steps behind her. "You have four blocks to attempt an explanation."

Eric nodded, looking penitent, and slid into the backseat of the rental car, allowing Layla to get in the front. Sadie buckled her seat belt and put the key in the ignition. "Four blocks," she repeated as she shifted into drive. She caught sight of Sergeant Mathews standing just inside the glass door of the police station, watching them. She grimaced, certain he thought she'd lied to him about not going with Eric.

Checking her blind spot, she pulled away from the curb as Eric moved to the middle of the backseat. He leaned forward between the front seats. She didn't look at him, but was only too aware of how close he was.

He took a deep breath and then let it out, seeming to signify the heaviness of what he had to say before he actually said it. "I think Megan's alive."

CHAPTER 17

Sadie wasn't that surprised to hear him say it, even though she thought she probably should be. Megan had been missing for three years. She'd never contacted him, but would he be up to his eyeballs in trouble like this if not for the fact that he thought it would take him to his daughter? What other reason would make sense of his actions? Not that she was saying his actions made sense.

"So where is she?" Sadie asked, keeping her voice even for fear that showing any emotion would somehow give up some of her control of the situation. Layla didn't react at all; she simply looked out the windows, watching the businesses and homes pass by. Eric's eyes were framed within the rearview mirror and he didn't even glance at Layla, watching Sadie intently instead. She was uncomfortable with him staring at her and tried to avoid looking in the mirror.

"I don't know that part," Eric said. "That's what I'm trying to find out."

"Why not tell the police?" Sadie asked calmly, though she was itching to hear the details.

Eric shook his head but kept watching Sadie in the mirror. His eyes boring into her made her increasingly uncomfortable. "The information I have is from someone who wants nothing to do with the police."

"Maybe you should take that into consideration. If whoever gave you this information is some kind of criminal, then they can't be trusted."

Eric looked away as Sadie made the final turn onto 4th Avenue. She couldn't help but frown a little. Her home on Peregrine Circle was the best-kept of any of her neighbors, while the homes in Layla's neighborhood sported untended flower gardens and more than a few yards had cars put up on blocks. The flat-roofed brick home across the street from Layla's even had a floral-patterned couch on the front porch, complete with a portly man watching them while he sipped his soda.

Sadie pulled to a stop in front of Layla's house, but didn't even shift the car into park. The police had removed the fire can and all its contents, as well as taken numerous photos—basically they'd done all they could do. Other than cordoning off the patio, they'd deemed the house cleared and no longer a crime scene. Sadie suspected their efforts at clearing it quickly had to do with Layla and why everyone seemed to treat her with a little more care than seemed necessary.

"Tia made chicken for sandwiches and a pasta salad for lunch," Layla said, opening the door of the car and swinging her legs out. Her sandals crunched on the gravely road while Sadie wondered, again, who Tia was.

"In a minute," Eric said, almost dismissively.

"It's past lunchtime," Layla said, surprising Sadie with the frustration in her tone—it was one of the few times there'd been any texture to what she said. "Tia made enough for everyone."

"Okay, Layla," Eric said in a somewhat patronizing voice as

though he was talking to a little girl and not his ex-wife. Nothing like how Larry had treated Layla. "I want to talk to Sadie for a few minutes, and then we'll come in."

We'll come in? Sadie didn't like his assumption that she was staying. Layla didn't look pleased either, and Sadie wondered if, in her own way, she was jealous. After another moment Layla shut the car door and went inside the house, pausing to pick up the cat sitting by the porch. She didn't seem to give the splintered wood of the door frame a second look.

Eric immediately leaned forward between the seats until Sadie didn't have any choice but to look into his face.

"I'm really sorry things happened this way," Eric said. "I shouldn't have presumed so much, and I swear I didn't mean to offend you."

But he *did* presume and she *was* offended, although she didn't like that word very much. Offense was rarely intentional, and often something the offended party came up with. And seeing as how she was the offended party, her own definition implied that she was *choosing* to be offended. And wasn't it Sadie who'd looked through a box that she didn't have permission to look through?

"I don't know what to think about all this," Sadie said. "I feel like I've been . . . taken advantage of somehow." She remembered how he had laughed on the phone, acting as though this was funny, like she was the butt of some joke.

"What, exactly, are you mad about?" Eric asked.

"You put my name down on the permission form," Sadie reminded him. "To me that says you *knew* I'd come out here, which makes it all feel very manipulated."

"I put your name down because other than Larry you're the only person I could think of that I'd trust the police to talk to. I admit I was hoping you would reconsider my invitation, but the last thing I expected was a call from you saying you were *here*."

Hmmm. That was an obnoxiously plausible explanation. She circled back to her early question of herself—was she more upset that he'd assumed she would come, or that she had come in the first place?

Busybody.

So much for Gayle's romantic notions; that part hadn't come to fruition at all and if anything she felt cautious with Eric rather than connected as she'd hoped.

When she didn't say anything, Eric continued, "Look, I knew there was a chance you would look in the box if I asked you to ship it. And I knew if you did that you might . . . want to be involved. I meant it when I said I wanted you to come with me." He smiled a soft, vulnerable smile that made Sadie feel a little soft and vulnerable too. "Have you thought about *why* I put your name on that paper? Why I invited you to come in the first place?"

In fact Sadie had not thought about that at all but didn't want to admit it so she just looked at him expectantly.

"You have a gift, Sadie," he said.

Sadie pulled her eyebrows together. *A gift?*

"You have a heart with room in it for other people's problems, you sincerely want to help, and you will do almost *anything* it takes to do the right thing. I understand why you wouldn't come with me when I asked you back in Garrison, and I respect that."

Sadie felt her cheeks heat up at the reminder of the almost-kiss two days ago, and she glanced away, but only for a moment before Eric took her chin in his rough hand and turned her to look at him. She felt herself slipping—he was such a smooth talker. Too smooth for her peace of mind sometimes.

"I also knew you truly wanted to help me, that you had sincere sympathy for what I was going through. It meant a lot to me to have that kind of support. It still does—more than ever."

Sadie liked the way he was summing this up, smooth talk or not. It was much better than being called a nosy busybody, but she still felt conflicted and didn't know what conclusion to draw from all of this.

Eric let go of her chin and pulled back a bit, looking out the car window at Layla's house. "Coming back to this world isn't easy for me. I moved to Garrison in hopes of starting a new life. I left my past here in the swamps of Florida." He smiled at his own description, but it quickly faded. "My past is now my present, and the next few days will be very difficult, regardless of what I learn about Megan. I could really use someone on my side, someone as genuine and compassionate as you. A little more of that Bonnie and Clyde thing we had going for us in the past."

Wow. It was hard to argue with that. The comment about Bonnie and Clyde took her back to when they'd met during another murder investigation. They'd made a good team back then, and she really did have a great deal of compassion for his situation which, she could only imagine, was as horrible as anything Sadie had ever faced.

Her cell phone rang and she gave him an apologetic smile as she pulled it out of her purse. It was Gayle. Now wasn't a good time to talk to her, so Sadie pushed the end button, sending the call to voice mail. Besides she was probably calling to tell Sadie the trailer was clean. She returned the phone to her purse and managed a smile for Eric. "I guess I *am* acting a little paranoid. I didn't tell you I was coming because I really thought you were in trouble."

Eric made a nodding-shrugging gesture. "I am in trouble, kinda."

Sadie lifted her eyebrows.

"But it's a good trouble, I think."

There was a good kind of trouble? Sadie thought, frowning at the concept.

Eric continued. "I'm close, Sadie," he said, his voice low and a little breathless. "I know I am. It sounds all mystical and stuff, but it's like I can feel her here."

"Here?" Sadie said. "In Homestead?"

"Maybe not in Homestead, but here, in Florida. It wasn't Megan's body the police found, but whoever it was is somehow connected to my daughter, and . . ."

"And?" Sadie prodded.

"I know I told you that the idea of her being alive all this time but unable to contact me was worse than believing she was dead. But that was before all this happened." He waved his hand through the air. "That was before I imagined what it would be like to look into my daughter's face again, to save her from whatever hell she's had to deal with. I have to do whatever it takes to find out whatever I can. Does that make sense?"

Sadie was a woman of faith, so what he said *did* make sense. She was once again overwhelmed by what this must be like for him.

Movement at the front door caught her eye and she turned slightly to see Layla standing in the doorway. She wasn't holding the cat anymore but she was looking at them. Eric followed Sadie's gaze and they both simply stared at Layla for a few seconds. She didn't move a muscle, and Sadie felt a chill rush through her.

"She wants us to come inside and have lunch," Eric finally said. He turned back to face Sadie with an invitation in his eyes.

Sadie balanced on the precipice—did she stay now that Eric had given such a heartfelt explanation? She'd told Mathews she was leaving, and her fight-or-flight instinct was begging her to catch that plane back to Colorado and take the time she needed to sort out her thoughts and feelings about all of this. But . . .

"You still haven't explained to me why you think Megan's alive," Sadie said.

"I have to meet someone in just over an hour, but after that I'll tell you everything I know," Eric said, his tone hopeful. "Then you can leave whenever you want to and I won't stand in your way, I swear."

Sadie bit her bottom lip. *Decisions, decisions!*

The slamming of the screen door caught her attention and she looked up to see Layla marching toward them. When she reached the car she knocked on the window and then put both hands on her hips. Her jaw was tight and her eyes narrowed. Sadie found herself shrinking back against the driver's side door, but Eric let out a sigh and then slid toward the back passenger door to let himself out. His jaw was tight too.

"Tia made chicken for sandwiches and pasta salad for lunch!" Layla yelled as Eric opened the door. "I have been waiting and waiting. It's past lunchtime!"

"I know," Eric said in a sharp voice that surprised Sadie since he'd been so soft with her moments earlier. "I'm coming. Just let me talk to Sadie for one more minute."

"You already talked to her," Layla said, practically screaming. "And it's past lunchtime. Tia made us a chicken for sandwiches and pasta salad!"

Sadie looked around to see if anyone was watching. The man on the couch across the street leaned forward on his knees as though watching his favorite TV show.

"I know that," Eric said, his words more clipped. "You've told me that like fifteen times, and I'm coming in right after I talk to Sadie."

"It's after lunchtime!" Layla screamed. The hands on her hips were balled into fists. *"Tia made us chicken for sandwiches and pasta salad!"*

Sadie couldn't take it anymore. She pushed open her door, grabbing her purse as she stood up from the car. "Okay, okay," she said, as she hurried around the car in hopes of diffusing some of the tension. She forced a smile and looked Layla in the eye. "Can I stay for lunch?" she asked in her sweetest voice.

"Tia made us chicken for sandwiches and pasta salad." Layla's voice was still raised, but she wasn't screaming.

"And it smelled wonderful when I was here earlier. I'm starving and would love to have some if you have enough."

Layla nodded, her face relaxing more and more. "She made enough for everyone."

"Wonderful," Sadie replied, still smiling although her concern for this woman's mental state was through the roof. "Thank you."

Satisfied, Layla nodded again and headed for the front door. Sadie followed her, avoiding any contact with Eric. A few steps from the front door Eric touched Sadie's arm and she turned to look at him. Her eyes were drawn to his shoes, still covered with a fair amount of mud. She wanted to know why.

"You're staying?" he whispered, his expression hopeful.

"For lunch," she said, not ready to make a decision but willing to entertain the possibilities. One choice made her a liar in the eyes of Sergeant Mathews, the other meant she really had wasted her time in coming here. Which one would be easier to live with?

Southern BBQ Slow-Cooked Chicken

1 (36-ounce) bottle ketchup
6 tablespoons brown sugar
2 tablespoons Worcestershire sauce
2 tablespoons soy sauce
2 tablespoons cider vinegar
2 teaspoons crushed red pepper flakes, or to taste
1 teaspoon garlic powder, or 2 to 3 cloves fresh garlic, pressed
6 boneless, skinless chicken breasts

Combine all ingredients for the sauce in the slow cooker. Add the chicken and coat it well with the sauce. Cook on high for 3 to 4 hours, or low for 6 to 8 hours, until chicken is fully cooked. Use two forks to shred chicken and serve over cooked rice or on rolls for sandwiches.

Serves 8.

*Makes great leftovers.

CHAPTER 18

L ayla immediately sat down at the kitchen table, waiting to be
served. Sadie didn't have to be asked to step in. It took a couple
of minutes to shred the chicken—in a slow cooker just as Sadie
had suspected—with two forks. If it hadn't been cooking for several
hours, the chicken wouldn't be so tender. What time had Tia started
it? There was a bag of hard rolls on the counter, but after going
through every drawer, Sadie was unable to find a knife she could use
to slice the rolls in half.

"Aren't there any knives?" Sadie asked, getting hungrier by the
moment and therefore, annoyed.

Eric pulled open a few drawers and looked around before shrugging. "I guess not."

"Why not?" Were they afraid Layla might hurt herself?

"I don't know," Eric said with another shrug as he dished himself
up some pasta salad. "I don't live here."

She had to resort to ripping the rolls in half before putting them
in a mixing bowl lined with paper towels; she couldn't find a basket.
Eric was halfway through his pasta salad by the time Sadie brought

over the plates she'd made for Layla and herself. Had he not noticed he was the only one eating and Layla was waiting for her meal?

Let it go, she told herself, and yet it was silly not to take note of how he acted in these situations. The key, she decided, was to observe these details without judgment. Could she push away her romantic feelings in order to see Eric objectively? She looked at him sitting across from Layla—the ex-wife he'd never talked about—and decided that she could. She had to, really. But, of course, observing Eric in new situations was secondary to the real issue at stake: Megan. By the time Sadie sat down at the table, she felt as though she had reset her expectations and objectives in regard to Eric.

The chicken for the sandwiches was wonderful, and Sadie savored every bite, determining the only thing she'd change would be to add a bit more heat to the chicken since the bread muted the flavor well enough that it wouldn't come across too strong. She was halfway through the sandwich before she took a bite of the pasta salad. She paused, and then took another bite, paying attention to the details that made up the unique flavors.

Grilled chicken, penne pasta, mandarin oranges—which Sadie had never paired with pasta in her life—snap peas, and a sweetened mayonnaise-based dressing. The flavors were divine. Pasta and fruit. Who knew they could be so good together? Sadie was definitely going to ask for both of these recipes, assuming she ever met the mysterious Tia. Pretty soon she was going to have to dig her notebook out of her purse and start making a list of all her questions: Who was Tia? What was wrong with Layla? Who knew the box was here? Why did they burn it? What made Eric think Megan was alive? And at any time during the day did the humidity turn itself off? Not necessarily in that order.

Eric finished first, and leaned back in his chair as he glanced at the clock on the microwave and then confirmed the time on his watch. "I've got to go," he said to Sadie, pushing back from the table.

"Go where?" Sadie asked. She knew he had a meeting, but that's as far as he'd gotten in the explanation. She needed more information.

Eric glanced quickly at Layla, who was eating quite daintily, one noodle or piece of chicken at a time. He looked back at Sadie and shook his head slightly, nodding toward the living room. Clearly, he didn't want Layla to know where he was going.

Sadie excused herself from the table and met Eric on the other side of the wall that separated the two rooms.

"I didn't get the chance to explain," Eric said softly, taking a step closer toward Sadie. Despite herself, Sadie felt his nearness trigger a wave of warm response that she tried to push away. Whether his soft tone was because he didn't want Layla to overhear or because he was feeling rather tender too, Sadie wasn't sure. "And I don't have time to explain it now, but can you stay until I get back?"

"How long will you be?"

"I don't know," he said simply.

"Maybe I should go with you," Sadie said. She was hesitant to put herself in the middle of this, but equally eager to know what he knew—what had spurred him to do so many things that seemed questionable.

"I have to go alone."

"Really?" Sadie questioned, folding her arms over her chest. "Or do you just not want to tell me?"

Eric let out a frustrated breath and stepped away, which, thankfully, allowed her body to relax. "I can't tell you right now." He glanced toward the kitchen again and then at his watch.

Sadie couldn't let it go. "Why do you want me to stay in Florida if I'm not doing anything?" But she didn't really *want* to do anything so she wondered why she was arguing that point in the first place. She knew why, though—because she still didn't know what was going on and it was making her crazy.

Eric paused thoughtfully for a few seconds. "You can ride with me, but I have to go to the meeting alone."

"Why can't I go to the meeting too?" Sadie asked, trying to feel around the edges of this meeting. Was he assuming she wasn't supposed to be there, or had he been given a direct order to come alone? The distinction made a big difference.

When he spoke his voice wasn't soft anymore. In fact it was downright annoyed. "Because he asked me to come alone and I'm not going to take any chances." He paused for a breath and softened his tone. "But you can drive with me so I can explain things."

The eager expectation in his eyes undid her. Again. He wanted her to go with him, even though she wouldn't be at the meeting and suddenly, against her better judgment, she wanted to go. It would only delay her flight home for a little while. "Okay," she said.

Eric instantly broke into a grin. "Great," he said. "Let me get my keys and then we can go."

Sadie nodded and went to the doorway of the kitchen. Layla was still eating and was seemingly oblivious to their entire conversation despite the fact that they were only ten feet away from her.

"Is she okay to be home alone?" Sadie whispered a minute later when Eric found her in the kitchen. She'd cleared her dishes—Eric had left his on the table—and rinsed them before putting them in the dishwasher.

Eric nodded. "As long as we don't let her watch *Renovation Nation*, we're fine." He knocked on the countertops. "She likes to learn about how things are made, so Larry thought she'd like those home improvement shows. He came over one day to find the kitchen countertops in five pieces in the front yard. Apparently she'd caught an episode about a new technique for removing the old Formica-based tops. So simple that one person could do it themselves."

Sadie turned back to look at Layla, the question of what was wrong with the woman on the tip of her tongue. But she didn't want to discuss it in front of Layla so she bit back her question and focused on rinsing her plate, realizing she had another reason to go with Eric, so she could find out what was going on with his ex-wife. Still, it seemed . . . irresponsible to leave her home alone.

"Layla," Eric said, leaning his elbows on the counter. "Larry said he recorded a few more episodes of *How It's Made*. Would you like me to turn one on?"

"Yes," Layla said, still eating.

Eric nodded and headed into the living room. Sadie hurried to catch up.

"Someone broke in and burned the box," Sadie reminded him when they were out of earshot. "Are you certain she's safe?"

Eric looked at the clock. "Tia gets home in a little while. She'll check in on her. Besides, the police will drive by every couple of hours. She'll be fine."

"And who's Tia?" Sadie asked.

"A neighbor," Eric said. "She helps keep an eye on things."

Five minutes later, with Layla engrossed in how jet packs were built, Sadie closed the front door and headed toward the carport, overwhelmed with the heat—again. "You're sure it's safe for her to learn about making jet packs?" Sadie asked, looking over her shoulder and feeling bad that they hadn't even said good-bye to Layla. Eric seemed so sure of things, but even that bothered Sadie a little bit. It was too easy to interpret his casualness as simply not caring.

"She doesn't have any jet fuel," Eric said. "She'll be fine."

Sadie couldn't think of a good argument for that. She lifted a hand to her hair, frowning at the way her hairspray didn't seem to have dried all the way, leaving her hair sticky and flat. On the way to the car she tried to fluff it back up, but it didn't seem to do much good. She wondered how women who lived in such heat did their hair. Her spiky, curly coiffure was certainly not a good choice for this climate.

Sadie slid into the passenger seat and hoped she was doing the right thing by going with Eric instead of heading for the Miami airport. After putting a stack of papers on the dashboard, he buckled his seat belt, shifted into reverse, and backed out of the driveway. Sadie waited until they were on the road before she asked the question she'd wanted to know the answer to all day.

"So, what's wrong with her?" she asked, trying to use her most diplomatic tone.

"Layla?" Eric answered, glancing at Sadie quickly.

Sadie gave him a look that said *Who else would I be talking about?*

Eric took a breath. "Layla," he said, almost sighing as he spoke her name. "Layla, Layla, Layla."

Fruity Pasta Salad

2 cups mayonnaise
1 teaspoon minced garlic
½ teaspoon celery seed
½ cup honey
1 teaspoon salt
½ teaspoon pepper
2 to 3 chicken breasts, diced*

1 (16-ounce) package tri-colored pasta (Rotini, wacky mac, penne, etc.)
2 (15-ounce) cans mandarin oranges, drained (Shawn likes fresh mangoes, for a more tropical taste)
¼ pound sugar snap peas, sliced diagonally
½ cup chopped green onions
Chow mein noodles

In a medium-sized bowl, mix the mayonnaise, minced garlic, celery seed, honey, salt, and pepper together. Cover and place in the refrigerator. Cook the chicken in a pan, then dice and place in a large bowl. While the chicken is cooking, cook the pasta, then drain and add to chicken. Add the mandarin oranges, sugar snap peas, green onions, and mayonnaise sauce to the bowl. Gently mix together until everything is covered with the sauce. Refrigerate for one hour before serving. Top with chow mein noodles.

Serves 12.

*Can use canned chicken in a pinch.

CHAPTER 19

Sadie tried to read into the tone of Eric's voice, wondering if there were any feelings for his ex-wife betrayed within it. She also realized she'd nearly forgotten about the little detail of Eric having stayed at Layla's last night. But after seeing Eric and Layla together, she didn't feel like her previous suspicions had any foundation. There was no chemistry left between them, and she'd bet a thousand dollars Eric had slept on the couch last night. Her wonderings came to a halt when Eric started talking.

"About eighteen years ago, Layla was in a car accident," Eric said, leaning toward the driver's side door and holding the steering wheel with his right hand. "She sustained a head injury that affected her frontal lobe and left her with a variety of problems including what they call *blunted affect*."

"I've heard of that," Sadie said. "Vietnam vets sometimes get it, don't they?"

A boy from the neighborhood where she had grown up had left for the war a high school basketball star and came home a recluse who didn't make eye contact or smile. He lived in a back room of his parents' house and, up until Sadie had moved away and lost contact, never recovered from whatever happened to him in Southeast Asia.

"It's similar to what some post-traumatic stress victims end up with, yes," Eric said. "But no two cases are the same, or so I hear."

"Eighteen years ago?" Sadie asked. "Were you married?"

Eric looked straight ahead as he rolled through a stop sign. "Yeah," he said simply. Sadie wondered if he was glad to be driving as they talked about this so that he had something else to focus on. Even though he kept his tone level, she could hear the deeply buried hurt beneath the layers. "And I was warned from the start that most relationships crumble under the pressure of brain injuries. I had hoped to avoid becoming a statistic, but it was harder than I could have ever imagined."

"She seems pretty functional," Sadie said. "Just kind of out of it." She hoped she wasn't sounding critical, but ending your marriage after your spouse sustained an injury, even a serious one, was hard for Sadie to justify automatically.

Eric shook his head, and Sadie noticed his jaw was set, making her wonder if he was feeling defensive. "At first she couldn't focus on anything, couldn't complete tasks. She got very angry and frustrated all the time. She went to all kinds of doctors and therapists and improved little by little for about nine months. Then she stopped improving. A couple months later, her neurologist dropped the bombshell—she had plateaued on her rehab. Whether it was due to her inability to cope or simply her lack of motivation, everyone felt she'd made all the progress she would make. The therapy stopped, the hope we'd been given disappeared, and she started watching TV all day. She's made some improvements since then— she can take care of herself and the house—but she still doesn't . . . *feel* anything. She doesn't think about how other people are feeling, doesn't comprehend other people's emotional responses to things. She doesn't cry or laugh or show affection. She just . . . *exists*. Except when she gets angry. And then she gets very, very angry."

"Wow," Sadie said, her heart softening as she imagined what Eric had been through. "That would be hard. How old was Megan when the accident happened?"

Eric began unconsciously rubbing his left thumb against his thigh as though trying to clean something off of his hand. "Seven." He took a breath. "Layla was a wonderful mother before then— parks, books, dress up; Megan loved to have her hair brushed, and every night Layla would sit with her on the bed and brush her hair out while they talked." He paused, and Sadie sensed he was very far away for a moment. "I'd sometimes stand in the doorway and just watch them. We called Megan Sweetie Pie—I know, lots of parents call their daughters that—but Layla had made up a song about her nickname, about how she was as sweet as pie." He paused again and took another deep breath. "We'd wanted more children, but were trying to get on our feet financially before we did. Layla had to work and didn't want to have another baby only to leave it in daycare, so I was working hard to grow my business; that's what brought us to Homestead."

Sadie wondered if he had ever told their story quite this way. Their story: his, Layla's, and Megan's.

After a few seconds, he continued. "Then Layla had her accident—it wasn't even that serious—but the head injury was enough to change her into someone else completely. She didn't like to be touched and had no patience anymore for a little girl. She'd stay up 'til three o'clock in the morning watching TV as though she thought it would disappear tomorrow. She'd lie if it helped her get what she wanted, or kept her out of trouble; she charged up a credit the normal thing to do in college." Sadie wasn't so sure of that—she hadn't partied in college, and it certainly hadn't hurt her. He kept talking. "They'd gone to a club of some kind on Friday, and Megan left early. I don't think she'd ever been to a bar in her life, so it was probably pretty overwhelming. She told Shay she was going back to the motel. No one saw her after that."

"No one?" Sadie said.

Eric shook his head. "It was spring break, with thousands of college kids overrunning Key West. Megan had never been one to stand out. By the time Shay dared tell anyone, it had been two full days since she'd seen her. She said she'd kept waiting for Megan to show up, and she didn't want to tell me or her parents for fear she'd get in trouble for going to Key West in the first place. Because of the delay, we lost precious time. The media didn't cover the story for very long. Megan was too old to garner the same attention a teenager would get, and there was literally nothing to go on."

"That's so horrible," Sadie said, realizing she'd learned more about Eric in the last five minutes than she had in the three months since she'd met him. She wished there was time to ask more questions—there was a kind of . . . abruptness to the way he told the story, but she was sure that was simply because he had to condense events.

"It has been horrible," Eric said. "I wouldn't wish it on my worst enemy."

Sadie looked at the freeway ahead of them while trying to think of what she could say next. It all looked so different from Colorado, with unbroken sky and almost as much tropical greenery as there were concrete buildings that rose up on every side.

"I assume the police investigated Shay and the boyfriend?" Sadie asked.

---

card she stole from my wallet. She'd leave the house and walk for hours and hours until I either found her or the police did. Her mom moved down from Gainesville so she could help while I was at work. We hoped and prayed that she would wake up one day. Instead she simply accepted that she belonged here and we were supposed to take care of her." He looked down at the spot where he'd been rubbing his pants as though surprised to notice he'd been doing it. "Her mom wasn't well, and taking care of Layla and Megan took its toll. After she moved back to Gainesville, everything just got worse—miserable, really."

Sadie was intent on the story, but noted that Eric had gotten on the interstate toward Miami. Miami was fifty miles away. They weren't going all the way to Miami were they?

Eric continued. "The rage subsided in part because her doctor finally put her on antidepressants that mellowed things out for her, but they also made her even more flat. Living amid the apathy for everything and everyone was like slowly drowning. She never called Megan Sweetie Pie after the accident, never brushed her hair before bedtime—it's like she didn't know Megan was her daughter."

"She feels nothing?" Sadie said, thinking back over the exchanges she'd had with her. Certainly Layla was withdrawn and unresponsive. "But she got really anxious when she saw the driver's license; she insisted it wasn't Megan and left the room."

"She did?" Eric said, looking at her quickly, surprised. He immediately turned his attention back to the road. "Really?"

Sadie nodded. "I mean, she wasn't crying or anything. She just said over and over that the photo wasn't Megan. Then she left and waited for me outside."

"I wish I'd been there to see that," Eric said, shaking his head with regret and changing lanes. "I'd have thought the only thing she'd worry about was the bracelet."

"Well, she asked about that, too," Sadie said after a moment, disappointed to have to share bad news. "What's so important about the bracelet?"

"Layla's father gave it to her when she graduated from high school; he died about a year later from colon cancer," Eric said. "After the accident, Layla's mom worried Layla would lose it or break it, so we decided to take it from her. She didn't notice it was gone, and I assumed she'd forgotten all about it, since a lot of her memories had been affected by the injury.

"When Megan turned sixteen, I gave the bracelet to her, as a kind of gift from Layla in a roundabout way. When Layla saw Megan wearing it, she got really upset and accused Megan of stealing. Meg thought she should give it back, but I wouldn't let her. After that, Megan only wore it when she wasn't around Layla, and when Megan disappeared, Layla was most upset because the police talked about how Megan was wearing the bracelet at the club that night. Layla kept saying that the bracelet was hers and she wanted it back. I'm assuming the police didn't return the bracelet?"

"They said it was evidence," Sadie explained.

Eric nodded. "Our daughter was missing, and yet Layla freaked out over a *bracelet*." He sighed before continuing, "It was a very ugly day for me."

Sadie could only imagine. "How did Megan handle Layla's problems? It must have been hard for her to grow up with that."

"For the most part she seemed to take Layla's injury in stride, but I know it was hard for her. Layla hated affection, got easily frustrated, and in time, Megan seemed to close in on herself more and more. One day when Megan was almost ten, I came home and found

her hiding in the closet. She'd broken something—I can't re: what—and Layla had just lost it. There were broken dishes the kitchen, and she'd ripped the pages out of Megan's ba while calling Megan horrible names and telling her she w girl over and over again. My little Sweetie Pie was shaking sl scared of Layla hurting her, and she melted into sobs wher her." Eric voice was soft.

"That's when I decided to leave. Until then I had thou ing the family together would be good for Megan, but t realized it wasn't anymore. I convinced Megan to go to a and for a little while it seemed to help, but it was exper we were really struggling to make things work. At some p had to trust that she could rise above all this." He paused wondered if he were questioning that decision.

"As Megan got older, she reminded me of Layla in so Layla after the accident, I mean. She wouldn't share h wouldn't react to things the way you'd expect someone like, because she had spent so many years trying to be ous, she didn't know how to be . . . normal anymore. decided to go to Virginia for school, I was optimistic t going to make her own way in the world. Seven mont was gone."

"How old was she when she disappeared?" Sadie asl

"Twenty-two, but it was her first year of college, living away from home. And she'd just broken up with friend." Sadie wondered if he was the boy in the pictu in the box. Eric kept talking. "She didn't tell me tha roommate, Shay, were going to Key West for spring br she was staying in Richmond to catch up on some scl honestly, I'd have probably encouraged her to go just

"Extensively," Eric said with a nod. "In the beginning I was convinced they knew something, but they both agreed to take lie detector tests and passed with flying colors. I honestly believe they told us everything they knew."

"But there have to be suspects," Sadie said. Every murder she'd been involved with had suspects. Without someone to look at, there was nowhere to look for answers. "Someone with a secret, a motive that, even if you can't prove it, is there and slowly unravels the more you pick at it."

Eric shook his head.

"And there were no other clues?" Sadie said, still wanting suspects. "I mean, did it look like she'd taken anything with her? How much money did she have?"

Eric glanced at her quickly. "You mean, like she left on purpose?" There was no mistaking the edge in his voice. He continued before Sadie could answer. "That's the police's favorite theory too, that she was depressed and struggling and just moved on. She wouldn't have done that. And no, she didn't take anything with her—nothing."

"Except the bracelet," Sadie said quietly.

CHAPTER 20

Eric heard her anyway. He clenched his jaw. "The bracelet, her purse, and the clothes she was wearing," he clarified, then leaned forward and grabbed the stack of papers he'd thrown on the dash, swerving slightly to the left. Sadie hurried to take the papers from him so he'd get back to driving in a straight line. "She had almost two thousand dollars in a bank account that hasn't been touched."

He nodded toward the papers in Sadie's hands. "There's a copy of the official police report in there," he said. "Shay listed everything Megan was wearing, and the police did an extensive search of Megan's apartment and car, which was in the motel parking lot."

Sadie thumbed through the papers until she came to one that looked official, with Megan's name broken into first, middle, and last name, followed by her physical description. Five foot two inches, a hundred and forty pounds, brown hair, blue eyes, no noticeable scars, tattoos, or piercings. She'd been wearing a green tank top, a denim skirt, and sandals, a hemp necklace with a shell on it, and one diamond tennis bracelet.

"Diamond?" Sadie questioned. "It was a diamond bracelet?"

"Kind of," Eric said. "Cubic zirconium, but still pretty pricey."

"Maybe someone thought it was real and tried to steal it," Sadie suggested.

"The police worked that angle," Eric said, "but it didn't lead anywhere. Nothing showed up in pawn shops, and now we know why."

Sadie thought about the body the police had found with the bracelet as she turned to another page. It was full of handwritten notes. She focused on one line. "'Body moved'?" she read out loud.

Eric nodded. "The grave they found the . . . woman in yesterday was fresh; they're pretty sure it was moved to that location, but it's been buried somewhere else for awhile. They don't know how long exactly, but things . . . break down pretty fast in Florida."

Sadie nodded, not wanting to get into details. Thinking about decomposition while discussing Eric's daughter—his Sweetie Pie—made her feel a little ill.

"Maybe Megan sold the bracelet," Sadie said, leafing through the other papers but not finding anything of interest. "If she had left on her own, and not taken anything, she might have needed the money."

Eric didn't answer for a moment so she looked over at him to see him staring straight ahead. Oh yeah, he didn't like the theory that Megan left on purpose.

"She didn't say good-bye," Eric said, his voice stubborn. "Not to me, or Larry, or Shay. If she had planned to leave, she'd have said something, or emptied her bank account, or taken something with her and, quite frankly, even at twenty-two, she struggled to simply get to class on time."

Sadie paused for a moment, but couldn't *not* say what she had in her mind. "But you *do* think she's alive."

Eric said nothing for several seconds. "She would have contacted me if she could." There was finality in his tone, and Sadie decided to let it go. It *was* hard to believe Megan would disappear on purpose—or, rather, the better explanation was that Sadie could see why it was hard for *Eric* to believe Megan would disappear on purpose.

"So, where are we going?" Sadie asked after they drove several minutes in silence.

"Miami," Eric said.

Sadie scowled; she'd been afraid of that. If she'd taken her own car then she could have headed right over to the airport when she was ready to go. But then she wouldn't have had this time to talk to Eric. Still, she could feel the circumstances pulling her in little by little, and although she was definitely intrigued, she was anxious about getting too involved.

"Why Miami?" she asked. "What's this meeting all about?"

Eric shifted in his seat, which Sadie chose to interpret as anticipation rather than nerves. "The short answer is that I'll be able to learn more about where Megan is."

"And the long answer?"

Eric paused for a few seconds and changed lanes. "Did Mathews tell you how they found the body?"

"No," Sadie admitted, wishing she'd thought to ask. "He didn't."

"They received an anonymous tip," Eric began. "I guess it would have been Wednesday morning. All the tip said was that there was a woman buried at some GPS coordinates near Redland. Megan disappeared in Key West, which is where the missing person's case was filed, so there was no immediate connection when the police went out on the tip. When they found the bracelet with the body, though, Mathews immediately thought about Megan. He read up on the case, the forensics team studied the purse found with the body, and then he called me."

"Okay," Sadie said. "That explains what the police know, but not why you're going to this meeting."

Eric let out a long, tortured breath. "I'm getting to that," he said. "I didn't get to Layla's until early Thursday morning, and I immediately crashed. Around 7:30 that morning I got a call from a man who gave me the same GPS coordinates he claimed to have given the police. He told me that he'd be calling me later with more information, but if I told the police, I'd get nothing."

"You didn't tell Mathews?"

Eric shook his head. "I met with him a little while later and, without telling him about the call, was able to verify the GPS coordinates. I was back at Layla's by ten, and the guy called me at 10:30. He told me the body wasn't Megan, but that she would lead me to my daughter."

"She?" Sadie said. "The . . . body?"

"I assume that's what he meant. I don't know. He said he had information the police would never find, but that it would cost me ten thousand dollars. If I did as he said, and didn't tell the police, he'd prove himself reliable. If I *didn't* do as he said, I'd never see Megan again."

"That's why you're selling the trailer," Sadie summarized, realizing this was the part where she'd become involved. "That's when you called me."

Eric nodded. "I called my neighbor Brian first. We'd taken the trailer hunting together once, and I hoped he'd want to buy it, but he thinks he's got a lay-off coming up and couldn't do it, although he offered to show it for me. Then I called you."

"Why did you need the box?"

"Mathews wanted it," he said with a shrug. "For things like hair and handwriting samples."

Sadie took a breath. If he'd told her even that much, she wouldn't have been as motivated to open the box at all, but he'd kept his reasons to himself, refusing to answer her questions and therefore allowing her mind to run wild.

Let it go, she told herself. Eric hadn't earned all the fault she wanted to heap upon his shoulders, and she was staying of her own volition. "Okay, so you started working on getting the money for the information this tipster offered you. And you kept working with Mathews in order to learn everything he knew as well."

"Yes," he said with a quick nod, devoid of any shame at working both sides.

"And you didn't tell Mathews any of this?" Sadie said for clarification.

"No," he said with an equally quick shake of his head. "Last night, the guy called back. After I assured him I was raising the money and was ready to work with him, he gave me another set of GPS coordinates. They weren't the same ones where the body had been found, but I could tell it was close by. When Larry came over, I told—"

"Wait," Sadie said, putting up her hand to halt the conversation for a minute. "I just remembered I was supposed to tell you that Larry came to the police station, but then had to go back to work. Now, in one hundred words or less, explain why Layla lives in Larry's house if they're divorced." They'd been talking about Larry as if Sadie knew everything about him, but she knew very little and needed a bigger picture.

Eric took a moment to collect his thoughts and then sighed. "Larry," he said as though it was a title for what he would say next. "Larry married Layla shortly after she and I divorced. He made it work for about three years before he threw in the towel, but instead of paying alimony, he purchased the house for Layla and agreed to maintain it. Layla is horrible with money, and this way she'd have somewhere to live for the rest of her life."

"Okay," Sadie said. "I should have given you two hundred words. Why did he marry her?"

Eric let out a breath. "Larry, Layla, and I have been friends since high school. He was always around; he's Megan's godfather and was pretty angry with me when I left." He glanced at Sadie quickly before turning his attention back to the road. "A few months after I left, he moved to Homestead, and a few months after that, they were married. He said it was so she could be on his insurance—he worked for the state and had great benefits—and he could take her to some new doctors. Bottom line, he wanted to fix her; it didn't work. For whatever reason, the nicer he was to Layla, the meaner she was toward him. He finally gave up, just like me."

"Oh," Sadie said. She pictured the timeline in her mind. "Was that . . . hard for you when he married her?"

Eric shrugged. "At first, I guess, but he had always been great with Megan, and then he took really good care of Layla—even though he didn't find any miracle to heal her—so I got over it for the sake of them, and he forgave me for leaving for the same reasons, and we've been okay ever since."

Men! Sadie thought. How did they deal with things so logically?

"And he works at the Speedway? Is that a grocery store?"

"No," Eric said, looking at her with genuine surprise. "The Homestead-Miami Speedway. NASCAR?"

"Oh," Sadie said, nodding. "Race cars."

Eric seemed a little startled by her simplistic answer. "It's one of the most famous tracks in the country and hosts more championship races than anyone else."

"So, Larry's a race car driver?"

"No," Eric said, almost chuckling. "He works in the back office—computers, printing; that kind of thing."

"Oh," Sadie said. She had more questions, but didn't want to get any more off track than she already was. "So you told Larry about the call you received and . . ."

"Right," Eric said, picking up the story. "It was eating me up not to talk to anyone."

Sadie bit back a comment about how she'd have talked to him about it if he hadn't purposely withheld the information from her.

Eric continued. "I knew he wanted information about Megan as badly as I did, and he even offered to loan me half of the ten thousand until the trailer sold. We decided to check out the GPS site together."

Sadie's heart rate increased as her eyes were drawn to his dirty shoes. "That's where you went this morning."

Eric nodded. "Before Larry had to go to work."

"What did you find?" Sadie said.

"A box buried under a couple inches of soil," Eric said.

"What was in it?"

"Megan's *real* purse—the one she had with her when she disappeared from Key West," Eric said simply, but the words seemed painful for him to say. "And this." He reached into the front pocket of his cotton, buttoned-up shirt and pulled out a business card, handing it to Sadie.

She held it along the edges, not wanting to get her fingerprints on it, though she feared that with both Eric and Larry having handled it, any fingerprints the caller may have left behind would be destroyed. The front of the card showed a speedboat jumping over a wave—obviously Photoshopped since there was no way a boat could catch a wave that big by the shore like that. To the side of the graphic was the name of a company: Motorways Powerboat, Inc., with an address on 51st Street in Miami.

"Look on the back," Eric suggested, and Sadie attempted to turn her hand, still holding the card by the edges. She had to tilt her head slightly to see the back since her wrist would only twist so far. In pencil was written today's date and the time of 2:30 PM above one word: *alone.*

"That's where you're going?" Sadie asked, turning the card over so she could read the address again.

"Yep."

Sadie handed the card back to Eric. "But you have no idea what you'll find there."

Eric returned the card to his pocket. "I'll find answers."

But was that enough? "I really think we should tell Mathews," Sadie said. "What if this is some kind of setup? What if something happens?"

"I don't care," Eric said calmly, shaking his head for emphasis. "I won't risk *not* learning what he knows."

"Did he *say* she was alive?" Sadie asked.

Eric shifted in his seat. This time he looked uncomfortable. "Not in so many words, but I think she is."

Sadie remained silent for a few seconds, trying to choose her words as best she could. "When you and I talked about her at the courthouse," she finally said, refusing to think about the almost-kiss like she did every time she remembered that afternoon, "you said you *hadn't* believed she was alive all this time."

"Why would he go to all the trouble of contacting me and leading me to her purse if he didn't have something important for me?"

Sadie pondered that for a while, reviewing all the motives for heinous crimes she'd encountered over the last few months. "In my experience, money is the lowest motive of all, meaning the people who seek it at all costs—no pun intended—are the least trustworthy.

If he wants money, then he can't be trusted once he gets what he wants."

"I don't *have* the money," Eric said. "The trailer's been listed for about five hours. But I withdrew all twelve hundred dollars out of my savings account—that's what took me so long this morning—and Larry got five thousand out of his. That gives me more than half. I'll tell him I'll pay the rest if I get Megan back."

Sadie shook her head. "This is a mistake," she said with absolute certainty. But she didn't like the way Eric was leaning away from her ever so slightly. If he took the defensive, *she'd* be the one losing *his* trust. She looked at Eric and allowed herself to embrace the compassion she really did feel for him right now. Maybe her understanding would open his mind better than her attack. "I know you want him to help you, but this thing has so many red flags it looks like it's on fire."

"It's all I've got," Eric said softly, but with just as much determination.

"Then give it to the police and let them figure it out. They're trained for this kind of work; they know what to do." She felt like a hypocrite for advising him on something she herself had never done, or at least not done well. "I know what this guy said, but if the police can get a hold of him, they can get the information you need." She looked at the dashboard clock. "We can call Mathews, and he can get something set up if we hurry." At least, she hoped he could.

Eric shook his head, then checked his blind spot and moved to the right. Their exit must be getting close, which only increased Sadie's concerns. "I *refuse* to take the chance of messing this up," he said.

"You recently pleaded guilty for withholding information during a police investigation," Sadie pointed out. "A second conviction might not go as smoothly."

"It doesn't matter," Eric said again, very calm and confident. "This is what I'm doing."

Sadie reflected on how differently he was behaving now compared to when they'd talked in the car before lunch. Then, he'd been gracious and sweet. Now he was rather dominating and dismissive of everything she said; he wasn't even trying to consider her thoughts on the situation. Gayle's assumption that Sadie's trip to Florida would give rise to some kind of romance seemed rather silly now. Maybe it was just circumstances . . . but maybe not. Sadie didn't dwell on those thoughts for long, however, they weren't what was important right now.

He moved into the exit lane and took the North Miami Avenue off-ramp. Sadie tried to think of another argument; surely there was something she could say that would help him see what she believed he was missing in the scenario. And yet she couldn't ignore the question of what she would do if this were her child. If she believed the police could ruin her chances of getting her child back, would she take that risk?

"I don't feel good about this," Sadie finally said. Eric had used his feelings that Megan was close to justify what he was doing. Surely her feelings of unease were just as real. "Something's not right."

"A hundred things aren't right," Eric clarified, coming to a stop at an intersection. "Believe me, I would prefer that he'd given all this information to the police instead of me; I would rather he wanted Megan's return more than he wanted my money, but that isn't what I've been given." Without warning he pulled into a gas station, taking Sadie off guard.

She glanced at the gas gauge—there was still nearly half a tank. When she looked from the gauge to Eric's face, however, she understood.

"I'm sorry you don't agree with what I'm doing," Eric said, sounding mostly understanding but a little bit disappointed, too. He'd wanted her to be a good sidekick and agree with him on everything. Apparently he didn't know Sadie as well as he thought he did. He pulled up in front of the food mart and turned to look at her. "Do you have your phone?"

Sadie didn't answer, battling inside herself on whether she should insist on going with him or not. No, she didn't like what he was doing, but was it worse for him to do it alone? Then again, she was sincere in her feelings that something was wrong. "I don't think this is safe, Eric," she said. "Let me go with you. I'll duck down in the back and stay in the car, but if something happens then you won't be on your own."

"No," Eric said, his tone final. "I can't take the risk. I'm sorry. I'll come back and pick you up when I'm done."

She looked at the gas station, unwilling to give in just yet. The food mart wasn't fancy, but it had a Burger King inside. There were tables where she could sit and certainly a selection of magazines that would keep her mind occupied. But Eric would be facing a difficult situation all by himself. Her gaze slid further to the side, taking in the other cars in the lot. After focusing on one in particular, she turned back to Eric and put her hand on the door handle. "I have my phone," she said. "If I don't hear from you by 3:00, I'm calling Mathews."

Eric hesitated, but finally gave a small nod, as though knowing he wouldn't win this one. "Quarter after," he said. "I've still got some distance to cover."

"Okay," Sadie said. "One hour—3:15." She looked at him and held his eyes. "Be careful."

"Yes, ma'am," he said with a dip of his chin.

Sadie bit back one more lecture and stepped out of the car. She could feel Eric watching her so she didn't look back as she pushed through the glass doors of the food mart. Once she was inside, Eric reversed out of his parking space. Sadie took a step closer to the front glass and watched until he'd pulled back into traffic. As soon as he was gone, she pushed the door open and took quick strides across the parking lot toward the far right gas pump.

"This yours?" Sadie asked as she approached a young man who was pulling the nozzle out of the gas tank of a white-and-black taxi. She actually preferred that the taxi wasn't bright yellow so that it wouldn't be as easy to spot.

"Yuh," the tall, thin black man said without looking at her, a Jamaican accent coming through with just the one word. His hair was cut short, not in dreadlocks or anything, and if Sadie had to guess she'd say he was in his early thirties. Whoever called New York the melting pot had never been to Miami.

"Good," Sadie said with a nod as she headed toward the back door. "There's a green Ford Tempo with an Avis rental car sticker on the back window that just pulled out of this station and is heading for 51st Street." She pointed in the direction Eric had turned. "I need you to catch up with him, but without him knowing."

"You be in some kinda trouble, lady?" the man asked, looking at her for the first time.

"Not me," Sadie said, giving him a confident look. "But he is. Can you catch up?"

The man looked at her for a moment. In the next instant his dark lips parted to show teeth that fairly glowed against his skin. "Certainly," he said, hanging up the nozzle.

Sadie nodded with relief, but immediately moved to the next worry on her list. It had been nearly a full minute since Eric had disappeared into traffic. Would they be able to find him?

CHAPTER 21

Sadie need not have worried about being unable to catch up. It only took two lights, and enough zigging and zagging between other cars to make Sadie grasp the door handle for balance, before Monty—the driver—pointed at a green Ford a few cars ahead of them as they slowed down for a light. "That be 'im?" Monty asked.

Sadie leaned forward and could just make out the Avis sticker. "That's him," she said, impressed. "Well done."

Monty shrugged, but he also smiled in the rearview mirror. "I know Miami," he said, obviously pleased with himself. "You wan' me to stay 'ere or get us closa?"

"Here is good," Sadie said, confident that if they somehow lost Eric, Monty would have no problem finding him again.

"What be on fifty-firs' he be want'n to fine?"

"A boat shop, I guess," Sadie said, thinking back to the business card Eric had shown her. "Motorways Powerboat."

Monty lifted his eyebrows and looked at her quickly in the mirror again. "What he be want'n with Motoway?"

Sadie shrugged, but honed in on Monty's interest. "I don't know. Do you know anything about the company?"

"Only dat dey be ba' business," Monty said with a nod. "Spected de owner done be selling 'is boats to Cuba 'gain."

"Again?" Sadie asked.

"Years ago FBI done talked to 'im 'bout rumors of 'im sellin' to Castro's men. Din't get proven, a'course, but some say he be back to work. Soon as people start a'talkin', though, 'e shuts down 'is shop."

"Shuts it down?" Sadie said. "So Motorways Powerboat isn't operating?"

"Not 'less he done open las' week," Monty said.

So, Eric wasn't only meeting an anonymous caller, he was meeting an anonymous caller at an abandoned business whose owner had possible ties to a communist regime. And he didn't think the police needed to be involved?

She looked up as the light changed and the cars started moving. Eric's car was in the lane to the left, and although there were several cars between them, she could see the outline of his head, leaning like he did against the driver's side door. She wondered if he was as nervous as she was.

"Dat be your fella?" Monty asked.

Sadie's eyes jumped back to the mirror, caught off guard. "Oh, uh, no," she said, managing a little chuckle despite the flush rising in her cheeks. "Just a friend."

Monty smiled again, embarrassing Sadie even more. "Sho', sho'," he said with a knowing nod. "Whe' you from, lady?"

Sadie was glad for the change of subject. "Colorado."

"Ooo, long way from 'ere."

Sadie nodded and thought to herself, *In more ways than one.*

Ahead of them Eric turned on his car's left blinker and pulled into the turning lane. Monty smoothly cut off another driver, ignored the ensuing honk, and moved in behind Eric. There were no cars between them now so Sadie sank down in the backseat, counting on Eric being preoccupied enough with the upcoming meeting that he wouldn't be checking out the passengers of a taxi.

The wait at the light seemed interminable, but finally Eric moved forward and made the turn. Another car made a right-hand turn before Monty could turn left. Sadie was relieved to have a car between them again. She kept waiting for Eric to turn in to a parking lot of one of the many businesses lined up on both sides of the road; 51st Street seemed to be part of a dedicated business district, though there were apartment buildings and condos sprinkled throughout the neighborhood as well.

Eric kept going. And going. And going. The car between them turned down another street, so Monty kept his distance and Sadie kept her head down. If only she'd brought a hat. The silhouette of her hair, kinda curled, kinda spiked, but always unique and rather . . . big, would give her away should Eric take the time to study the taxi's interior.

It seemed they drove a few miles, stopping at a light every other block, before the buildings became more spread out, with fences around the paved portions of industrial space. They passed a used car lot, then an auto-body shop, what looked like a vitamin company, and then, finally, Eric turned on his right blinker.

Sadie held on to the edges of both front seats, leaning forward while Monty slowed the car so as not to get too close to Eric before he completed the turn. A sign mounted on the fence read Motorway Powerboats, Inc., using many of the same colors and graphics as the business card had.

"Drive past it," Sadie said, then, remembering her manners added, "please." As they passed by, she craned her neck to watch Eric as long as possible. He'd pulled into a fenced lot with an open rolling gate, but instead of parking in the front lot—which was empty—he headed down a driveway that ran along the right side of the building. Then he turned left, moving out of sight. She'd have to follow him on foot. Wonderful.

Glancing around, Sadie spotted a cabinet shop across the street. The parking lot wasn't so full that she thought Monty would get in trouble for parking there—she knew small businesses could get persnickety with their parking sometimes—but the lot faced Motorway. It looked right down the driveway, in fact.

"Can you wait in there?" Sadie asked, pointing to the lot.

"Sho', sho'," Monty said. "De meter got to keep running, though, even if de motor don't."

"I understand," Sadie said, digging in her purse as he turned into the lot and maneuvered the car so that it was facing Motorway. She dug out a twenty, even though the fare meter said she owed twenty-two, and handed it over the seat as he shifted into park. She worried that if she gave him too much, he'd take off and desert her, yet she had to give him enough now for him to know she was good for it, too. "I'll pay the rest when I get back," she said.

For the first time, concern entered Monty's expression. "Whacha goin' ta do?"

"Just . . . look around," Sadie said. "I don't think I'll be too long."

"Isn't safe for ladies ta go 'round on deir own like dat," Monty said, nodding toward the buildings around them. Most of them were fenced, and no one was walking up and down the sidewalks here. "S'pose I go wit you?"

"Uh," Sadie said, not sure what she thought about that. On the one hand, having a big strong bodyguard would provide a nice sense of security, and yet she still didn't know what she was getting into, therefore she was hesitant to involve anyone else. Not to mention that she feared Monty wouldn't blend very well. Sadie, on the other hand, knew how to blend into tight spaces and cramped situations. She finally shook her head. "Thank you for the offer. You're very kind, but I'll be okay. I just want a peek is all." She put her hand on the door release and pushed it open.

Monty wasn't pleased, but suddenly reached into a pouch strapped to his visor and pulled out a slightly bent business card. He handed it to her with a nod. "You need me, you call me, okay?"

Sadie took the card and smiled her thanks as she got out of the car and stuffed the card in her back pocket. She considered leaving her purse in the car, but no matter how chivalrous Monty seemed, she was not an idiot. Or at least not that big of one.

She shut the door and tried to ignore her racing heart as she waited for a few cars to pass before darting across the street. She eyed the windows of the two-story metal building Eric had driven behind and hoped no one was watching her. The windows had a reflective tint on them, so she couldn't see in. When she reached the side of the building, she placed her back against the wall and tried to repeat some positive affirmations to boost her confidence.

"You're doing great," she told herself. "What would Eric do without you, anyway?" Sadie continued whispering as she moved down the building. "Like it or not, he's better off with you looking out for him. One day I'm sure he'll realize it and find a way to thank you."

When she was only ten feet from the far side of the building, she slowed down and stopped talking to herself, listening for other voices instead. All she could hear was the rush of traffic coming from 51st Street behind her as well as whatever street was on the next block over—52nd probably. Once she reached the corner, she squatted down so she wouldn't be at eye level with anyone else, and gingerly poked her head around the edge of the building.

Eric's car was there, along with a sporty red car parked close to the building itself. Eric was nowhere to be seen. *Has he gone inside?* she wondered as she scanned the back lot. Surely he wasn't dumb enough to go into a private building with a suspicious stranger. But there was no one in the yard. Instead, it was full of stuff she thought surely made sense to people who knew boats. There was metal stuff, funny-shaped stuff, and bright plastic-looking sheets of stuff. There was also a line of boat trailers against the far side of the fence, which, she realized, was about ten feet tall with loops of razor wire along the top. The way she'd come in seemed to be the only way back out, which meant she would need to keep herself within view of the exit at all times.

Once assured no one was in the yard, she turned the corner. Monty wouldn't be able to see her from here on out, and although she was glad she hadn't asked him to come with her, she was equally glad to know he was there. Still pressed against the edge of the building—which was rather warm, thanks to all the Florida sunshine it had been soaking up all day—Sadie moved toward the double doors set smack dab in the middle of the back wall. The glass doors aligned almost perfectly with the trunk of the red sports car.

Sadie crouched down as she approached the double doors and held her purse close to her chest so it wouldn't bang against anything. When she reached the edge of the doors, she poked her head slowly forward, allowing her a look inside. She saw a carpeted entryway but, like the yard, the lobby, with its fake plants and empty reception desk, was unoccupied. Fluorescent lighting brightened the interior even though the sunlight coming through the glass doors seemed to provide more than enough light. Light or not, however, Eric was nowhere in sight.

"Oh biscuits," Sadie said under her breath, leaning forward even farther to make sure she hadn't missed anything. But her first assessment had been the right one. No one was there. Not in the entryway, at least. It took a few seconds before she dared check the door to see if it was unlocked. When it moved outward, she immediately let it go, overcome with the panic of what could happen to her inside this building. It was one thing to prowl around the outside of a building, but to go *inside* was something else entirely. Especially a building owned by a man suspected of selling boats to communists.

Sadie liked to think she was brave, but going inside was beyond her. Whether that made her a coward or a genius, she wasn't sure, but she liked the sound of genius better. Her hesitation didn't change the fact that if Eric was in there, and if she was trying to figure out what was going on, then staying out here simply meant she'd wasted her time. For the moment, however, wasting time still seemed a better option than cornering herself.

Her eyes were drawn to the sports car. The license plate was from Texas. She looked quickly at the doors of the building to make sure the coast was still clear on the inside, and then ran past them, immediately pressing herself against the wall of the building on the other side of the doors, holding her breath to better hear if someone was coming. After ten seconds she let out the breath and assured herself she'd made it. She glanced cautiously at the door, then walked to the driver's side window of the car, cupping her hands around her eyes so she could see through the tinted glass.

There was a pair of sunglasses on the dashboard and an iPod on the passenger seat, a cord stretching between it and the CD player. What looked like a jacket or sweater was crumpled on the driver's seat and in the middle console between the seats was a Diet Coke bottle—half full—in one of the drink holders, a pile of change in the other one. It was obviously not a rental car.

A GPS unit, similar to the one Sadie had bought at Walmart, was plugged into the cigarette lighter, making Sadie wonder if the driver of the car was from out of town. Someone had directed Eric and the police to certain locations near the body by using GPS coordinates. In Sadie's mind that confirmed the car owner's identity—definitely the tipster. She felt better knowing that, by all appearances, Eric was contacting and dealing with only one man. But the man was still a criminal, and Sadie would be wise to remember that.

After scanning the front seat, she moved to the back window. There were some papers folded up on the backseat. The color, light yellow, set them off from the black leather upholstery, but after squinting in an attempt to see what they were, she realized the tinted windows made them impossible to read. She scanned the interior of the car a little more, looking for anything that would lead her to say, "Aha, I found a clue!" But there didn't seem to be any clues at all, and within a minute, she was out of things to do.

Her eyes went back to the glass doors. Eric had been in there for at least seven or eight minutes. What were they talking about? Maybe she wouldn't have to sneak around if she went inside. She could simply call out for someone and ask to use their restroom or something as a ploy to explain her presence. But the idea was not a pleasant one. What if Eric gave away that they knew each other? What if the guy Eric was meeting was armed? He was already an extortionist; who's to say he wouldn't also shoot first and ask questions later?

She looked back at the car, wishing she could get inside it. If nothing else, there might be locations stored in the GPS unit that would tell her where the tipster had come from or where he was going later. And then maybe she could check his glove box to see if there was anything in there. The trunk! She could pop the trunk. Maybe he had luggage that would tell her more about him. On an impulse she reached for the handle, just in case the tipster hadn't locked his door. Her fingertips were wrapped around the handle when she realized she was acting too fast, and she pulled her hand back.

This was Miami, and this man had a lot to hide. He probably had a car alarm. She peered into the car, scanning the dashboard for a light that would indicate the car was armed. She didn't see anything, so she scanned the windows, looking for a decal that indicated an alarm system. She didn't see one of those either and turned her attention back to the car. She couldn't see a lock being up or down on the door and felt her eyes drawn back to those papers on the backseat. Her thoughts once again turned to the trunk and what it could be holding. Wouldn't it be ridiculous if it turned out that the car held the answers to any number of her questions and she hadn't even tried?

She decided it absolutely would be ridiculous. Things had fallen into place so far. She reached for the handle again, and then held her breath in anticipation, truly believing that the chances were good the car was unlocked.

The ear-splitting sound of sirens caused Sadie to jump at least a foot in the air. When her feet returned to the ground, she couldn't breathe, but realized the alarm that had just taken five years off her life was coming from the car. Looking around wildly, the blood pumping loudly in her ears, she looked for somewhere to hide. She didn't dare pass the glass doors for fear that the owner of the car was, right now, on his way outside.

The nearest pile of metal stuff caught her attention, and she made a run for it, crouching low to the ground and muttering,

"Oh please, oh please, oh please," under her breath as she ran. She ducked behind the pile and put her hand over her mouth in case the fear got the better of her and she screamed. With her hand holding her purse, she attempted to cover her left ear as best she could; even with fifteen yards between her and the car, the alarm was excruciating.

No sooner had she wondered how long it would go on, when the sound stopped. Sadie's ears continued ringing even as she made out the sound of the glass door opening. She wasn't surprised someone had come, but she had really, really hoped they wouldn't. Her entire body froze, and she held her breath in case her breathing was as loud to him as it was to her. She sounded like Darth Vader, and her ears were ringing like Christmas bells.

"You said you came alone," an unfamiliar voice said, sounding displeased. The tipster? The ringing made it hard to hear, but Sadie was only fifteen yards away. She leaned toward the voices. Her heart continued to race.

"I *did* come alone," replied a voice Sadie definitely knew. Eric. Relief washed over her knowing he was safe, and she told herself she had accomplished what she wanted to accomplish, though she hadn't wanted to do it quite like this. "It's just me," Eric said. "A bird probably landed on your car or something."

Good save, Eric, Sadie thought, wondering if she'd ever be able to tell him that to his face. To do so would mean telling him she was the one who had set off the alarm, and she wasn't sure she wanted him to know that.

There was silence, and she waited, sure they'd go back inside and finish their discussion now that Eric had given a plausible excuse for the alarm being set off. Then she would sneak out past the doors and down the alleyway where Monty would whisk her back to the gas station. It was a good plan. A really good plan. But moments later she heard what sounded like a gut punch and a groaning exhale. A scuffle followed, ending with a metallic thud that Sadie imagined was the sound of someone being pushed up against the building. Her heart sank. It didn't seem likely that Eric would be the one to take a swing at the tipster.

"The alarm doesn't go off unless someone tries to break into the car," the unidentified voice said. He was definitely angry this time. "Who came with you?"

"No one," Eric groaned, though he sounded angry too. "You saw me pull in. No one else was in the car."

Sadie cringed as she heard another sound, one like a closed fist against Eric's head. If only she'd have let Monty come with her. Looking around for any means of escape, Sadie came to the quick and devastating reminder that she was fenced-in on every side. Literally.

How did she get herself into this situation in the first place? If not for the fact that she was hiding, she'd have screamed in frustration. Why, oh why, was she not on a plane right this very minute?

The internal tantrum lasted only a few seconds before it burned out, and she was forced to face the full reality of her present situation.

She was trapped. Eric was pinned. She let her eyes drift closed as she sent up a silent prayer for help to get herself, and Eric, out of this one. Poor Eric. And yet, she couldn't help but shoot him a little "I told you so" in her mind. She'd said this meeting was a bad idea, but her caution didn't change the fact that Eric wouldn't be pinned against the wall if she hadn't followed him here. She willed the man to let Eric go.

She winced at the sounds of another hit, another groan, and

another round of shouted questions. It was more than Sadie could stand. She couldn't wait here and listen to Eric take a beating because of her. The alternative wasn't all that appealing either, but Sadie was crafty and thought she could pull it off.

Without allowing enough time to second-guess herself, Sadie stood up and took two steps to her left, leaving the security of the metal stuff that had given her sanctuary. Just as she'd thought, Eric was up against the building with a man standing in front of him, one hand holding the front of Eric's shirt against his neck. The man's back was to Sadie, so she couldn't see his face, but Eric saw her over the man's shoulder, and his eyes went wide, which caught the attention of his attacker. The other man turned and looked at Sadie, surprised to see her there, but not at the expense of his anger.

"I'm s-sorry," she said quickly, trying to stay above the fear that was grasping at her with ten-fingered hands. "I was looking for a bathroom and hit against your car. I'm afraid the handle caught on the edge of my purse." She lifted her wine-colored, boxy purse for emphasis. "When the alarm went off, I kind of panicked. Please don't hurt that man on my account."

Don't hurt me either, she nearly added. Then all she could do was steel herself for his response and continue praying silently for deliverance.

CHAPTER 22

The man holding Eric against the wall was of average height and frame, shorter than Eric even, but the muscles in his arms and the set of his chest showed that Eric—who wasn't out of shape by any means—didn't stand much of a chance. Sadie had become used to seeing every shade of brown and black skin since arriving in Florida; this man ran in the lighter end in the spectrum, but had dark eyes and longish, dark hair anchored in a ponytail at the back of his head—not unlike Eric's own hair, though this man's head was shaved beneath the ponytail itself.

He wore a leather shoulder harness, but there was no gun in the holster. A closer look, however, revealed the gun to be in the hand not pressing Eric against the siding. It always amazed Sadie how fake real guns could look. This one was black and small, but with what she could only assume was a silencer on the end, making the barrel unusually long. She pretended not to notice the gun at all. This was Miami, after all; everyone waved guns around, right?

"I'm so sorry," she said again, moving toward the strip of drive-way which was the only way out of the yard. "I, um, saw a cabinet shop across the street. I'll see if maybe they'll let me use their rest-room instead."

"No," the man said suddenly, releasing Eric as he took a step back and holstered his gun in one fluid movement. "You can use ours," he said, and though his tone was friendly, his eyes were not as he watched her intently. He had a slight accent—nothing like Monty's—but still apparent in his words. He was in his late-thirties, she'd guess, with lines around his eyes and the beginning of jowls he would not appreciate in another fifteen years.

Eric attempted to smooth out his shirt, but the part of his neck the man had been pressing against the wall was red, showing the force that had been holding him there. He wasn't looking at Sadie; she wondered if that was on purpose. She was avoiding Eric's eyes as well, not wanting to give anything away. It took every ounce of in-ternal strength for Sadie to keep from running back to the cab. "It's okay, I don't want to disturb you any—"

"You've already done that," the man said, folding his arms across his chest as he continued to stare her down. He moved to the door and pulled it open. "May as well not waste any more time by making all this irrelevant."

Sadie paused, studiously avoiding looking at Eric for fear he would betray their connection, while desperately searching for a way out of this. "Thanks anyway," she said, swallowing the fear and try-ing to convince herself that everything was fine. She moved forward, but the man moved in front of her, blocking her way.

"I insist," he said evenly, and Sadie realized that other than screaming and attempting to run, she had no choice. Taking a deep breath, she tried to convince herself everything was okay, that he was simply testing her story. If she really needed to use the restroom bad enough to have come back here, she'd follow through, right?

"Okay," she said, hoping she sounded brave. "Thanks."

She'd go into the bathroom for thirty seconds, then thank him and make her getaway. It was possible for it to be that simple, right? She tried very hard to believe it as she walked into the building, the man close enough behind her that she could hear him breathing. She suppressed a shiver and thought courageous thoughts, taking confidence in the fact that Eric was here. If worse came to worst, he'd defend her.

"It's down that hallway," the man said, his arm extending past her shoulder as he pointed straight ahead to an unlit hallway with two doors on either side. "Second door on the right."

Sadie nodded, unable to verbalize a second thank-you with her heart thumping in her throat. He continued to follow right behind her as she headed for the door. She half-expected him to go into the bathroom with her, but he stopped right outside the door.

"I'll wait for you here," he said, managing a smile that gave Sadie no comfort. Eric had followed the two of them as well, but Sadie still refused to look at him, though she could sense his tension. As she stepped over the threshold and pushed the door closed behind her, she remembered her chiding him about going to this meeting at all, about how unsafe it was. What a hypocrite she was.

The door clicked, and Sadie turned the lock. For a moment she listened, wondering if the man was staying right outside the door. She didn't hear him walk away, but maybe she wouldn't be able to hear through the door.

She glanced around the small room. Now what? She didn't have much time. That's when she remembered Monty's card in her back pocket. Moving carefully, she pulled the card from her pocket and then slowly opened her purse and pulled out her cell phone.

She hoped that Monty texted. Gayle didn't like to, which,

despite Sadie's lack of skill when it came to texting, was very annoying when a text would be easier and faster than having a conversation. But Monty was young, and from what Sadie had learned about young people, they always had texting enabled.

Using her foot to flush the toilet, she typed as quickly as she could.

Come inside in 3 minutes.

She wanted to add "please" as a way to abate the presumptuousness of her request, but the toilet stopped flushing, and she was out of time. Monty would know the text was from her, right?

She went to the sink and turned on the water, using it to mask the sound her phone made as she sent the text. She watched the screen of her phone as long as she felt she could, but no one washed their hands for more than twenty seconds, so she finally had to put it away. She shoved Monty's card back into her pocket and the phone back in her purse. After running her hands under the water, she pulled a paper towel from the dispenser and dried them before unlocking the door and pulling it open, startled to find the man planted in the doorway only inches away from her.

His arms were folded across his chest and although he was only a few inches taller than Sadie, he might as well have been eight feet tall for the imposing figure he cut. With her peripheral vision, Sadie saw Eric standing against the far wall of the hallway, a few feet closer to the exterior doors. She didn't need to make eye contact to feel how tense he was—or perhaps *angry* was a better description.

"Where are you from?" the man demanded.

"Uh, I'm from Georgia," Sadie said. Since she was trying to keep her connection to Eric a secret, admitting she was from the same state Eric was from, assuming the man knew where Eric was from, didn't seem wise. Then again, she didn't talk like someone from Georgia and felt the need to strengthen her story. "Well, not originally," she said, offering a slight smile. Her mind was whirling with ideas on how she could make herself sound more believable. "My husband and I moved there from Wyoming a few years ago. You know, snowbirds and all that. We sure do like the sunshine, though; it does wonders for my husband's arthritis, which was just about as bad as it could be that last winter we spent in Cody." She'd managed to confuse people before with too many words and hoped she could be so lucky again.

"What are you doing in Miami?" the man asked, having not moved even a fraction of an inch away from her. She could smell his cologne and didn't like it.

"Um, we're . . . buying a car," she said, remembering the used car dealership half a block down the street. "We came out to visit Neil's brother in our old Dodge, but it broke down about fifty miles out of town. We had to get it towed to his brother's house, if you can believe it, and, rather than fix the old hunk-a-junk, Neil decided to get us a new car—well, new to us anyway. I can hardly stand listening to him haggle, though, so I decided to take a walk." Her story, rather than getting stronger, felt as though it was unraveling.

"Alone?" he asked.

She added the rest in her mind—*in downtown Miami?*

"Neil was trying to get another five hundred dollars taken off the purchase price," Sadie explained. "I didn't want to interrupt him—five hundred dollars is five hundred dollars after all—but I still don't like to listen to all that, so I walked down the block. I was on my way back when I saw a car pull into this lot so I thought you must be open and, if you were, you might have a restroom I could use, and it would probably be cleaner than whatever the used car lot had to offer. I'm not much of a fan of public restrooms, if you know what I mean. Then my purse caught on the handle and all that drama ensued." She made her smile a little bigger and waved her hand through the air in hopes it would make it all seem silly. "Sorry for interrupting your meeting, though," she said, more eager than ever to leave. She finally dared glance at Eric, worried that at this point, not looking at him, and therefore not including him in her apology, would look more suspicious than ignoring him. His right cheek was red and a little swollen, but she was glad he didn't look too mad. Instead, he looked really nervous—scared even, and that undid some of Sadie's confidence.

The man still hadn't moved, so she took a step forward and slightly to the left, hoping he would step aside. He didn't.

Sadie glanced at Eric, who looked even more anxious. His hands were balled into fists at his sides. She didn't let her eyes linger very long before she looked up at the man blocking her way. "I'd better get back to my husband," she said, unable to keep the fear out of her voice any longer.

He still didn't move, and Sadie found herself holding her breath, worried that Monty didn't have texting on his phone after all and wasn't coming. Surely it had been three minutes by now, right? Maybe he'd given up on her altogether and left with the twenty dollars she'd given him.

Finally, the man began turning to the side, allowing just enough room for her to slip past him. But as soon as she took a step forward, he moved like lightning, raising his right forearm and pressing it against her neck while pulling his gun from the holster with his left hand and pointing it at Eric's head before Eric had time to do so much as flinch. Sadie attempted a scream, but the arm crushing her trachea prevented any sound from coming out of her mouth. She could only make a gurgling, coughing noise as she stared up at her captor with shock and fear rushing through her veins.

He stared at her with those shark eyes of his, holding her with the intensity of a look that was as strong as the muscles in his arm. "Who are you?"

CHAPTER 23

The silence was profound as Sadie tried to look at Eric, but couldn't turn her head enough to make eye contact. The man stared at Sadie while keeping the gun trained on Eric. "Who sent you?"

He moved his arm from her neck to her collarbone so she could answer. She had to cough three times before she felt as though she could speak; her throat throbbed. "I told you, I'm from Georgia and—"

The click of the safety being taken off the gun caused the rest of the lie to stick in her throat. She looked at Eric, who had suddenly stiffened.

"I'll kill him." The man's cold tone convinced Sadie he really would pull the trigger.

Should she attempt another lie? The look in the man's eyes told her not to. "My name is Sadie," she finally admitted, seeing Eric slump a few feet away. "Eric told me he was coming here, but . . . he refused to let me come with him." She turned to look at Eric. "I'm so sorry I followed you," she said, meaning every word of it.

"You weren't supposed to tell anyone," the man shouted, turning toward Eric, who startled at the volume of the man's words.

"I'm sorry," Eric said. "I didn't think she'd interfere."

The words were a slap, one Sadie knew she deserved.

The man turned his eyes back to her. "Have you gone to the police with this?"

"No," Sadie said, suddenly hoping she was a bad enough liar that he would instantly recognize she was telling the truth now. "I only learned about it on the way here. Eric dropped me off so he could continue alone. I was just worried about him, I swear."

The man's eyes continued to bore through her. "This complicates things," he muttered. He moved his arm from Sadie's chest, but only to clamp his hand on her right arm, tightly enough to convince her that now wasn't the time to try the skills that had gotten her out of similar situations in the past. Still pointing the gun toward Eric, the man dragged Sadie toward the doors. Partway there, he suddenly shifted and pointed the gun at her head instead of Eric's. Sadie forgot to breathe for a few stumbling steps. Then, in one fluid movement the man turned around, keeping Sadie with him. He looked at Eric.

"She's coming with me," he said. "And the price just went up another five grand."

"Fifteen thousand dollars?" Eric sputtered, shaking his head. "There's no way I can get that kind of money. The sixty-two hundred was all I'd been able—"

"Find a way," the man countered. "There's a practice race at the Speedway tonight at 6:00. We'll be in section C. Find us, bring the money, and I'll give you your woman back as well as your daughter."

At the mention of Megan, Eric's face drained of both tension and color, as though realizing how seriously Sadie's interference had jeopardized his chance to find Megan.

At the look on his face, Sadie felt the emotion she'd been holding back threaten to break free. "I'm so sorry, Eric," she said as tears rose in her eyes.

The man's grip on her arm tightened as he pulled her toward the door. She tripped over her own feet and nearly dropped her purse. He steadied her without looking at her, but it surprised her that he'd bothered.

"I hope you understand how serious this is," the man said to Eric. "I've now got double coverage. You'll have to give up ever seeing your daughter again if you choose to do something stupid." He shook Sadie's arm for emphasis.

They'd reached the glass doors. Though Sadie envisioned elbowing this man in the stomach, kicking him in the groin, and making her getaway, she didn't so much as try to pull away. She'd caused enough trouble for Eric and didn't dare compound it. The man pushed the door open and turned back to look at Eric, who stood in the middle of the entryway. So many feelings were playing over his face that Sadie didn't have time to identify them. "Get out here so I can lock up."

Eric paused for a moment then came forward, passing Sadie and the tipster in the doorway. Sadie tried to catch his eye, but Eric avoided her gaze. He exited the building and headed for his car. When he reached it, he dropped his chin, keeping his back to Sadie. She kept watching, waiting for him to turn around. Then she asked herself what she wanted him to do. Tell her it was fine when they both knew it wasn't? Still holding her arm, the man pulled her completely out of the building. Sadie squinted against the blinding sunshine.

The door closed, and Sadie watched the man turn the key in the lock of the door before pulling on the handle to ensure it was locked. "You'll wait here for five minutes before you leave," he told Eric. "Following us will only make things worse. I've given you enough information for you to know *I* can be trusted; you have not earned my trust nearly as well."

The man dragged Sadie around the car to the passenger side. "You understand how this arrangement works?" He released her arm and pulled open the door. It took her a moment to realize he was talking to her. He still had the gun in his hand, but wasn't pointing it at her anymore. He didn't need to. "You don't scream or run or do anything to draw attention to yourself while you're with me."

Sadie nodded. "I won't do anything else to make this worse," she said. "I want Eric to find his daughter."

"Good," the man said. "If you do something stupid, *you* will be responsible for him never seeing her again."

She nodded her understanding, looking at the ground, feeling Eric's eyes on her—eyes she couldn't bring herself to meet.

He motioned with the gun for Sadie to get into the car. She didn't have to be told twice—or once, really—and she obediently moved the iPod off the seat and sat down. She put on her seat belt while the man made his way around the car and then she zipped up her purse and held it tightly in her lap. Moments later he pulled open the driver's door and removed the jacket from the front seat. He slipped it on, covering the shoulder holster he wore. He slid the gun into the holster, and Sadie wondered how he could wear a jacket in this heat. The very idea increased her own internal temperature.

Sadie did not try to catch Eric's eye again. She'd messed everything up. As the magnitude of the situation descended on her, she winced at the ramifications. Could she live with herself if she was the reason he didn't find Megan?

"Give me your purse," the man said once he had sat down and pulled the driver's door closed.

Sadie clutched the handles of her purse closer to her chest. After all this, he was going to rob her too?

When she didn't comply, he reached for it. Sadie automatically slapped his hand, surprising them both.

"I'm sorry," she said before realizing it was ridiculous to apologize to him.

"I'm going to put it in the backseat so you don't get any crazy ideas."

"What kind of crazy ideas?" Sadie said, wondering just how dangerous a purse could be. But then she thought of hitting him with it repeatedly, or sneaking her phone out when he wasn't paying attention, or finding a pen and using it to defend herself. Not that she would ever really do any of those things and put finding Megan at risk, but thinking about the options helped her realize why he didn't want her to have it. She handed it over before he could ask for it again, and he threw it over the seat. Sadie winced as she heard it land, all the items inside crashing into each other. Now, instead of a meticulously organized arrangement, her purse would be a mess. So far things were off to a *fabulous* start.

He picked up the GPS unit, and Sadie watched him press a series of buttons. She'd been right; he wasn't from Miami. But where were they going? What was he going to do with her for the next three hours? Of course, she didn't want to know badly enough to actually ask. Not that he'd tell her anyway.

"Your route is being calculated," the female voice from the GPS said as he returned it to the cup holder. A moment later the voice added, "In twenty yards, turn right."

Only then did he start driving. As he pulled out of his parking space, Sadie met Eric's eyes, which were watching her from where he stood in front of his car. "I'm sorry," she mouthed. He didn't say anything back, just stood there, helpless. Sadie had to look away. She felt awful.

The tipster was pulling away from the building a few seconds later when Sadie saw the black-and-white taxi across the street. She'd forgotten all about Monty. He hadn't texted her back, but he was still there, still waiting for her. Her stomach sank—again—as she made eye contact with Monty.

She felt horrible about not having paid him fully. She did have his card, however, so maybe she could call him when this got resolved and pay him the balance. He wouldn't try to follow her, would he? Panic rose in her chest at the thought of him stepping in somehow. Sadie shook her head quickly, hoping to communicate that Monty wasn't to follow her. His expression didn't change, but he nodded and Sadie made a note to be *sure* and find a way to pay him the full fare she owed. He was a very nice young man. Hopefully she hadn't cost him any jobs while he'd waited on her.

She didn't turn her head to watch Monty until he was out of sight, but she sure wanted to. He was the last link to what she *knew*, instead of whatever lay ahead, all of which was what she *didn't* know. After a few more seconds, she dropped her chin, reprimanding herself for being so blasted curious all the time. When would she learn? And she hadn't even *wanted* to be involved in this one.

They traveled several blocks in a silence that pressed on Sadie until she thought she would explode. The man had made it perfectly clear that Sadie was a liability. She'd seen enough CSI shows to know what that meant.

"Are you going to kill me?" she blurted out. For whatever reason she felt better having said it out loud—there was no room in this little red sports car for the two of them and the elephant. She waited for an answer, wondering what she would do if he said, "Why, yes, I am going to kill you."

He cleared his throat, and Sadie braced herself.

"I'd rather not," the man said, his tone surprisingly casual. "Other than showing up in the first place, you seem like a pretty nice lady." He glanced at her and settled into his seat a little more. "So long as you abide by the rules, I don't *need* to kill you. I need that money, and Megan's father wants you—and her—back badly enough to give it to me."

"He *wants* to pay you the money," Sadie said. "I tried to talk him out of going to meet with you at all, but he insisted he'll do whatever it takes. You don't need me as extra insurance on that."

He shrugged. "Hopefully he won't be trying to pull off a partial payment the next time we meet up then."

Sadie wanted to insist he wouldn't, but she had no idea where Eric was going to come up with the rest of the money.

"Look," he said a moment later, his tone reasonable. "You seem like a sturdy woman."

Sturdy? Was he making a crack about her weight? She'd recently lost seven pounds, thank you very much!

"If you can just keep from freaking out and making me crazy, then when we meet Megan's dad at the track tonight, I'll hand you over, get my money, and we can part ways as friends. Understood?"

Friends? She wasn't inclined to argue with a term he was obviously using rather loosely. "I understand," she said.

They drove in silence for a few more minutes, while Sadie pondered her options and came to terms with her predicament. Not ideal, for sure, but she didn't feel as though she was in any kind of danger. Not right now, at least.

"Where are we going?" she asked. He'd practically said he wanted them to get along. This was his chance to confirm it.

He didn't answer. Sadie let out a breath, annoyed with his hypocrisy even as she thought of another tactic she could use—humility and sincere regret. "For what it's worth, I really am sorry about following Eric," she said, hoping to clear the air and make sure he understood her motives. "And he really didn't know I was there; I followed him. He didn't set it up."

"Oh, I figured he didn't," the man said, smiling slightly. "Why would he have someone like you along as backup?"

CHAPTER 24

Sadie clenched her jaw, frowning. It was tempting to tell him that she had skills—skills that had saved her life more than once and that became particularly honed in moments of extreme peril—but in the unlikely event that he believed her, he would then view her as a possible threat. She wouldn't be using her kung fu skills anyway, since she refused to create more stumbling blocks for Eric. However, even if her captor didn't know what she was capable of, Sadie took courage in knowing that she could defend herself if she needed to. The seven pounds she'd lost over the last couple of months was due in part to the kickboxing class she'd enrolled in at the local women-only fitness club in Garrison. Her blocks and jabs had become increasingly more reflexive. It was a mistake for him to underestimate her, but she wasn't about to say so.

"Well, anyway, I am sorry," Sadie said.

"Don't be sorry on my account," he said. "An extra five thousand dollars will go a long way." He glanced at her and winked.

Five thousand dollars?

Until that moment, Sadie hadn't thought about how ridiculously small the amount of money was, even with the extra five grand he had demanded. Fifteen thousand dollars? The man was going to all this trouble, breaking all kinds of laws, for an amount of money that wouldn't even buy a new car? Well, maybe a Hyundai.

"How do you know Megan's father?" he asked.

Sadie looked at him quickly. She'd told him she was from Georgia by way of Wyoming. Should she stick to that story? Would keeping to her original lies make her seem more credible in some totally twisted way?

When she didn't answer right away, he went on. "The cars at Best Buy Used Cars are a front for a money-laundering scheme. No one buys a car from them unless they are involved in guns, drugs, or . . . other things just as bad." He slowed down for a red light. "I don't imagine you're a kingpin in any of those industries?" His gaze flickered to her left hand. "And you aren't wearing a wedding ring, so everything else you said is suspect."

Shoot, Sadie thought, rubbing her finger that hadn't had a wedding ring on it for many years.

What could she say now? The light turned green, and they pulled forward, merging into the right lane per the GPS voice that told them to turn right at the next intersection. He did as he was told, turning right, then right again, and then left before Sadie was completely turned around and had no idea where they were or where they'd been. She'd done pretty well at keeping track while they remained on 51st Street.

"Believe it or not," he said after they'd driven several blocks with only the GPS providing conversation. "I'm actually one of the good guys, or at least I'm trying to be—it's a lot harder than I expected."

Hmmm. "If you're one of the 'good guys,'" Sadie said out loud, choosing her words carefully. "Then who are the bad guys?"

He didn't answer.

Sadie tried again. "Did the bad guys take Megan?" She knew that a good hostage wouldn't ask so many questions, and certainly not in a way that betrayed the fact that she really wanted to figure out what was going on, but he was the one who started the conversation. Sadie had learned that if people wanted to talk, you did everything you could to accommodate them.

"Take?" he repeated, then shook his head. "No, they didn't take her."

Sadie furrowed her brow. "So, you're saying she . . . left?"

"There's lots of things to run away from in this world," he said quietly. "And lots of places to run *to* if you know how to find them."

Run away? He couldn't have said it any clearer than that. It changed so many things, twisting them just enough to make them look very different—almost unrecognizable. Sadie's chest tightened as she imagined what that information would do to Eric. "Does Megan want to be found?" It was a painful question to ask, and she feared it would be just as painful an answer to hear.

The question surprised her captor, but he only let it show in the slight shifting of his eyebrows. He kept his mouth shut, but it was answer enough.

Megan didn't want to come back.

Wow.

A traffic jam of questions crashed into her mind. "Why would she want to disappear?" Sadie asked while reviewing everything Eric had said about his daughter. "What was she running from?"

"I'm done talking," he said.

"Well, you're being so cryptic that it doesn't make much sense anyway," Sadie said, folding her arms over her chest and pouting a little as her emotions got the best of her. This had become a very strange conversation.

He managed a chuckle. "Cryptic? I guess you can see it that way if you want. You'll learn all these answers eventually; I just need you to not know them yet."

"Why?"

"I'm not answering any more questions."

Sadie leaned back against the seat, processing what he'd said. What would Megan be running away from? She had a father who loved her, and a mother . . . who didn't seem to know what love was anymore.

"You're trying to help Megan, aren't you?" she heard herself asking, even though he'd told her himself that he wasn't going to answer any more questions. She regarded him carefully. He was the same man who had held her against the doorway and who'd pointed a gun at her head, but there was more to him than that. His square jaw was tense, but his eyes reflected sincerity, and when he answered her question, the softness in his tone was not feigned.

"Yes, I'm trying to help her," he said.

"But you're not bringing her to the track tonight, are you?" If Megan didn't want to come back to her old life, Sadie didn't imagine this man would be forcing her to come to a public place. Beneath the confusing signals he was sending out, Sadie sensed he *cared* about Megan.

"No," he said. "But I'll give her father all the information he needs to find her." He glanced at Sadie quickly. "And she's safe until then."

"Are you hiding her somewhere?" Sadie imagined Megan bound and gagged in a closet.

"No."

"Is she close?"

He turned and gave her a look that clearly said he wasn't going to tell her that. But Megan must be close, Sadie was sure of it.

"And after you tell Eric what you know, you're going to disappear, right?"

It was the only explanation for why he wouldn't tell Sadie right now.

He clenched his jaw and stared through the windshield.

Okay, she was pushing too hard. Was there another topic she could bring up to keep him talking without making him defensive? Scanning the car, her eyes landed on the GPS unit, reminding her that someone had given Eric coordinates to Megan's purse and had known it was 200 yards from where the other woman's body had been found. She couldn't keep her mouth shut. "You're the anonymous tipster who told the police about the body, aren't you?"

"I think we should change the subject," he said, his voice heavy.

But his reply had given Sadie the answer she needed so she was willing to let it go. She leaned a little closer to the passenger door and a little farther away from him, studiously looking out the window. At some point they'd exchanged the run-down apartments and industrial buildings for retail stores, restaurants, and gas stations.

He slowed down as he pulled into a turning lane. The GPS voice immediately said she was recalculating his route, meaning this stop wasn't what he'd programmed into the gadget. Sadie decided to call the GPS Dora. She wasn't sure why Dora was the name that came to mind, she just sounded like a Dora to Sadie's ears, and Sadie preferred giving the voice an identity. It was like getting directions from a friend.

He pushed the mute button, and Sadie scanned the nearby parking lots. Where was he going?

"You understand that if you try to run, or scream, or draw

attention to yourself you'll ruin everything for Megan's father, right?" he asked as he came to a stop in the middle lane, waiting for a break in traffic.

"Yes," Sadie answered.

"Good," he said, sounding relieved to have that out of the way. "Are you hungry?"

"Um, not really," Sadie said, shaking her head. How could she be expected to eat at a time like this? If she were being offered something wonderful, like authentic hush puppies or more of Tia's pasta salad, maybe, but Del Taco, Burger King, and Panda Express did nothing for her. She looked around for a true Southern restaurant—one that advertised shrimp Creole, or fried okra or . . . gumbo! Her brother, Jack, made the best gumbo; she'd love to put his recipe up against another version. Alas, they were in a strip mall that could exist anywhere in the United States. How disappointing. Maybe Jack would make her some gumbo when she got home to make up for her limited options. She hadn't even seen mention of key lime pie since her arrival—not that she'd really had much time to think about it, but still. She thought of Eric's nickname for Megan—Sweetie Pie—and her heart ached all over again. Where was Megan, and how was she connected to this man?

"You sure?" he said as he pulled in behind half a dozen cars in the drive-thru of KFC.

"I'm sure, thank you," Sadie said. She had a coupon for a buy-one-get-one-free meal in her purse, but wasn't about to offer it to him.

"So, your name is Sadie?" the tipster said. "I've never heard that before."

Apparently he wasn't a big Barbara Streisand fan. Sadie had had "Sadie, Sadie, married lady" sung to her most of her life. Listening to his tone now, it was difficult for Sadie to believe he was the hardened man who hadn't thought twice about pinning her against the doorway with a gun to her head. Difficult, but not impossible. Sadie would make sure she didn't forget it.

"It's a nickname," she said, realizing that, defenses aside, the next three hours until they met Eric at the Speedway would be more comfortable if some of the tension subsided. "It's short for Sarah Diane."

"Huh," he said, nodding as though he cared about the origins of her name. They edged forward, and he ordered a number five combination meal.

"Do you have a name?" Sadie asked after they inched forward toward the drive-thru window.

He paused, and Sadie realized he was trying to come up with a name. He hadn't planned to have a hostage any more than she'd planned on becoming one. He was flying by the seat of his pants just like Sadie was. She wasn't sure why that understanding was important, but it stood out to her so she filed it away. After a few more seconds, he said, "Call me Joe."

"Joe," Sadie repeated, knowing it was a fake name, but she hadn't expected he would use his real name anyway.

He rolled up to the drive-thru and exchanged his money for food. He set the bag in the space between their seats. Sadie had to admit it smelled good, but she still didn't want fast food.

"So, Joe," she began. "Where are we going now?"

"A park," Joe said.

"A park?" she repeated.

"What else should I do with you?" he asked, sounding frustrated as he wove his way out of the parking lot and back to the street.

"You could let me go," Sadie offered. He looked at her like she was crazy, so she hurried to explain herself. "I already gave you my word that I wouldn't do anything or say anything that would risk Eric not finding his daughter. And you are obviously concerned enough about Megan to orchestrate all this. The longer I'm with you, the more I'll figure out. So, with that in mind, it seems as though it's in your best interest not to have to deal with me at all, therefore having more control over what I know and having more to offer Eric when you two meet at the Speedway."

He was still for a moment and then laughed out loud. "Do you really think I'm *that* stupid?" He un-muted Dora, once again in need of her direction.

"No," Sadie said with sincerity. "I think you're that *smart*. I understand why you had me come with you—to show Eric that you weren't to be taken lightly. I get that, and you played the role very well. But you achieved that goal, so why put up with me any longer than you have to? I can be very aggravating, or so people tell me."

"Yes," he said slowly, studying the traffic. "I can see where people would get that idea."

Sadie just smiled. It was all part of her plan. She'd agreed not to yell, scream, run, or in any other way get him caught, but she'd said nothing about not talking his ear off—especially now that she had the sense he wasn't interested in hurting her. "I won't do anything to mess things up if you let me go," she said. "You have my word."

"You'd go to the cops," he said as Dora told him to make a left-hand turn.

Sadie shook her head. "No, I wouldn't." From the backseat she heard the ascending ring of her phone—it was a Michael Bublé song this week. Sadie wondered who was calling and remembered that she hadn't listened to Gayle's message yet.

Joe spotted a hole in traffic and shot forward to cross all four lanes.

Sadie's phone stopped ringing as she grabbed the door handle and was pushed back against the seat due to the forward momentum of the car.

"If I did let you go, what would you do?"

Oh, good, he's considering it! Sadie straightened. "Well, I would call Eric and see if he needed help getting the money together." Joe ought to like that part. "Then, I would . . ." She trailed off, wondering if she should tell this part, but she couldn't expect him to trust her if she didn't tell him the truth. "I would tell him what you've told me about Megan so that he'll be a little better prepared."

"*Prepare* him," Joe said under his breath, shaking his head slightly. Sadie watched him carefully and replayed his reaction in her head. He cleared his throat. "Look, you were right when you said I wanted Megan to be found. I do, which is why I can't take the risk of you getting in the way of that—no matter how tempting it is to be rid of you."

He checked his blind spot and switched lanes, glancing at the GPS. As if on cue, Dora told him to turn right in one-quarter of a mile. As they were coming up on the intersection, Dora reminded him about the right turn. He followed her instructions.

"Okay, then," Sadie said. "We have a couple hours' worth of conversation ahead of us, don't we? So, tell me more about yourself. Where are you from? If you were a native of Miami you probably wouldn't need a GPS."

"Spoken by someone who has no concept of how confusing Miami can be, even if you know the city."

"But you're not from Miami, are you?"

"I'm not telling you where I'm from," he said blandly.

"We could play twenty questions for it," Sadie said. "Is it east or west of the Mississippi River?" Maybe she should have asked if it was north or south of the Rio Grande.

Jack's Gumbo

2 tablespoons olive oil
12 ounces chicken breast or thighs, diced
1 small yellow onion, chunked (double onions for Jack)
1 red pepper, seeded and chunked (double peppers for Jack)
2 stalks celery, chunked
6 ounces formed sausage, sliced (Andouille if you can find it, though Kielbasa works fine)
1 quart chicken or ham stock
2 bay leaves
2 cloves garlic, sliced or crushed
1½ tablespoons Creole blend spice
¼ cup roux (can use other mode of thickening to save time)
Salt and pepper to taste

Heat oil in a 4-quart saucepan. When hot, add chicken and brown. Remove chicken and add onion, red pepper, and celery to pan, sautéing until golden. Add cooked chicken, sausage, stock, bay leaves, garlic, and Creole spice. Simmer for 30 minutes.* Add roux with a whisk, stirring constantly till thick. Season with salt, pepper, and additional Creole spice to taste.

Serve as a soup or over cooked rice.

Serves 8.

*I like to add half a pound of shrimp 20 minutes before serving. (If the shrimp is added too early, it gets tough.)

Ham Stock

1 ham hock
2 quarts water
2 stalks celery

Combine all ingredients in large soup pan. Simmer for 6 hours. Strain and discard ham bone and celery. This stock also freezes well.

Roux

½ cup butter
½ cup flour

Melt and brown butter in saucepan; the browner you cook the butter, without burning, the richer the flavor of the roux. Add flour; cook for at least 2 minutes. You can store roux in the refrigerator for up to 4 months; use as a savory thickener for soups, sauces, and gravies.

CHAPTER 25

Joe gave her a withering look, but Sadie felt sure he was starting to warm up to her. Dora told him to make a left turn in point-eight miles.

"It makes sense that you don't want to tell me where you're from," Sadie said, keeping her tone conversational even though the conversation was distinctly one-sided. "So, let's talk about something different. How long have you been in Miami?" Obviously not very long or he'd know his way around. But he knew about the car dealership being a money-laundering scheme. "How did you know about Best Buy Used Cars?"

"You ask a lot of questions you'd be better off not knowing the answers to."

Sadie shrugged. "I'm just trying to make conversation. Is there something you'd prefer to talk about? I don't know much about sports or politics, but I'll do my best."

He chose not to answer. Sadie thought it might be a long couple of hours. Dora piped up to say their destination was on the right. Sadie glanced out the window to confirm that they had indeed reached a park.

Joe entered the parking lot and headed to the far side, where there weren't many cars. He pulled into a spot and shut off the car. Without a word, he let himself out, grabbing the sack of food as he stood up and then bent down to look at Sadie expectantly. She nodded her understanding and let herself out. Once she shut the door, Joe used his key fob to lock it.

As Sadie walked around the back of the car, her eyes were drawn to a small sticker in the lower left-hand corner. It showed a flag of some kind with four red stripes, three white ones, and a blue triangle coming in from the left-hand side like a pennant. There was a single white star in the center of the triangle. Sadie wasn't sure she'd seen the flag before but wondered if it could be a clue to something.

Joe headed across the grass for a cluster of trees, under which Sadie could see a single picnic table. She glanced over her shoulder as she followed him to see if anyone was watching them. It felt strange that he was so comfortable having her with him in public, but then she wondered what his alternatives really were. He wasn't from around here, which meant he was probably staying at a hotel somewhere and wouldn't want Sadie to see him in his own space. She also realized that he must trust her, at least a little, to not only bring her here but to walk twenty paces ahead. If she chose right now to scream and run he'd be sunk. But Eric would be sunk too, and Joe believed she would do anything to help Eric get the information he needed.

And he was right, she would.

By the time Sadie reached the table, Joe was seated and pulling his meal out of the bag. She noticed he had soft hands and strong arms. Not a laborer, and yet he didn't come across as exactly white collar, what with the ponytail and shaved head. He had nice eyes though. She wondered if he had a wife or children. She found family men so much more trustworthy, though that was a strange word to attribute to the man who had abducted her at gunpoint. Still, she felt he wasn't a bad guy by nature.

Sadie was grateful they were in shade; it diffused the heat better than shade did in Colorado, where the dry air exacerbated the heat. She wondered what they would do after the park—go bowling, maybe?

"How can you wear a jacket in this heat?" Sadie asked.

Joe looked up at her. "It's not so bad today."

"It's like ninety degrees," she said, sliding onto the bench across from him.

"Nah," he said dismissively. "It's barely eighty."

"And a hundred and sixty percent humidity," she added.

He gave her a half-smile and shook his head.

She knew he wore the jacket to conceal the gun, but why did he think he still needed the gun? Hadn't she convinced him that she wasn't a threat?

"You really should have gotten something," he said, popping off the clear plastic cover.

Sadie scowled at the fast food. KFC was one of the better ones, but it was still cheap, fast, poor nourishment. "I'm a home-cooking snob," she said without an ounce of humility. "And my digestive tract is pretty upset with the liberties I've been taking since I headed out here. I don't dare offend it any further."

He managed a smirk at that comment, even though Sadie wasn't trying to be funny. She picked up his utensils and tore off the plastic covering, careful not to touch the eating end of the spork as she put both it and the napkin down in front of him. He didn't say thank you, but she read it in the strange look he was giving her nonetheless.

"I've never been to Miami before," Sadie said, folding her arms on the tabletop and looking around. "Parts of it are really pretty." She waved toward the trees. "I like how green it is. Colorado hasn't greened up much yet, even though it's been raining a lot."

"You haven't been to the beaches, have you?" he said, scooping up a bite of coleslaw with a spork. "They're the real draw."

Sadie shrugged. "I'm not much of a beach person. I gave up swimsuits around the age of forty, and the ocean stinks."

He paused and looked over at her. "The ocean stinks?"

Sadie nodded and wrinkled her nose for emphasis. "Stinks bad."

He took a bite of food, shaking his head. Sadie didn't mean to offend him, but not everyone liked the beach. Give her mountain breezes and a campfire any day of the week over sand in her toes and salt water drying out her skin. She watched him take another bite of the coleslaw and felt her mind turning toward food again.

She still hadn't come to terms with her disappointment over the biscuits and gravy. Tia's pasta salad, while delicious, wasn't really Southern, and now Joe was eating coleslaw from KFC—the exact same coleslaw Sadie could get in Garrison.

"Is Florida even considered Southern? I mean, other than geographically?" she asked, reflecting on her woefully lacking education of her country. "They talk about Louisiana and Georgia, even Texas, and call them the South, but all this"—she waved her hand to encompass the park—"doesn't really feel Southern at all. It's more like California but with more humidity, heat, and bugs."

Joe shrugged and picked up one of his two pieces of chicken. "I've never really thought about it."

"Never mind that this trip hasn't turned out to be anything like I expected it would," Sadie said when he didn't add anything else.

"But it's somewhat disappointing to find Florida so . . . lacking in personality."

Joe pulled the chicken away from his mouth and grabbed his napkin to wipe at the grease left behind on his lips. The look on his face showed a little more interest in her than she was used to seeing from him. "Most people say Miami has too much personality," he said. "So many cultures, classes, and interests clashing together in one of the smallest big cities in the world."

Sadie looked around. "Small?"

"Compared to most large cities, yes. But it makes up for it in the fact that it's surrounded by ports, which means industry and tourism. You've only been in the city so you haven't really seen Florida. Ever been to Key West?"

Sadie shook her head. Megan had, though; she'd disappeared from there. Was it a coincidence that Joe had brought it up?

"Key West is awesome. I'd live there if I could."

"Why can't you?" Sadie asked.

"It's pricey, really remote, and—" He stopped himself, but she could read in his eyes that he'd been about to say more than he wanted to. He went back to his food without finishing his thought.

"I hear they don't even grow key limes in the Florida Keys any-more," Sadie said, resorting to her comfort zone of food once again and hoping to keep him talking.

"I have no idea," Joe said. "But I'd be surprised if any farming was being done down there. In answer to your question about Florida being Southern, though, I think it is up in the panhandle, but down here—nah, it doesn't have the same influences. It's more diverse."

"That fits what I've seen so far," Sadie said. "I bet they have good Cuban food here though. Cuba's pretty close, right?" She was trying to subtly ease into topics that might lead her to answers.

"Ninety miles or so from Key West, I think," Joe said.

Sadie nodded. "I heard that if a Cuban makes it to American soil he's a citizen."

"He gets a green card," Joe said. "As a refugee. North Koreans get one too."

"Hmmm," Sadie said. "So we can't buy their cigars, but we can take their people?"

Joe shook his head. "It's a little more complicated than that."

"Have you ever been to Cuba?" she asked innocently, hoping he didn't pick up on how she was deftly steering the conversation.

He looked up at her as though puzzled by her question, then went back to his food and took a bite of mashed potatoes. "So, did you come down with Megan's dad?"

"No," Sadie answered, frustrated by the change in subject. She wished they'd have stayed on the Cuba topic long enough for her to see what he knew about the illegal selling of boats. Still, she was glad he was asking questions. Maybe they'd get back to it in a little while. "I came after he said he needed money and the box."

"The box?" Joe repeated.

Sadie nodded, wondering how much she should tell him. Then again, there hadn't been anything important in the box. "Eric had a box of Megan's things at his house in Colorado. He needed it, so instead of shipping it, I brought it down myself. I thought he might need my help."

"Why did he want the box?"

"The police wanted it," Sadie said. "For hair samples and things. I guess they don't need it though, since the body wasn't Megan. But you know all that, right? I mean, you are the one who called the police with the coordinates."

Joe's hand slowed, but he continued eating, trying to pretend that he wasn't bothered by her bringing up the body again or revisiting a topic he'd already refused to discuss.

"Who is she, Joe?"

Joe swallowed and looked away from her.

Sadie jumped in, sensing he was wavering. "You said you're one of the good guys. If that's true, tell me who that girl was so she can be laid to rest properly. Can you imagine how her family is feeling right now? Not knowing where she is?"

Joe looked back at her. "They know where she is," he said with a spurt of anger. "They put her there."

Sadie couldn't understand what he was saying. "What do you mean?"

Joe stabbed his spork into his potatoes. "When Megan is back in the picture, you can tell the police that she knows who it is. They can make her tell."

Megan knowing the dead woman's identity was not good news. "I don't get it," Sadie said. "You want Megan found, and yet you're implicating her in something very serious at the same time."

Joe looked up from his food and held her eyes for a few moments. She could sense him struggling to decide how much to say. He finally dropped his eyes back to his food, apparently choosing to say nothing. Sadie moved past her frustration, not wanting to belabor the conversation to the point where he'd stop talking. She'd come back to it later.

"Is that what the fifteen thousand dollars is for?" Sadie asked. "To get away? How far do you think you'll get on it?" She quickly shut her mouth when she realized she could be giving him the idea to ask for more money.

"The money won't last long," Joe said, meeting her eyes again. "But like I said, there are lots of places to run to."

Run, Sadie repeated. "And lots of things to run from."

He nodded.

"And what if they catch up with you?" Sadie asked, having no idea who *they* were but hoping he'd give something away.

"They *will* catch up." His voice was low and serious. "But until then I'll have a little time to live with a clear conscience. It's been a long time coming."

Sadie held his eyes, trying to see past them to the core of this man. "You're telling me that you believe helping Eric find Megan will lead to your own death?"

Joe smiled as though trying to lighten the mood. "A hero's death doesn't sound so bad, does it?" He chuckled, but without any humor. "Look, I haven't necessarily lived a life I've been proud of, and Megan gives me the chance to do something right for once. The money gives me a chance to get away and enjoy the freedom for a little while. What happens after that is anyone's guess, and I'm willing to take it as it comes."

Sadie felt her respect for this man swell up in her chest, assuming what he told her was the truth. "Just tell me where Megan is, Joe," she said sympathetically. "Tell me everything you plan to tell Eric, and then let me go. I'll tell him for you, and you can get a head start."

"And how would I get my money?"

"Oh, I hadn't thought about that part," Sadie admitted, lacing her fingers and putting them on the table. "What about Western Union? They can send money anywhere."

Joe gave her a half-smile as he scooped another bite of potatoes. "Too risky," he said after he swallowed.

"I'm worried about Megan," Sadie said. "I'm worried she's in trouble. The sooner we can reunite her with her father, the better, right? I mean, you're trying to help her, so why wait any longer than you have to?"

"I'll tell you this much. Right now," he pointed his finger and jabbed it at the table, "Megan is safer than she has been for a long time. I am *trying* to make sure she doesn't go back, and I'll do whatever it takes to make that happen, but I can't do it without that money—cash."

"Make sure she doesn't go back?" Sadie repeated. "Back where?"

"That's all I'm saying," Joe said, but Sadie didn't believe him. He wanted to talk. If he didn't, he wouldn't have said so much already.

As she reviewed everything he'd told her, she realized he hadn't known about the box until she'd told him about it. Granted, he could be pretending, but she didn't think so—there was something very solid about Joe once he didn't feel threatened.

So, if Joe hadn't known about the box, then he wasn't the one who burned it, which meant there was someone else involved in this very strange game. Were the people who burned the box the same people Joe was running from?

"What?" Joe asked, interrupting Sadie's thoughts. "What are you thinking about?"

She looked up from the table where she'd been staring and met his eyes. She quickly scanned the immediate surroundings in search of something she could improvise as the topic of her thoughts since she wasn't about to tell him the truth. Her search ended at his plate of food. "Coleslaw," she said quickly.

"Coleslaw?" Joe repeated.

"There's this little Cajun restaurant in Fort Collins—that's the largest city near where I live, about an hour away from Garrison—that serves this amazing coleslaw. It's a little spicy, but a little sweet, too. Nothing in it but cabbage and the dressing. And they serve key lime pie—the official pie of Florida."

"I thought the state pie was pecan pie," he answered. "Pecans grow all over the place."

Sadie shook her head. "That might be so, but key limes are so very Florida, and you can find pecans in other states. In fact, it's the state nut of Alabama so if they ever lay claim to a pie, it will probably be pecan."

He blinked at her, encouraging her to convince him that she was an expert on things like this.

"There are only two other states with state pies, you know. Vermont has apple pie, even though Johnny Appleseed is buried in Indiana, which happens to be the other state with an official pie— sugar cream. Massachusetts has Boston cream pie, but it's not really pie at all, it's cake. Then of course Louisiana has Natchitoches, but it's a meat pie so I don't really count that one either. Key lime pie is definitely Florida's official state pie."

"Ri-ight," Joe said, looking at her with a bland expression. "It's good to know the politicians don't have enough social issues to deal with and can therefore focus on things like state pies."

"It's pie, Joe," Sadie said. "One must not be cynical about pie."

Joe shrugged and went back to his food.

Sadie sighed wistfully. "I was really looking forward to enjoying some key lime pie during my trip, but, well, things haven't gone so well."

"We could always stop at the Key West Key Lime Pie Company on our way to the Speedway," Joe said, wiping his mouth. "I remember hearing they make the best key lime pie in the state—assuming they're still here in Miami. They've got a lot of stores in Key West, but they used to have one here in Miami too."

"That would be wonderful," Sadie said, forgetting for a moment that she was a prisoner. She smiled at the anticipation of dessert. A good slice of pie would see her through any difficult times ahead, she was sure.

He lifted his spork, pointing it at her. "But I still think the state pie *should* be pecan," he said with emphasis, but as he shook his spork at her, he knocked his biscuit off his plate. It rolled off the tabletop and disappeared.

Joe swore.

"Don't swear," Sadie reprimanded him before bending down to see where the biscuit had landed.

"But it's been on the ground, now," Joe said from the other side of the table.

"Haven't you ever heard of the ten-second rule?" she answered, spotting the biscuit a few inches past her feet. She reached down, her entire back under the table, and picked it up, not sure that she'd eat it either. At home there was no question about it, but at a public park with bugs and pets and things? She was just beginning to straighten when she heard a thud, a groan, and another thud from above the table. She startled, hitting her head on the bottom of the table, and then inhaled sharply as Joe slid off the bench and landed in a crumpled heap at her feet.

CHAPTER 26

For one full second Sadie stared at Joe's body. His ponytail had pulled loose slightly, leaving his hair disheveled, and his mouth hung open, eleven herbs and spices not yet wiped away from his lips. The spork lay a few inches away. Then Sadie's eyes moved past Joe to see a pair of denim-clad legs standing behind the bench where Joe had been sitting. Hoping Joe's attacker hadn't seen her, Sadie stayed where she was, bent in half with her torso and head under the table. The fantasy was shattered when the newcomer spoke.

"Ya okay, lady?"

Monty?

Sadie emerged from under the table to see Monty standing across from her, looking at her with concern. She looked between him and the place where Joe had been sitting. "What have you done?" Sadie asked, breathless as she attempted to make sense of what had just happened.

Monty didn't seem to hear the dismay in her tone. Instead he smiled broadly, his white teeth once again looking luminescent against his skin. He pointed a finger at Joe. "I know trouble when I see it, lady, and dis boy be trouble."

"But . . . but you . . . what did you do?"

Monty held up a short, black stick that Sadie recognized as a billy club—police officers in old movies often swung them back and forth as they walked down the streets, whistling. "You hit him with that?"

"Sho' did," Monty said, flipping the billy club around before catching it under his armpit and holding it against his side. He knew how to handle that stick. Sadie bent down to look at Joe again. He was out cold.

When she sat up again, she put her elbows on the picnic table and covered her face with both hands. She was in so much trouble.

"Wha' d' mattah?" Monty asked.

Sadie spread her fingers wide enough to look up at him. He wasn't smiling anymore. "I promised him I wouldn't try to escape," Sadie said. "And he's the only person who knows something I need to know."

Monty's eyes flicked to the body under the table. "I taught you wer' in trouble. You done sen' me dat text but den lef."

"I know, I know," Sadie said, lowering her hands and trying to think of what to do next. "And I appreciate you coming to my rescue; it's just that I'm in even more trouble now."

"Why?"

Could she really *not* tell him now that he was involved? In a few sentences she explained how she'd made a deal with Joe in order to help Eric get the information he needed. When she finished, Monty looked down at Joe, who still wasn't moving and simply said, "Oh."

"You didn't kill him, did you?" Sadie asked, finally standing up and coming around the table. If Joe was dead she would really be in a pickle.

"'Course not," Monty scoffed. "I jus hit 'im in de back o' de head, but den 'e done hit 'is head on de table when 'e fell too." He seemed a little concerned but then looked at Sadie and repaired his expression. "'E be okay in a minute."

Sadie wasn't so sure. She'd been knocked unconscious before, but had been out only a few seconds. Even then she'd had a terrible headache, and it had taken a little while for her brain to work correctly again. She crouched down and put two fingers against Joe's neck. He had a strong pulse, and being this close to him, she could see that he was still breathing. Good.

"Can we get him out from there?" she asked. He had basically fallen under the table, but his left arm was at an awkward angle under his body and it seemed weird to leave him in such an odd position.

"Sho'," Monty said, and Sadie stepped aside so he could drag Joe out from under the table. Sadie looked around to see if anyone was watching them. Joe had picked their location well; there wasn't anyone close by. They were still in a public park, however, which meant that sooner or later someone was going to wonder why an unconscious man was lying next to a picnic table. Monty pulled him a few feet from the table and let him fall on the grass. Joe's head rolled to the side. Maybe people would think he was asleep.

"He is going to be so mad when he wakes up," Sadie said, thinking about her promise not to mess things up and how she could explain what had happened when he regained consciousness. She'd felt like she'd been gaining his trust, but surely that was ruined now.

"Well, den let's go," Monty said. He grabbed Sadie's arm, but she resisted. Why did everyone have to grab her arm?

"I can't just leave him here," Sadie said. Joe was supposed to give Eric the information he needed to find Megan. She heard laughter and looked up to see a young couple walking their dog on the other side of the trees. Luckily they didn't notice the drama unfolding, but it was one more reminder why Sadie couldn't stay here. She thought briefly about having Monty pick up Joe and take him to the cab with them, but what if someone saw them carrying a body to the car? And then her thoughts turned in a new direction. Joe had been unconscious for two whole minutes. What if he was really hurt? What if he didn't just end up with a headache? He might need a doctor.

"I need my phone," she said, bending down and checking Joe's pockets—delicately—until she found what felt like keys in his front left pocket. She reached in only as far as she had to in order to grab the keys, then looked up at Monty. "Can you stay with him for a minute?" she said. "My phone is in his car."

Monty looked around, obviously concerned about someone seeing them, but finally nodded.

"I'll hurry," she said, running for the car without waiting for his answer. When she was a few feet away, she pushed the unlock button twice and immediately opened the back door on the driver's side where Joe had so rudely thrown her purse, which was still upside down on the seat. Shaking her head in annoyance, she picked it up and a stack of papers caught her eye. But at the same moment, her phone rang.

After a quick glance at Monty, who was walking in a slow circle around the table with his hands in his pockets—Sadie could barely make out Joe's body in the shadows—she turned back to the car and quickly dug her phone out of her purse. It was Gayle. Confident in her ability to multitask, Sadie answered the call and held it against one ear while picking up the papers with her other hand. She gave herself twenty seconds to skim the papers and talk to Gayle.

"You're all right," Gayle said with relief. "I got nervous when you didn't call. Is everything okay?"

At the top of the papers was a seal that read University of Miami Hospital. Why did Joe have hospital admission forms?

"Everything's fine," Sadie said, distracted. The patient's name on the form was Liliana Miriam Montez. She was twenty-nine years old.

"So, what's happening?" Gayle asked. "How's Eric?"

Eric's name broke her out of her distraction as regret washed over her again. He was either worried sick or incredibly angry right now. Maybe both. While she was tempted to share her burden with Gayle, it seemed impossible to explain. Things were completely different than she'd imagined they would be since the last time she'd spoken with Gayle.

"Well, it's complicated," Sadie finally said.

"Really?" Gayle's tone was brimming with intrigue.

"I'll have to tell you about it later," Sadie said, forcing her thoughts away from Eric and back to the name on the hospital forms—Liliana Miriam Montez. Was this woman Joe's wife? He hadn't been wearing a wedding ring. Could Liliana be his sister?

"I called Pete."

Suddenly Gayle had Sadie's full attention again. "Oh?" she said as evenly as she could manage. "How did that go?"

"Okay, I guess," Gayle said. "I think he might need more time than you thought, though. He mostly asked me about you. He said he'd stopped by your house this morning, but you weren't home."

"He stopped by?" Sadie repeated, a hopeful flutter tickling her heart. She'd been so sure when she left Garrison that Eric was the direction her heart was leading her. Now she wasn't so sure. Was Pete unsure too? "Did he say why he was looking for me?"

"No," Gayle said, sounding a little disappointed. "I mean, we talked about going to the Renaissance dinner—he's going to call me back when he checks his schedule—but he seemed more concerned about where you were."

The word "concern" sparked a whole slew of them in Sadie's mind. "You didn't tell him I'd come here, did you?" Sadie asked in a panic. Would Gayle throw Sadie under the bus in hopes of bettering her chances with Pete?

"Of course not," Gayle said, allowing Sadie to exhale. "But the conversation as a whole just didn't bode well for eternal bliss between him and me, ya know?"

"I'm sure that's not it," she said, though the feelings competing inside her chest were confusing. "He can be difficult to read sometimes."

"Yeah, maybe that's it," Gayle said. "So, what are you doing right now? Was Eric glad to see you?"

"Um, yes," Sadie said, answering the last question instead of the first one. "But I need to go—can I call you later?"

"I guess," Gayle said. "Oh, and I finished cleaning the trailer."

"Oh, right." She'd forgotten all about the trailer. "Thank you. I'm sorry, Gayle, but I really do need to go."

"Okay," Gayle said. "But don't leave me hangin'. Call me as soon as you can."

"I will," Sadie said and hung up the phone. Pete had stopped by? She shook her head. No time to think about that, never mind that if Pete knew where she was and why she'd come, he wouldn't be stopping by ever again.

Sadie went back to the paperwork, scanning all the details she could find. She froze when she read that Liliana had been admitted to Labor and Delivery yesterday. Liliana was pregnant? Why would Joe be running around town if a woman important to him had just had a baby? He said he needed the money to leave. What about this woman? What about the baby?

Gayle and Pete were suddenly of very little consequence. She read through the form again, aware that Monty was waiting for her and that she was taking a lot longer than she should be. At the bottom of the second page was Liliana's signature. Sadie barely glanced at it at first, nearly convinced she was being silly to think these papers were important, but then something stood out and she gave it a second look. Well, a *first* look, since she hadn't *really* looked at it before. It was just a signature, in swirling letters. What had drawn her eye?

Wait.

Her eyes went to the M at the front of the middle and last name. Something was familiar, and instantly Sadie had a flashback of the gas station receipt she'd glanced at when she'd been pawing through the box at Eric's house. Megan had signed the receipt with a typical signature except for the swirly M at the front of her name. Sadie had never seen anyone get that creative with the letter M, which is why she'd noted it in the first place. The M in *Miriam* and *Montez* were exactly like the M on Megan's gas receipt.

A rush of adrenaline ran through her veins as Joe's words filtered back to her. "She's safe," he'd said. "For now."

Megan was Liliana Montez—and *she* was having—or had already had—a baby.

CHAPTER 27

Sadie paused for only a moment, and then began scouring the car. This was Joe's car, so it had to have important information in it. Information the police would need. She opened her purse and threw the GPS device into it; she could look up those coordinates Joe had given Eric and the police. There were a few receipts in the middle console and she stuffed those in her purse as well. A briefcase or planner would have been nice, but she didn't find anything like that. Even the trunk was empty except for the basic roadside necessities. She slammed it closed and jumped at the sound it made—louder than she'd expected it to be.

"Deep breaths," she told herself. Her nerves were getting the better of her so she consciously slowed down her movements and stopped trying to rush.

She moved to the front seat for a final look, but she had already taken everything of interest. Finally, after having spent way too much time on this—Monty had to be freaking out by now—she reached to close the driver's side door when she saw a piece of paper wedged between the middle console and the driver's seat. She leaned back into the car, pulled out the paper, then shut all the doors. She scanned the paper on her way back to Monty. She was only halfway there when she froze in her tracks. The paper was an itinerary—a flight plan for a reservation made online.

"Paris?" Sadie said. The flight left from Miami tomorrow morning, stopped over in New York, and then continued on to Paris. The itinerary was for one person by the name of Hugo Montez.

Montez? Like Liliana Montez?

Was Joe's real name Hugo? And was Hugo Megan's husband?

"You're back."

Sadie looked up, having forgotten all about Monty for a minute. She started walking toward him again. She folded the paper and shoved it into the side pocket of her purse; she'd already zipped up the fuller-than-ever interior. "I'm sorry that took so long," she said, shaking her head. "I got . . . distracted."

There was no time for any more distractions now, though. During the search of the car, Sadie had made some decisions, and she needed to follow through with them.

"I need his phone," Sadie said when she reached Monty. She put her heavy purse on the picnic table and moved toward Joe, who didn't seem to have moved at all other than his head being a bit more to the side. It couldn't be good that he'd been unconscious this long. She thought back to Eric's explanation of Layla's injury, how he'd said it hadn't been a serious accident, but it had been enough. Monty stepped in front of her and shook his head before kneeling down in her place. Such a gentleman.

"'Is phone?" he asked, checking Joe's pockets.

"Yes." Sadie nodded, grateful she didn't have to look for it. She tried not to look at Joe's face—or should she be calling him Hugo?—but couldn't help it. He looked paler, which only confirmed that Sadie's plan to get him some help was a good one. Monty pulled the phone out of Joe's jacket pocket, handing it to Sadie, who accepted it with a smile. "I'm still on your clock, right?"

He nodded as he stood up, but he'd lost his smile somewhere.

"Good," she said. "I'm going to call someone to come help Joe, but then can you take me to the University of Miami Hospital?"

"Sho'." He looked as though he wanted to ask more questions, but he didn't. Sadie was glad for that, since she wasn't sure how she would explain that she was basing everything on a single letter of the alphabet.

That settled, she looked at the phone again and nearly talked herself out of calling for help for fear of what the repercussions of her involvement would be.

"Maybe we should take him to the hospital with us," she said.

"Not a man like dis," Monty said, shaking his head. "'E be trouble. Like I tow you, 'e be best right 'ere."

Sadie looked up. "You think so?"

Monty nodded, and Sadie wondered if he would get in trouble for knocking Joe out. She certainly didn't want that. Monty had thought he was helping. Besides, she needed to see if Liliana was Megan, and although Joe was out cold, she knew there was someone else involved—the box burner. What if they beat her to Megan?

She also wondered if maybe getting Joe to a hospital would give him a chance to talk to the police, perhaps sparing his life in the process. He'd said he wasn't proud of some of the things he'd done, and obviously he was involved in some illegal things, but he also knew where Megan had been. Maybe he could trade what he knew about her situation for some help with his own. Sadie knew he didn't trust the police, but they might be the very people to save him from what he'd already accepted as his fate.

One more look at Joe, who was partially blocked from view by

Monty, convinced her that she had to call. Eric had said Sadie was willing to do anything in order to do the right thing. Getting Joe some help seemed to be the most right thing she could do. Before she could argue the point with herself any longer, she punched in 911 and waited as a dispatcher came on the line.

"Nine-one-one. What is your emergency?"

"Um, yeah, there's a man unconscious at—" She scanned the park desperately; she hadn't noticed the name of the park. She looked to Monty for help.

"Tropical Park," Monty said.

"Tropical Park," Sadie replied. "I think he hit his head."

"Did you see him hit his head, ma'am?"

Technically, she hadn't, but she wasn't going to say anything more anyway. Instead she bent over to put the phone next to Joe. Monty, once again, cut her off. He took the phone and placed it on the ground next to Joe's hand. It almost looked as though Joe had dropped the phone himself.

The operator's muted voice continued. "Ma'am? Ma'am, are you there?"

"Sorry, Joe," Sadie whispered, then looked up at Monty. "And I'm sorry to you too, Monty. I don't want to get you in trouble."

Monty's expression was flat as he looked down at Joe. He'd thought he was helping Sadie and seemed to be realizing that it hadn't quite worked out that way.

"I think I found the information he was going to give to my friend," Sadie said. "Can you take me to the hospital?" She scanned the park, imagining that in a town like Miami there were police all over the place who would be responding to her 911 call any second.

Monty must have been thinking the same thing because he too was looking around. He reached out and took Sadie's hand in his large one. "We bettah 'urry," he said, pulling her in the opposite direction from where Joe had parked. "De' meta's runnin'."

"After you drop me off, you can go," Sadie said a minute later as she put on her seat belt in the backseat. "You've done so much for me, and I'm afraid things are only going to get worse from here on out."

Monty pulled out of the parking lot and turned left. There were no mountains for reference so Sadie had no idea which direction they were headed.

"I kin wait fo' you," he said with a nod as he pulled up right behind another car and honked to get them to pull to the right. The car complied, and he hit the gas again, throwing Sadie against the seat.

"Are you sure?" Sadie asked, holding onto the door to brace herself. "I really don't want to get you in trouble."

"No trouble," he said, glancing at her in the rearview mirror before making a hard right turn. "I not be leavin' a lady like you to face dis alone. 'Sides, dis be de best time I had in weeks." He smiled and winked.

Sadie smiled slightly, reminded of her son, Shawn, and how he was the same way—unable to absorb the severity of what was happening, seeing life as one big adventure. Kids. The taxi zoomed past a restaurant with a marquee that read "Key Lime Pie $3.99" and Sadie frowned. Joe had offered to take her to get some key lime pie. Oh, she hoped he was okay.

"Well, why don't I pay you now?" Sadie said, opening her purse. "Just in case you need to go while I'm inside."

Monty shook his head. "I wait fo' you, lady, an' you be payin' me when you come back."

Sadie hoped his insistence wouldn't put him in a bad position, but she finally nodded her acceptance of his terms. She'd been very clear with him, and he was choosing to remain involved. She couldn't deny that it felt good to have someone else on her side, and she was glad that her knack for finding good people in difficult times was still holding. Even if he had knocked Joe out and complicated things a whole heck of a lot, Monty had still rescued her.

Remembering that her phone had rung while she'd been in the car with Joe, she pulled it out of her purse to see who'd called.

A shiver ran through her as she saw Pete's number next to a tiny picture of him. Her daughter, Breanna, had showed her how to customize her phone so that a person's picture came up with the number. The tiny Pete looked up at her, a slight smile on his face, and she realized that she missed him. Immediately she felt ridiculous. They hadn't really had a relationship in the first place, they just both had really *wanted* to have one, and she'd chosen to cut it off.

He'd left a voice mail, and Sadie took a deep breath to prepare herself before she pushed the button to listen to the message. Gayle's message was first. As Sadie had expected, she was reporting that the trailer was cleaned and ready to go—and that Eric's neighbor, Brian, was kind of cute. Sadie shook her head, but felt a fledgling hope that maybe Brian would help distract Gayle from Pete.

Speaking of Pete, he was the next message on her phone, and she bit her lip as his voice elicited another wave of . . . what? Nostalgia? Regret? Tenderness? She focused on his words instead of his voice. "Sadie, I just received a strange call from a police sergeant in southern Florida. He had a lot of questions about you and Eric." Pete paused and Sadie cringed. "I had no choice but to share the information about your conviction with him, but I did try to emphasize that it's your only run-in—ever—and that you pled guilty and are nearly finished with your sentence. On a personal note, I'm not sure what to think about any of this. Please call me back."

What Sadie wouldn't do for a rewind button! Then she wouldn't have looked in the box, and she wouldn't have come to Florida and led Pete to believe she had come here with Eric. She was so embarrassed, and yet she couldn't think of anything she could say to Pete if she called him back right now. What must he think of her? Was he wrong to think it? She *had* chased Eric to Florida, and she was in the middle of yet another investigation. But therein lay her redemption—she was on the brink of possibly finding Megan, which would justify everything she'd done so far. She couldn't regret that entirely, no matter how much Pete's good opinion of her mattered.

She looked out the window as she tried to be confident in what she was doing and attempted to distract herself by focusing on the city beyond her window—a city that she hoped to leave behind as quickly as possible. As soon as she did just one more thing.

It seemed she'd traveled all over Miami today, yet Joe had said it was small for a big city. To Sadie it just kept going and going and going; she hadn't seen the beach yet, though she'd seen glimpses of ocean now and again. Gayle had said Florida was one of the most romantic places in the country. Sadie wished she could see that side of Florida. The next thought she posed to herself was if she'd *want* to see that side of Miami with Eric. She wasn't sure she did.

Her phone rang from inside her purse, and she nearly shouted "Hallelujah," glad to have a reprieve from her miserable thoughts— until she realized it could be Pete calling her back. When she recognized the Florida area code she almost relaxed—until she realized it could be Eric. Was he calling her from Layla's house instead of on his cell phone? Her stomach sank as she wondered what she could say to him right now with so many whirling thoughts taking place in her brain. Chickening out wasn't the answer either though. On the third ring, she took a deep breath and answered.

"Hello?"

"Mrs. Hoffmiller?"

"Yes," Sadie said, recognizing the voice immediately. "Sergeant Mathews?" She didn't want to talk to him either and wished she'd let the call go to voice mail after all. Too late now. *What does he know?* she wondered. What could she say without making everything worse? Was there any way he could know she'd placed that 911 call?

"Are you still with Mr. Burton?"

She thought back to when she'd been leaving the police station and insisted that she wasn't with Eric. She'd worried then that Mathews thought she was lying. Knowing she was still in town must make him pretty certain she had lied. She paused before deciding to tell him as much of the truth as she could. "No, I'm not."

"Are you on your way back to Colorado?"

Sadie wished she could tell him she was about to get on a plane right that minute. "No," she said simply.

He waited for more, but she remained silent.

"Then where are you?"

"I'm sorry, Sergeant, but I can't tell you that."

CHAPTER 28

Mathews was quiet for what felt like a long time. Sadie shifted in her seat trying to shake off the tension that built with each second Mathews didn't say anything.

"Mr. Burton is withholding information," Mathews said, his voice cool. "And while he likes to think that we can't charge him with anything, he's mistaken. We're giving him some space because of what he's dealing with, but he is not in good standing with us right how. I want to make sure you understand the predicament that puts you in if you are currently acting on the information he's with-holding from us."

Sadie swallowed. That was perhaps the most professional repri-mand she'd ever heard. There was no way to argue with him about what he'd said, but neither was she inclined to tell him everything that had happened since she'd left the police station. Not yet. "I'm not acting on anything Eric's told me," she said. Joe had told her what she was acting on now. "Thank you for your concern, Sergeant." She hoped she sounded confident but not snotty. She couldn't believe she was creating problems with yet another police department. "I appreciate your concern, and you'll be the first person I call if I learn anything concrete."

Mathews let out a breath laced with disappointment and frustration. "That's not good enough," he said. "I know you understand how serious it is to withhold information, Mrs. Hoffmiller. It would be a shame to add a charge so soon after the one you received in Colorado."

Sadie felt her cheeks heat up. "Sergeant Mathews," she said. "I swear I'm not trying to be difficult, it's just that what I know won't be helpful unless I—"

"I am asking you to come into the police station as soon as possible. The case may rest upon you following this direction."

"I don't know where Eric is," Sadie hedged. "And I don't know what he's involved in other than he really wants to find his daughter and he believes that working with the police will prevent that."

"I need to know what you know," Mathews said.

"I don't know anything," Sadie said, and it was true. She didn't *know* a single thing, but she *suspected* several things, and she was working on confirming those details. "When I do know something, you'll be the first person I call."

"Mrs. Hoffmiller," he said in a warning tone.

She felt horrible doing it, and could only imagine the trouble she was getting herself into, but she pressed the end button, hanging up on Sergeant Mathews. She hoped he'd assume the call had simply been dropped at an inopportune moment.

She stared at the phone in her hand. "Did I really just do that?" she asked herself out loud.

Yes, she answered herself silently. *I did.*

Ugh, she hated being so disagreeable, but she wasn't sure how to explain what she was doing, or what had happened with Joe.

She wished Sergeant Mathews could understand that she wasn't being coy or trying to hide something; she had to make sure she didn't ruin Eric's chances of finding his daughter. Sadie didn't know what she would do if Liliana Miriam Montez wasn't Megan. And knowing that Megan didn't necessarily want to come home made this meeting an even more precarious situation.

"Main doe's?" Monty asked, and Sadie looked up to see a huge white building half a block in front of them.

"Wow," she whispered in awe, unable to answer him directly. The sunlight reflecting off the windows and white stone—or stucco—walls made the building look as though it were glowing. There were palm trees reaching toward the upper floors, and Sadie wondered how on earth she was going to find Megan—or Liliana Montez—amid that many rooms.

Monty drove up to the main entrance and stopped in front of the large glass doors.

Sadie took a deep breath. "Wish me luck," she said, tucking her purse under the backseat and hoping she wasn't an idiot to leave it behind. She couldn't pretend to be a hospital volunteer with a purse on her arm, and Monty had given Sadie no reason to distrust him— quite the opposite, in fact.

"You'll wait here?" she asked, even though he'd already said he would.

"Yes, mum," he said, smiling back at her.

She stepped out of the car and let her eyes travel up the front of the building. She had butterflies in her stomach as she moved forward and worked on gathering her wits about her. She hated not knowing what her plan was after she found Megan, assuming the woman in the hospital was Megan in the first place. She'd call Eric, certainly, but then what? Would she go to Mathews? Would she return Pete's call? A glance at the clock behind the reception-ist's desk said it was a quarter after four. She would need to call Eric before he headed for the track where he would *not* be meeting Joe at six.

A pink-haired elderly woman at the front desk smiled as Sadie approached. Sadie smiled back at her. "Hello," she said when she reached the desk, looking at the woman's name tag that read "Volunteer." "I'm here to visit with Liliana Montez," she said. "She was admitted to Labor and Delivery yesterday morning." Would she still be in Labor and Delivery, though? Having adopted her children, Sadie wasn't sure how it all worked at a hospital.

The woman continued smiling and blinked behind her thick glasses. "I'm sorry, we don't give out patient room information."

"She's expecting me," Sadie lied. "And with the baby and all, she forgot to tell me the room."

"We don't give out patient room information," the woman re-peated, still smiling.

"But I just need to—"

"We don't give out patient room information."

Sadie tried for another two minutes to get the information she wanted, but the woman wouldn't budge no matter how many ways Sadie tried to ask her. Where was a plate of Butterfinger cookies when she needed it? No one could resist them; Sadie felt sure that if she had some to offer, this woman would be putty in hands, privacy laws or no privacy laws.

When the woman's smile began to fall and her eyes behind the glasses began to narrow, Sadie stopped mid-sentence and took a breath, forcing a smile she knew looked like stone. "Thanks anyway," she said, determining that since she knew what unit Megan was in, she could find her easily enough. "Thank you."

She headed toward the elevators before realizing the receptionist was likely still watching her. She looked over her shoulder to find she was right. The old woman's eyes burned through her thick glasses. Were Sadie an ant and this woman's eyes the sun, she'd have been incinerated.

She kept her smile fixed and headed . . . *right*, toward the cafeteria and emergency room. There had to be an elevator over there as well so it would be convenient for the nurses to grab an egg salad sandwich when the craving hit them.

A big sign hung from the ceiling pointing to the elevators ahead. She hurried forward, almost passing the hospital pharmacy and gift shop before she came up short. After the receptionist's less-than-warm welcome, would Sadie simply be able to walk into Megan's room? And what was she going to say when she got there? If Megan had left of her own accord, which it seemed she had done, then she was likely pretty uncomfortable being back in Miami.

Sadie needed a cover. She distinctly remembered Eric mentioning how Layla would brush out Megan's hair every night before bed back when Megan was little and Layla was still well. Sadie checked her pocket, verifying that she still had her travel cash with her. Perfect.

A few minutes later, she left the gift shop with a bottle of lotion, a hairbrush, and a plain blue scrub top that she hoped made her seem more official, even if it was absolutely shapeless. With her head held high, she continued to the elevator and became even more optimistic that she could pull this off when a directory sign listed that Labor and Delivery was on the third floor. Perfect. She'd start there since it was the unit Megan had been admitted to, and then move on to Maternity if she didn't find her.

The doors on the third floor seemed to go on forever, but as

Sadie approached the nurses' station she saw a big, dry-erase board with last names and a few columns of statistics. At the end of each row was a room number. Sadie slowed down enough to find Montez at the very end of the list, with a couple spaces between it and the next highest name on the list. She wondered why it was set apart from the others, then followed the line across to room number 323. So much for patient privacy.

She took a breath and let it out slowly, nodding politely to a nurse who was hurrying down the hall. Room 323 was at the very end of the hall, and a pink sign placed above the room number read "Surgical."

Sadie frowned at the sign and looked around, realizing this room was set apart from the rest of the unit just like the name Montez had been separated on the sign. Hopefully, within the next few minutes Sadie would know why there was so much differentiation between Megan and the other women in Labor and Delivery.

Please let this work, she thought to herself before pushing open the door.

Butterfinger Cookies

½ cup butter, softened
⅔ cup sugar
¾ cup brown sugar
1 egg
1¼ cup peanut butter (chunky or creamy)
1½ teaspoon vanilla
1·cup flour
½ teaspoon baking soda
¼ teaspoon salt
5 (2.1-ounce) Butterfinger candy bars, chopped* (about 2 cups)

Preheat oven to 350 degrees. Cream butter and sugars. Add egg; mix. Add peanut butter and vanilla; mix until smooth. Add flour, baking soda, and salt. Mix well. Add Butterfingers; mix. Roll into 1-inch balls, use a 1-inch scoop, or drop by 1-inch spoonfuls onto ungreased baking sheet. Bake 10 to 12 minutes, just until browned. Allow cookies to cool 2 minutes on baking sheet before moving to cooling rack.

Makes 4 dozen.

*Chop Butterfingers with a chef's knife or put in a zip-top bag and crush with a rolling pin. Food processors make the pieces too fine and you lose the crunch.

CHAPTER 29

Sadie had made it this far by pretending she knew what she was doing, but she was at the most important part of her journey now; the stakes were higher than ever.

Taking a breath, she pushed the door all the way open, then closed it behind her, holding the hairbrush and lotion she'd bought at the hospital gift shop. The curtain was drawn around part of the bed, hiding it from Sadie's position at the door.

"Hello, hello," Sadie said, using her "everything's great" tone as she moved forward. She reached out a hand and pulled back the curtain. The sight of a woman curled on her left side with her hand on her swollen belly was a shock. Sadie kept her smile in place, however, and continued forward as the woman's big blue eyes opened and then blinked up at her. Blue eyes just like Eric's. Sadie's stomach flipped to have the visual evidence in front of her. It *was* Megan, she had no doubt about that, and not only was Megan alive, but she seemed to be well . . . and very pregnant. But she'd been here for two days, and the note on the door had said surgical. Was there a problem with the pregnancy?

Megan's hair was cut into a bob, shoulder length, and while she didn't have any makeup on, the acrylic nails and the highlights in her hair attested to the fact that she'd been taking care of herself. Sadie was grateful for that. Ever since realizing Joe had wanted to help Megan, Sadie had worried the poor girl was being mistreated somehow. Seeing her up close put many of those fears to rest; Megan could have passed as a soccer mom.

"Hi," Sadie said. "I'm . . . Connie, one of the hospital volunteers. I wondered if you'd like to have your hair brushed, or maybe some lotion rubbed on your feet?"

"No, thank you," Megan said. Sadie realized her eyes were somewhat red and swollen. She'd been crying. Not in the last few minutes, but not long ago either.

"Are you sure, sweetie?" Sadie said, cocking her head to the side. "The very best medicine is often a little pampering. Just to help you relax a little bit."

Megan looked at her again, her eyes traveling to the brush in Sadie's hand. "My mother used to brush my hair when I was a little girl," she said, a sad and wistful tone in her voice.

Sadie almost said "I know," but stopped herself just in time. "It's even an antistatic brush," she said lightly, holding it up for inspection. "I can brush your hair as long as you like without making you look like you put your finger in a light socket."

Megan managed a small smile, which Sadie took as an invitation. She moved around the bed so Megan's back was toward her. Megan made no move to sit up, so Sadie simply focused on the side of Megan's head that wasn't against the pillow.

"So, how are you doing?" she said as she pulled the brush through Megan's hair. As her hair moved to the side, Sadie saw a small tattoo, just beneath Megan's hairline, centered on her neck. It took a few seconds for Sadie to read what it said, but she thought it was the name "Alex" in fancy lettering.

"Okay, I guess," Megan said, her voice still soft. Still scared.

"And the baby?" Sadie said. "I bet you're excited to meet him or her about now, aren't you?" *Could the baby be named Alex?* Sadie wondered. But would a pregnant woman get a tattoo?

Megan didn't answer, but she dipped her chin and seemed to curl into herself a little more.

"I've said something wrong," Sadie said, worried she'd ruined her chances right out the gate. "I'm so sorry. I didn't mean to upset you."

"No," Megan said in a tiny voice that made her sound young and vulnerable. "It's not your fault. It's just . . . hard."

Sadie put a hand on the girl's shoulder and gave it a squeeze. "I'm sorry," she said, and although she wanted to ask what was hard, she knew that would be too pushy. "I'm sure everything will be okay, though. When are you due?"

"Not for three and a half more months," Megan said.

Sadie looked at the size of Megan's belly. Three more months? That couldn't be right.

"Twins," Megan said, but she still sounded upset, making Sadie wonder if she didn't want to be pregnant. But then she realized that Megan's emotion must be related to the "Surgical" sign on the door. She looked at Megan's extended belly again. It wasn't as big as Macy Nelson's had been when she had her twins a few years ago. Macy had looked impossibly huge, but Megan didn't look much bigger than a typical woman did at full term, which made sense if she was only two-thirds of the way through her pregnancy.

"That's wonderful," Sadie said, trying to choose her words carefully but, with Megan's back to her, unsure of how well she was doing. "Girls or boys? Or one of each?"

"Boys," Megan said, and Sadie could finally hear the tenderness that laced itself within those words. Even though it had been many years since Sadie had come to terms with not giving birth to her own children, that tone of wistful motherhood still caught her in the gut. For a long time it had nearly reduced her to tears when other women took on that glow, both in words and in expression, when they talked about their pregnancies. Sadie would never begrudge God the gift her adopted children were, but there were still moments when she wished she'd had the whole experience.

She pulled the brush through Megan's hair again and put those thoughts back where they belonged, far behind her gratitude for two wonderful children, a husband who had loved them all, and a full life which held very few regrets. Not everyone had it so good.

"Congratulations," she said, and she really did mean it.

"I hope so," Megan whispered, almost too quiet for Sadie to hear. She turned her head into the pillow.

"Oh, sweetie," Sadie said, stilling the brush and laying a hand on Megan's shoulder. Megan cried for a moment before getting a hold of herself.

Sadie was hesitant to push, but then again, that's why she'd come—to learn everything she could about Megan and the new life she was living. "What's going on?"

"You don't know?" Megan asked.

Sadie dissected the tone, looking for suspicion, but only heard surprise.

"They don't tell volunteers much about the patients," she said, glancing toward the door and praying no one else came in for a few more minutes. "I don't mean to pry, though," she said, hoping that would encourage Megan's continued trust.

"They call it TTTS," Megan said, pausing for a breath.

"Twin-to-Twin Transfusion Syndrome. It means one of the babies is getting too much blood, too many nutrients, and the other is . . . the other isn't getting enough."

"Oh dear," Sadie said. She wanted to move around to the front of the bed and take Megan's hand, try to give her a hug or something, but she just kept brushing her hair instead for fear that was all the comforting Megan would allow. Even though Megan was talking, Sadie still sensed a ring of caution in everything she said. "But the babies are okay?"

"So far," Megan said. "But the doctors say it's serious. Without surgery, they aren't sure Carlos will make it. That's why I had to come here; this is the closest hospital that can do the surgery."

"Carlos is the twin who's in trouble?" Sadie asked for clarification.

Megan nodded, her head still against the pillow as she raised an IV-laden hand to wipe her eyes. Across the back of her wrist, above the tape that held the IV tubing against her arm, was a three-inch scar that stood out against her tanned skin. It was wide in the center and a little puckered, attesting to the fact that she hadn't had it stitched up, but probably should have. Sadie thought back to the police report she'd read in Eric's car. It had clearly said Megan had no noticeable scars. No tattoos either. What had Megan been through since she left home? Her heart ached a little more for this poor girl—this woman—who was obviously facing a very difficult time. Was Alex the father of these babies? Sadie wondered.

"When is the surgery?" she asked.

"Tomorrow morning," Megan said, her voice quivering. She was so scared; it caused a lump to rise in Sadie's throat. She wanted to tell her that her father was in Florida, just a phone call away. He'd be right beside her, help her through this.

"And the babies' father?" Sadie asked, thinking about Joe's trip to Paris. "Is he here with you?"

"No," Megan said, and her voice cracked. "He had to stay with the boys until he could make arrangements."

Boys?

"You have other children?"

"Yes," Megan said. "Two boys—five and three."

They couldn't be Megan's children, then. She'd only been gone three years. "Oh, how fun," Sadie said out loud, still brushing while her brain tried to piece the information together in a way that would make sense of it all. She scanned the counters and tables in the room in hopes of finding a family picture, but there wasn't anything personal in the room. "Will your husband be here in time for the surgery?" Sadie asked, hoping that Megan was married and not part of one of those modern relationships where marriage was considered obsolete. She glanced quickly at Megan's left hand—wedding ring; thank goodness.

"No," Megan squeaked, then took a deep breath as though trying to calm herself. "He hopes to come next week though."

"How long do you have to stay in the hospital?" Sadie asked.

"Ten weeks."

Sadie's mouth dropped open and her hand stilled until she realized what she was doing and went back to the methodical brushing. "Ten weeks?" she repeated. "You can't go home after the surgery?"

"It's too far," Megan said, crying again. "I have to be on bed rest until the babies are born, and I can't fly or sail home, so I have no choice but to stay here until I can deliver. Even then the babies will be about a month early."

Sail? A flight, Sadie could understand, but where did Megan live that sailing provided an option of getting home? Megan didn't mention a car. It had to be an island, right? No roads. Cuba was maybe a couple hundred miles away, but going back and forth was pretty much impossible, wasn't it? Key West? But that was drivable thanks to the highway that connected the Keys to the mainland.

Sadie heard voices outside the door and held her breath, thinking they were coming in. They moved on, but Sadie was reminded that time was of the essence. Every question mattered.

"You don't look old enough to have a five-year-old," she said, looping the conversation back to the earlier topic, even though she knew Megan was twenty-five years old—plenty old enough to have a child that age.

"I'm twenty-nine," Megan answered.

She was *adding* years to her age? But then Sadie remembered the hospital admission forms—Liliana Montez was twenty-nine.

"You don't look a day over twenty-five," Sadie said.

Megan didn't answer, but Sadie sensed a change in the feel of the room. "I'm sure everything will turn out fine," she said, hoping to restore the younger woman's comfort. "You said one of the twins was named Carlos. What about the other one?"

"Jorge," she said, using the Spanish pronunciation of George that sounded like Horhay. Two Latin-American names.

"Good strong names," she said. "Strong names for strong babies."

"I hope so," Megan said, her hand rubbing her stomach as though comforting her unborn children.

"Ten weeks is a long time to be in the hospital," Sadie said, digging for more information. "I hope you have some family close by who can help you out."

She immediately realized she'd said the wrong thing again. Megan tensed and didn't say anything at all for a few seconds, then she pulled forward on the bed a couple of inches—away from Sadie. "Thank you," she said. "I'm going to try to get some sleep now."

Sadie mentally kicked herself. For a moment she considered laying it all out to Megan, telling her who she really was, that Eric was worried sick over her and doing everything he could to find her. But Joe had said Megan didn't want to be found. And Megan was facing serious complications. Adding to her stress wouldn't be good for the babies.

In addition, the fact was Megan had come to this hospital because she had to, not because she wanted to. Joe, therefore, was taking advantage of her situation to help her be found. But why exactly?

"I didn't mean to upset you," Sadie said, stepping away from the bed but hesitant to leave. She picked up the lotion from the bedside table and turned it in her hands. She wished she could think of something to say that would take them back to the vulnerable girl who seemed to like having someone to talk to, even if she didn't say very much.

"You didn't upset me," Megan said, trying to sound causal, but failing. "It's been a difficult couple of days, and I'm really tired. I need to rest up for tomorrow. But thank you."

"You're welcome," Sadie said, accepting that she'd been dismissed. She headed for the door and took one final look at Eric's daughter, who had closed her eyes as though to demonstrate just how tired she was. Turning away, Sadie moved toward the door and had almost reached it when it was pushed open from the hallway. Sadie startled more than the circumstance warranted, but quickly tried to cover up her reaction.

"Oh," the thickly built woman with spiky, unnaturally red hair said as she came up short. She wore bright purple scrubs and had a stethoscope around her neck. "I'm sorry. I didn't realize Mrs. Montez had visitors."

Sadie nearly accepted that title, but realized Megan was only a few feet away, listening. "I'm a volunteer," she said quickly. "I was just brushing out Mrs. Montez's hair—to relax her, you know."

The woman held her eyes. "A volunteer?"

Sadie nodded and smiled as she moved past the other woman, intent on reaching the hallway. She could feel the nurse pivoting to keep her eyes on Sadie, and when Sadie stepped out into the hall, the woman came with her, shutting the door to Megan's room behind her. Sadie pretended she didn't think it at all strange and kept walking.

The woman caught up with her after taking a few heavy steps. "Wait a minute," she said, her tone sharp.

Sadie turned to her with an innocent expression and raised her eyebrows expectantly. *Please let her ask to borrow the lotion,* Sadie asked silently. She'd even hand over the hairbrush if it would erase the skeptical look on this woman's face.

"We don't have volunteers in Labor and Delivery."

"Oh?" Sadie said, feeling her heart rate increase.

"We're a transitional unit," the woman said, her eyes narrowing slightly.

Sadie suddenly had a vague memory of someone once explaining that Labor and Delivery was where a woman was before the baby was born, and Maternity was for recovery. She snapped her fingers. "Duh," she said as though realizing her mistake, which, in fact she just had. "They said to go to Maternity, and I just didn't differentiate—it's my first day. I'm so sorry for the mix-up. They're probably wondering what happened to me, I better get over to the Maternity ward . . . uh, wing . . . uh, unit. Again, I'm really sorry."

She made it one step before the woman reached out and grabbed her arm. Sadie immediately pulled away. "I said I'm sorry. I won't make the mistake again."

"If it's your first day, why aren't you shadowing someone?"

Sadie scrambled for an answer. "They didn't have enough volunteers," she said. She took another step away.

"What floor is Maternity on?" the other woman asked.

Sadie felt she had no choice but to stop again. Surely there was something she could say that would get this woman off her back. "Look, I'm sorry that I—"

"What floor?" the nurse asked. "You said you were new, surely they told you which floor to go to. It makes me wonder how you ended up here."

"I don't remember," Sadie said, scrambling to remember what floor she was on. Third! That's right. "I thought they said the third floor, but they must have said something else. I'm afraid I'm not very familiar with this hospital, so I'm not sure what floor—"

"The fifth," the woman said. "Did they say it was on the fifth floor?"

Sadie paused as though trying to remember, but in truth she was simply trying to calm herself down. She didn't understand why having a volunteer on the wrong floor would be such a big deal, but it obviously was, and she was feeling frantic. She wanted to get out of there. "That's right," she said. "Fifth. I remember now. I don't know why I chose the third, I'm so sorry. I better get back there before they fire me . . . Can they even fire volunteers? I've never done this before, and here I am making a mess of it. I better go."

She forced a smile and began walking again. The other woman didn't follow her this time.

"Fourth," she said from behind Sadie. "Maternity is on the fourth floor. You'd better come with me. I'll get my supervisor."

Sadie's shoulders slumped in defeat, and she turned around. The woman looked relieved and turned around herself before heading back the way they had come, expecting Sadie to follow her. It was all the opportunity Sadie needed. The nurse had no sooner turned her back than Sadie turned again and began moving as quick as she could down the hallway, trying to make as little noise as possible, but moving quickly enough to create some distance. She was around the corner before she heard the woman yell, "Hey!"

Sadie said a little prayer in her mind, and then took off in a full run.

CHAPTER 30

She couldn't hear any footsteps over her own as she reached the elevator, but she knew they were there. A man stepped out and Sadie slid through the opening instead of heading for the stairs she'd been planning to use. The door caught her bad shoulder, and she winced as the contact triggered the doors to open again, but she didn't let it slow her down. She turned and pushed the "Close Doors" button fifteen times before they finally obeyed. The man whom she'd pushed out of the way was staring at her from the outside; she offered him a smile as the doors closed. At the last possible moment, she saw the man turn to look in the direction she'd come, and she heard the voice of the nurse say, "Stop that elevator!"

It was too late for the nurse. Sadie took a breath as the door sealed shut. She lifted her hand to push the button with the glowing number one on it to take her to the first level, then hesitated and pushed the button for the second floor instead. There had been security at the front doors when she walked in, not to mention the Doberman of a receptionist who would likely take great pleasure in seeing Sadie thrown to the ground.

When the elevator door opened a moment later, she

half-expected to find a security guard posted in front of it, but there wasn't anyone there so she turned right, passed the stairwell, and headed down the hall to the elevators by the cafeteria, making an extra effort to walk normally and hold her head up while she attempted to catch her breath. There was a red fleece vest on the back of a chair in one of the waiting areas. She nonchalantly traded her brush and lotion for it, leaving both items on the chair. She tucked the vest under her arm, wrinkling her nose at the smell of stale cigarettes.

She passed a nurse who smiled at her, and she smiled back, then a doctor, who didn't even look at her, which was just as well. The hallway was circular, but she kept following it, sure there had to be another set of stairs by the original elevators she'd taken up to the third floor. Her anxiety increased with every second. The longer it took her to get out of the building, the better her chances of getting caught.

There was a cart on one side of the hallway, and she barely glanced at it, then stopped and walked backward two steps until she reached it again. She grabbed a trial-sized bottle of talcum powder and kept walking, looking side to side to see if anyone had noticed. People passed her now and again, but no one seemed to be looking for her here. Not yet, anyway.

Finally she saw the elevators she'd used on her way up, as well as a sign for stairs, and she gratefully hurried toward them. Once secure within the stairwell, she draped the vest over the handrail. She put some talcum powder in her hands and rubbed it through her hair, leaning forward so she wouldn't get too much on her clothes. She knew the powder wouldn't turn her hair white, but it might gray it enough to let her get out of the building. With the way the humidity had left her hair products sticky, the talcum powder ought to adhere pretty well; hopefully it wouldn't look like she'd just rubbed a bottle of talc through it.

She pulled the scrub top over her head and used it to wipe the powder from her face and neck before putting on the red vest, scowling again at the offensive smell. She hurried down the single flight of stairs, both hoping for and dreading the prospect of passing a mirror. When she reached the door marked "First Floor," she took a breath and pushed through it, keeping her chin up and trying not to be too furtive as she looked around to see if a security guard was barreling toward her.

A sign on the wall outside the stairwell said the main entrance was to her left. She turned right, but avoided the cafeteria for fear it was centralized and wouldn't have an exit. The Emergency Room would have a way out, though. Her heart was racing as she pulled her phone from her pocket and texted Monty.

Emgncy Rm Exit

She turned a corner and held her breath as she moved out of the way, allowing a heavy man in a wheelchair to pass, and then continued following the signs. A few people looked up at her as she walked through the waiting room, but no one stopped her, not even the security guard who was flirting with the receptionist at the check-in desk. Thank goodness for cute, giggly girls.

She was almost to the door, unable to breathe, when she heard something crackle on the guard's walkie-talkie behind her. She didn't even slow down. Once outside, she cut across the ambulance bay and hurried through the parking lot. She heard the swish of the automatic doors open behind her and looked back to see the security guard step outside. She didn't pause long enough to see if he spotted her, but kept going, scanning for Monty's taxi. The parking lot was huge. She couldn't wait at the entrance for him so she simply headed for the street, hoping he would recognize her.

The red vest!

She texted him quickly that she had a red vest on, and then kept moving toward the street. Finally, she caught sight of the black-and-white taxi making its way through the rows of cars on its way to the emergency entrance. She course-corrected and headed toward it, walking as fast as she could without breaking into a run.

Monty saw her as she emerged from behind two cars a few yards in front of him. He slowed down, and she unzipped the vest as she headed to intercept the car. She laid the vest on the trunk of the nearest car, hoping someone would return it to its original owner.

She was dying to turn and see if the guard was still behind her, but didn't dare. Without slowing down, she pulled open the front door and slid into the passenger seat of the taxi, smiling thankfully at Monty. She craned her neck around to see the security guard running through the parking lot after her. Her heart jumped into her throat.

"Go!" she shouted, ducking down in the seat. The guard would have seen her take off the vest. He knew it was her.

Monty didn't need to be told twice. He took off like a rocket, glancing in the rearview mirror to see what it was Sadie had seen.

"Maybe he wasn't close enough to see your license plate," Sadie said, peeking over the seat to watch the security guard head back to the hospital with long, quick steps. "I'm so sorry," she said, turning to face front again. "I'm getting you in so much trouble."

"Don' worry 'bout me," Monty said, shaking his head for emphasis. "I'm worryin' 'bout 'ow much trouble you be in."

Sadie let out a breath. "Honestly? I'm not sure." She couldn't help but peek out the back window again. The hospital was a full block away, and there were no flashing red lights coming up behind them. A phone rang; she reached into her pocket before realizing it wasn't her phone.

Monty fished his phone out of his own pocket and put it to his ear. "Yeah," he said, then paused before saying it again.

Sadie tuned out Monty's voice and took a deep breath, trying to force herself to relax. *You didn't do anything wrong,* she told herself. But if that was true, why did she feel so awful right now?

"Okay, I be dere," Monty said into his phone before shutting it off and putting it back in his pocket. "Sorry 'bout dat."

"Don't be sorry on my account," Sadie said, meaning every word. She reached over the seat to pull her purse out from under the back-seat where she'd stashed it.

When she sat back down in the front seat and put on her seat belt, Monty reached out and touched Sadie's hair. He gave her an inquiring look, and Sadie raised her hands to touch her hair. Between the hair care products that never quite dried in this climate and the talcum powder she'd rubbed all over her head, her hair felt cakey and gross. Did she dare look?

"A rather lame attempt at a disguise, I'm afraid," Sadie explained. Steeling herself for the shock, she flipped down the window visor, sighing with relief when she saw there was no mirror. She vowed to wash her hair as soon as she could.

"So, whe's ya fella?"

He's not my fella, Sadie wanted to say once she realized Monty was asking about Eric, but she knew that would be rude. "I don't know," she said with a heavy sigh. "He was going to meet us—the guy at the park and me—tonight at the Speedway, but now that I've found Megan—"

"Who be Megan?"

"Oh, my . . . fella's daughter. We've been looking for her." She'd forgotten that she hadn't given Monty many details when she'd given him the overview back at the park.

Monty nodded. "She been lost?"

Sadie considered that. Had Megan been lost? She thought back to what Joe had said about Megan being kept and not taken. "Not really," she said. "At least, that's not what seems to have happened, but her father thought she was." It was impossible to boil the story down to make any sense, mostly because there were still so many holes. Why would Megan leave in the first place? Where had she been? Sadie knew why she was in Miami right now—she needed the surgery to save her babies—but why was she alone? She said she had other boys, but they couldn't be hers. And who was Joe, and why did he want Megan found, but didn't want to be the one who found her?

"An' de man from de park?" Monty said. "'E be helpin' your fella?"

"Kind of," Sadie said, trying to figure out the right words. "He wanted money for what he knew. My friend was having a hard time getting it together."

"But you found de' girl, right? You don' need de money now."

"Yes," Sadie said, but there was uncertainty in her voice. "But Joe—the man in the park—probably had more information. He could have helped make sense of why things happened the way they did. Without him, I'm just not sure how things fit together. I'm not sure what to do next."

Monty was quiet as he made a right-hand turn. Sadie wondered where they were going, but was mostly glad to be far away from the hospital. What she needed now was a new plan. No matter how much Monty insisted on driving her around, she couldn't justify allowing him to continue helping her. Sadie didn't know much about taxi drivers, but she knew that most cities only allowed a certain number of people to carry taxi licenses. She imagined that once a license was lost, it was lost for good. This was his career, his livelihood, and she was putting that all on the line for him, knowing it likely wouldn't end well.

It was time to part ways; it was the best option. She opened her purse and grabbed her wallet. When she opened it, however, she frowned. She only had eighty dollars in cash. Surely she owed Monty more than that. She'd spent most of her travel cash at the hospital. She fingered through the bills to make sure that was all she had, but although she did find the buy-one-get-one-free KFC meal coupon, she didn't find any spare hundred dollar bills.

"I've only got eighty in cash," she said, embarrassed to be making excuses after all he'd done for her today. "How much do I owe you?"

He tapped the fare machine: $112.50. "Sorry. It be the com'ny car, and dey track de fares so I can't give a discount."

Sadie wondered how on earth people survived in big cities if they took taxies everywhere. Then again, they likely didn't spend two hours driving all over town.

"Oh, I understand," Sadie said. "Can you take me to an ATM?" She was tempted to ask Monty to find the nearest Globe Bank so she wouldn't have to pay the two-dollar ATM fee, but there was no point in getting cheap now. She'd just spent twenty-four dollars on a scrub top she'd worn for eight minutes, not to mention the fact that she had left the brush and lotion behind as well.

"Sho'," Monty said, and took another right. Sadie couldn't be sure but she thought they were moving toward the interstate. That reminded her that she still hadn't called Eric, and another thrill rushed through her. Complicated or not—and it most certainly would be complicated—she'd found Eric's daughter.

She took a deep breath and picked up her phone, staring at it for a moment before dialing Eric's number. It amazed her how much could happen in an hour.

CHAPTER 31

S adie?"

    She wondered if the frantic tone in Eric's voice was fueled by relief to hear from her or fear that her calling him was a bad sign. "Where are you? What's happened? He let you call?"

"Eric," she said very slow and even, making a calming motion with her hand, even though only Monty could see it. "I have something to tell you, and I need you to listen very carefully."

"Did he hurt you? Are you okay?"

"Are you listening?" Sadie said, frustrated that he wasn't paying attention.

"I'm listening," he finally said, but the words were obviously difficult for him to say.

"I found Megan."

The other end of the line went completely silent.

"You what?" Eric asked after a few seconds.

Sadie took a breath, both excited and scared to death about what this news meant to him. "She's at the University of Miami Hospital," she said. "In the Labor and Delivery unit."

Silence again. "What?"

Sadie recounted everything about her meeting with Megan, stopping only to breathe when she absolutely had to. When she finished, Eric was, once again, silent.

"I can't believe this," Eric said. "I . . . what about that guy?"

"Um, don't worry about him," Sadie said as lightly as possible. "I got that all wrapped up, but I think you should get to the hospital as quickly as you can. I had a little trouble getting out of there after I talked to Megan, and I'm worried they might try moving her to a different room or something." Immediately she realized that there was one person who might be able to stop all that from happening. "You need to call Mathews."

Eric let out a breath. "I can't believe this," he said again. "I just . . . I don't know what to do."

"Go to the University hospital!" Sadie said loudly. "Go now! But call Mathews on your way, okay? I think you'll need him to get into her room. Tell him everything I told you."

"Okay, I'll call him, and I'll head to the hospital. Where are you? Are you okay? I can pick you up on my way."

"I'm fine," Sadie said. She paused before continuing, part of her waffling on her goal. "Don't worry about me, I'll tell you all about it later."

"But, that guy—"

"Go to your daughter," Sadie interrupted. "She needs you *right now.*"

Without giving him a chance to voice any more arguments, she clicked the END button on her phone and stared at it as she returned to her internal ponderings. She hoped that after she gave her statement to the police she would be able to see Megan and Eric together—a visual closing on all that had happened today.

Had this really all happened in a single day? She thought back and realized she hadn't caught her flight to Miami until five o'clock last night. A quick glance at the dashboard clock told her it had been just over twenty-four hours since she'd decided to come to Florida. It seemed impossible for so much to have happened in such a short period of time.

She startled when her phone rang. She took a breath, feeling unprepared to talk to anyone right now. She didn't know the number, but it was a Florida area code, and her phone recognized it, which she quickly worked out to mean that it had to be Mathews again. She'd liked the idea of Eric being the one to break the news to the sergeant, but realized he'd have had to call her for verification. She pushed the TALK button and accepted that she couldn't simply avoid the things she didn't want to do.

Mostly Sadie listened to Mathews explain to her that she needed to go to the police station right that minute and make a full report; Eric had called him and apparently told him everything he knew.

"Do you understand what I'm saying, Mrs. Hoffmiller? We need a full statement from you before you leave town."

"I understand," Sadie said, letting out a breath that seemed to hold all her hope of getting herself untangled from all of this. She wanted to ask about Joe, but not yet. Not until Monty was safely out of the picture. "I won't leave until I've been told I can. I'm on my way right now. Are you at the police station?"

"Yes," Mathews said, sounding relieved—as though he'd expected her to argue.

"Okay," Sadie said. She looked around the freeway for a sign that would tell her how far she was from Homestead, but there weren't any signs close by so all she could do was gauge the time. "I think I'm about forty minutes away."

"I'll be waiting for you," he said before hanging up.

For all her determination to do the right thing, the idea of confessing her part in Joe's situation made her insides shrivel. And Monty—what would she do about him? He was the one with the billy club, but the last thing she wanted to do was get him in trouble. However, lying in her statement wasn't an option either.

"I'll wai' fo' you 'ere," he said a few seconds later as he pulled into a parking lot near an ATM.

"Thanks," Sadie said, letting herself out of the car. She hurried inside, put her card in the machine and entered her PIN. It took less than a minute to complete the transaction. She used that minute to plan what she needed to do. She had to let Monty go, even if he was her one security right now.

When she returned to the cab, she went to the driver's window instead of the passenger side. Monty rolled down the window. She handed him two hundred dollars in cash. "This should make up for all the trouble I've been," she said.

He looked at the money he'd taken from her, then looked at her with a question in his eyes.

"If you get pulled over and I'm not in the car," Sadie explained, "you might have a better chance of getting out from under this mess." She thought of something else and pulled her mini-notebook out of her purse, removed the specially sized pen from the spiral binding at the top, and proceeded to write down her number. "If you do get in trouble for all this, call me, okay? If I can help you, I will."

Monty shook his head and put his hand out the window and over her hand, stilling it in the process of writing down her contact information. "I not be leavin' you 'ere, lady."

"I feel horrible enough already," Sadie said. He wasn't looking at the whole picture. "You could lose your license for this; I can't live with that responsibility and you've already done so much. It's better that I let you get back to work."

Monty was shaking his head before she finished speaking. "To 'ire my cab for de' day is four hun'red dollas." He nodded toward the ATM. "You get dat much fo' me, and I be your cab driver, no one else. I'm a good storytella, and I not be getting in any trouble fo' dis, I promise." He paused. "Dis city be full a' people you can't trus'. I can't be leav'n you to dat."

Sadie was torn. He seemed to mean what he'd said, and she'd given him every chance to move on. She also had lots of reasons to believe that finding anyone else she could trust in this town would be just as hard as he'd said. From what she'd heard so far—and based on all the episodes of *CSI Miami* she'd watched over the years—it seemed as though everyone here were a criminal of one kind or another. Monty was willing to help her, and he had already proved himself reliable. Would it be foolish for her to turn her back on that?

She lifted her eyes and scanned the buildings around them, focusing on three teenage boys at the bus stop across the street. Had they seen her withdraw cash out of the ATM? She'd told Monty she was worried that if the cops pulled him over with her in the car it would be bad for him. But she had a connection with Mathews, and she would be able to verify what she'd been doing, and in the process, she might be able to lobby for fair treatment of Monty. The deciding factor was that Monty was already in trouble for helping her, and while he might get in more trouble for staying with her, he certainly wasn't going to be in any less trouble for what he'd already done.

She looked back at his dark eyes that were watching her carefully. He seemed to genuinely want to help her. "Are you sure?" she asked, giving him one more chance.

Monty broke into a grin. "I'm sho'."

Sadie couldn't help but smile at the relief she felt. She wouldn't be alone. That was powerful. "Okay. Let me get the rest of the money."

Monty nodded and sat back in his seat, satisfied with their arrangement. It only took another minute to enter her PIN, but she'd hit her daily ATM limit and hoped she wouldn't need to make any other withdrawals. She sat in the front seat again and handed him the rest of the money. He folded the bills over and put them in the back pocket of his worn-out jeans.

"Can you take me to Homestead?" Sadie asked.

"What be in 'omestead?"

"Something I wish I didn't have to do," Sadie said with a sigh.

"Sho', I can take you to Homestead."

They were ten minutes into the drive when a chime from Sadie's phone informed her that she had a text message. It was from Gayle, which was a surprise; Gayle hated texting.

You haven't called me back. Are you okay?

Sadie smiled at how formal Gayle was with her texts; she hardly ever used abbreviations like everyone else. Sadie texted back, not wanting to have a conversation with Monty right here.

I'm fine. I'll call you when I can.

It took a full minute for Gayle to respond.

Pete and I are going to the Renaissance dinner. Are you sure you're okay with this?

Sadie closed her eyes as her chest started to ache. How could she have given her blessing? She again pictured her analogy of the love triangle she'd first thought of when she'd sat down in front of that lousy key lime pie. Pete had stepped out of the picture, and Sadie had come to realize her interest in Eric wasn't what she'd thought it might be. What did that leave? Feelings on Eric's part, perhaps? She opened her eyes and let out a breath before turning her attention back to the phone. She couldn't bring herself to lie, but she had to say something.

Have a great time ☺

The smiley face might have been too much, but Sadie realized she was trying to convince herself as much as Gayle that she was fine with Pete and Gayle dating. But telling herself it didn't bother her didn't make her chest ache any less. Pete had made plans with Gayle so quickly that Sadie should feel reassured that whatever feelings existed between them hadn't been deep enough for a real relationship. She *should* feel reassured, but she didn't.

She looked out the windshield and hoped she could hide her feelings when she returned to Garrison where she would see them both—together probably. How on earth would she pull that off?

"So, Monty," Sadie said, desperate for a distraction. "Tell me about yourself? Do you have a family?"

Monty smiled. "Sho' do," he said and proceeded to fill the last twenty minutes of the forty-minute drive. Monty showed Sadie a picture of his two-year-old son, and she oohed and aahed over the chocolate-skinned toddler with shiny cheeks and puppy-dog eyes. Sadie told him about her kids as well. When they got off the interstate, Sadie gave him Layla's address and tried to ignore the sorrow of their upcoming parting.

"Thank you, again," Sadie said as some of the familiar streets and businesses came into view. "For everything. You've made all the difference today."

"You done pay for de whole day, lady."

"I know," Sadie said. "And it's far less than you deserve, but I can make my own way now. I really do appreciate all you've done," she said sincerely, smiling at him. "You're a good man."

"No probl'm," he said, making Sadie think of Bob Marley. "I prob'ly stay in 'omestead and pick up work fo' de next few hours. If you need me, you give me a call, okay? You got my card?"

"Oh, sure," Sadie said. "But don't be staying in Homestead on account of me."

"No," he said, shaking his head. "I'm licensed with the county, an' it be good to get out of de city now an' again. I'll jus' let dispatch know where I be."

"Okay," Sadie said. "It's the second street up there, on the left." She pointed to emphasize her directions.

Monty nodded and a few seconds later turned onto 4th Avenue.

Sadie immediately sought out Layla's house and noticed an unfamiliar car parked out front, behind Sadie's rental. She told herself she didn't care and it didn't matter, but she was taking in details as fast as she could while Monty pulled into the driveway. The car was a newer model Acura, silver, with upgraded wheels and tinted windows. Not flashy, but definitely a nice ride. It was very much out of place in this neighborhood. Heck, Sadie's rented Kia was out of place in this neighborhood.

"You sho'?" Monty asked as she put her hand on the door handle.

"I'm sure. Thank you so much."

He nodded, and Sadie stepped out of the car, moving away so he had room to pull out. After waving to him one last time, she opened her purse to get her keys and saw the GPS unit she'd taken from Joe's car. She'd forgotten all about it.

Maybe I should . . .

No, her stronger, wiser self said. *You are not going to follow the coordinates. No way, no sir, no how.* Sadie let out a breath. Of course she wasn't going to. She was going to give the GPS unit to Mathews. Ugh. She was not looking forward to that meeting. Maybe now that he knew about Megan, he wouldn't be so mad at her when she told him she was the one who'd found her.

It took a few seconds to find her keys, and she was turning toward her car when she caught movement from across the street. Already suspicious of the Acura, her sleuthing reflexes took over, and she hurried to hide behind the garbage can placed at the edge of the carport. Then she crouched down, counting on the shadows to conceal her. Her Spidey-senses tingled. Something was afoot, and she was once again right on the edge of the action.

After taking a breath to fortify herself, she peeked around the garbage can, paying strict attention to every detail only to realize what she'd seen was the neighbor across the street settling himself back onto the blue couch, opening another soda—Dr. Pepper she thought. *Has he been there all day?* Sadie wondered as she stood up and smoothed her shirt, looking around to make sure no one had seen her little overreaction. That would be embarrassing.

Luckily, no one was around but the neighbor, and he wasn't looking her way. Her dignity would stay intact. She resumed her walk to the rental car, glancing at the neighbor and wondering how he could simply sit there all day. Sadie had a hard time sitting still long enough to watch *The Office* once a week. She and Pete used to watch it together, and the only reason she stayed on the couch and wasn't up doing something in the kitchen while she watched was so she could be close to him. Sadie wondered if Pete would catch next week's episode with Gayle. She really needed to call him back; she just worried about what she'd say.

Using the button on the key fob, she unlocked the car door and put her purse on the passenger seat. She was halfway in the car when she looked at the neighbor one last time and found herself frozen in place by one simple thought.

Had he been there all day?

CHAPTER 32

"Hi, I'm Sadie, a friend of Layla's," Sadie said less than a minute later as she came to a stop at the base of his wooden porch; it was badly in need of a new coat of paint. She'd left her purse in the car so she tucked her keys into the front pocket of her capris. It made an unsightly bulge, but she didn't think he would notice.

The dark, round face of Layla's neighbor looked at her. He'd watched her walk all the way across the street and up the gravel sidewalk with heavy eyes. He looked to be in his thirties, but it was hard for Sadie to tell for sure. He was wearing gray cutoff sweats and a blue T-shirt that stretched across his ample stomach, not quite concealing all of it. He didn't say anything, but Sadie didn't let that deter her. As she'd crossed the street she'd promised herself this was the last thing she was going to do before she went to Mathews, but it would be irresponsible to miss this opportunity. Five minutes, then she was done.

"And you are?" she asked, dipping her head.

He continued watching her, then took a swig from his drink. "Max," he said, resting the soda can on his thigh.

"Well, I'm glad to meet you, Max," Sadie said, folding her arms but keeping her shoulders slack so that she wouldn't give off the wrong vibe. Without her purse to hold, she didn't know what to do with her hands. "I couldn't help but notice you seem to spend a lot of time out here. Not that I can blame you—the weather is incredible. I'm from Colorado, you see, and while spring is pushing through, it's never anything like this." She took a moment to look around, validating her appreciation of the weather. She kept her thoughts about the humidity to herself.

He didn't respond, which, after a few seconds, made Sadie realize she hadn't asked a question. She was feeling awkward, which made her instinctively try to fill all the spaces with words. But it was rarely effective, so she held back.

"I'm sure the police have already talked to you," she said, "but I was wondering if you saw anyone here earlier today, after I left with Layla?"

"Lots of people been here today," he said simply.

"Yes," Sadie agreed. "I suppose that's true, but between us leaving in that little red car"—she pointed to her rental car—"and us coming back in the same car, did anyone else come to the house?" *And kick in the front door*, she almost added since that was the real question she was asking.

Max looked away from her and took another swig of his Dr. Pepper. He knew something, she could feel it.

"Did the police ask you about this already?" Sadie asked, wondering if they would have specifically told him not to talk to anyone else about it.

"Yep," he said, returning his drink to rest on his thigh once more and still not meeting her eyes.

"Did you see anyone?"

He turned the can in a circle on his leg, still avoiding her eyes.

That was suspicious, right? But he obviously wasn't about to answer her. At least not easily. He was in need of some motivation, and Sadie had just the thing.

"Max," Sadie asked, looking at the soda and remembering he'd been drinking one earlier in the day as well. "Have you eaten anything today?"

He made eye contact this time, and the momentary excitement in his eyes said everything. His size attested to the fact that he was more than meeting his recommended caloric intake, but was he really being *nourished?*

"Can I make you something to eat?" Sadie offered, smiling at him. "I can work with whatever you have inside or grab something from Layla's house, but you look like a man in need of a good home-made meal."

CHAPTER 33

Sadie had braced herself for a kitchen that reflected Max's personal hygiene and ambitious nature and was therefore stunned to find the inside of the house almost pristine. Even cleaner than Layla's house—and Layla's house was *clean.* The countertops were a cream-colored Formica, and although they were old and showed a few burn spots and knife marks, they were spotless and in good repair. The stainless steel sink was empty and practically sparkled it was so clean. The white painted cupboards gleamed in the sun coming through the windows that were topped with a bright floral valance.

"Are you married, Max?" Sadie asked as she came to a stop at the point where the light-green linoleum met up with the gray carpet of the living room. "I don't want to step on anyone's toes by using another woman's kitchen; us women can be a little territorial."

"I'm not married," Max said from behind her. Right behind her.

She felt herself tense at him being so close. Was it really such a good idea to be inside a house with a man twice her size when no one else knew she was here?

Another thought it would have been good to explore before

she'd acted on an impulse. Max moved away from her and pulled out a kitchen chair. Again, not new by any stretch, but clean and in good condition. The table, Formica top with chrome legs, was not much different than the table Sadie's parents had had in their house for many years. Max dropped himself into the chair and looked at her expectantly. Oh, right, lunch . . . or dinner . . . maybe linner.

Sadie entered the kitchen, pleased that she wasn't working amid squalor, and pulled open the door to the refrigerator. The bottom rack was filled with beer and more Dr. Pepper. The next rack up held butter, jam, and some yogurt containers. The top shelf was full of chocolate milk, SunnyD, and regular milk. The door was, of course, filled with condiments.

"How about a sandwich," Sadie said, pulling open the deli drawer and smiling to find bologna and that fake cheese stuff. Very unhealthy, but even Sadie could admit it tasted pretty good.

"Okay," he said.

Sadie grabbed mayo and mustard from the door before turning away from the fridge and kicking the door closed with her foot. "You should think about adding a few more vegetables to your next gro-cery list," she said, keeping her tone light in hopes he wouldn't be offended. "All I saw was cabbage and apples."

"I don't do the shopping," he said, watching her. He held his Dr. Pepper and took another sip.

"Well, who does?"

"Tia."

Sadie paused. "Tia?" she asked. The woman who made the deli-cious lunch at Layla's? "Does she help take care of Layla?"

"Yeah."

Sadie took another glance around the kitchen and wondered

how she could have not noticed the woman's touch that suddenly seemed to be everywhere. "She lives here?"

Max nodded. "She's my sister."

Oh, Sadie thought to herself. Things were making a bit more sense, which meant even more questions popped into Sadie's head. "Will she mind that I'm in her kitchen?"

In answer, Max just shrugged.

Sadie looked at the collected ingredients on the counter and didn't think it was fair to go back on her offer to make Max a meal just because he lived here with his sister.

Onward and upward. It was the best she could do.

She found some bread on the opposite counter and then turned back to the task at hand as she undid the twist-tie.

"So, Max," she said, hoping to ease into things by building a trusting relationship with this man who didn't seem inclined to be very helpful. Sadie wondered if he might be a little slow too, and lacking in social skills, but she had no way of knowing that for sure. "Did you grow up here in Homestead?"

"No."

"So, when did you move to Homestead, then?" she asked, laying two slices of bread on the counter and picking up a piece of the fake cheese.

"Been here six years," Max said.

He was going to be difficult to get information out of, she could tell.

"And what brought you here?"

"Layla."

Sadie looked up at that, her hands pausing in the process of unwrapping the plastic from the cheese slice. "Oh," she said in surprise. That wasn't what she'd expected him to say. "Layla?"

"Tia got a job to take care of her," Max said. "So we moved."

"I see," Sadie said, returning to her sandwich-making duties while they talked. "And how does their arrangement work? She gets paid to take care of Layla?"

"Yeah."

"And who pays her?"

"Larry."

"Oh," Sadie said for the second time. She was doing a lousy job of concealing her surprise at his answers, but she didn't think Max noticed or even cared. "Larry pays Tia to take care of Layla?" *And* he paid the expenses for Layla's house? Sadie had never heard of such a generous ex-husband. She felt the familiar threads of suspicion begin creeping their way into her mind. She'd told Eric that in order to get to the bottom of things, there had to be suspects. She may have just found one.

Max nodded and drank more Dr. Pepper.

"And do you work as well?" Sadie asked while opening the bologna package.

Max looked at the table and shook his head. "Hurt my back."

Sadie gave him a sympathetic smile. At least there was a reason he lounged around on his porch all day. Poor guy.

She laid the bologna on top of the cheese and lifted the jar of mayonnaise. "Mayo?"

"That's remoulade."

Hearing Max speak French took her by yet another surprise. He'd even pronounced it right: ray-moo-lahd. Impressive. She looked back at the jar, which said mayonnaise quite prominently. But as she looked closer, she could see that it had a bit of a pink tint with some spices mixed in. Did that mean it was homemade remoulade that had been put back into the mayonnaise jar?

Sadie couldn't help herself, the mere thought of homemade remoulade took hold. She opened the jar and took a finger swipe. She put it in her mouth and groaned out loud as the creamy spiced mixture filled her mouth with all the flavors the South was famous for. She closed her eyes to give the creation proper respect. After a few more moments, she opened her eyes to see Max watching her strangely. "It's delicious," she said, almost sighing. "Did Tia make this?"

Max nodded.

"It's amazing," she said. The flavor reminded her of something, but it took her a moment to make the connection. "Coleslaw!"

CHAPTER 34

"U h, what?" Max asked.

Sadie could barely contain her excitement as she went back to the fridge and pulled out the head of cabbage. *May Tia forgive me if I'm ruining her dinner plans.* Within thirty seconds, she'd found a chef's knife and a cutting board and was slicing through the head of cabbage.

"What are you doing?" Max asked.

Sadie glanced up at him before looking back at the cabbage. She was a fast chopper—top of her class in home-ec back in high school—and didn't want to accidentally cut off her finger. "See, I'm from Colorado," Sadie explained, using the knife to push the already sliced cabbage to the side so she could continue chopping. "And we don't have much Southern food there. But there's this little Cajun place in Fort Collins, and they have the most *amazing* coleslaw I've ever had in my life. It's spicy like this remoulade. And so I can't help but wonder if I combined the remoulade with the cabbage, if that might be how they make their coleslaw. I mean, it's a unique flavor so I assumed it was complicated and specific, but you guys use remoulade for lots of things down here, right?" She looked up long enough to see him nod before keeping her eyes on her fingers again. "Right, that's what I thought."

She shook her head and muttered under her breath, "Genius."

With the cabbage shredded, Sadie banged through a couple of cupboards before she found a bowl large enough to hold the cabbage. Then she found a big spoon and scooped some of the remoulade into the bowl before using that same spoon to toss the ingredients to-gether. She may have used too much sauce, which could have used a little thinning, but she kept stirring to coat the cabbage, and within a couple of minutes, she had what looked like the very coleslaw she'd been craving.

"Do you want some?" she asked Max as she pulled a couple of bowls out of the cupboard.

"Sure," he said, but he continued to watch her carefully, as though she might burst into flames at any moment. "Do I still get a sandwich?"

Oh, yes, the sandwich. That was why she'd come in here, wasn't it? "Of course," Sadie said, smiling as she scooped some coleslaw on a plate and took it to him with a fork. On her way back to the coun-ter, she turned around to face him. "Have you ever used remoulade on your sandwich in place of mayo?"

"That's how Tia always makes it."

Which explained why it was in the mayo jar in the first place. Sadie liked how this woman thought.

Before she dug into her own bowl of slaw, she finished making his sandwich. Tomatoes and lettuce, and maybe a few caramelized onions, would have made it nearly perfect, but she'd done the best she could. She took the plate to Max and then returned to her food.

"Mmm," she heard herself say as she took the first bite. This was it—Cajun coleslaw: cabbage and remoulade. She'd figured it out! In her mind a heavenly choir began singing.

She just loved food.

"Do you like it?" Sadie asked as she dished herself up another bowl a minute later.

"It's good," Max said. He was alternating between bites of the sandwich and bites of the coleslaw. Sadie figured he probably wasn't the type to gush over the discovery of a recipe so she just smiled and took his compliment as simply that, a compliment.

It wasn't until Sadie was nearing the bottom of her second bowl that she remembered that Cajun coleslaw wasn't her reason for having come over here. As soon as she remembered that, everything else came flooding back: Mathews, Megan, Eric. Food was so distracting sometimes. She busied herself with cleaning up the mess she'd made, even reluctantly putting plastic wrap over the Cajun coleslaw and returning it to the fridge. She wished she could take it with her.

"So," she said as she wiped down the counters, invigorated by her success. "We were talking about what you saw this morning after Layla and I left. Have you had some time to think about that?"

Max stared into his coleslaw bowl while Sadie patiently waited for him to answer. After nearly a full minute, she worried he wasn't going to answer at all. If food hadn't done it, what would help him open up?

A few seconds later, Max stood and carried his dishes to the sink. "Thank you for the sandwich," he said, then opened the fridge for another can of Dr. Pepper and headed out of the kitchen.

Sadie let out a huff as the screen door slammed. She was losing her touch if someone like Max—nice enough, but not necessarily sophisticated—didn't give her what she wanted. She rinsed the dishes, left them in the sink, and then headed toward the front door, wondering if maybe cold, hard cash would make a difference.

On her way to the porch, she glanced around the small living room again, giving it more attention than she had on her way in. There were two recliners facing the TV and a small table between them. Sadie moved toward the table and picked up a silver paperweight in the shape of a three-dimensional star. As she expected, it was heavy for its size, and as Sadie turned it in her hand, she read the words engraved on the front: "Thank you for being one of our service stars." Beneath it in smaller letters were the words, "Lighthouse Rescue Mission." *What a nice gift*, Sadie thought, putting it back.

As she turned toward the door, she saw a frame on the wall between the door and the window. There were several cutouts in the matte board, allowing more than one photo to be displayed within a single frame. She took a few steps closer and looked for a picture of who must be Tia. She found one of a large woman who had a round face like Max and a smile so big and so proud that Sadie couldn't help but smile back. She was standing next to two boys in wheelchairs, each of them holding up a medal. The next photo was a younger, thinner Max in high school graduation regalia. He wasn't smiling, but he looked pleased all the same. There was a picture of Tia hugging an elderly woman, and then Sadie's eyes stopped on a photo of Tia, Max, Layla, and a teenaged Megan.

Tia stood between Max and Megan, her arms thrown around their shoulders. Layla stood a little apart from the other three, looking like a deer in the headlights, her expression flat, her eyes staring straight ahead. Everyone was looking at the camera, except Megan who, instead, had turned her head to smile at her mother. Sadie looked between mother and daughter. What had their relationship been like? If Sadie could base her judgment solely on this photo, she would have said that Megan was completely comfortable with Layla, perhaps even trying to encourage her to smile for the picture. It was very sweet.

Sadie took a closer look at Tia, ticking off the details she knew about the woman. Tia was good cook, a caretaker for both Max and Layla, and, by the looks of the photos and the thank-you paper-weight, an avid volunteer. Good for her.

Sadie took another look at the picture with Megan in it and wondered if Eric had ever seen it. Then her stomach flipped; by now he was with his daughter. It was surreal to think about, and she hoped that, despite the things she'd learned from Joe, their reunion would be a happy one. She wondered if it was too soon to call Eric and ask for a report.

She put her hand out to push open the screen door and looked across the street at Layla's house. There was a perfect line of sight from where she stood to Layla's front door, obstructed only by Sadie's car parked on the street. Sadie could see into Layla's front door and thought she could see someone coming toward the door. Thinking it might be the owner of the silver Acura, she paused and took a step back from the door in the hopes of simply putting her curiosity to rest. The afternoon sun was moving behind the house, casting Max's front porch in shadow, which she hoped would conceal her.

A moment later Layla's screen door opened, but it wasn't Layla who exited. Instead, Larry headed down the steps, his right hand holding his phone to his ear. Hadn't he said he had to work? He was quite animated in his conversation, and Sadie watched as he went to the Acura, pulled keys out of his pocket and pushed the button that unlocked the car. But he didn't open the driver's side door. Instead, he popped the trunk and, a few seconds later, pulled out a cardboard box big enough to hold reams of paper. It even had the Staples logo on the side. He lifted it with only one arm, which meant it couldn't be full of paper—paper was too heavy.

Larry didn't head back to Layla's house. Instead he shot a cursory glance in both directions and took long strides across the street while still talking on the phone.

He was coming to Max and Tia's house.

Sadie looked around wildly for somewhere to hide, but the living room furniture was basic and sparse. She did the only thing she could think to do and jumped to the side of the door, pressing her back against the wall just to the side of it and trying not to knock the picture frame to the floor.

It was a good position for Sadie to have chosen because, as Larry got closer, she could hear his end of the phone conversation. Not that it did her any good; he was speaking Spanish. She picked up a few words though—*tomorrow* and *iron* . . . or was it *mistake?* They were very similar in Spanish. Sadie's breathing became more and more shallow the closer Larry came to the house, and she realized that while her position supported eavesdropping quite well, it wasn't at all optimal should he decide to come inside.

She heard a few hurried words in Spanish, and then Larry said, "Hey Max, how'd things go?"

"Fine," Max said with all the luster he'd used when he'd spoken to Sadie.

"Good."

Sadie listened to the sound of shuffling paper—money maybe?

"Here you go," Larry said. "Did the police ask you about having a key?"

"Yeah," Max said simply. "I said I did, and they went away."

Key? Sadie nearly gasped out loud. Had Max broken into Layla's house and burned the box? If he had a key, the police wouldn't suspect he'd break in. And Larry put him up to it?

Larry interrupted her thoughts. "Tia's going to take care of this for me," he said. Was he talking about the paper box he'd brought from the car? "Can I put them inside?"

Sadie's heart froze, and she found herself looking around the room again just in case a good hiding place had become available in the last twenty seconds. There were no curtains to hide behind, no large furniture other than an entertainment center, but it was pushed up against the wall. She looked longingly across the doorway at the space behind the front door. If only she'd thought to hide there, she might have had a chance. She heard the screen door creak open and inched herself to the side, pressing against the wall even more while clenching her eyes shut and preparing for a very awkward conversation.

"You can leave that out here," Max said.

Sadie's eyes shot open. She looked at the shoe-clad foot poised on the threshold.

"You sure?" Larry said. "I don't mind taking it into the office."

"I'll take it," Max said.

Oh, bless you, Max, Sadie thought, but she still didn't breathe.

"Well, all right then," Larry said, letting the door shut. Sadie heard him put something down on the porch. "Tell Tia I'll call her later. Thanks."

Max didn't reply, but Larry's voice immediately picked up in Spanish again—had he not ended his phone call from before? Sadie could hear him getting farther away.

Sadie stayed pressed against the wall until she heard the car engine start and then fade away. Only then did she turn and push open the door a few inches. "Thank you, Max," she whispered.

He took a sip of his soda while he stared at Layla's house. He didn't say anything.

"Why'd you do it?"

"He said he was leaving."

Sadie pulled her eyebrows together. "Larry said he was leaving?" she repeated. She hadn't heard him say that—he'd just left.

"He said if I'd get rid of the big box, he'd leave."

"You mean he'd leave Homestead?"

"Leave Layla."

Cajun Coleslaw

2 teaspoons sugar
1 cup remoulade
1 (14-ounce) bag coleslaw blend (or equal amounts of green and
  purple cabbage, sliced thin)

Mix sugar and remoulade. Add coleslaw mix and stir until cabbage is well-coated. Refrigerate until serving.

Remoulade

2 cups mayonnaise
3 tablespoons ketchup
2 tablespoons Creole, Cajun, or deli-style mustard (not yellow)
1 tablespoon fresh parsley, chopped
1 tablespoon lemon juice, freshly squeezed
2 teaspoons prepared horseradish
2 garlic cloves, chopped
1 teaspoon Worcestershire sauce
1 teaspoon celery salt

1 teaspoon paprika
1 teaspoon cayenne pepper

Mix all ingredients together, adjusting spices according to taste. Refrigerate overnight so that flavors have a chance to blend.

Makes about 2½ cups.

*Tastes great in place of mayo on sandwiches and in deviled eggs.

CHAPTER 35

Sadie glanced at Layla's house. She could hear the faintest sound of applause coming through the open screen door. Then she looked back at Max, making the connection. "You like Layla?" Sadie asked, wondering how it was that a woman with a brain injury could still be so appealing to so many men. But as she looked at Max, she thought maybe she did understand. Layla was simple. Max was too, and probably lonely. Was it better to sit next to someone than to sit alone?

Max didn't answer the question, but she noticed him blush, and she suppressed a smile. In Garrison, Judy Bellows and Stan Highland, both of whom were mentally disabled, had gotten married about ten years ago. They lived in Judy's mother's basement and walked two miles together every day. Judy was almost sixty, and Stan was thirty-six. They always went to Bingo on Saturday nights, and it was impossible to see them together without feeling that while perhaps not traditional, their relationship worked.

"Did you burn the box I brought to Eric?" Sadie restated, wanting to make sure she understood what had happened.

He didn't answer, but she noticed that he'd started tapping his foot.

"I'm not mad that you did it," Sadie said, keeping her voice neutral. "Did Larry tell you to burn the box?"

After a few seconds, he nodded.

Interesting. "Why?"

"I dunno," Max said. "He said he might get in trouble if I didn't."

"And he paid you to do it?"

Max shrugged, but Sadie could see the slight outline in his T-shirt pocket of what looked like it could be folded bills. Sadie wondered how much burning the box had been worth to Larry. But whatever he had wanted hidden was gone. She hated that he'd succeeded.

She looked at the Staples box by the door. "What's in there?" she asked, nodding toward it.

"Deliveries," Max said. He actually engaged enough in the conversation to look at the box. "For Tia."

"Would you like me to take it into the office so you don't have to get up?" It was a subtle way to push for how much he might offer, but Sadie didn't know if he would catch it.

He shrugged, and Sadie stepped farther onto the porch so she could pick up the box.

The first door on the right in the hallway was definitely Tia's room—it was floral and tidy. The bedroom on the left had to belong to Max—a queen bed topped with rumpled sheets. She pushed open the third door and scanned the home office, taking in the plastic table that served as a desk, a couple of filing cabinets, and a bookshelf. A certificate of appreciation from the Salvation Army hung on the wall with the name "Tia Gerald" written in as the recipient.

And there were a few more photos of Tia posing with people holding medals. Special Olympics?

She pulled her attention away from the photos and scanned the room to see if anything stood out, but quickly realized the box she was holding was the main topic of her interest. She hurried to the desk and set the box down, then pulled off the lid. Inside were several letter-sized manila envelopes. At least eight. Max had said they were deliveries. But deliveries of what? She picked up an envelope and turned it over so that the metal brad was facing her. The envelope wasn't sealed, and she pinched the metal prongs together and opened the flap.

Inside, she could see two sheets of paper, one letter-sized and one smaller. She dumped the envelope upside down on the desk, then turned the papers over. The larger one was a birth certificate from Louisiana for someone named Sonia Maria Hernandez, and the other was a social security card for the same name.

Sadie replaced the papers and opened the next envelope. It held the same kinds of documents, but for a Reynaldo Miguel Hernandez. The third envelope had documents for another person, including a driver's license. The fourth envelope was similar—birth certificate, social security card, driver's license—but the state of issue was Colorado.

Sadie stared at the papers for several seconds. She was very familiar with Colorado's documentation, and if not for the fact that she was looking in a box full of various identifications from various states, she would assume these were legitimate. However, she could not think of one legitimate reason why Larry would be bringing a box full of this stuff to Tia.

She was replacing the envelopes when she heard a car engine. Leaning forward, she could see through a space in the partially closed slats of the mini-blinds as a green sedan pulled into the gravelly driveway of the house. The sun reflected off the windshield so that Sadie couldn't see who was inside, but she could only guess it was Tia.

Moving fast, she put the lid on the box and hurried out of the office, pulling the door shut as quietly as possible before heading for the front door. Realizing she wasn't going to make it outside in time, and being extremely curious about this woman, Sadie went left toward the kitchen instead of right toward the front door.

She heard a woman talking to Max on the front porch and took a deep breath. She needed to be peppy and act as though her being here was completely reasonable. The hinges on the screen door creaked, and she turned on the water in the sink, rinsing dishes she'd already rinsed just to have something to keep her busy, as well as to let the running water warn Tia that someone was in her kitchen, giving her time to prepare. Not watching the entryway, Sadie picked up the washcloth, ran it under the water, and then rung it out. When she turned as if to wipe the counter, she found the woman from the photographs standing by the table, looking at her.

"Who are you?" the woman asked, putting her purse on the table and a hand on her hip. The other hand held two white plastic grocery bags. The woman's dark hair, slightly gray at the temples, was pulled into a knot at the back of her head. She was dressed in light blue scrubs and a lanyard around her neck held some kind of ID badge. "And what are you doing here?" Her face was tight, her eyes narrowed, and her tone not the least bit inviting.

Sadie forced her smile to stay despite being thoroughly intimidated. She'd hoped Tia was sweet, soft, and meek.

"Oh, hi," she said, putting the rag in the sink and drying her hands on a dishtowel. "I'm Sadie, a friend of Layla's." She reached her hand across the counter that separated them. Tia looked at it, and then looked back at Sadie expectantly, seeming to let her gaze linger on Sadie's hair, which likely looked as though it was coated in paste by now. Tia didn't wear any makeup and probably didn't know what an eyebrow wax was, but was quite pretty in an understated way.

"You're no friend of Layla's," Tia said darkly, still staring Sadie down as Sadie lowered her hand, giving up on the handshake. "I ain't never seen you before."

"Well, I guess I'm more of a friend of Eric's," Sadie said. "You know Eric, right?"

By the further tightening of Tia's expression, Sadie suspected that Tia *did* know Eric, and wasn't necessarily a fan. "What are you doing in my home?"

"I made Max a sandwich," Sadie said in her most confident tone, as though it was perfectly normal for a complete stranger to make Max a sandwich. "And I made some coleslaw with your remoulade." She paused and clicked her tongue. "It was amazing. Would you like me to get you some?"

"No, I would not like you to get me some," she said, putting the bags of groceries on the table next to her purse and crossing her arms over her chest, which made her seem even more imposing. Lucky for Sadie, Tia was rather short—not more than five feet, which meant Sadie at least had the advantage of being the taller of the two. "What are you doing making Max a sandwich?"

"Just trying to be a good neighbor," Sadie said, feeling a tremor in her voice. Being taller than Tia wasn't giving her the confidence she'd hoped it would. "I came over to . . . introduce myself. When I asked if Max would like a sandwich, he said I could come in. I didn't mean to upset you . . . Tia, isn't it? You keep a lovely home."

Tia continued to glare, but Sadie kept the smile up and reminded herself that she'd charmed people even pricklier than this woman before. Hadn't she?

"I had some of that pasta salad and the chicken you made," Sadie said, grasping at anything to release some of the tension and hoping that food could build a bridge. "They were both wonderful."

"At Layla's?" Tia asked.

Did Sadie note the smallest softening in her tone or was she looking too hard?

CHAPTER 36

Y es," Sadie said, nodding her head and feeling her nervous habit of talking too much taking over. "We were at the police station during lunch, and she was getting really antsy. It was so nice to come home and have it all right there, ready to eat. You take excellent care of her and, I have to admit, one of the reasons I came over to talk to Max was to meet you and ask you for those recipes. Have you ever tried the salad with mangoes?"

Again, Tia was silent for a few moments, and Sadie's mind started moving a million miles an hour, trying to think of what to say next while at the same time forcing herself to keep her mouth closed so she didn't keep rambling and making a crazy fool of herself.

"I think the oranges would overwhelm the subtlety of the mangoes," Tia finally said. "But I suppose it's worth a try."

Sadie exhaled. She'd found an in. "You might be right," she said, nodding thoughtfully even though she still thought mangoes would be a nice touch.

When Tia didn't offer anything else to the conversation, Sadie couldn't help but fill the silent spaces. "I have this recipe book at home. I call it my little black book, but it's not what you think." She laughed and could feel that her nerves were still in control. "It's for recipes—my favorites, ya know—and I would love to add both the chicken and the pasta salad to it when I get home. They were really, really good."

Tia continued to glare at her for a few seconds before she spoke. "It weren't nothin' fancy," Tia said, but her tone was improving, and she unfolded her arms. Sadie could feel the change in the air and patted herself on the back for taming this particular lion.

"I'm not a fancy cook," Sadie said, looking around for her purse in order to get her notebook out of it before realizing she'd left her purse in the car. Sadie had seen a couple legal pads in the office but wasn't about to admit she'd been in there. "But I love good food, and I thought the fruit with pasta was wonderful, and the peas added just the right crunch."

Sadie sincerely hoped that Tia wasn't one of those women who didn't share her recipes—that was just uncharitable in Sadie's mind—so she continued to smile and watch the battle playing out on Tia's face. She was still suspect of Sadie, but couldn't find anything to prove Sadie was any kind of threat.

Finally, after what seemed like forever, Tia moved to the computer desk against the wall by the back door. "I think I have some paper in here," she said, pulling open the drawer. Sadie smiled even wider. Once again, Sadie's theory had been proven correct: Food was the universal common ground.

"Oh, and while you're at it, can I get your remoulade recipe, too? It was delicious."

Tia nodded, though she looked a little unsure. Still, she wasn't able to withstand the flattery, and, if nothing else, Sadie was going to get the recipes, which made her very happy. Now to get something else equally important—information about Larry, assuming she could find a way to get it without triggering Tia's defenses more than she already had. Hopefully their common interest in good food would build a bridge strong enough to support additional topics.

"So," Sadie said, as Tia found a notebook and then came to the counter to get a pen out of a mason jar near the phone. "Where do you work? Other than taking care of Max and Layla."

"Crestview," Tia said, making a swirly line on the top of the paper to make sure the pen worked. It did. "It's a nursing home."

Another caretaking job. "Are you a nurse?"

Tia shook her head but didn't look up. She had bubbly handwriting, like a young girl, and Sadie took it as one more sign that underneath it all Tia was a kind person, never mind her gruff exterior and probably illegal activities. "I'm a recreational aide," Tia said. "Just part-time, ya know. I need to be around for Max and Layla as much as possible."

"Of course," Sadie said. "You help with the activities for the residents at Crestview?"

Tia looked up briefly and nodded.

"That's wonderful," Sadie said. "I sometimes volunteer at a nursing home in my town. The ladies like having their fingernails painted now and again."

"They do love that," Tia said, and Sadie saw the slightest smile on her face. Progress. She continued to make small talk as Tia wrote, asking many of the same questions she'd asked Max and getting the same answers as to how long they'd lived in Homestead and what Tia did for Layla. Tia obviously took both pride and satisfaction from caring for other people, something Sadie could relate to.

Max had called the envelopes in the box "deliveries," and Sadie wondered if Tia's role in whatever was going on was based on the responsibilities Tia felt toward these other people in her life.

Recreational aides didn't make a lot of money, especially working part-time. Were the documents extra income? In Sadie's mind it was a stretch to justify the illegal behavior as means of caring for the disabled people in Tia's life, but then Sadie had never needed to consider such things. Neil had left her well cared for when he died, and she was industrious by nature.

"You take care of everyone, it seems," Sadie said. "Max, Layla, your residents. And I saw those pictures by the door—was that one photo of the boys holding up their medals taken at the Special Olympics?"

Tia nodded, her countenance brightening considerably. "Paralympics, for people in wheelchairs. Them boys made it to regional that year."

"Congratulations," Sadie said. "It's sure a blessing to serve, isn't it?"

Tia nodded and offered her second small smile of the conversation. "It does my heart good to help people, ya know. Helps me forget about my own problems and feel like I'm making a positive difference."

"I completely understand," Sadie said, though her thoughts were still on the box full of what she could only assume were forged documents. That wasn't making much of a positive difference.

Tia looked over what she'd written, added one more sentence, and then ripped off the paper, handing it to Sadie, who nearly giggled with excitement as she held the paper with both hands. Even though most recipes didn't make it into the book until she'd made them several times, she couldn't imagine that these would be difficult to replicate—they were pretty straightforward.

"Thank you so much," Sadie gushed, reading over what Tia had written down. "I can't wait to make these myself." She looked up and made eye contact. "You've made my day." Granted, after the day Sadie had had that wasn't hard to do.

They fell into silence, and Sadie sensed the need to make a transition. What could she say that would be of enough value to Tia that she wouldn't notice Sadie was seeking information? She decided to jump in with both feet and simply see how Tia reacted. "Did you hear about Megan?"

Tia had been putting the notebook back in the desk drawer, but turned quickly, her eyes wide. "What about her?" she asked.

Sadie noted the anxiety in Tia's spontaneous reaction. "The body they found wasn't her," she said.

Tia almost looked disappointed. "Oh, I knew that. Larry told me."

Aha, she'd opened the door to a conversation about Larry. "I guess you work pretty closely with Larry, huh—what with Layla and all?"

Tia nodded, but she didn't meet Sadie's eyes. Tia was clearly uncomfortable talking about him.

Tia opened one of the grocery bags she'd brought in and began unpacking the food. She pulled out a container of sour cream and a block of cheese, then made her way to the fridge. After she opened the door, she picked up the bowl of coleslaw and looked at it in confusion.

"The Cajun coleslaw I told you about," Sadie said. "It's really good."

Tia looked at her doubtfully, but put the bowl on the counter before returning to the fridge again. Sadie hoped she'd like it. Tia took eggs out of the fridge and set them on the counter before returning to the grocery bags and pulling out a mango from a produce bag.

"What's that for?" Sadie asked automatically, watching intently.

Tia had already proven herself a good cook, and the prospect of getting another of her delicious recipes was clouding Sadie's objectives.

"Mango corn bread," Tia said.

"Mango corn bread?" Sadie repeated, a little bit breathless. "That sounds wonderful. Are you making it right now?" She watched Tia pull a box of corn bread mix from one of the grocery sacks and felt a twinge of disappointment. Maybe she and Tia didn't have so much in common. "From a mix?"

"My friend Lizz came up with it," Tia explained. "It's easy and fast and a real crowd pleaser. We've got a fund-raiser planning meeting over at the Boys and Girls Club tonight."

Sadie watched every move Tia made, committing it to memory. After putting the mix in a bowl, Tia peeled one of the mangoes with a paring knife, letting the peel trail off in one long strip.

"Do you mind if I watch?" Sadie asked, realizing that would fulfill both of her interests: extend her time with Tia and learn the recipe for mango corn bread.

"Fine with me," Tia said, and Sadie was glad that she seemed flattered rather than annoyed by Sadie's interest. After the mango was peeled, Tia sliced the fruit while it was still clinging to the pit by making vertical cuts from the top of the mango to the bottom. Sadie usually cut the fruit off pit first, which was always such a pain.

Sadie glanced at the clock on the stove. It was 5:20. She felt okay about not calling Eric since he was having a reunion with Megan. In the next moment she realized that while she'd told Tia the body wasn't Megan, she hadn't said anything about having actually found the real Megan. Sheesh, how did she forget that?

"About Megan," Sadie said, deciding to get more information before she dropped the bombshell. "You knew her?"

"Of course I knew her," Tia said, still slicing. "She came down to see her mama every chance she got."

"That's sweet," Sadie said, remembering Eric's explanation of Megan's relationship with her mother. He'd talked about making a distance between Megan and Layla, but then Sadie thought about the picture she'd seen in the living room. The look on Megan's face didn't reflect *distance*. "Did she come down a lot, then?"

"Until she went away to school, yes," Tia said. "Once or twice a month, even if it meant taking the bus down if Eric"—she said his name with a twist of her mouth—"was busy with other things."

"And what was it like when she came down? What did she and Layla do together?" Eric had said Layla was volatile and kept Megan at a distance. Had things gotten better as Megan had grown older? Sadie wondered.

Tia started cutting horizontally across the vertical cuts in the mango, creating a grid pattern. "Megan would do some of the cleaning, laundry, and then she and Layla would watch TV together." She glanced at Sadie. "Their relationship was different," she said, making a point, "but they loved each other."

But Eric had said Layla couldn't feel things like love. "It must have been hard for Megan, though, to deal with Layla's problems."

Tia nodded and started cutting the fruit away from the pit. Chunks of mango fell into the bowl, perfectly diced. Brilliant! "She loved her mama every way Layla would let her. Sure, Megan had her hard times, but I was real proud of the way she handled everything. Not everyone would be able to do what she did for as long as she did it."

"As long as she did it?" Sadie repeated. "What do you mean?"

Tia looked up, startled as she seemed to review what she'd just said. She looked away quickly. "School, of course," she said, talking too fast for Sadie to take it at face value. "It was real far away."

Sadie nodded, trying to make everything she'd learned line up in a way that made sense. "That night she disappeared—wouldn't she have driven right past Homestead on her way to Key West for spring break? Did she stop in for a visit?"

"She was with a friend," Tia said, but her hands were moving faster, and she wasn't meeting Sadie's eyes. Did that mean Megan *had* stopped by? Eric hadn't said anything about that, and Sadie didn't imagine Tia would be lying about it now if the police had been told. "You could never be quite sure how Layla would react so Megan would have never brought a stranger by to meet her."

Yet Tia had said Megan came to see her mom every chance she got.

"You best be goin'," Tia said, grabbing some oil out of the cupboard. "I've got to get Max fed and make myself presentable for the meeting."

There was only one thing Sadie could think of saying that might prolong this visit.

"I found Megan."

Tia spun around so fast that she nearly dropped the oil she'd been pouring into the bowl. As it was, she spilled some of it on her scrubs, but didn't seem to notice. "What did you say?" she demanded.

"I found Megan," Sadie repeated, surprised by the reaction but trying not to show it. "In a hospital in Miami."

"A hospital?" Tia said. She put a hand to her chest. "She hurt?"

Sadie shook her head. "No. She's pregnant and—"

"Pregnant?" Tia cut Sadie off. She inhaled sharply. "She's having a baby?"

"Twins, actually," Sadie said. "But she's having some trouble.

She's scheduled for a surgery in the morning and then will be in the hospital for several weeks until the babies are born."

Tia closed her eyes and muttered a prayer under her breath, then looked around as though unsure what to do.

"Her dad's with her now," Sadie said, hoping to relieve Tia's obvious concern. "She's okay."

That information didn't seem to make Tia feel any better. She put the oil back on the counter. "I need to call Larry."

"I'm sure he knows already," Sadie said. "I'm sure Eric told him."

Tia didn't respond. She hurried for her purse and pulled out her phone. She pushed a single number and then the talk button before putting it to her ear.

"Larry," she said moments later, with Sadie looking on, "is Megan really in the hospital?" She paused for a moment. "This lady was here with Max. She told me . . . I don't know." She looked up at Sadie and then switched to Spanish, turning away from Sadie as she continued the discussion.

If only Sadie had paid more attention in her high-school Spanish class. As the conversation increased in volume and speed, Sadie watched Tia's body language—her anxiety was growing. Sadie considered all the reasons why Tia would be so intense about this discovery. After a full minute, Tia turned to look at Sadie and began to calm down, but it seemed unnatural, forced. Was she being told to relax? The only reason Sadie could think of as to why Larry would be telling her to calm down was because Tia's reaction gave something away. He was a smart guy.

Sadie was careful to keep her own thoughts and emotions contained, but she could feel her mind speeding up, looking for connections between the bits and pieces she'd been learning all along the way. A little from Mathews, a little from Eric, Joe, Max, and now Tia.

Tia nodded, said something else, and then hung up.

"I'm just so surprised," Tia said. It was all Sadie could do not to roll her eyes at the attempt Tia was making to sound causal. Sadie kept her expression carefully guarded as Tia continued. "I mean, after all these years?" She tried to chuckle, but it sounded more like a cough. "It's just amazing."

"I bet Larry's excited too," Sadie said. "I understand he and Megan were very close."

Tia looked down. "Larry loves that little girl like his own daughter," she said, almost under her breath.

Sadie couldn't help but wonder if Tia was somehow putting Eric down with that statement.

"I'm sure he does," she said out loud. "Well, I'd better go," she said. Tia was on guard now, and staying would likely do her little good. "Thank you again for the recipes," she said. "I really appreciate it."

"Of course," Tia said. "It was . . . nice to meet you."

"You too," Sadie said. She headed for the front door. "Bye, Max," she said, glancing at him quickly as she strode to her car.

Larry and Tia were involved in illegal documents.

A driver's license with Megan's picture but a different name had been found with the body.

Reunion or no reunion, Sadie needed to talk to Eric.

Lizzy's Mango Corn Bread

2 cups flour
2 cups cornmeal
2 tablespoons baking powder
1 teaspoon salt
½ teaspoon cinnamon
¼ teaspoon nutmeg
1 cup butter
½ cup sugar
4 eggs
2 cups milk
1 mango, chopped
1 tablespoon sugar

Preheat oven to 350 degrees. Combine dry ingredients and set aside. Cream butter and sugar. Add eggs and milk. Add in dry ingredients, stir until just mixed. Add mango. Stir to combine. Pour batter into a greased 9x13-inch pan. Bake 35 to 45 minutes or until toothpick inserted into the center comes out clean. When bread is done baking, sprinkle top with sugar. Serve with softened butter.

Makes 12 servings.

Note: Can use a corn bread mix. Follow package instructions to prepare batter, then add cinnamon, nutmeg, and mango. Mix according to recipe.

CHAPTER 37

Certain that Tia was watching her, Sadie got in her car and drove around the block before pulling over in front of an elementary school. She was reaching for her phone to call Eric when it rang. She picked it up, then bit her lip as Pete's face looked back at her from her phone, reminding her she hadn't returned his last call. And she couldn't answer this one either. Not yet. She felt horrible letting it go to voice mail, and she promised—cross her heart and hope to die—that she'd call him as soon as she possibly could.

A quick scroll through her recent calls showed that Gayle had called while she'd been at Max and Tia's as well. After she talked to Pete, which would be after she talked to Eric, she would call Gayle back too.

Without hesitating any longer, she called Eric, organizing her thoughts so that she could tell him what she'd learned in the most concise way possible. It wasn't until the third ring that she considered he might not answer at all.

Eric's voice mail kicked in. *No!*

"You've reached Burton Locks. Please leave a message, and I'll get back to you as soon as possible. Thanks."

"This is Sadie. I know this isn't great timing, but I need to talk to you about . . . well, anyway, call me as soon as you get this message."

She clicked off the phone and let her head fall back against the seat. Now what?

She could go to Mathews, but what if she was wrong about Larry? She kept picturing him at the police station, the way he'd been so solicitous to Layla, the sincere concern he had for her welfare. He'd married Layla in order to take care of her.

What if there was a reasonable explanation for the documents? What if he somehow didn't know what was in the Staples box?

If she didn't go to Mathews, however, was she just going to sit and wait for Eric to call back? Idling away time had never been her forte, especially when there were things that needed to be done.

She looked at her phone lying on the passenger seat. She had promised herself to call Pete and she suddenly had time to do it. Was she ready to try explaining what she was doing, and why she had come to Florida? The idea made her both queasy and . . . eager. For whatever reason, she wanted to hear Pete's voice, wanted to take comfort in knowing that, even if he was angry, he was also genuinely concerned for her as well. Even after all that had happened between them the last couple of days, she knew he still cared about her. He must be really worried that she hadn't answered any of his calls.

She took a breath, gathered her confidence, and dialed his number, which was still on speed dial, hoping that this was a good decision.

"Sadie," Pete said after only one ring. "I'm glad you called."

His voice caused a confusing reaction of warmth to spread throughout Sadie's body. Knowing he was going to be disappointed in what she'd done, however, made her take his reaction with a grain of salt, but it also urged her to not beat around the bush.

"You might not be so glad in a minute," Sadie said, determined to be fair to him.

Pete was silent for a minute. "You're up to your neck in this, aren't you?"

"I might be a little further in than that," Sadie said. It was a lame attempt at a joke.

"I just got off the phone with Sergeant Mathews again. He said you told him you'd come in, but he hadn't seen you yet. I worried that something had happened." He wasn't going to ask her about going to Florida? Make her tell him what she'd been doing? In fact he seemed up-to-date and rather—could it be possible?—accepting.

When she didn't answer, he spoke again. "Are you okay, Sadie?"

More warmth flooded her and . . . homesickness? "I'm okay," she said. "Just . . . involved. More than I should be."

Pete's laugh took her off guard, and she pulled her eyebrows together. "Are you laughing at me?"

"No," Pete said, but there was a smile in his voice. "It's just that you think you should be involved in everything, so it's funny to hear you admit that you shouldn't."

Sadie was almost offended, but Pete was right. She really was a busybody, wasn't she?

"*Are* you okay?" Pete asked again before Sadie could think of what else to say. "Are you safe?"

"I'm safe," Sadie said. "And I am going to go to Mathews. I just have to do one more thing first. I'm sorry I didn't call back sooner— it's been . . . crazy, but I don't want you to worry. I really am okay."

Pete was silent, and Sadie prepped herself for a reprimand. Instead he said, "How can I help?"

"What?"

"I know I could try to talk you out of it, tell you to go straight to the police, but I realize that your faith in the police isn't the same as mine, and you won't do it until you feel like you've done everything you can anyway. So, if I can help you get to the bottom of whatever you're looking into, I can speed things up a great deal, right?"

"Ri-ght," Sadie said cautiously. Was he teasing her?

"So, what can I do to help? I already vouched for you with Mathews, convincing him that, while you might be overly involved, you want justice and truth as much as he does. I think it bought you a little more time. What else do you need?"

Really? It's not that she doubted him—Pete had always dealt with her honestly—but it was so far beyond what she'd expected of him. "Won't you get in trouble for helping me?"

"I have some wiggle room," Pete said. "But only for a few minutes. I've got a department meeting in a half hour."

Sadie's dashboard clock said it was five-thirty—a little late for a meeting. Oh, wait, Pete was in a different time zone. "Are you at the station, then?" Sadie asked, ignoring her hesitations. She trusted him. If he was offering to help, he meant it.

"I'm at the station," he confirmed.

"Do you think you could look up a name for me on that fancy database?"

"I can do that," Pete said. "I might not be able to tell you everything I bring up though. Not unless it's public record."

"That's fine," Sadie said, actually feeling better about him setting limitations. Despite the wiggle room he claimed to have, Sadie doubted helping her would be smiled on by his superiors, and she didn't want to get him in trouble. She could hear the clicking of a keyboard in the background.

"Okay," Pete said. "I'm logged in. Who are we looking for?"

"Lawrence McCallister. Originally from Gainesville, currently living in Homestead, Florida."

More tapping. Then a pause. "Okay," Pete said. "What do you want to know about him?"

"Does he have a criminal record?" Sadie asked.

"Nope."

"Really?"

"You sound disappointed," Pete commented. "Was there something you hoped he'd done?"

"Well, no," Sadie said, deciding not to hide anything from Pete. "It's just that he had a box of documents, and I thought maybe he'd have some kind of history that would make sense of that."

"What kind of documents?"

"Birth certificates, social security cards, driver's licenses," Sadie said. "For several different people."

"Really," Pete said. "There's nothing on his record, and he has an extensive file here. Looks like he used to work for the state."

"Oh?" Sadie said, remembering that Eric had said something about Larry being employed by the state and therefore having good health insurance for Layla. But she didn't know why that was important to Pete.

Pete continued, "Yeah, it looks like he worked in vital records for Miami-Dade county."

Sadie sat up a little straighter. "That's the department that maintains . . . documents, right?"

"Right," Pete said, following Sadie's thoughts. "They're pretty careful about who they employ there for the very reason of how tempting it can be to do a little moonlighting, if you know what I mean." He paused. "You realize that my knowing Mr. McCallister might be brokering identities means I have to turn that information over to Sergeant Mathews."

"Of course," Sadie said. She wished he could wait an hour but didn't think it would be appropriate to ask for that. She'd assumed Larry was involved in *moving* the documents he'd left with Tia, but what if he was *making* them instead? "It helps me know what I'm dealing with, though. He doesn't work in vital records anymore?"

"No," Pete said. "Looks like he quit about a year ago. I could request his job history and see if there are any red flags, but it will take a day or two to get it."

"Well, I'm assuming it's going to come out eventually, so making a request—or having Mathews make one—will probably be an effort in efficiency." Sadie very much appreciated efficiency.

"Good point. So who is this guy?" Pete asked.

"Eric's ex-wife's ex-husband," Sadie said, shaking her head at how that sounded. "I know, it's really bizarre. Can you look up another name?"

"Sure."

"Liliana Miriam Montez," Sadie said. If it was a fake name, it wouldn't be in the system, right?

It felt like she waited forever for Pete to bring up the information. "No criminal history."

"But she does have a history?" Sadie asked.

"Yes. Born in Puerto Rico, but looks like she lived in Miami for a few years after she got married."

"She's a real person then," Sadie said, confused. How could Megan be using the name of a real person? And then she thought of the body the police had found. A woman who wasn't Megan.

"Wait. This is interesting," Pete said.

Sadie gripped the phone tighter. "What?"

"*She* doesn't have a criminal history, but her husband was brought up on charges of defying the embargo with Cuba by selling speedboats. The case was thrown out based on lack of evidence, but the family moved back to Puerto Rico after that."

Puerto Rico? Megan had said she couldn't fly or take a boat home until after she had her babies. Monty had said that Motorway Powerboats had been accused of selling boats to the Cubans. Sadie pictured the flag sticker she'd seen on the back of Joe's car. "Pete," she said, "what does the Puerto Rican flag look like?"

"Um, it's red, white, and blue, like ours, but it's got a triangle on the side instead of a blue square."

"And one star in the blue triangle?"

"I think so," Pete said. Sadie heard voices in the background, and when Pete spoke, he was quiet. "Why?"

"Well, there was this guy who kind of kidnapped me," Sadie said. Boy, did that sound strange. "But he was nice. He said he was trying to help Megan, and I believed him. He had that flag on his car."

"Believed him?" Pete asked. "Why the past tense?"

"Oh, well, we were at this park, and he, uh, hit his head and was knocked unconscious, but don't worry, I called 911."

"And Mathews knows about this, right?"

"Not yet," Sadie said, "but he will. I just didn't want to . . . well, it's complicated, and you probably don't have time to hear the whole story."

The voices in the background were getting louder. "Actually, you're right, I don't," Pete said. "But I want to hear more about it later, okay?"

"Deal."

"I've got to go. You'll talk to the sergeant as soon as you can, right?"

"Yes," Sadie said. "Thank you."

"Be safe," Pete said.

"I will," she said, touched by his concern and his willingness to help do something she could never have done on her own. "And thank you, Pete, for calling and for . . . caring." It sounded cheesy, and she blushed.

"Anytime, Sadie," Pete said, a husky tone to his voice. "Anytime."

CHAPTER 38

After ending the phone call, Sadie thought of one more thing, but knowing Pete was going into a meeting, she sent him a quick text.

What's Liliana's husband's name?

She hit send and then sighed. Was she feeling all soft and squishy toward Pete because he was far away? Hard to get? Was Eric less appealing because no glittery thoughts surrounded him anymore? Or did having a fuller view of him and his life give her reasons to wonder if she had been simply attracted to some of him, but not the entire package?

"I don't know!" she snapped to no one. "And I don't know how I'm supposed to figure it out." And why was she even trying to figure out her stupid love life when there were bigger things at stake? That was so ridiculous and self-centered.

She needed to talk to Eric, and then she needed to go to Mathews.

Her phone rang in her hand, and she jumped. She looked at the caller ID and breathed a sigh of relief to see it was Eric—who didn't have a picture or a speed dial button on her phone.

She pressed talk and put the phone to her ear. "Eric," she said. "How did it go?"

"She's gone," Eric said, his tone hollow.

"What?" Sadie said, her fingers tightening around the phone.

"They're checking the cameras, and I've been talking to security, but apparently there was some kind of distraction, and she slipped out of the hospital."

"Why would she do that?" Sadie said, her heart sinking. "What about the surgery?"

Eric said nothing. The full weight of Sadie's actions fell across her shoulders. If she hadn't gone to see Megan, would she have stayed? She knew Eric was thinking the same thing and closed her eyes. "Eric, I'm so sorry."

"Yeah," he said. "Me too." The way he said it sounded like an accusation.

"I thought going to see her would help," Sadie tried to explain. "I didn't want to call you if it wasn't her. I was just going off of some papers in the car; I had no way of knowing—"

"I know you were only trying to help," he said. "But . . . well, I don't know."

Sadie felt as though she'd been slapped. Although she felt the defensiveness rising, she kept from reacting to the feelings. Eric was in a horrendously stressful situation, and now he was worried about Megan more than ever. Of course he would be angry with anyone who got in the way of that.

They sat through a few seconds of uncomfortable silence while Sadie tried to think of the words that would diffuse his anger, defend her intentions, and help them move past this. Nothing came to mind.

Eric broke the silence. "The Miami police have an APB, or whatever it's called, out for her, so hopefully they'll find her." They were pretty words, but he didn't seem to feel them, and therefore Sadie didn't really either. "Anyway, I better go. I got a call from Larry a while back and ought to—"

"Larry!" Sadie said loudly, instantly reminded of what she needed to say to Eric. "Sorry," she said, realizing she'd taken Eric by surprise. "I've learned some things about Larry that might be important."

Eric was quiet for a moment before he spoke. "Like what?" He didn't seem to have high hopes.

"Did you know he worked in vital records when he was employed with the state?"

"Yes," Eric said. "So?"

"And did you notice that he drives an awfully nice car for someone supporting three households and having a new job?"

"Three households?" Eric said.

"Layla, Tia and Max, and his own."

"He doesn't support Tia," Eric said. "He gives her a couple hundred a month to keep an eye on Layla."

"Nope," Sadie said, shaking her head. "Tia works part-time, and I'd wager she cooks for Layla every day. Not that she's not compassionate and wouldn't help anyway, but she came to Homestead six years ago *specifically* to take care of Layla—that was the whole reason."

"Where are you going with this, Sadie?"

She took a breath. "I think Larry is dealing in illegal documents, and I think he asked Max—that's Tia's brother, he's disabled or something—to burn the box of Megan's things."

Eric was quiet again. "Larry?" he finally said.

"Yes," Sadie said, and she proceeded to relate to Eric the details of everything she'd seen and overheard at Max's house. "Remember when I said we needed suspects, and that suspects have secrets? Well, Larry has a secret, and it's too much of a coincidence to imagine that his secret has nothing to do with Megan's original disappearance."

He took a deep breath, and when he spoke, Sadie was disappointed to hear him sounding almost patronizing. "So what do you want to do about this little theory of yours?"

"Oh, well, I hadn't thought all that out just yet," Sadie said. "But maybe we should talk to Mathews about it and let him take it from there."

"Mathews." Eric said it as though it were a dirty word. "I'm in enough trouble with Mathews right now; I'm not going to give him some unsubstantiated tip."

Sadie remained silent, letting Eric work things through in his mind.

"Where are you right now?" he asked.

"Parked in front of a school around the corner from Layla's house," Sadie said.

"Meet me at Layla's then," he said. "I'm about five minutes away."

"You didn't stay in Miami?"

"I was stuck talking to the Miami cops for over an hour, then I bailed. It's not like Meg's going to go back there."

Sadie cringed all over again. Why would Megan leave? Where would she go?

Eric continued. "I think we should go to Larry's and see what he has to say."

"Then we can go to Mathews with the whole story," Sadie suggested, though confronting Larry didn't sound like fun.

"Okay. Meet me at Layla's."

Sadie shifted into drive and hoped this would give her a chance to redeem herself with Eric a little, show him she was as determined to get to the bottom of this as he was. "I'm on my way."

CHAPTER 39

Twenty minutes later, they crouched beside the gate and waited for Larry to leave. Once they'd arrived, Eric had decided to look around Larry's condo before they talked to him. Sadie wasn't entirely comfortable with that, but she felt so badly about Megan leaving the hospital that she wasn't inclined to argue.

They knew there was an event at the Speedway—Eric was supposed to meet Joe in section C—and while they waited for Larry to leave, Sadie could feel Eric's breath on her cheek. The evening light created shadows among the trees across the street from the condo Eric said was Larry's. Eric's arm around her waist, and the warmth of him pressed against her back, was nice, and yet strangely uncomfortable.

Turning her head slightly, she found her face inches from his. His eyes glittered with the glow from the streetlight to the left of them. She couldn't deny that he was a good-looking man, and she dug deep for the sparks that, in part, had brought her here.

"What?" he whispered.

Sadie continued to look at him, remembering their exchange on the courthouse lawn two days ago and the complicated feelings she'd been having ever since. There were things she'd learned about him in the last forty-eight hours that just didn't sit right. Yet, her eyes traveled to his lips, and his words came back to her: *Mark my words, Sadie Hoffmiller, the first time our lips meet, it will be you kissing me.*

Did she even want to kiss him now?

She turned away, embarrassed by the direction her thoughts were taking at a time like this. No sooner had she turned away, however, when she felt Eric's hand on her chin, turning her back to face him. She waited for him to say something, but he didn't. Instead he leaned toward her. It wasn't until their faces were close enough to touch that she realized what he was doing.

He's going to kiss me! she said in her mind, feeling herself pulling back. This wasn't how it was supposed to happen. He'd given her the lead on this!

And then his lips met hers, and his hand on her chin moved to the back of her head, preventing her from pulling away.

Sadie froze, waiting for the euphoric rush of heat and adrenaline despite being unprepared for it. A tiny part of her wondered if this was what she needed to make sense of the feelings battling themselves out within her. Maybe this kiss was the answer.

His lips pressed against her own and she waited for the fireworks that would fix all the confusing thoughts in her mind.

She felt nothing.

Was she doing something wrong? Was the fact that he'd turned this moment over to her and then yanked it away preventing her from fully enjoying the kiss? Regardless of all the emotional baggage, this *was* their first kiss, it was important, and she needed to get over herself. She moved her hands into Eric's hair, really putting herself into the kiss as she sought for . . . something, anything, to capture what this moment was supposed to be.

Nothing.

How was that possible? She'd felt the tingle when she first met him; felt the giddy nervousness when he was close to her since then. Even Pete had said she lit up when he was around.

Pete. Where did that thought come from?

But had she felt that giddiness since coming to Florida? Instead of the passion and connection she'd imagined this moment should have, she noticed that Eric's beard felt scruffy against her skin and that he needed ChapStick . . . and gum or something. Sadie could count on one hand—okay, maybe two—the number of men she'd kissed in her life. Not one of those exchanges had been as disappointing as this one, and as Eric took over, deepening the kiss even more, Sadie found herself completely turned off.

After a few more seconds, she pulled away and cleared her throat, not sure what to do as embarrassment crept up her neck. Casually lifting her hand to tuck her hair behind her ear, she used the movement as an excuse to move away from him.

"Gosh, what's that in your hair?" Eric said, and she looked back at him to see him wiping his hand on his jeans.

She was even more embarrassed and wished he hadn't kissed her at all. Would it have been different if they weren't in the bushes waiting to see what Larry was up to? Somehow, she didn't think so. In fact, as the moments ticked by, she couldn't shake the feeling that no matter how that first kiss had happened, she'd be feeling just like this.

An instant later, Eric stiffened slightly and whispered in her ear, "There he is."

Sadie nodded, grateful for the distraction even if she wasn't looking forward to what came next. Eric moved around her, gently pushing her behind him. She didn't fight him, simply relieved that he wasn't trying to kiss her again.

"I'll wait for him to pull out before I go up," Eric whispered. "You stay here."

Not on your life, Sadie said in her mind, taking a quick glance at the bushes on either side. Surely they were teeming with spiders, maybe even cockroaches—she knew what kind of creepy crawlies lived in tropical climates—but telling Eric she had no intention of obeying his orders would only waste time.

Meanwhile Larry headed to his car, talking on his phone again. Sadie wondered who was on the other end. His latest customer, maybe?

Eric hunched slightly, like a lion ready to pounce, and Sadie felt the air electrify with tension. They watched silently as Larry got into his car and pulled out of his parking space. Only when his car was gone and the complex silent did Eric move forward, crouching as he looked around. It wasn't until he was on the porch and reaching for his tools in his back pocket that he realized Sadie was right behind him.

"I thought you were going to wait in the bushes," he whispered, looking around even as he unsnapped his case and opened his pick set. The tools really did look like glorified bobby pins.

"You were wrong," Sadie said, also looking around to be sure they weren't being watched.

Eric made a huffing sound and then turned back to the door, extracting one of his picks and handing the case to Sadie. After wriggling the pick into the lock, he paused, then wiggled it some more, then held it in place with one hand while reaching for another pick from the case Sadie held out to him. He chose a second pick while Sadie continued to serve as the lookout, increasingly uncomfortable.

Within seconds, she heard the final click, and Eric pushed the door open.

"Eric," she said as he stepped forward, "isn't this breaking and entering?"

Eric looked at her but said nothing, simply walking through the door.

Sadie paused only a moment before slipping in behind him and moving to the side so he could shut the door.

She didn't know if she was okay with this and yet, she was here. They were here. Did Larry's criminal involvement justify them breaking the law just a little? She didn't think so, and now she regretted agreeing to Eric's plan.

Eric pulled a penlight from his front pocket and turned it on before scanning the room as he crept forward. It wasn't dark, but evening had deepened the shadows and made it hard to see the details of the apartment. The penlight helped, but not very much. Sadie watched him for a minute, then saw a light switch and flipped it.

"Hey," he said, spinning around to face her. He still had the two picks in his hand, and she held the kit out to him. "Low profile, remember?"

"Like his neighbors keep track of when he is and isn't here," Sadie said. She knew she was being a little snappy and wondered if it was because of the stress that had been building all day or because she was frustrated by both the kiss itself and the fact that Eric had been able to blow it off completely. "We're breaking the law. We need to hurry and get this over with."

Eric looked as though he might argue, but finally took the case she offered and returned his tools inside before clipping it back on his belt. Without a word he turned back to the apartment.

They were standing in the entryway but could see into the living room that ended with French doors on the other end. Through an arched doorway to the left was the kitchen, and perhaps a dining room beyond that. On the right was a wall that separated the living room from a hallway, off of which there were two recessed door-ways—bedrooms, Sadie assumed.

"I'll start in here," he said, turning toward the living room and, more specifically, a computer desk.

Sadie glanced at the front door. For all her self-assurance, she was terrified of Larry coming back and finding them here. She'd been caught where she didn't belong enough times to know exactly how scary those situations could be, but she turned her attention to the search at hand, trying not to freak herself out too much.

Larry took more after Layla than Eric in regard to cleanliness, and Sadie appreciated his sense of organization—a place for every-thing and everything in its place. Sadie took note of the furniture. It wasn't elaborate, but neither did it scream economy—much like Larry's car and clothing. She headed toward the hallway, specifically the first door, which was open but dark inside.

She flipped on the light and found her eyes immediately drawn to the open drawers, the stack of clothing on the bed, and the two suitcases half filled on the floor. The obvious signs of packing con-firmed what Larry had told Max—he was leaving. She moved into the room, scanning it for anything obvious, like more of those enve-lopes he'd taken to Tia.

Her phone chimed, indicating she'd received a text message, and she pulled it out of her pocket. It was from Pete.

Alejandro Montez Rosado

Alex was a nickname for Alejandro. Sadie pictured the tattoo she'd seen on the back of Megan's neck. Alex *was* her husband. So how did Joe, a.k.a. Hugo, factor in?

"I wonder where he's going," Eric said from behind her, and she startled, having not heard him approach.

She put the phone in her pocket and returned to the task at hand, which was pulling open drawers. She didn't want to talk about Megan with Eric right now. She still felt horrible for being part of her escape, and she sensed that Eric hadn't quite come to terms with it either. She might have expected the kiss to soften things, but then it hadn't been much of a kiss so it made sense that she wouldn't get optimal results.

"Me too," she said, sliding open the closet door and fingering through the hangers. Eric joined her, and eventually she stepped back, since he seemed intent to be the one searching the closet. She was also uncomfortable being so close to him. Had the kiss changed everything or had it sped up the process of her realizing that Eric wasn't everything she may have thought he was? Not that he wasn't a good guy, she just wasn't sure he was the *right* guy.

"I'm going to check the other room," Sadie said when she finished with the drawers, leaving Eric to fumble through the closet. She headed for the other door she'd seen farther down the hall.

She opened the door to the second bedroom and turned on the light, instantly disappointed to find a guest room. There was a double bed placed against the middle wall and a simple white dresser next to it with an artificial flower arrangement. It was only the black leather rolling office chair at the end of the bed that seemed out of place. It was a strange piece of furniture for a guest room, especially since the chair faced the closet. There was also a smell in the room that didn't fit either. Metallic but also dry—crisp somehow. She turned around to see all three-hundred-and-sixty degrees of the room but couldn't see anything she could attribute the smell to. It reminded her of the copy room at the school where she used to teach.

Her eyes landed on the closet with two sets of sliding doors that filled one entire wall of the room. It was a big closet for a guest room—bigger than the one in the master bedroom, even. She approached it and attempted to pull the door open by pushing it along the track. It was stuck. She pushed harder, but it still didn't move. Luckily, Sadie could be flexible. She didn't have to open *this* door. She moved to the other door and pulled on it. It was also stuck. She felt a rush of heat travel through her chest. Two stuck closet doors. What a coincidence.

"Eric," she said, a little louder than she intended. But hadn't she been the one who said they needed to hurry more than they needed to prowl?

He came into the room a few seconds later. "What?" he asked, and she looked up at his sharp tone. "Sorry," he quickly said. "I guess things are getting to me."

Sadie nodded toward the closet doors. "They're stuck," she said. "But do you smell that?" She sniffed again, and Eric did the same thing.

"I don't smell anything," he said, but moved toward the closets anyway, almost as though he were humoring her.

"You don't smell anything?" she repeated, surprised. "Bedrooms are supposed to smell like fabric softener or lavender, maybe musty if they aren't aired out. This one smells like a . . . a print shop."

That was the smell—ink, electronics, paper. She looked at the closet doors, moving her eyes around the edges. "I'll bet the closet is full of equipment—printers and whatever else Larry used to make those documents he took to Tia."

Eric pulled on the door, paused, and then pulled again

before stepping back and moving his head as he scanned the doors. "They're locked," he said.

"How can sliding doors be locked?"

Eric didn't answer, instead he continued scanning, his eyebrows pulled together, before he moved forward and bent down, running his fingers along the interior panel of the door.

Sadie watched him, not sure what he was feeling for, when suddenly he stopped. Sadie moved so she could get a better view as Eric pulled back a six-inch portion of wood paneling on the edge of the door. She crouched down to get a better look at the keyhole hidden beneath the piece that seemed to fit into place like a tongue-and-groove wooden floor.

Without a word, Eric snapped his tool kit off his belt and flipped it open, choosing a smaller bobby pin than the one he'd used on the front door. Sadie watched in fascination as he wiggled the pin into the lock. She was going to learn how to pick locks some day; it was such a useful skill. Almost immediately the lock clicked. Eric slid the door back, and Sadie moved around him so she could see what had been so expertly hidden.

"Wow," she breathed as she scanned the floor-to-ceiling equipment built into the closet. She recognized several printers of different sizes as well as a computer, but there were half a dozen machines that she didn't recognize at all. She looked at a pile of papers sitting on top of the computer keyboard. Larry's current work in progress, perhaps? Or maybe his own ID that would take him away from all this.

"I'm no expert," she said, cocking her head to get a better look at the papers without having to touch them. "But this looks like a birth certificate to me." The top sheet had the state seal of Delaware on the top.

Eric stood beside her and picked up a square piece of plastic that had been sitting next to the keyboard—perhaps on the only empty space on the built-in countertop. Sadie wasn't sure getting his fingerprints all over it was such a good idea, but Eric didn't look to be in the mood for advice. He turned the plastic over, and Sadie realized that it was printed with the back of a driver's license. The front was blank.

"I can't believe this," Eric said softly under his breath, shaking his head. Sadie watched Eric's face as the details of the betrayal sank in. He turned the plastic over in his hand, from the blank side to the printed side and back again. "Larry," he said, as though it were a sigh.

"What?" said a voice from the doorway.

Both of them whipped their heads around to see Larry standing there, looking very much like an office employee at the Speedway and nothing like the identity broker they'd just realized he really was.

CHAPTER 40

S adie sucked in a breath.

Eric lifted his chin defiantly.

Larry just stared at them. He held a grocery sack in one hand; Sadie didn't know what was inside it, but it explained his leaving the house. They'd thought he was going to the track to help with the event, instead he'd just gone around the corner. Despite having struck what Sadie assumed was supposed to be a casual pose, leaning against the door frame the way he was, Larry looked uncomfortable—a mix between the insecure man from the police station and the confident one from Max's porch. She wondered now, though, if part of his discomfort at the station had been due to his "extracurricular" activities. If he'd made the ID from the wallet found with the body, did he worry the police would somehow trace it back to him? Was that why he was leaving now?

"What did you do with Megan?" Eric finally said, his voice low enough that it sounded like a growl, which was probably a pretty good description of how he felt.

"I did what she wanted." There was resignation in Larry's voice, as though he'd avoided this conversation for a long time, but could tell he had little choice but to admit to what he'd done now that he'd been asked a direct question.

Eric did growl this time, deep in his throat. His jaw tightened, and Sadie sensed the rest of him following suit. She put a hand on his arm, hoping it would calm him. He pulled away, and she let her hand fall to her side.

"I don't believe that," Eric said.

"You think I somehow *forced* her to take on a new identity and start a new life?"

Eric clenched his jaw but didn't answer. Sadie was surprised he didn't have a comeback.

"She wanted a new life," Larry said when Eric simply continued to glare. "You saw it, Eric. You saw her stuck inside Layla's world—it was killing her."

Eric shook his head. "She was doing fine."

"No, Eric, she wasn't," Larry said, an edge to his tone.

Sadie took a step back. With about fifteen feet between the two men, she didn't want to be caught in the crosshairs of an altercation if it came to that, and, gauging Eric's tension, it might just come to that.

"So you sold her off? Pulled her out from under me, sent her on her way, and let me live without knowing the truth all these years?"

"She'd wanted it for a long time, and I finally ran out of excuses not to help her."

"What do you mean?" Sadie asked, trying to collect important information before Eric lost his temper.

Larry's eyes settled on Sadie. "Megan knew I was dealing in documents." He waved toward the equipment staring back at them from the closet. "She was fourteen, and staying with Layla and me for the weekend, when she came across some papers." He glanced at

Eric. "You were spending a week in Atlantic City with, what was her name, Rita?"

Sadie looked up at Eric, whose neck reddened as he held Larry's eyes. He said nothing. After a few seconds, Sadie couldn't take it. "Who's Rita?"

"Just an old girlfriend," Eric said, insinuating with his tone that it wasn't important. And it wasn't. Sadie had dated, was even engaged six months ago, and dating someone else up until two days earlier. It was the defensiveness in Eric's words that caught her attention and gave her pause.

"Not *just* a girlfriend," Larry said. "A girlfriend Eric took up with *before* he divorced Layla."

Sadie lifted her eyebrows and looked at Eric again. He was shooting such daggers at Larry that she feared he'd lunge toward the other man at any minute. Sadie thought back to Eric's explanation of how Larry had been angry with Eric when he learned about the divorce, feeling as though he'd abandoned Layla. Perhaps Larry had a good reason to feel the way he did.

Larry continued, directing his words to Sadie. "Let me guess, he told you he was a saint during that marriage, right? That he took care of Layla, did everything he could to help her get better?" The sarcasm was sharp. "The truth is that he resented Layla for not being who he wanted her to be, and he left her with nothing but monthly disability checks that barely paid for a one-bedroom apartment."

"Larry," Eric said in a warning tone.

Larry ignored it. "He also said he left *purely* for Megan's sake, right?" He shook his head before Eric or Sadie could respond, turning his attention to Eric and narrowing his eyes. "Megan's never believed that, and neither have I."

Sadie was trying to think of what to say when Eric beat her to it. "I made some mistakes," Eric said, shaking his head but sounding more angry than repentant. "But no one knows what it was like watching Layla ignore Megan every day. No one can understand how hard it was trying to pretend we were still a normal family."

"I do," Larry said. "But even when I reached my breaking point, I didn't abandon Layla."

"You didn't have a daughter to worry about," Eric said.

Sadie reflected on the words Eric had used when he'd explained things to Sadie: "slowly drowning." She didn't doubt that was true, even in light of this new information, but . . .

"That's not why you left," Larry replied, his words even sharper.

"I did my best for as long as I could," Eric continued, but he didn't meet Sadie's eyes despite her watching him closely. "And I finally broke. It was no good for Megan, and—"

"No," Larry broke in. "You *didn't* leave for Megan. You left for yourself—for Rita, then Karen, and then Naomi. Megan wanted to stay. She told you that."

"You can't understand!" Eric practically yelled. "And it was better for Megan to leave, even if she didn't want to. It was too much for her to try to make sense of."

"But she could come stay with us on the weekends when you had better things to do?" Larry asked in a mocking tone. "She could spend her summers here when you wanted to hit the beach with whoever your hottie was that season?"

Eric's cheeks began turning red, and Sadie found herself not wanting to talk about this anymore. She had no reason to know these things about Eric, but wasn't sure how to segue into something else.

Larry continued, "You can't have it both ways, Eric. Layla wasn't good for Megan except when you didn't want her *cramping your style,* then it was okay for her to have a relationship with her mother." He waved toward the equipment again. "You think I do this because I like it? Because this is the kind of contribution I want to make to society? I did what it took to make sure Layla was okay, Eric. I risk my future every day to make sure she's taken care of."

"But you're leaving now, too, aren't you?" Sadie cut in quickly, watching as guilt sprang into Larry's eyes. "Everything that's happened has made your situation precarious, so you're leaving."

"That's right," Eric chimed in, obviously looking for a way to turn things on Larry. "You're willing to take off and leave now that the heat is on. Some hero you are."

Larry didn't have an answer for that, and Sadie wondered if he'd thought through his actions in that light or if he was just in a panic, seeing circumstances closing in around him.

"Megan came to see Layla the night she disappeared, didn't she?" Sadie asked, worried Larry would clam up if she didn't keep pushing.

Larry looked surprised but didn't say anything.

Eric, on the other hand, turned to look at Sadie. "What?" he snapped, as though he had some reason to be angry with *her*.

Sadie glanced between both men, one surprised and one confirming her suspicions by the look of surrender on his face. "Megan wasn't a party girl, and she missed her mother," she began. "Maybe going away to school was her attempt to break free, I don't know, but she was suddenly a few hours away from home, feeling insecure, and so she came back to the one thing she wanted more than anything—her mother."

Both men just looked at her, stunned for different reasons. "How do you know that?" Eric finally asked, sounding offended.

"Megan was twenty-two when she chose to go away to college," Sadie said, looking him in the eye and silently pleading with him to open himself up to the possibilities. "She visited her mother every chance she could get. She was obviously looking for something, Eric, and running away from it at the same time." She paused for a breath and glanced at Larry, who was hanging on her every word, before focusing her attention back to Eric. "You said you left Layla because you broke under the pressure. Megan broke too. She broke that night she came back here, but she needed more distance than you did."

Eric shook his head. "Her car was still at the motel."

"That doesn't mean she didn't leave by choice," Sadie said, feeling a mixture of frustration and compassion. He needed to accept the possibility that Megan could be *that* unhappy if he were going to deal with whatever else was lying ahead of him. "It wouldn't have been difficult for someone to return her car to the motel. Her friend didn't look for it until the next morning anyway."

She looked at Larry and asked quietly, "She *always* came back to Layla, didn't she?"

She waited for Larry to refute what she'd said so far. He didn't. "You said she'd wanted to leave for a long time, and that she knew you could help her. Why did you run out of excuses to help her that night?"

He blinked, but then lowered his head and allowed his shoulders to fall forward—his first sign of defeat. "She *did* go to school in an attempt to get away from her past. She hoped that college would fill her life and help her forget how much it hurt not to matter to her own mother."

"That's not true," Eric cut in, shaking his head. "She went to school because she—"

"I'm the one who talked to her a few times a week, Eric," Larry said, slapping his own chest for emphasis and squaring his shoulders once again. "You shut her down every time she tried to talk to you about how she felt; you told her not to worry about it so much. You told her that she needed to move on. She *couldn't* move on, and I was the only person she could talk to about it because I understood—I couldn't move on either. I couldn't make peace with what had happened or simply pretend that Layla wasn't *Layla* anymore." He looked back at Sadie. "Megan just wanted to sit next to her mom on the couch and watch TV that night—just be close to her. She didn't even realize she was wearing that stupid bracelet until Layla saw it. Tia called me around two o'clock, freaking out and telling me Megan was hurt. When I got to the house, Tia was holding a bloody dish towel to Megan's arm—apparently Layla had tried to cut the bracelet from Megan's wrist."

"That's why there were no knives in the kitchen," Sadie said, remembering the broken rolls they'd had with the barbeque chicken. She also pictured the ugly scar she'd seen on Megan's forearm that hadn't been in the police report. "You didn't take her to the hospital?"

Larry shook his head. "Megan was afraid Layla would get in trouble so Tia and I bandaged up her arm as best we could. Megan was an absolute wreck." He looked at the floor for a moment as he put his hands in his pockets. "Layla had attacked her, and it caused everything to implode. Megan couldn't stand it anymore and begged me to help her, begged me to make her into a new person the way I'd been doing for other people. She wanted me to use my contacts and send her somewhere she could start over—*really* start over—and she was willing to leave everything behind to make it work. I couldn't say no." He looked at Eric, and Sadie saw the glimmer of him *wanting* Eric to understand. "She was so miserable."

"You should have talked to me," Eric said, still angry, still tense. "If I'd known she was struggling, I'd have gotten her help."

"That's just it," Larry said, sounding frustrated. His expression,

303

which had softened moments earlier, hardened again. "You *didn't* know, but it was so obvious. She planned to contact you when the police had stopped looking for her and she was strong enough to explain what she'd done and why. By the time she was ready, you'd already left Florida and started over in Colorado. Your old numbers were disconnected—it sent a pretty strong message."

Eric finally got it. He'd been on the defensive, but he now looked as though he'd been punched in the stomach. Sadie wanted to reach out to him, but wondered if he needed to fully face this, no matter how painful it was.

"Don't you get it?" Larry cried now that Eric seemed to understand what he'd said. "Layla's abandonment was painful, but it wasn't something she did on purpose—it was a horrible accident. But you abandoned Megan in a completely different way. When I agreed to help her that night, she didn't *want* you to know where she was because she didn't think you would let her go. And because of what you've done since then, she still doesn't trust you. How did you think she'd contact you if she were alive, Eric? Did you even once consider that moving halfway across the country might make it impossible for her to come back? To find you?"

"I thought she was . . ."

"Dead," Larry finished when Eric didn't. "And you know what, she wasn't the only one who thought maybe you wished she was. Maybe you wished you could free yourself of the problem of Megan just like you'd freed yourself from the problem of Layla."

Eric looked down, and it seemed as though he'd shrunk two inches in the last thirty seconds. His bursts of defensiveness had been spent. Larry had finally made his point, and Eric was reeling, perhaps looking at himself in a new light—a very painful one.

"You kept in touch with her?" Sadie asked Larry, purposely

keeping her voice calm, hoping it would ease some of the tension in the room. She took a step toward Eric and reached for his hand. He let her take it, but didn't return the squeeze she offered him. The other women Larry had mentioned came to mind, but Sadie wasn't worried about that. She wasn't Eric's girlfriend—would never be one of *those* women—but she was his friend, and he needed to know he wasn't alone.

"Occasionally," Larry said, and he was the wary one now. "I had to be very careful. As time has gone by, she contacts me less and less. She doesn't want the connections to her old life anymore."

"Did you send her to Puerto Rico?" Sadie asked.

Larry shook his head again. "A friend in Texas helped her out in the beginning. Puerto Rico came later."

"A friend?" What kind of friend helped a man with something like this, Sadie wondered.

"A client," Larry clarified. "He coordinates documents with me, then helps people become established."

"Hugo Montez?" Sadie guessed, causing Larry's eyes to go wide and his mouth to open for only a moment. "The tipster," she said to Eric as he looked at her with confusion. "His license plate was from Texas, and he was trying to help Megan be found." He was also somehow related to Megan—well, to Liliana anyway.

Larry looked between the two of them before folding his arms across his chest. "Hugo found her a job at a bakery in Galveston. She worked there while I set up her identity."

"Lucile Powell," Sadie said. The name from the driver's license found with the body.

Larry nodded. "She found friends who didn't feel sorry for her because they didn't know they should. She took a lot of pride in her work at the bakery and moved into her own studio apartment. Once she'd been known as Lucy long enough to have confidence in the new identity, she called me and said Hugo had found her a nanny job in Puerto Rico." He flicked a glance at Eric before turning his attention back to Sadie.

She was beginning to feel a little silly holding Eric's hand when he didn't seem to notice, so she loosened her grip and he let her go.

Larry kept talking, and she folded her arms over her chest and listened intently. "She felt Puerto Rico would be the ultimate new start—a new country, a new life altogether, and she wouldn't even need a passport to get there."

"Well, she definitely got a new life," Sadie said, glad she wasn't the one who would have to feel responsible for what had happened between then and now. It would be a heavy burden to shoulder, and as she looked at Larry, she wondered how he'd managed it so far. "I'm guessing the new employer was Alex Montez, who had two sons and a wife named Liliana."

Larry couldn't hide his surprise . . . again. "How did you know that?"

"Megan's been living as his wife, using his wife's name—Liliana Montez—and, I suspect, raising her children." By the look on Larry's face she could tell he hadn't known that bit of information. Megan was keeping secrets from everyone it seemed.

Eric was staring at her too.

"I think the body the police found was the *real* Liliana Montez," Sadie explained. "Hugo must have come to regret the part he'd played, so when Megan came to Miami for this surgery, he started setting things up for her to be discovered—preventing her from returning to Alex. I don't know how the bracelet ended up with Liliana, but it certainly got the police looking for Megan, didn't it?"

They were all silent for several seconds. She kept her eyes fixed on Larry, hoping he would keep talking. She wasn't disappointed.

"When you live off false papers, you have to exist in the margins of typical society. I explained that to Megan when I first sent her with Hugo, and she seemed to understand. When she told me about the job in Puerto Rico, I looked into Alex. He'd had some trouble, but nothing serious. I had no idea he was . . . the man she told me she'd married. She seemed so . . . happy. Just as I wanted her to be."

"Did you know she was in Miami?" Sadie asked. "Did she call you?"

Larry shook his head and seemed a little bit hurt by that fact.

"Why did you have Max burn the box?" Sadie asked, trying to fit in as many questions as possible.

"I was just . . . scared, I guess. Hoping I could buy some time; worried that she might have something in there that would lead the police to me."

"How can you live with yourself?" Eric asked in a harsh whisper, glaring at Larry with his fists clenched at his sides. His eyes were narrowed, and Sadie took a step away from him.

"I could ask you the same question," Larry said coolly. He lifted his eyes and seemed to appreciate the aggression Eric had restored to the conversation. It was likely easier for both men to rely on their anger with one another than on the guilt of what they'd done. "The irony is that I've been haunted about my part in this, and you've never once thought about yours."

Eric sprang forward and landed a fist on Larry's nose before Larry finished speaking. Larry yelled and swung wildly, catching Eric's right ear with the bag he was still holding. They both went through the doorway and slammed into the wall of the hallway.

Sadie probably should have yelled at them to stop, but she just watched and sighed in aggravation. Not that fighting was silly—they both obviously had some rage they needed to work out—but now was the time to act like rational adults, not teenage boys with no self-control.

Larry tried to get up, scrambling toward the living room, and Eric knocked him to the floor again, creating a gap in the doorway wide enough for Sadie to slip through. She did just that, careful not to get caught by a stray leg as the men rolled across the floor. She hoped they wouldn't seriously hurt one another; men in their forties didn't heal as well as sixteen-year-olds.

"You should have told me!" Eric yelled, followed by a particularly crushing punch that made Sadie wince. She didn't look back—boxing had never been her thing, and this wasn't a game—as she headed for the kitchen. She picked up the phone and dialed 911 for the second time that day.

"Nine-one-one. What's your emergency?"

"I'm at the Garden Grove condominium complex, number 27. A couple men are fighting. I think they need some intervention." There were groans and curse words and the sound of body punches from behind her.

She answered all the questions the dispatcher asked, even giving her name this time. Pete would be so proud of her. But though the woman asked her to stay on the line, Sadie hung up once she'd given all the important information. She could wait around here for the police, or she could get her car from Layla's, go to the police station herself, and keep herself as distanced from the rest of this as possible. Then, when she'd finished her statements and explanations, she could really leave. She hoped.

Sadie thought it was at least a mile walk to Layla's, but she didn't mind a good stretch of the legs while she got her thoughts in order.

There was plenty to think about, plenty of details she needed to put into order in her mind. Among them was sorting out her feelings for Eric. The kiss had worried her, but it was only one part of the equation. Seeing him in this environment had been uncomfortable from the start. Hearing Larry's accusations hadn't helped, but neither did they change everything. The change had been happening all along—bit by bit, she had glimpsed another side of this man. She let herself out the front door, taking a final look back. Eric was pinned beneath Larry, who was shouting rather than hitting. Sadie had a feeling this had been a long time coming for both of them.

She pulled the door closed behind her and headed down the snaking streets that led out of the complex, wishing she hadn't left her purse in her car. At least she had her phone. The main entrance was in sight when she saw a police car turn in with no lights or sirens. Lowering her head, she tried to look inconspicuous. The car sped by, and she looked over her shoulder in time to see it turn the corner she'd just rounded.

She quickened her pace, but then stopped when she got to the street. There were no mountains, and she'd left her GPS in her car, which meant she had no idea which direction to go. Hadn't Eric made a right-hand turn into the complex? She started walking that direction, but the homes didn't seem familiar. The last thing she needed was to get lost on top of everything else. She started walking the other way, but within a few steps was unsure of that direction too. The sun had almost set, burnishing everything with a coppery light that subdued details she might otherwise have noted.

Monty.

She pulled her cell phone and Monty's card from her pocket and stopped at the corner where she'd be able to read the coordinates off the street sign. With a little luck he was still in Homestead. If not, maybe he could tell her which way to go—he had an amazing sense of direction.

"Hallo?" Monty said on the other end of the line after just two rings.

"Hi, Monty," she said. "It's Sadie Hoffmiller. Is there any chance you're still in Homestead?"

"Sho' am," he said. "It be Friday night, and the bars be hoppin'."

"Do you think you could pick me up and take me back to my car? I'll pay fare, of course."

"Sho'. Where you be?"

"On the corner of 400 Northeast and 18th Avenue. Do you know where that is?"

"Sho', sho'. I am not fa'."

"Thank you," Sadie said as she watched another police car turn into the complex. She hung up the phone, hoping Monty would hurry.

Less than a minute later, a quick honk caught her attention. She couldn't suppress a smile as Monty pulled smoothly to the curb. He wasn't kidding about being close.

"Thank you, Monty," Sadie said, sliding into the passenger seat. She didn't feel like a customer anymore. "You have been such an amazing help to me today."

"Sho', sho'," he said, nodding. He had opened the window on his side, and Sadie tried to convince herself that it didn't bother her. But the thick air flowing into the taxi as he pulled away from the curb wasn't the least bit relaxing. Still, it was his cab, and she wasn't about to demand he close the window.

"I just need a ride back to my car," Sadie said. "It's in the same place it was the last time you dropped me off. Do you remember where that is?"

"Sho', sho'," Monty said, turning left at a stop sign.

Her phone rang just as she put her seat belt on. The call was from Pete, and she knew it was officially time to go to Mathews. She also knew Pete would be glad to hear it. She shot a quick smile at Monty and put the phone to her ear.

"Sadie," Pete said. There was intensity in his tone that hadn't been there during their earlier conversation, and she immediately feared he was angry with her about something. "Where are you?"

"I'm on my way to talk to Mathews right now, I swear I'm—"

"The guy you left in the park," Pete interrupted. "You said he hit his head and was unconscious, right?"

"Right," Sadie said, bracing herself for getting in big trouble.

"I just got off the phone with Sergeant Mathews. He said the Miami PD did find a body at a park following an anonymous 911 call, but the man wasn't unconscious. He was dead."

Sadie gasped. "No, he wasn't dead," she said as her stomach fell. "He was breathing and everything—I checked!" She distinctly remembered checking his pulse after Monty pulled Joe out from under the table.

"Sadie," Pete said, "did you see anyone else at the park when you were there? Was anyone watching you?"

"No. I was right there when . . . he hit his head. I saw him fall, and I checked his pulse. He wasn't—"

"He didn't die because he hit his head," Pete said. "He had a gunshot wound to the back of his skull."

Sadie froze, her entire head buzzing. "That's impossible. He just—"

She was cut off when the phone was snatched from her hand. By the time her mind caught up with what had happened enough to turn her head, her phone was sailing out the open window.

CHAPTER 41

I should have done that a long time ago," Monty said. The accent was gone, and when he looked at her, there was no smile, no teeth, and no compassion in his expression. It was as if it wasn't Monty at all anymore.

Her breath froze in her chest and a tremor ran down her spine, starting in her head and moving all the way to her toes. She should say something—anything—but all she could do was stare while fear filled her chest. When she finally got hold of herself and looked out the car window in search of some means of escape, she saw the sign for the freeway entrance. Monty wasn't taking her to her car.

She grabbed the handle of the door and pulled while ramming her shoulder against the door. She'd rather roll across pavement at thirty-five miles an hour than be stuck on the freeway with this man. The door didn't budge, and although she pushed the unlock button multiple times, nothing happened. When she was with Joe, she'd never felt this trapped.

Monty didn't say a word, but she felt the car accelerate as they reached the freeway entrance. Sadie stopped struggling and leaned her forehead against the window, taking deep breaths and telling herself that if she was going to get out of this one, she would have to keep her wits about her. Apparently her heart didn't believe her; it was racing so fast she could barely distinguish the individual beats.

"I don't understand," she finally said, still facing the window, still attempting to calm her racing thoughts and heart.

"That's the beauty of it," Monty said with a nod. "You are so utterly clueless that you played right into my hands."

Sadie replayed every conversation, every movement he'd made, but none of them came off as suspect.

"You were at the gas station," Sadie said, finally turning to face him. He still didn't look like Monty. Everything had changed. "*I* found *you*."

"But you didn't see me following you from Homestead," Monty said, arrogance creeping into his tone. "You didn't notice that I pulled into the gas station right behind Megan's father. I saw you look at me, take note of the taxi. I could tell you were upset with him, and I knew he was on his way to meet Hugo. You came to me, saving me from having to follow blindly. It worked out quite perfectly for me."

"You're with Hugo?" Sadie asked.

Monty shook his head. "No, I'm most certainly *not* with Hugo."

Pete had asked if Sadie had seen anyone else at the park. "*You* killed him," Sadie said, almost breathless with the discovery.

Monty lifted his shirt and pulled a gun from his waistband. A toy-looking gun with a silencer on the end Sadie had seen before.

Joe's gun—Hugo's gun.

She looked at Monty. "When I was at the car?" It was a question because it still seemed utterly impossible. The gun had a silencer, but Sadie knew silencers only quieted the sound of a gunshot enough to disguise it. She'd have heard it. Then she remembered how she'd jumped when she slammed the trunk at the park. It had been too loud, but she'd blamed it on hypersensitivity triggered by nerves. Had Monty been watching her when she'd been at the car? Waiting for her to slam a door—or the trunk—so it would hide the sound? "How could I not have noticed he was dead?" she said, almost to herself.

"I didn't let you get close to the body once you came back," Monty replied. And Sadie had just thought he was being chivalrous when he bent down to get Joe's phone. "You didn't notice the pool of blood forming under his head either—that was the part I was most worried about, but the grass hid it pretty well."

Sadie thought about how pale Joe had looked. It had increased her concern, but he was already dead by then. She closed her eyes and tried to keep the nausea from rising in her throat. Was Joe's death her fault? Had she caused it?

"Trust is a dangerous thing, lady, and you have far too much of it to play these kind of games. Patience, on the other hand, is a virtue, and I have been very, very patient until now, letting you dig around, helping you gather the information I needed as much as you did and staying close at all times. All in all, I think I've played my part incredibly well." He smiled smugly, and Sadie looked away, feeling her nose tingle with suppressed emotion she couldn't give in to now. "I almost left after I dropped you off at your car, but when I turned the corner and looked back, you were crossing the street—off for more information. So I bided my time a little longer, wondering what you were up to. When I followed you to Larry's condo, I knew you knew too much." He smiled again. "Imagine my surprise when *you* called *me* for a ride after I'd already convinced myself I was going to have to find you alone somehow to finish things up."

She still couldn't believe what had happened, but knew she

would have to find some way to "play" this kind of game if she hoped to get out of this alive. She looked out the window at the trees and the occasional utility pole that sped past the windows. It was starting to get dark and some of the highway lights were on. They were traveling eighty miles an hour and, Sadie realized, they weren't heading north, toward Miami. There were buildings all along the interstate going north. All Sadie could see now was trees, greenery, waterways, and the occasional car that, even though it was only a few feet away, seemed impossibly far away.

"Where are we going?" she asked.

"You'll know soon enough," Monty said, speeding up even more. "I'm afraid you've made me late."

"You work with Megan's husband, don't you?" Sadie said. "You knew Joe—Hugo—was trying to help her get found, and you were sent to stop that from happening."

Monty nodded. "I've been tracking Hugo for two days, trying to figure out what he was up to. You managed to fill in many of the blank spaces for me."

Sadie was sick to realize she'd given him the answers he needed. "What happened to Liliana?"

"She wore out her welcome."

"And Megan took her place."

"Quite well, as I hear it," he answered. "Megan wanted to be someone else, and Alex wanted a new Liliana. Hugo was supposed to be watching out for Liliana while she was here in Miami—Alex has to be careful about keeping his distance—but something was off, which is why I got involved."

Sadie reviewed the things Hugo had said about Megan being safer than she'd ever been, about her knowing what happened to the real Liliana, and how he knew he'd be found eventually, but wanted to live the rest of his life with a clear conscience. "Who is Hugo to Alex?" Sadie said. "His brother?"

"Very good," Monty said. "Alex gave him everything he needed to have a successful life, and Hugo turned his nose up at it one time too many."

Hugo had said Liliana's family had killed her. Had he been a part of it? Had it haunted him ever since? They came up on a construction sign, and Sadie hoped Monty would keep speeding like he was—maybe he'd catch the attention of a police officer. Monty saw the sign, too, however, and slowed down to meet the new speed limit.

"The police have all the pieces," Sadie said, watching the first orange barrels show up on the side of the road. "They'll figure it out."

"But they won't find me, will they? You didn't tell them anything about me." He turned to her and smiled. "Thanks for that, by the way." He adjusted his position in his seat.

"Megan knows what Alex is, doesn't she? She knows what he does?"

"Megan?" he repeated, lifting his eyebrows. "You mean Liliana."

"I mean *Megan*," Sadie said sharply. "Liliana is dead, which is exactly where Megan will end up."

"I wouldn't count on that," Monty said. "Megan's proved herself quite . . . malleable. Alex likes that."

"She's hungry for the security Alex can give her," Sadie whispered, feeling the pieces come together. Megan was willing to accept who he was and what he did—though Sadie wasn't sure what those things were exactly, other than that they were illegal—because he could give her the security she wanted so much. It bothered Sadie to be able to make sense of that.

"I told Alex not to let her come to Miami," Monty said. "It was too risky for her to come back to where it all started. He wouldn't listen to me, but now he wants her back. Alex believes she'd be difficult to replace."

That meant Megan was the one who wanted to come to Miami for treatment. Perhaps Alex didn't have as strong a hold on her as Sadie feared. Yet Megan *had* left the hospital. "And her babies?" Sadie asked. "Aren't Alex's babies hard to replace?"

"Alex already has children," Monty said casually. "And Megan can have more if she wants to. Life is full of hard lessons."

Sadie clenched her eyes closed, wishing she could get those words out of her head. The flippancy was disgusting. She couldn't imagine that Megan was so cavalier about her unborn sons. Sadie had seen the tenderness; she'd felt Megan's fear for them.

"Where is she?" Sadie asked.

"Funny you should ask that," Monty said. The car started slowing, and Sadie looked ahead to see a truck stop several yards off the side of the road. If he stopped, this could be her chance. She carefully surveyed the area, thick with woods that hadn't been manually cleared. She could run into the woods, find somewhere to hide. If only she had her phone! Would she even have reception, though? It seemed so remote.

A minute later, he pulled into the parking lot and drove past rows of semitrucks, past the café and food mart, and around the back of the building. The lot was fenced along the perimeter, and the building blocked the back corner from view. Unless an employee came out the back doors to have a smoke or take out the trash, no one would see them. Monty stopped behind a loading dock and pulled his phone from his pocket.

Sadie's hand inched toward the door handle.

"I'm the only one who can control the locks," Monty said casually, putting the phone to his ear. He held up a finger, indicating for her to wait a minute, then placed the gun on his thigh. He raised an eyebrow as though issuing her a challenge.

"I'm here," he said into the phone. He clicked his phone shut without saying anything else and put it back in his pocket. He reached across her and opened the glove compartment. He pulled out half a roll of duct tape and dropped it in her lap, keeping his other hand on the gun.

"Tape up your hands," he said.

"No," Sadie said, folding her arms over her chest.

Monty looked at her for a moment and then glanced out the window behind her and smiled. Sadie wanted to see what he was looking at, but didn't dare take her eyes off of him long enough to do so. She heard the click of the locks a moment before the car's back door opened. She looked to see who was there.

Her mouth dropped open as Megan slid into the backseat, her hand on her belly as she relaxed against the seat and took deep breaths, causing her belly to rise and fall. She was dressed in maternity denim shorts, leather sandals, a white billowing shirt, and a light blue, cotton jacket. Her cheeks were flushed, and her eyes were frantic. How had she gotten here?

Monty barely allowed Megan time to pull the door closed before he picked up the gun and pointed it at her head. Megan inhaled sharply, and her eyes went wide. Monty looked at Sadie and nodded toward the duct tape. "Tape up your hands."

Sadie looked from him to Megan. Her face had paled, and her eyes darted around the car as though wondering what she'd just gotten herself into. Sadie had no choice and pulled the tape back with a zip. She wrapped it around one wrist, then wriggled around in order to wrap it around both wrists, her palms touching. She had to use her chest to brace the roll of tape and use her teeth to move it, always waiting for him to help her, but he didn't. She tried to keep it loose, but couldn't make it work; she couldn't pull the tape without tension.

When she'd done three awkward turns, Monty finally set the gun down and grabbed the roll, finishing three more turns before ripping off the end.

"Good girl," he said. He returned the duct tape to the glove box and then turned to look at Megan. "Give me your phone."

Megan hurried to obey, digging in her purse for the phone, when Monty snatched the whole purse from her, causing her to gasp in surprise before pulling back against the seat.

Monty tucked the gun in the waistband of his pants. Holding the straps of Megan's purse in one fist, he reached his other hand for the door handle. "I need to make a call." He gave both of them a challenging look.

Megan nodded quickly, looking terrified. Sadie looked away when Monty turned his eyes to her, hoping it hurt him somehow to be snubbed by her. But she watched as he tucked Megan's purse under his arm and pulled his phone from his pocket. He popped the trunk, dialed a number, and then pushed opened the driver's door while putting the phone to his ear. Sadie watched him intently. He was leaving her alone with Megan?

When Monty caught her watching, he moved the phone from his mouth and stared her down. "I won't be far away," he said. "And I'm not nearly as nice as Hugo was."

Sadie looked at her taped-up hands and pretended she hadn't heard him as she tried to come up with any possible option of escape.

He moved the phone back in place. "Yeah, it's me. I've got her and—" He shut the door and plunged the inside of the car into silence.

At least for the moment.

CHAPTER 42

Sadie was sure that this crisis had sharpened her senses, honed in her thoughts, and she tried to take confidence in the fact that she'd been in situations that looked bleak and hopeless—she'd even had her hands locked together before—and she'd managed to get out alive. However, she couldn't deny that this situation was different from anything she'd faced before. She was in an unfamiliar location, with no way to contact anyone who might be able to help her. But she couldn't afford to linger too long on those thoughts. Instead, she took a deep breath and gathered her courage together, saying a silent prayer before she exhaled slowly.

Feeling centered, Sadie looked out the window at Monty, then down at her hands taped together, the ends of her fingers red from the lack of circulation. She didn't dare look over the seat to make eye contact with Megan; Monty was watching them while he talked on the phone a few feet away from the taxi. Instead, she dropped her chin and turned her head away from him so that he couldn't see her mouth.

"Do you have any idea what you are doing, sweetheart?" Sadie said, keeping her tone light and maternal.

Megan didn't answer.

Sadie took a breath and continued. "You don't have to do this," she said quietly. "There are other options."

Seconds ticked by, and Sadie had almost given up on having any communication when Megan spoke. "You can't understand."

"I understand that you chose a new life and feel like you have to live it now, no matter what, but you don't. There are so many people who love you, Megan, so many people who would do anything to see that you and your babies are cared for. I know your father, and I've met Tia and Larry and Max." She left out Layla. "They can help you—I can help you."

Megan was quiet for a few seconds. When she spoke her voice was sad and certain. "Every single person in my life before I left was better off after I was gone."

Did she really believe that? Sadie thought to herself. A quick review of what she'd learned about Megan's life up until she disappeared helped Sadie see things from Megan's perspective. A disabled mother who couldn't love her and a distracted father who she couldn't trust. Larry and Tia loved her, certainly, but they were Layla's caretakers first. And they'd been part of sending Megan away. Even if leaving was what Megan had wanted—asked for—wouldn't it still be painful to know they were willing to let her go?

"You got the short end of several sticks," Sadie said, still looking forward with her head turned away from Monty. "I can't argue with you on that, and it's certainly not fair that you were at the mercy of your parents' tragedies and poor choices." She chose her next words carefully. "But you're a grown woman now and have already proven your ability to start again, create a new life. None of us can choose our past, but we have the future ahead of us every single day. And you do have people here who love you, miss you, and want to be a part of your life again."

"Those are very pretty words," Megan said, "but they aren't realistic. I was only able to come to the hospital with strict instructions on what to do if anything happened. When the hospital freaked out about you, I had no choice but to leave."

Sadie closed her eyes, stung by the accusation. "I'm sorry. I wasn't trying to cause you problems, but going back is not the solution."

"I don't have a choice," Megan said.

"And you're willing to put your unborn sons on the altar of that belief?" Sadie said, aching at the thought that Megan would even consider it. "Carlos is already in trouble, and you've got three and a half months left. Monty just held a gun to your head. You're not safe there."

She heard a sniffle. "I have to go back."

She was as stubborn as her father! Sadie took a breath and looked out the driver's window to see that Monty was heading for the back of the car. Watching carefully, she saw the trunk lift— blocking her from his view. She took the opportunity to turn in her seat and make eye contact with the scared woman in the backseat. "Do you *want* to go back?"

Megan's eyes filled with tears. "It doesn't matter," she said in an emotional whisper. "I have to. People would . . . suffer if I didn't."

Sadie felt tears rising in her eyes as well. "Hugo's already dead," she said, causing Megan to jolt.

"What?" Megan asked, her face both pale and scared.

"He was trying to help you, trying to get you found without putting himself in the crosshairs, but it didn't work. He knew it wasn't safe for you to be with Alex—and he died trying to keep you from going back. Doesn't that mean something? If he thought you could live apart from that life, then isn't there a chance you can?" She paused for a breath. "Your father is in Florida right now and has a lot of making up to do, Larry and Tia love you so much and would do anything—have done anything—they can to help you." Never mind that they were both likely going to jail—she'd bring that up later. "And you should know better than anyone how much power a parent can have in the lives of their children." She looked down at Megan's belly before raising her eyes to meet Megan's once again. "Do you really think you won't be haunted by this choice for the rest of your life?"

The tears overflowed as Megan clenched her eyes shut and shook her head as if clinging desperately to the lies she'd been told—perhaps even been telling herself. But Sadie knew she couldn't deny the fact that Alex was willing to sacrifice these babies. No way could Megan be okay with that—not really. Megan placed her hands on her belly and bowed her head, tears dripping from her face as emotion took over. She looked so anguished that Sadie instinctively lifted her hand to reach out to her before realizing she was still taped up.

"Megan," she said, gently, "the police are going to figure everything out. They have Liliana's body—Hugo's too—and they will find out what happened to them and why."

Megan looked up in surprise, and her face reflected desperation. "I didn't know about Liliana," she whispered. "Not for a long time. They told me she left Alex and abandoned the boys. When Hugo told me the truth, I didn't believe him. I loved Liliana; she was my friend."

Sadie was so relieved to hear that and wished she had more time to discuss the particulars of just how Megan had justified *becoming*

Liliana if she truly believed Alex's first wife had left on her own. But there was no time. "Even if you go back to Puerto Rico, the police won't be too far behind. You can't return to the life you left there, Megan—even if you love Alex, the life you've shared with him is over one way or another." Understanding was beginning to show on Megan's face, and abject fear was replacing her sorrow and earlier confusion.

Sadie continued. "You're the only one who can get any of us out of this." She glanced down at Megan's rounded stomach to indicate just how many lives were depending on her. "You won't get another chance to—" She heard the click moments before a hand clamped around Sadie's right arm and pulled her through the passenger door before it was even opened all the way. Her shin caught on the door, and she yelped in pain.

She was immediately slammed against the side of the car, her head snapping backward and causing her to bite her tongue. Before she could lift her head and focus on Monty's face, his hand connected with her left cheek, causing her to cry out as her head twisted sideways. With his other hand he held her against the car, crushing her chest and making it hard to breathe.

The sight of the ground, the open trunk, and the trees spun as she tried to process what had happened. The taste of blood filled her mouth, and the left side of her face throbbed. She tried to focus on one thing in order for her vision to adjust. In the next moment, she could feel Monty's breath on the side of her face, only inches away. She didn't look at him, but felt her body shaking involuntarily.

"I have my orders, but there are always circumstances that call for split-second decisions and I have no reservations relieving Alex of dead weight again—if you know what I mean."

"You think I don't already know you're going to kill me?" Sadie said, though she didn't believe it. Not yet. As long as she was alive there was hope she'd get out of this.

"I wasn't talking about you," Monty said, his voice even lower and his face even closer. His breath smelled like mint, which Sadie felt was yet one more thing that made him seem so harmless. Evil people should have evil breath . . . and crooked teeth.

"Alex wants her back," Sadie said, her stomach sinking. She kept her head turned so that she wasn't looking at him. Less than a minute ago she'd been trying to convince Megan not to go back to Alex, and now she was trying to convince Monty that she had to return. She felt the cold metal of what she could only assume was the gun against the side of her face. The coolness almost felt good against the swelling of where he'd hit her moments earlier, but mostly served as a reminder of who was really in control.

"There's an endless supply of stupid women in this world," Monty said. "Alex will have no trouble finding a replacement. And I'll have no trouble getting rid of that one too, if needed. Alex didn't lose much sleep over Liliana; he won't waste time mourning this one either."

This one. Megan wasn't even worthy of a name to this man. "Then why take her back at all?" Sadie said, unable to keep the words back. "Why bother?"

"Because Alex is very generous when he gets what he wants," Monty said. "Alex makes it possible for me to have the means of a better lifestyle, while the cab gives me the cover that so often comes in handy—such as today. I do things his way as much as I can."

"Like killing Hugo?" Sadie said.

"Dead weight," Monty said. "Hugo should have done as he was told, not make up new rules based on his current view of morality."

"People like you don't win forever," Sadie said, wanting to make sure he understood that though he'd obviously gotten away with horrible things, it wouldn't last. It couldn't. She finally looked at him, feeling her eyes narrow at the arrogant look on his face.

"I don't need forever," Monty said. "Today is good enough."

"They saw your cab at the hospital."

"They'll never trace it, and no one else saw me but you. So, in a sense I've already gotten away with it, but we're on a tight schedule, and I'd rather you disappear a little better than Liliana did—which is going to take time I don't have at the moment. So, you hang in there, keep your *faith* alive, and behave yourself until we get things sorted out—all for her, of course." He nodded toward the car before meeting Sadie's eyes again. "I've heard all I can stand of your voice today, so if you open your mouth again for any reason, I'll let you watch her bleed to death in the backseat."

There was no doubt in Sadie's mind that he meant what he said. In fact, she imagined it would give him a great deal of satisfaction to show her what he was capable of. She clamped her lips together as the situation fell heavy around her shoulders. Liliana was dead, Hugo was dead, and Megan and her babies would be next—closely followed by Sadie herself—if Sadie didn't keep quiet. It really was a brilliant plan on Monty's part. Sadie's own life was worth risking, but Megan? Two unborn children? There was no comparison.

"So, do I have your word that I won't have to resort to such measures?" Monty asked in a purely conversational tone.

Sadie nodded, feeling spineless even while knowing she had no other option. "I'm holding you to that, then," Monty said, tapping the gun against her swollen cheek, causing Sadie to wince.

This was a promise she wouldn't break, but it might very well cost her her life.

CHAPTER 43

They started driving, and it took only a moment for Sadie to realize they were continuing south, toward the Florida Keys. The construction cones and equipment continued alongside the road, and patches of water began appearing intermittently on either side of the road. It was too dark to be as beautiful as it probably was during the day, but she watched the light reflecting off the surface of the water and wished she could dive in and swim away from all this. It was so surreal outside the car, and so utterly frightening on the inside.

Monty turned on the radio, some icky rap music that certainly didn't make Sadie feel any better. Now and then she'd feel him looking at her. She refused to meet his eyes and simply watched the scenery, sprinkled with construction paraphernalia, pass by. She took deep breaths to calm herself, and continued saying internal prayers for guidance and help.

She came up with a hundred scenarios that could lead to her escape, with Megan of course—a police barricade, an accident, Monty eating peanuts and going into anaphylactic shock due to an unsuspected allergy—but as the miles stretched on, both ahead of and behind them, she found it harder and harder to imagine how she'd get out of this.

There were a few other cars on the road, but it was fully dark now, and traffic was sparse. Sadie imagined people preferred not to drive this road after dark. It was remote and lifeless, and she was sure the water was full of snakes and alligators and all kinds of tropical critters.

Unable to ask questions out loud, she asked them in her mind, then made up answers.

Where are we going?

Key West, of course.

Why?

So I can smuggle Megan back to Puerto Rico and throw your body to the sharks, of course.

Or,

Could we stop for some key lime pie in Key Largo?

Is that what you want for your last meal?

The questions all seemed to end the same way so she tried not to ask them anymore, focusing instead on anything that might come in handy should an unknown opportunity present itself.

Her kung fu skills, obviously, were a huge asset. Her hands were taped and going numb, but she had fingernails and quick reflexes. She could also spit and scream, and . . . she looked around the cab, noticing it had an emergency brake between the front seats and what looked like a road atlas in the passenger door pocket. She wasn't sure road atlases counted as an actual weapon, but it was all she had to work with. Yet all the thinking and planning didn't block out the fact that she was responsible not only for her own life, but for Megan's and her children as well.

They were several minutes, and miles, down the road ahead of them when Megan spoke. Sadie couldn't hear what she said, the music was too loud, but after she said it again, louder, Monty turned down the radio.

"Where's Hugo?" Megan asked. Her voice was quiet and scared. Sadie wished she'd at least try to sound confident instead of so weak, and yet she understood why Megan was feeling the way she was.

"Can't say that I know," Monty answered. He reached for the volume knob again.

"Is he dead?"

Sadie felt Monty look at her as though suspecting she'd told Megan, which she had. She didn't meet his eyes. "Now why would you ask such a thing?" Monty said, his voice patronizing.

"He's the one who brought me here," Megan said. "Alex said he would look out for me. You were only his backup, right?"

"Now I'm looking out for you," Monty said, looking in the rear-view mirror.

"What happened to Hugo?" Megan asked.

"Stop asking stupid questions," Monty said, turning up the volume of the radio, though not as loud as before. "Alex will explain everything when we get there."

"Is he sending a boat?" Megan said loudly in order to be heard over the music. Even though it was only an increase of volume, it made Megan sound stronger.

"He'll meet us in Nassau," Monty said.

"He's not meeting us in Marathon?" Megan asked.

"Of course not," Monty said, laughing and shaking his head. "Alex has more important things to do than clean up other people's mistakes." He looked in the rearview mirror again, and Sadie assumed he was looking at Megan. "Which would be a good lesson for you to learn."

Sadie cringed inside. What a horrible thing to say to anyone, let alone a woman in Megan's situation. Megan didn't say anything else, but Sadie could hear a slight sniffling from the backseat. Monty turned the music up even more.

A few more miles passed—monotonous with clusters of trees, waterways, and construction cones. Sadie wondered if the road would look like this all the way to Marathon Key, where she assumed there must be a marina where Megan would get on a boat, and Sadie would be left to Monty and whatever fate he had in store for her. She looked down at her hands, which were tingling, yet balled into fists, and forced herself to unclench her fingers. Her palms pressed together as though she were praying.

"What are you doing?" Monty asked, turning down the music.

Sadie thought he was talking to her, which was downright rude since he'd told her not to talk, but when she turned to him, he was looking in the rearview mirror again.

"I'm j-just taking off my jacket," Megan said. "I'm too warm."

Monty didn't respond, and Sadie looked over her shoulder long enough to catch a look from Megan as she shrugged out of her jacket before Monty's hand grabbed Sadie's chin and faced her forward.

"Don't look at her," he said.

Sadie clenched her teeth together to keep from talking and forced herself to look at the endless road ahead of them. But she kept thinking about that look from Megan. She'd looked directly at Sadie, holding her eyes as though wanting to say something but being unable to. Did it mean something or was Sadie desperately grabbing for any hidden meaning that might offer her some hope?

There was a light ahead of them on the road. At first Sadie thought it was an exceptionally bright streetlight, but as they drew closer, she realized it was a huge halogen lamp lighting up the road for a construction crew. People.

Monty swore and started slowing down per the illuminated speed limit sign flashing his speed at him and telling him to slow down.

"Hide your hands," Monty said to Sadie. "If they stop us . . ."

Sadie appreciated that he didn't finish the thought out loud since she was certain it was another threat against Megan, and Megan didn't need any more stress. Sadie put her hands and wrists between her thighs, as though she was cold, which, she realized she was. The night had cooled off considerably, even though the air was still thick. Yet, Megan had taken off her jacket, claiming she was warm.

They had almost reached the area of active construction. Sadie could make out a couple of men working against the far left-side rail, not paying any attention to the cars that drove by. The huge lamps lit up the area around the construction crew until it almost looked like daylight. Sadie had to squint in order for her eyes to adjust to the artificial brightness.

Sadie was just getting used to the lighting when they began moving away from it. No one had looked twice at them. There was no salvation here, and she had resigned herself to the fact that there would be no rescue when a flash of blue out of the corner of her left eye caught her attention.

She instinctually pulled toward the door and turned her head to see what the blue was, only to see Megan's jacket loop over Monty's face and pull his head against the headrest. Megan yanked back on the sleeves of her jacket while Monty yelled and grabbed at the fabric covering his face—letting go of the steering wheel in the process.

Sadie's heart leapt into her throat as the car hit a construction barrier. She flinched, but then caught Megan's frantic eyes as Megan attempted to tie the sleeves of the jacket in a knot behind the headrest. Sadie jumped into action, and she lunged forward, grabbing the emergency brake with both hands and pulling up as hard as she could. The car struck another cone.

"Hold on!" she screamed as the wheels locked. Monty yelled again, and the car went into a spin. Still holding onto the emergency brake, Sadie tried to brace herself as best she could as the car went around and around, disorienting her completely.

An orange barrel bounced off the hood and then the windshield. Megan screamed, and Sadie prepared herself for the next thing she needed to do as the car continued to slide before coming to a stop at an angle, hood down. Assuming they were on the shoulder of the road, Sadie pushed herself across Monty, who was still frantically pulling at the jacket over his face, and pushed the unlock button on the driver's door—the only unlock button in the car that worked.

"Get out!" Sadie yelled just before Monty pulled up his knee, catching her in the throat as she tried to get out of his way. "Run," she said with a cough. She felt a hand grab her hair. Then she heard the back door whoosh open.

She pulled away and Monty's hand slid off her icky hair; the gooey hair product and talcum powder making it impossible for him to keep his grip. She scrambled toward the passenger door, gravity pulling her toward the dashboard as her feet were suddenly immersed in cold water.

She grabbed for the door release with her conjoined hands. *Oh please, oh please, oh please.*

She'd managed to grab the handle when she heard the door locks click again. She looked over her shoulder in time to see Monty lunge across the seat at her, the jacket held in one balled fist. She managed to turn toward him and lifted a knee, hitting him squarely in the face. Looking past him, she could see that Megan's door was open. She was gone.

The only way out of the car was through that door, but as soon as she moved toward the space between the two front seats, Monty was on her again, this time throwing his whole body weight on her, pressing her against the corner between the dashboard and passenger door.

She grunted, feeling the air knocked from her lungs. She started kicking and used her taped-together hands as a weapon, swinging them back and forth wildly, trying to protect her neck and face as best she could. She caught his face with one of her backhand swings, and managed to knee him in the thigh, but it didn't stop him, and within seconds, he had one hand on her neck and his full body weight pressing against her chest. The chill on her back told her the water level was rising.

Monty's eyes were on fire, his too-white teeth looking ferocious as he snarled at her. "You . . . are a . . . very foolish . . . woman," he said between clenched teeth, tightening his grip on her neck. There was no warning in the strength of his hand; he'd like nothing more than to snap her neck in two. Her hands were pinned against her chest so she could barely move.

She heard voices, and tried to yell, but it was beyond her as pressure began building in her head. She could feel her eyes bulging even as the water level continued to rise past her waist, traveling inch by inch up her chest. If Monty didn't kill her soon, she'd drown. Light began popping in her peripheral vision, and she realized she'd stopped fighting.

"Was she really worth saving?" Monty hissed, his eye taking on a glint of excitement. "She'll die anyway, you know. I'll make sure of it now."

His threat brought on a renewed burst of energy. Despite Sadie's vision beginning to swirl, she tried to kick, tried to raise her hands, but she was losing strength almost as quickly as she could feel her consciousness slipping. There was no fight left, no oxygen to rejuvenate her muscles. She closed her eyes as darkness began to take over. She didn't want Monty's face to be the last thing she saw and felt tears leak out of her eyes. She wasn't going to get out of this one. He was going to win.

Her thoughts began to spin with thoughts of Monty, Eric, the key lime pie she hadn't had, and Megan's bracelet. Her children. Pete. Her throat was on fire, her eyes feeling as though they were about to pop out of her head, when suddenly the voices she'd heard got louder.

The pressure around her neck suddenly lessened, but it took a few moments for her to comprehend what that meant. She looked up to see Monty being pulled away from her. He clawed toward her face, swearing and cursing, but it made no difference. One minute he was crushing her, the next he was moving backward, and in the next instant she was looking up into another dark face, this one staring back at her in horror. "Are you okay, lady?" he said in a voice so similar to Monty's Jamaican accent that Sadie felt a rush of fear overcome her before realizing this man had saved her.

She opened her mouth to speak, but all that came out was a raspy cough. Water filled her ears, but she lacked the strength to pull herself up. The man yelled for help as he reached for her, grabbing her arm awkwardly due to the angle of the car. Brackish water splashed into her mouth before more hands grabbed her other arm and pulled her up, across the seats, and out of the car before laying her on the ground. The first face she'd seen hovered over her again, his dark eyes frantic with concern. She took deep breaths, trying to recover from the lack of oxygen as she looked around. She could see two workers lying on top of someone putting up a fight—Monty. Craning her neck around, she looked for Megan and tried to say her name, but the words still wouldn't come.

"She be okay, lady," the man said, smoothing Sadie's wet, slimy hair back from her face.

She looked up at her rescuer, and tears began to rise as she reached up with her taped hands and grabbed his shirt. "Thank you," she mouthed, unable to speak.

He smiled, though he still looked scared. "An ambulance be comin' from Key Largo," he said. "Jus' 'old on, okay? You be alright."

Sadie could feel her whole body begin to shake as shock set in. She forced herself to relax her head back and close her eyes, tears streaming down her face and pooling in her ears.

"You be alright," the man said again as he began pulling at the duct tape holding her hands together. "I promise, you both be alright."

CHAPTER 44

"You're sure you're okay?" the emergency room nurse asked as he helped Sadie stand. He was Hispanic, about six-two, and totally ripped—as Breanna would say.

Sadie nodded. Her throat was still raw and hurt like the dickens, so she didn't dare talk much. She was exhausted and ready to go home, but then she thought of the report she needed to make to Mathews and the phone call she owed Pete—both a little hard to do when she couldn't talk. And then there was Megan.

"Megan!"

Startled to have her thoughts repeated out loud, she looked up in time to see the curtain surrounding her gurney-bed-thing be yanked to the side. Behind the curtains stood Eric, his eyebrows up, a black eye swollen shut. He looked at Sadie and froze for a moment, then he moved forward, coming to a stop a foot or so from where Sadie stood beside her bed.

"Sadie?" he whispered, raising his hand to her neck. She'd seen the bruises; it wasn't pretty. She grabbed his hand before he touched her and shook her head.

"Can I help you, sir?" the ER nurse cut in, taking a step toward them as though planning to come between them if necessary.

Sadie gave him a look and smiled. "It's okay," she said in a horrible whisper. She lowered her hand still holding Eric's wrist and let go.

The nurse looked between the two of them and nodded. "I'll be right out there," he said, pointing through the curtains before stepping through the gap Eric had made. He didn't pull the curtains closed, and Sadie could see his shoes stop to the side of the opening; he was waiting to make sure Eric didn't try anything, she assumed.

She looked from the shoes to Eric's face. "You haven't seen Megan yet?" she whispered, trying not to cringe at the pain speaking caused.

"I just got here," Eric said, still looking at her neck with sympathy in his expression. "They said she was brought to the emergency room. Mathews brought me." No sooner had he said Mathews's name than the police sergeant appeared in the opening of the curtains. He caught Sadie's eye, then nodded and stepped out of view. But she could see his shoes too.

Sadie turned her attention to Eric and shrugged to show she didn't know where Megan was. They hadn't transported her and Megan in the same car, and no one had come to talk to her about anything yet. "Labor and delivery?" she whispered.

Eric nodded and finally met her eyes. "What happened?"

Sadie shook her head; it didn't matter right now. "Let's find Megan," she said. She moved her hand to his forearm. He surprised her by pulling back, and she turned to face him.

"Sadie," he said. "About the things Larry said back at the apartment, I—"

Sadie shook her head quickly. She really didn't want to discuss that right now. How could she explain that she'd had reservations about a future with Eric before she'd heard any of that? Certainly what Larry had said made an impact, but it wasn't the reason for her change of heart. There was something thrilling about Eric, and he certainly wasn't a bad guy by any stretch, but she also couldn't see herself snuggled up in front of a fire with him, or opening presents with grandchildren on Christmas Day. There had been chemistry, but chemistry wasn't enough.

"We'll talk later," she whispered and began walking again, pulling him with her.

Sergeant Mathews and the nurse, as well as the female police officer who'd brought Sadie in, were waiting for them. Eric explained the situation, the officer called someone on her walkie-talkie, and a minute later they were in an elevator Sadie had already used twice that day.

When they reached the doorway to Megan's room, Eric paused and took a breath. A curtain was drawn around the bed, blocking most of the room from view. Eric turned to look at Sadie, and she gave him a reassuring smile and nod. He stepped into the room. Sadie had every intention of following him, but her feet wouldn't move. Despite all her involvement, she realized that this moment didn't belong to her.

"Sweetie Pie?" she heard Eric say in a nervous voice.

She felt tears in her eyes and winced as she tried to swallow the emotion that came with it.

"Daddy?" came a voice that at that moment sounded like a very scared little girl. "I'm so sorry."

CHAPTER 45

It was two o'clock Sunday afternoon when Sadie's plane began its descent into Denver. Her ears popped, and Sadie braced herself for the moment the wheels touched down. A few minutes later the plane came to a stop, but the butterflies were just getting started. What would she say when she faced Pete? How would she explain the bruises? They'd texted back and forth, and Sadie knew he'd talked to Mathews, but the anxiety of having an actual discussion about what had happened was eating her up.

The pilot thanked them for their patronage, and Sadie tucked her hair behind her ears. She'd spent all day Saturday giving her statement and answering questions. Last night she'd met Eric for dinner and tried to let him down easy. He was still convinced it was the things Larry had said that had made her change her mind; she finally gave up trying to convince him otherwise and just wished him well. Eric was staying in Miami to be close to Megan, and Sadie was glad for that on many levels. He and Megan needed to create a new relationship, and Sadie was relieved that Eric wouldn't be in Garrison for a little while.

As soon as the plane came to a stop, passengers began popping open luggage compartments and fighting to be the first ones off. Sadie didn't even stand, content to let the plane clear out and therefore avoid the chaos. She was in no hurry.

Finally, when the plane was nearly empty, she stood and threw her purse over her arm, glad she'd checked her bag instead of carrying it on with her. She walked through the airport in a daze, not smiling at the people she passed, not browsing the magazines or books like she usually did. The only stop she made was to buy a ridiculously expensive multicolored silk scarf she immediately looped around her neck so that she didn't feel so self-conscious about the bruises. She'd looked for one at the Miami airport, but apparently scarves weren't in high demand when it was 85 degrees outside.

By the time she arrived at the baggage carousel, there were only a couple suitcases left. It was easy to spot hers—bright blue with an orange poppy painted on the front pocket. She'd painted the poppy herself a couple years ago after returning from a trip only to find herself with someone else's suitcase.

Not wanting to chase the bag, she simply waited for it to make the round and come back to her. When it was a few feet away, she stepped forward. Then she felt a hand on her arm.

"Let me get that for you."

Sadie turned and felt her mouth fall open as Pete smiled at her. Immediately her hands went to her scarf-covered neck, and she wished she'd reapplied her lipstick before getting off the plane. "Pete," she said in her raspy voice. "Wh—what are you doing here?"

"Making sure you arrived safely, of course."

Sadie blinked at him and felt the tears well up in her eyes. "You came all the way down from Garrison for me?"

"I took the airport shuttle," he said with a nod. "I figured after all that's happened you might not be fit to drive." He pulled her scarf a few inches away from her neck, making a sympathetic face as he looked at the evidence of what had happened in Florida.

Sadie moved the scarf back into place, smiling sheepishly as she did so. She hated him seeing her broken, and yet . . . he was here.

She met his eyes again and felt warmth and *longing* begin filling her head and chest. She wiped at her eyes. "I'm sorry," she whispered, glancing away, embarrassed.

Pete reached down and lifted her chin so she was looking at him. "Are you okay?" he asked in a tender voice.

Sadie didn't nod, she didn't blink; she only stared at him and realized that whatever she'd thought she felt for Eric was almost silly compared to *this* moment. Pete had been the same man in every situation she'd seen him in. He was solid, he was trustworthy, and he was here even though he had every reason not to be. Gayle came to mind, and Sadie felt conflicted. She'd given her blessing . . . but Pete had come to Denver. Even after everything that had happened.

"Gayle said you never got a decent piece of key lime pie," Pete said, interrupting Sadie's thoughts by nudging a grocery bag near his feet that seemed to be holding a bakery box of some kind.

"I guess I'd forgotten about that," Sadie said. The last two days were a blur.

"Well, Gayle made one for you and insisted I bring it with me. She thought we might like to have a slice while we . . . talk."

Sadie felt her eyes widen and her chest expand with the dangerous emotion of hope. "Gayle knew you were coming to meet me?"

Pete held her eyes. "Gayle knows."

They were simple words, but Sadie thought she heard a deeper meaning in them than Gayle simply knowing he had come to the airport.

"She's not really my type, Sadie," Pete said in a low voice.

Sadie's cheeks heated up; he knew she'd given Gayle the green light to spend time with Pete. She didn't know how to explain herself, especially since she regretted ever having done it. "I'm sorry," she said. "I thought . . ." She'd thought so many things she didn't know where to start.

"So can we talk?" Pete asked. "Over pie."

Sadie looked up into his face and the thoughts she'd been having about him exploded into words. The setting was all wrong, and yet that didn't stop her. It had to be said.

"Maybe I was afraid of how I felt," she began, "or maybe I just wasn't ready to admit it, but either way I didn't trust you the way I should have and didn't give us a fair chance. I'm sorry." For a moment, he just looked at her.

"So . . . what happened with Eric?" Pete said, and she saw him pull back a little bit. Maybe not physically, but he was guarding his emotions, protecting himself. She knew what he was afraid of. Had Sadie explored a relationship with Eric only to come running back to Pete when she was disappointed? Perhaps in a sense she had, but not like he thought.

"I saw the big picture," Sadie said. Eric had seemed mysterious, flattering, and adventurous. Now she realized that though he might be in his late forties, he had a lot of growing up to do. "I wish him only good things, but he's not the kind of man I want to spend my life with."

Pete held her eyes, questions still lingering in his face. "You sound so certain."

"What I had with Neil and what you had with Pat was powerful, and maybe we both thought we could never find that again. Maybe we can't. But we've been there, Pete. We have loved *that* much, and we have been loved that much in return. Who else could understand that the way we can? Who better to make it happen again?" She was still whispering, but he was listening intently.

Pete watched her carefully for a few seconds. "I'm not willing to settle for anything less than that," he said.

She lifted both her hands, ignoring the protest of her left shoulder, and put them on either side of Pete's face. He was tall, so she rose up on her tiptoes and then waited for him to come down to her. If they were going to try to have a relationship that moved toward a life together, she was done driving in the slow lane.

"I don't know when it happened," Sadie said, feeling his breath on her face as she stared into his eyes. She had to clear her throat before continuing; she was getting raspier by the minute. "And I don't know how I didn't notice it before, but somewhere along the crooked path we've taken, I fell in love with you."

"Sadie," he whispered.

Sadie stared up at him, hoping to tell him with her eyes the things words couldn't say. Yet she braced herself as the events of the last few days marched through her mind. Eric, Florida, Gayle. He had so many reasons to say no, but she prayed he wouldn't.

There were a hundred other things she wanted to say—about seeing firsthand how quickly lives could change, about how much hurt there was in the world, about how certain she was that she could prove herself to him—but she didn't say any of those things. She watched his eyes and waited. This was up to him now, and she'd have to live with whatever choice he made.

He watched her carefully, and she held her breath, waiting for his answer and trying to ignore the ache developing in the balls of her feet as she continued to stand on her toes so that their faces were as close to one another as she could possibly make them. She'd about given up when he leaned forward quickly and pressed his lips against hers that had parted slightly in surprise by the time he reached her.

Any fear that had lingered between them was banished in an instant. Sadie wrapped her arms around his back, pulling him close and forgetting everything—and everyone—else. The creaking of the baggage carousel disappeared, and the people around them were inconsequential.

As the kiss deepened and warmth spread through her body only one word came to mind.

Fireworks.

Key Lime Pie

4 ounces cream cheese, softened to room temperature
1 tablespoon grated lime zest
½ teaspoon salt
1 can sweetened condensed milk
1 egg yolk
½ cup fresh lime juice (about 4 limes; if using key limes, use about ⅓ cup of juice, add more to taste)
whipped cream (for garnish)
sliced limes (for garnish)

Preheat oven to 325 degrees.

Using electric beaters, mix cream cheese, zest, and salt until creamy. Add sweetened condensed milk and mix until incorporated. Add egg yolk, mix until combined. Add lime juice and stir until well blended. Mixture will thicken slightly. Pour filling into your choice of prepared crust (pastry, crumb, sugar cookie) and bake until set, about 20 to 30 minutes. Cool to room temperature. Cover and refrigerate 2 hours before serving. Garnish with whipped cream and sliced limes.

Serves 8.

Sadie's Favorite Crumb-Crust

1½ cups animal cracker crumbs (not the frosted kind)
3 tablespoons brown sugar
6 tablespoons butter, melted

Preheat oven to 325 degrees. Mix ingredients together and press into a 9-inch pie tin. Bake 18 to 20 minutes or until golden brown.

ACKNOWLEDGMENTS

This book will forever stand as a reminder not to procrastinate my deadlines. Many sacrifices by many people made it possible.

First and foremost: my husband, Lee. When I told him I had six weeks to write two-thirds of the book, he didn't blink an eye and simply asked what he could do to help. That help resulted in my being out of the house two to three nights/days a week while he chauffeured kids, made meals, orchestrated household things, and kept up with his work schedule. The kids were equally supportive, looking out for each other when I was gone for full days while Lee was out of town, leaving me alone when I locked myself in the basement, and acting quite pleased to be having frozen pizza for dinner . . . again. Much thanks to Schwan's and Costco for the part they played in my family's survival.

I had asked five friends to edit the manuscript for me, only it wasn't completed by the time I'd arranged. Every one of them agreed to read it unfinished and help where they could. Every one of them edited it in less than five days; a couple of them did it in less than forty-eight hours, which meant their kids were having frozen pizza too. I would never have been able to finish the story and say what I wanted to say the right way without them: Crystal White (my friend and my sister), Heather Moore, Julie Wright, Annette Lyon, and Melanie Jacobsen. Thank you, ladies! You better let me repay this one!

Throughout the writing process, Sadie's Test Kitchen was crankin' and my friends and chefs continue to be an absolutely vital part of this series, both for helping perfect the recipes I come up with, and for offering up some of their favorites. Danyelle Ferguson (Fruity Pasta Salad), Whit Larsen (Southern BBQ Slow-Cooked Chicken and Super Sausage Gravy), Laree Ipson, Michelle Jeffries, Don Carey, Barbara Dallon, Annie Funk, and our new baker, Megan O'Neill, were absolutely priceless.

Once all these people finished helping me with the writing, the book moved into the ever-competent hands of the Deseret Book staff. Big thanks to Jana Erickson, product director; Lisa Mangum, editor; Shauna Gibby, designer; Rachael Ward, typographer; and the dozens of other Deseret Book employees who had a hand in taking the story and making it into a book. Once it's in book form, Roberta Stout and Leigh Dethman do their magic. Thank you, thank you.

Beyond all these hands, I am most grateful to my Father in Heaven, for bringing these people into my life and for giving me more than I ever dreamed of.

Enjoy this sneak peek of

Blackberry Crumble

Coming Spring 2011

CHAPTER 1

Q uiz me," Sadie said, straightening the row of cherry chocolate chip cookies she'd laid out on the platter. Pete Cunningham, her *absolutely-certain* boyfriend, was also laying out cookies—blueberry muffin tops to be exact. The Fourth of July had been several weeks ago, but she'd chosen the color scheme of red, white, and blue for the annual Latham Club summer picnic, which made the cookies a perfect fit.

"Okay," Pete said in his rich voice, placing a final cookie in his row—you couldn't really stack or layer blueberry muffin tops, but he was doing a wonderful job of arranging them as attractively as possible. More points in his favor, though he didn't need extra credit. Their relationship had moved to a new level over the last few months, and Pete had proved himself a hundred times since then. "How many exits?"

"Three," Sadie said with confidence; that was an easy one. She popped open a plastic clamshell container of chocolate chip cookies and tried not to be offended. She'd have made more cookies if she'd known the other people on the food committee were bringing store-bought desserts. "Double doors straight ahead, single doors to the close left and far right. The doors behind us don't count because they lead to the kitchen, which leads to the fenced parking lot."

"Good," Pete said. "But always assume you're in the six position on a clock and specify exit locations by the hours they represent. That would make the double doors eleven o'clock, since they are slightly right of straight ahead. The single doors would then be at eight and two."

"Got it," Sadie said, a little thrill of discovery rushing through her. People said you couldn't teach an old dog new tricks—and at the age of fifty-six Sadie could certainly be considered a mature student—but she was proving the cliché wrong under Pete's excellent tutelage. "What else?"

"How many chairs are along the walls?" Pete asked. "That will give you an idea of how many people are expected to be here."

"About seventy," Sadie said, glancing quickly at the left wall and estimating that there were twenty-something chairs lined up. Two other walls had what looked like equal numbers of chairs, and the fourth wall had the tables for the food. However, since she'd helped plan the event, she already knew how many people were expected. Originally, the annual picnic-style dinner was supposed to be held outside, but Garrison, Colorado, was in the grip of a hot spell so the event had been moved to the city hall—a former elementary school with a nice-sized gymnasium and overzealous air conditioning system. It was 5:30 in the evening, ninety degrees outside, and yet Sadie had goose bumps since it was a chilly sixty-five degrees inside.

"And where are your keys?"

Sadie's head snapped to the side, and she looked at Pete in surprise. "My keys?" she asked, confused. In the weeks since she'd started asking him to quiz her about her surroundings—honing her skills of observation—he'd never asked about anything other than the place they were at or the people they were with.

Pete glanced at her as he straightened the row of M&M's cookies he'd been putting out and then wiped the crumbs off on his apron. Sadie thought he looked very cute in the apron. "If you had to leave in a hurry, you'd need your keys. Where are they?"

"Um, in my purse."

"And where is your purse?" Pete asked, turning to face her and crossing his arms over his chest. His silver hair caught the light streaming in through the high windows, but Sadie was in no mind to appreciate it the way she normally would.

"In the kitchen," she said, defeated. "With the other half a dozen people helping with the food."

"Not to mention anyone who can come in through the back door, which is unlocked to make it easier for helpers to come in and out." He gave her an understanding smile, but didn't stop there. "I counted three other purses on the counter next to yours, each one of them likely holding wallets and keys. With no one specifically assigned to stay in the kitchen at all times—not that that's foolproof either—there's no one to keep an eye on those purses. They're a prime target for theft, especially since the gate is open, and Goose Park, a common hangout for transients and drug users, is right across the street."

Sadie's shoulders fell. "It's not fair," she said, suddenly petulant. "I don't have any pockets. Even if I wanted to keep my keys with me, I can't."

"Don't you have a code on the door of your car? You can leave your purse in the trunk of your car where it's safer."

"That's gotten me in trouble before. I need to keep my cell phone close by."

"So keep your phone on your person."

"Pockets," Sadie reminded him, lifting the sides of her skirt to demonstrate how pocketless she was.

Pete shrugged and smiled at her. "Then wear clothing with pockets when you know you'll be unable to keep your purse with you."

Sadie narrowed her eyes at him. "Easy for you to say," she said, half serious and half playful. "You're a man. Everything you buy comes with pockets."

Pete grinned back at her in a superior way. "I believe, however, that men's clothing doesn't have a corner on the market."

"But some styles don't offer a pocket option," Sadie continued, reflecting on the women's clothing industry as a whole. Because of the patriotic theme that had helped her choose the types of cookies to bring, she was wearing what she called her Betsy Ross dress—a navy blue, cotton sundress sprinkled with white polka dots. Upon closer inspection, however, the dots revealed themselves as stars. The bodice fit well, with a wide, navy blue belt that set off her waist, even if it did make her hips look a little more prominent. Pockets on a dress like this would pad her hips even more and keep the A-line skirt from falling correctly.

"Then don't buy those styles," Pete said. He took a step closer to her, and Sadie felt the now-familiar zing as the protons between them started dancing. She loved the zing, something she hadn't felt between them for too long. Now, however, was not the moment for protons.

"O-okay," Sadie said, finding it hard to stay focused as Pete moved even closer. His hand brushed her arm as he tucked her hair behind her ear, trailing his fingers down her jaw and neck. Her breath shuddered slightly at his touch even as she felt herself leaning into him. They were alone for the moment, creating the perfect moment for him to steal a kiss . . . or three. The rest of the food committee could be heard through the door behind them; they were all in the kitchen. The scent of Pete's cologne mingled with the smell of cookies—was there a more perfect combination than baked goods and Peter Cunningham?

"Just remember that if someone takes your keys, you're stranded, and whomever it was you were supposed to be going after is getting farther and farther away."

Shop talk or not, he was totally flirting with her, and she was completely under his spell.

When words failed her and she was feeling herself pulled into the reservoirs of his beautiful hazel eyes, he spoke again. "I've got two words for you, Sadie Hoffmiller."

"What?" Sadie breathed, thinking of all the things he could say that were only two words. *Kiss me* made the top of the list.

"Voice mail."

"What?" Sadie said, pulling her eyebrows together in surprise as Pete stepped back.

"If you can't keep your purse with you, chances are you're too busy to answer your phone anyway. Let them leave a message, and you can enjoy the peace of mind of knowing your personal items are safe."

"Oh," Sadie said, trying to hide her disappointment. "That's a really . . . smart idea."

"Well," Pete said with a shrug and another of his adorable smiles as he tapped her nose playfully and moved away, "I didn't find my shiny badge at the bottom of a Cracker Jack box." He wiped his hands on his apron again, and in the process drew attention to the very badge he was referencing, clipped to the waistband of his pants.

At that precise moment, it caught the same light that had caught Pete's hair a few moments earlier. The metal gleamed heroically and initiated a wave of . . . envy in Sadie.

She looked away, chastising herself for being silly. She was not, nor would she ever be, a police detective. She was a retired school-teacher, for heaven's sake. And yet she'd had several adventures over the last eight months that had created a longing for . . . something. She didn't know what, exactly, but listening to Pete talk about his work—the details he *could* talk about—ignited something inside her that drew her toward his expertise. It had also drawn her to a few Web sites about how to become a private investigator, but she hadn't told anyone about them and felt rather silly for having even thought about something like that. Instead, she peppered Pete for tricks of his trade and had him quiz her about details or procedures while continuing on with her community-oriented life as though it hadn't somehow lost some of its appeal.

The squeaking of a hinge caused both Sadie and Pete to look up as a young woman entered the room. Sadie didn't believe she'd ever met this woman, and Sadie had been part of the Latham Club—a nonprofit community service group—for several years. Maybe the woman was a guest, but she'd entered alone. Was that a newspaper tucked under her arm? Sadie's observation skills were getting better all the time.

A voice from behind them broke into their study of the new ar-rival, however. "Detective Cunningham?"

Sadie and Pete both turned toward the doors that led to the kitchen. Glenda Meyers stood in the doorway. "I'm so sorry to inter-rupt, but it seems we filled the punch bowl so full that none of us can carry it. Would you mind helping us bring it out?"

"Of course not," Pete said.

Sadie sprang into action, stacking emptied cookie containers in an attempt to clear the tables. There needed to be room for the trays of lunch meat and veggies, not to mention the punch bowl, chips, and the array of salads the club members would be bringing with them. Initially this was supposed to be a lunch, but after juggling schedules it became a dinner . . . of lunch-type foods since no one wanted to do much cooking—other than Sadie.

"Would you mind throwing these away?" Sadie said as Pete moved toward the doorway. "Be sure to keep half a dozen or so for leftovers." There were always store-bought cookies left over, unlike her homemade varieties, which disappeared quickly. A fine argument for why being late to these types of events might be fashionable, but not wise. Pete nodded, and Sadie handed over the stacked containers. He winked at her while turning toward the doorway and the awaiting Glenda. Sadie's toes tingled in her sandals. ·

Once they disappeared, Sadie's eyes were drawn back to the woman who'd entered the gym . . . alone and uninvited. To Sadie's surprise, however, the woman was no longer standing at the far end of the room looking out of place. Instead she was striding toward Sadie with purposeful steps.

There were only a few yards between them, and Sadie finished assessing this woman as quickly as she could. Shoulder-length, strawberry-blonde hair tucked behind her ears, no bangs. Blue-gray eyes and a fair complexion with a smattering of freckles that made her look younger than what Sadie believed to be her thirty-something years. Her makeup was minimal, and she wasn't wearing a wedding ring. The woman's jeans fit her widish hips well, and the purple tank top, while not quite the right color for her hair, went quite well with her figure, which, while full, was shapely. The woman was of average height, maybe an inch shorter than Sadie's five foot six inches. Her purse was a large, ornate, white leather number which, if Sadie wasn't mistaken, was rather high-end—making it look out of place on a woman who didn't seem particularly polished. Perhaps it had been a gift?

"Hi," Sadie said with a smile as soon as the woman came to a stop on the opposite side of the table. She put out her hand. "I'm Sadie Hoffmiller. I don't believe we've met. Are you part of the Latham Club?"

"No, ma'am," the woman said. She took Sadie's hand, gave it a single firm shake, and dropped it before unconsciously wiping her hand on her jeans. She was nervous. "I came to talk to you."

"Me?" Sadie said, surprised. Granted, her name was on all the posters and things advertising the luncheon, but the urgency in the other woman's voice and intent of her words didn't seem to have much to do with that.

"A neighbor of yours said you'd be here," she said as she took a cursory glance at the three-dimensional, crepe-paper watermelon slices and real beach balls dangling from the ceiling. "I'm afraid I'm in a bit of a hurry."

"O-kay," Sadie said carefully. "What can I help you with?"

"I'd like to hire you," the woman said as her eyes snapped back to Sadie.

"Hire me?" Sadie repeated. "For what?" She looked down at the cookies. "Catering?" Sadie enjoyed helping with the food for community events, but cookies and cakes didn't seem to fit what this woman wanted. Who needed emergency catering?

"Investigation stuff," the woman said, leaning closer and lowering her voice as though fearful she'd be overheard.

Sadie couldn't deny feeling flattered, but her attention was drawn to the newspaper in the woman's hand. The woman must have stumbled onto an article about the unfortunate incidents Sadie had been involved in. Some of the situations she'd found herself in made Sadie sound rather heroic, but there hadn't been anything written for weeks, and most of the mentions Sadie had cut out of the paper had been short and tucked between public notices and ninetieth birthday announcements.

"Oh, I'm not an investigator. I just have really bad luck." She tried to smile at her own joke.

The woman shook her head. "You're exactly what I need. Someone obscure, who can help me make sense of things."

Sadie wasn't so sure that being called obscure was all that complimentary. "I don't understand what you're asking," she said. "I'm not . . . for hire." Though wouldn't it be cool if she were? She remembered that wave of envy she'd shrugged off a few minutes earlier in regard to Pete's badge and her own fantasies about private investigation work.

"I can pay whatever it takes to make this worth your time," the woman said, keeping her eyes trained on Sadie. She was beginning to sound a little desperate. "Twice that if I need to."

"But I'm not an investigator," Sadie explained again. "I don't know what you've heard, but it was likely overstated and—"

The woman cut Sadie off by putting the newspaper on the table.

Sadie couldn't help but look down. Her own face stared up at her. She immediately looked to the masthead. *The Denver Post*—a paper Sadie was very familiar with as it was the largest paper in Colorado. Sadie wasn't aware of the *Post* having run anything about her for several weeks. Where was that photo from, anyway? Her hair looked fabulous.

"I realize asking you this way isn't exactly proper," the woman said, drawing Sadie's attention away from the newspaper. "But I don't have time to waste. I don't know if you believe in fate, Mrs. Hoffmiller, but I do. I believe in cosmic forces playing out in our lives from time to time, and I believe this article coming out right now is no coincidence." Her voice was soft, but intent, confident and yet not overbearing.

Right now? Sadie looked back at the paper, noticing the date for the first time. Friday, August 10th. That was *today*. She read the headline—"Modern Miss Marple a Magnet for Murder?"—and felt a swirling heat take hold of her stomach as recent insecurities began rising from the corner of her mind where she'd been trying to stash them.

"Mrs. Hoffmiller," the woman said, causing Sadie to look up again. "I really do need your help." The woman's face changed in an instant, her expression falling and her eyes filling with tears. "I think my father may have been murdered."